W9-CAJ-547

PRAISE FOR

Tidelands

The first book in the Fairmile series

"Superb . . . A searing portrait of a woman
that resonates across the ages."
—*People*

"A gripping novel . . . This book will leave readers eagerly
awaiting the next installment in the series. Fans of
Gregory's works and of historicals in general will
delight in this page-turning tale."
—*Library Journal* (starred review)

"The author crafts her material with effortless ease.
Her grasp of social mores is brilliant, the love story rings
true, and the research is, as ever, of the highest quality."
—*Daily Mail* (UK)

"As with all good historical fiction, the novel offers
that uncanny combination of distancing detail and themes
that feel only too close to us today. . . . Spellbinding."
—*The Independent* (UK)

"Richly detailed and brimming with secrets . . .
a captivating portrait of a brave woman."
—*Shelf Awareness*

"A dramatic roller-coaster ride full of drama, intrigue, and family secrets." —*WOMAN'S WORLD*

PRAISE FOR

PHILIPPA GREGORY

"The queen of royal fiction."
—*USA Today*

"There's no question that she is the best at what she does."
—Associated Press

"A mesmerizing storyteller."
—*Sunday Telegraph* (London)

"One of historical fiction's superstars."
—*Historical Novels Review*

"Gregory . . . always delivers the goods."
—*New York Post*

"Gregory defines what it means to be a writer of
historical fiction."
—*RT Book Reviews*

BY THE SAME AUTHOR

History
The Women of the Cousins'
War: The Duchess, the Queen,
and the King's Mother

The Plantagenet and Tudor Novels
The Lady of the Rivers
The Red Queen
The White Queen
The Kingmaker's Daughter
The White Princess
The Constant Princess
The King's Curse
Three Sisters, Three Queens
The Other Boleyn Girl
The Boleyn Inheritance
The Taming of the Queen
The Queen's Fool
The Last Tudor
The Virgin's Lover
The Other Queen

Order of Darkness Series
Changeling
Stormbringers
Fools' Gold
Dark Tracks

The Wideacre Trilogy
Wideacre
The Favored Child
Meridon

The Tradescants
Earthly Joys
Virgin Earth

Modern Novels
Alice Hartley's Happiness
Perfectly Correct
The Little House
Zelda's Cut

Short Stories
Bread and Chocolate

Other Historical Novels
The Wise Woman
Fallen Skies
A Respectable Trade

The Fairmile Series
Tidelands

Children's Books
The Princess Rules
It's a Prince Thing

DARK TIDES

A NOVEL

PHILIPPA GREGORY

WASHINGTON
SQUARE PRESS

ATRIA

New York   London   Toronto   Sydney   New Delhi

WASHINGTON
SQUARE PRESS

———

ATRIA

An Imprint of Simon & Schuster, Inc.
1230 Avenue of the Americas
New York, NY 10020

This book is a work of fiction. Any references to historical events, real people, or real places are used fictitiously. Other names, characters, places, and events are products of the author's imagination, and any resemblance to actual events or places or persons, living or dead, is entirely coincidental.

Copyright © 2020 by Levon Publishing Ltd.

All rights reserved, including the right to reproduce this book or portions thereof in any form whatsoever. For information, address Atria Books Subsidiary Rights Department, 1230 Avenue of the Americas, New York, NY 10020.

First Washington Square Press/Atria Paperback edition June 2021

WASHINGTON SQUARE PRESS **/ ATRIA** PAPERBACK and colophon are trademarks of Simon & Schuster, Inc.

For information about special discounts for bulk purchases, please contact Simon & Schuster Special Sales at 1-866-506-1949 or business@simonandschuster.com.

The Simon & Schuster Speakers Bureau can bring authors to your live event. For more information or to book an event, contact the Simon & Schuster Speakers Bureau at 1-866-248-3049 or visit our website at www.simonspeakers.com.

Manufactured in the United States of America

1 3 5 7 9 10 8 6 4 2

The Library of Congress has cataloged the hardcover edition as follows:

Names: Gregory, Philippa
Title: Dark tides : a novel / Philippa Gregory.
Description: First Atria Books hardcover edition. | New York : Atria Books, 2020. | Series: The fairmile series ; vol 2
Identifiers: LCCN 2020033249 (print) | LCCN 2020033250 (ebook) | ISBN 9781501187186 (hardcover) | ISBN 9781501187209 (ebook)
Subjects: LCSH: Domestic fiction. | GSAFD: Historical fiction.
Classification: LCC PR6057.R386 D37 2020 (print) | LCC PR6057.R386 (ebook) | DDC 823/.914—dc23
LC record available at https://lccn.loc.gov/2020033249
LC ebook record available at https://lccn.loc.gov/2020033250

ISBN 978-1-5011-8718-6
ISBN 978-1-5011-8719-3 (pbk)
ISBN 978-1-5011-8720-9 (ebook)

DARK TIDES

Reekie Wharf, Southwark, London, Midsummer Eve

Dear Ned, my dearest brother,

I have to tell you that we have had a letter from ~~Rob's wife~~ from Venice.

It's bad news. ~~It's the worst news.~~ She writes that Rob is ~~drowned dead~~ drowned. Rob's ~~wife~~ widow says that she is coming to England with his baby. I write to you now ~~as I cannot believe it~~ as I know you would want to know at once. But I don't know what to write.

Ned—you know that I would know if my son was dead. I know he is not.

I swear to you on my soul that he is not.

I will write again when she has come and told us more. ~~You will say—~~I think you will say—that I am lying to myself—that I cannot bear the news and I am dreaming that everyone but me is wrong.

~~I don't know. I can't know. But I do think I know.~~

I am sorry to write such ~~a bad~~ a sad letter. It is not possible that he be dead and I not know it. ~~I would have felt it its not possible that he could be drowned.~~

How could I have come up out of deep water and twenty-one years later it hold him down?

Your loving sister, Alinor.
Of course I pray that you are well. Write me.

MIDSUMMER EVE, 1670, LONDON

The ramshackle warehouse was the wrong side of the river, the south side, where the buildings jostled for space and the little boats unloaded pocket-size cargos for scant profit. The wealth of London passed them by, sailing upstream to the half-built new Custom House, its cream stone facade set square on the fast-flowing river, as if it would tax every drop of the roiling dirty water. The greatest ships, towed by eager barges, glided past the little wharves, as if the quays were nothing but flotsam, sticks, and cobbles, rotting as they stood. Twice a day even the tide deserted them, leaving banks of stinking mud, and piers of weedy ramps rising like old bones from the water.

This warehouse, and all the others leaning against it, like carelessly shelved books, shuddering along the bank towards the dark channel at the side, were hungry for the wealth that had sailed with the new king in the ship that had once been Oliver Cromwell's, into the country that had once been free. These poor merchants, scraping a living from the river trade, heard all about the new king and his glorious court at Whitehall; but they gained nothing from his return. They saw him only once, as he sailed by, the royal pennants flying fore and aft, once and never again: not down here, on the south side of the river, on the east side of the town. This was never a place that people visited, it was a place that people left; not a place that ever saw a grand carriage or a fine horse. The returning king stayed west of the City, surrounded by aristocratic chancers and titled whores, all of them desperate for promiscuous pleasure, jerked back from despair by gamblers' luck: not one of them earning their good fortune.

But this little house clung to the old puritan principles of hard work and thrift, just as the buildings clung to the quayside: so thought the man who stood before it, staring up at the windows as if he were hoping to catch a glimpse of someone inside. His brown suit was neat, the white lace at his collar and cuffs modest in these times of fashionable excess. His horse stood patiently behind him as he scanned the blank face of the warehouse—the pulley on the wall, and the wide-open double doors—and then turned to the murky river to watch the lumpers throwing heavy grain sacks, one to another from the grounded flat-bottomed barge, grunting a monotone chant to keep the rhythm.

The gentleman on the quayside felt as alien here as he did on his rare visits to court. It seemed as if there was no place for him at all in this new England. In the glittering noisy palaces, he was a dowdy reminder of a difficult past, best clapped on the back with a quickly forgotten promise. But here on the quayside at Bermondsey he stood out as a stranger: a rich idler among laboring men, a silent presence amid the constant scream from the pulley of the crane, the rumble of rolling barrels, the shouted orders and the sweating lumpers. At court, he was in the way of a thoughtless round of pleasure, he was too drab for them. Here, he was in the way of the passage of work, where men were not individuals but moved as one, each one a cog; as if even work was not work anymore; but had been atomized into a new painful machine. He thought the world was not whole anymore; but sundered into country and court, winners and the lost, protestants and heretics, royalists and roundheads, the unfairly blessed and the unjustly damned.

He felt very far from his own world of small luxuries taken for granted—hot water in a china jug in the bedroom, clean clothes laid out for the day, servants to do everything—but he must enter this world of work if he were to make right the wrong he had done, bring a good woman to happiness, heal the wounds of his own failure. Like the king, he had come to make a restoration.

He hitched his horse to a ring on a post, stepped to the edge of the wharf, and looked down into the flat-bottomed barge which was grounded heavily on the ramp beside the quay. "Where have you come from?" he called down to the man he took to be the master of the ship who was watching the unloading, ticking off the sacks in a ledger.

"Sealsea Island, Sussex," the man replied in the old, familiar drawling accent. "Best wheat in England, Sussex wheat." He squinted upwards. "You've come to buy? Or Sussex-brewed ale? And salted fish? We've got that too."

"I'm not here to buy," the stranger replied, his heart thudding in his chest at the name of the island that had been his home: her home.

"Nay, you'll be here for a dance in the ladies' great hall?" the shipmaster joked, and one of the lumpers gave a crack of a laugh as the gentleman turned away from their impertinence, to look up at the warehouse again.

It was on the corner of a run of shabby three-story warehouses built of planks and old ships' timbers, the most prosperous of a poor row. Farther along the quay, where the River Neckinger joined the Thames in a swirl of filthy water, there was a gibbet with a long-ago hanged man, a few tatters of cloth holding the bleached remaining bones. A pirate, whose punishment had been to hang, and be left to hang as a warning to others. The gentleman shuddered. He could not imagine how the woman he had known could bear to live within earshot of the creak of the chain.

He knew that she had no choice, and she had done the best she could with the wharf. Clearly, the warehouse had been improved and rebuilt. Someone had gone to the expense and trouble to build a little turret at the downriver corner of the house, looking out over the Thames and the River Neckinger. She could step out of the glazed door and stand on a little balcony to look east: downriver towards the sea; or west: upriver to the City of London; or inland along St. Saviour's Dock. She could open the window to listen to the cry of gulls and watch the tide rise and fall below her window and the goods come into the wharf below. Perhaps it reminded her of home, perhaps some nights she sat there, as the mist came up the river turning the sky as gray as water, and she thought of other nights and the thunder of the tide mill wheel turning. Perhaps she looked across the turbulent river to the north, beyond the narrow street of chandlers and victuallers, past the marshes where the seabirds wheeled and cried; perhaps she imagined the hills of the north and the wide skies of the home of a man she had once loved.

The gentleman stepped up to the front door of the warehouse which was clearly home, business, and store combined, lifted the ivory handle of his riding crop, and rapped loudly. He waited, hearing footsteps approaching, echoing down a wooden hall, and then the door opened and a maid stood before him, in a stained working apron, staring aghast at the glossy pelt of his French hat and his highly polished boots.

"I should like to see—" Now that he had got this far, he realized he did not know what name she used, nor the name of the owner of the warehouse. "I should like to see the lady of the house."

"Which one?" she demanded, wiping a dirty hand on her hessian apron. "Mrs. Reekie or Mrs. Stoney?"

He caught his breath at her husband's name and the mention of her daughter, and thought that if he was so shaken to hear this, what would he feel when he saw her? "Mrs. Reekie," he recovered. "It is she that I wish to see. Is Mrs. Reekie at home?"

She widened the gap of the front door; she did not open it politely to let him in, it was as if she had never admitted a visitor. "If it's about a load, you should go to the yard door and see Mrs. Stoney."

"It's not about a load. I am calling to visit Mrs. Reekie."

"Why?"

"Would you tell her that an old friend has called to see her?" he replied patiently. He did not dare give his name. A silver sixpence passed from his riding glove to the girl's work-stained hand. "Please ask her to receive me," he repeated. "And send the groom to take my horse into your stables."

"We don't have a groom," she answered, pocketing the coin in her apron, looking him up and down. "Just the wagon driver, and there's only the stables for the team horses and a yard where we store the barrels."

"Then tell the wagon driver to put my horse in the yard," he instructed.

She opened the front door just wide enough to admit him, leaving it open so the men on the quayside could see him, standing awkwardly in the hall, his hat in one hand, his riding crop and gloves in the other. She walked past him without a word, to a door at the rear, and he could hear her shouting from the back door for someone to open the gate to the yard, though there was no delivery, just a man with a horse that wouldn't stand on the quayside. Miserably embarrassed, he looked around the hall, at the wood-paneled doors with their raised stone thresholds to hold back a flood, at the narrow wooden staircase, at the single chair, wishing with all his heart that he had never come.

He had thought that the woman he was visiting would be poorer even than this. He had imagined her selling physic out of a quayside window, attending births for sailors' wives and captains' whores. He had thought of her so many times in hardship, sewing the child's clothes with patches, stinting herself to put a bowl of gruel before him, turning this way and that to make a living. He had thought of her as he had known her before, a poor woman but a proud woman, who made every penny she could; but never begged. He had imagined this might be some sort of quayside boardinghouse and hoped she worked here as a housekeeper; he had prayed that she had not been forced to do anything worse. Every year he had sent her a letter wishing her well, telling her that he thought of her still, with a gold coin under the seal; but she had never acknowledged it. He never even knew if she had received it. He had never allowed himself to find the little warehouse on the side of the river, never allowed himself even to take a boat downriver to look for her door. He had been afraid of what he might find. But this year, this particular year, on this month and this day, he had come.

The maid stamped back into the hall and slammed the front door against the noise and glare of the quayside so he felt that he was at last admitted into the house, and not just delivered into the hall like a bale of goods.

"Will she see me? Mrs. Reekie?" he asked, stumbling on the name.

Before she could answer, a door farther down the hall opened, and a woman in her thirties stepped into the hall. She wore the dark respectable gown of a merchant's wife, and a plain working apron over it, tied tightly at the curve of her waist. Her collar was modestly high, plain and white, unfashionable in these extravagant days. Her golden-brown hair was combed back and almost completely hidden under a white cap. She had lines at the corners of her eyes and a deep groove in her forehead from frowning. She did not lower her eyes like a puritan woman, nor did she coquet like a courtier. Once again, with a sense of dread, James met the direct unfriendly gaze of Alys Stoney.

"You," she said without surprise. "After all this time."

"I," he agreed, and bowed low to her. "After twenty-one years."

"This isn't a good time," she said bluntly.

"I could not come before. May I speak with you?"

She barely inclined her head in reply. "I suppose you'll want to come in," she said gracelessly, and led the way into the adjoining room, indicating that he should step over the raised threshold. A small window gave the view of the distant bank of the river, obscured by masts and lashed sails, and the noisy quay before the house where the lumpers were still loading the wagon, and rolling barrels into the warehouse. She dropped the window blind so that the men working on the quay could not see her direct him towards a plain wooden chair. He took a seat, as she paused, one hand on the mantelpiece, gazing down into the empty grate as if she were a judge, standing over him, considering sentence.

"I sent money, every year," he said awkwardly.

"I know," she said. "You sent one Louis d'Or. I took it."

"She never replied to my letters."

"She never saw them."

He felt himself gasp as if she had winded him. "My letters were addressed to her."

She shrugged as if she cared for nothing.

"In honor, you should have given them to her. They were private." She looked completely indifferent.

"By law, by the laws of this land, they belong to her, or they should have been returned to me," he protested.

Briefly, she glanced at him. "I don't think either of us have much to do with the law."

"Actually, I am a justice of the peace in my shire," he said stiffly. "And a member of the House of Commons. I uphold the law."

As she bowed her head, he saw the sarcastic gleam in her eyes. "Pardon me, your honor! But I can't return them as I burned them."

"You read them?"

She shook her head. "No. Once I had the gold from under the seal, I had no interest in them," she said. "Nor in you."

He had a choking sensation, as if he were drowning under a weight of water. He had to remember that he was a gentleman; and she had been a farm girl and was now passing herself off as the lady of a poor warehouse. He had to remember that he had fathered a child who lived here, in this unprepossessing workplace, and he had rights. He had to remember that she was a thief, and her mother accused of worse, while he was a titled gentleman with lands inherited for generations. He was descending from a great position to visit them, prepared to perform an extraordinary act of charity to help this impoverished family. "I could have written anything," he said sharply. "You had no right . . ."

"You could have written anything," she conceded. "And still, I would have had no interest."

"And she . . ."

She shrugged. "I don't know what she thinks of you," she said. "I have no interest in that either."

"She must have spoken of me!"

The face she turned to him was insolently blank. "Oh, must she?"

The thought that Alinor had never spoken of him in all these years struck him like a physical blow in the chest; knocking him back in his hard chair. If she had died in his arms twenty-one years ago, she could not have haunted him more persistently than she had done. He had thought of her every day, named her in his prayers every night, he had dreamed of her, he had longed for her. It was not possible she had not thought of him.

"If you have no interest in me at all, then you can have no curiosity in why I have come now?" he challenged her.

She did not rise to the bait. "Yes," she confirmed. "You're right. None."

He felt that he was at a disadvantage sitting down so he rose up and went past her to the window, pulled back the edge of the blind to look out. He was trying to contain his temper and, at the same time, overcome the sensation that her will against him was as remorseless as the incoming tide. He could hear the rub of the fenders of the barge as the water lifted it off the ramp, and the clicking of the sheets against the wooden masts. These sounds had always been for him the echoes of exile, the music of his life as a spy, a stranger in his own country; he could not bear to feel that sense of being lonely and in danger once again. He turned back to the room. "To be brief, I came to speak to your mother, not to you. I prefer not to talk to you. And I should like to see the child: my child."

She shook her head. "She cannot see you, and neither will the child."

"You cannot speak for either of them. She is your mother, and the child—my child—has come of age."

She said nothing but merely turned her head away from his determined face, to gaze down at the empty grate again. He controlled his temper with an effort but could not stop himself seeing that she had matured into a strong, square-faced beauty. She looked like a woman of authority who cared nothing for how she appeared and everything for what she did.

"The child is twenty-one years old now, and can choose for himself," he insisted.

Again, she said nothing.

"It is a boy?" he asked tentatively. "It is a boy? I have a son?"

"Twenty-one gold coins, at the rate of one a year, does not buy you a son," she said. "Nor does it buy you a moment of her time. I suppose that you are a wealthy man now? You have regained your great house and your lands, your king is restored and you are famous as one of those who brought him back to England and to his fortune? And you are rewarded? He has remembered you, though he forgets so many others? You managed to elbow yourself to the front of the queue when he was handing out his favors, you made sure that you were not forgotten?"

He bowed his head so that she should not see the bitterness in his face that his sacrifice and the danger he had faced had done nothing more than bring a lecher to the throne of a fool. "I am fully restored to my family estates and fortune," he confirmed quietly. "I did not ever stoop to curry favor. What you suggest is . . . beneath me. I received my due. My family were ruined in his service. We have been repaid. No more and no less."

"Then twenty-one pistoles is nothing to you," she triumphed. "You will hardly have noticed it. But if you insist, I can repay you. Shall I send it to your land agent at your great house in Yorkshire? I don't have it in coin right now. We don't keep that sort of money in the house, we don't earn that sort of money in a month; but I will borrow and reimburse you by next week."

"I don't want your coins. I want . . ."

Once again her cold gaze froze him into silence.

"Mrs. Stoney." He cautiously used her married name and she did not contradict him. "Mrs. Stoney, I have my lands, but I have no son. My title will die with me. I am bringing this boy—you force me to speak bluntly to you, not to his mother, and not to my son, as would be my choice—I am bringing him a miracle, I will make him into a gentleman, I will make him wealthy, he is my heir. And it will be her restoration too. I said once that she would be a lady of a great house. I repeat that now. I insist that I repeat it to her in person, so that I can be sure that she knows, so that she knows exactly, the great offer I am making her. I insist that I repeat it to him, so that he knows the opportunity that lies before him. I am ready to give her my name and title. He will have a father and ancestral lands. I will acknowledge him . . ." He caught his breath at the enormity of the offer. "I will give him my name, my honorable name. I am proposing that I should marry her."

He was panting as he finished speaking but there was no response, just another void of silence. He thought she must be astounded by the wealth and good fortune that had descended on them like a thunderclap. He thought she was struck dumb. But then Alys Stoney spoke:

"Oh no, she won't see you," she answered him casually, as if she were turning away a pedlar from the door. "And there's no child in this house that carries your name. Nor one that has even heard of you."

"There is a boy. I know there is a boy. Don't lie to me. I know . . ."

"My son," she said levelly. "Not yours."

"I have a daughter?"

This threw everything into confusion. He had thought so long of his boy, growing up on the wharf, a boy who would be raised in the rough-and-tumble of the streets but who would—he was certain—have been given an education, been carefully raised. The woman he had loved could not have a boy without making a man of him. He had known her boy, Rob, she could not help but raise a good young man and teach him curiosity and hopefulness and a sense of joy. But anyway—his thoughts whirled—a girl could inherit his lands just as well, he could adopt her and give her his name, he could see that she married well and then he would have a grandson at Northside Manor. He could entail the land on her son, he could insist the new family took his name. In the next generation there would be a boy who could keep the Avery name alive, he would not be the last, he would have a posterity.

"My daughter," she corrected him again. "Not yours."

She had stunned him. He looked at her imploringly, so pale, she thought he might faint. But she did not offer him so much as a drop of water, though his lips were gray and he put up a hand to his neck and loosened his collar. "Should you go outside for air?" she asked him, uncaring. "Or just go?"

"You have taken my child as your own?" he whispered.

She inclined her head; but did not answer.

"You took my child? A kidnap?"

She nearly smiled. "Hardly. You were not there to steal from. You were far away. I don't think we could even see the dust behind your grand coach."

"Was it a boy? Or a girl?"

"Both the girl and the boy are mine."

"But which was mine?" He was agonized.

She shrugged. "Neither of them now."

"Alys, for pity's sake. You will give my child back to me. To his great estate? To inherit my fortune?"

"No," she said.

"What?"

"No, thank you," she said insolently.

There was a long silence in the room, though outside they could hear the shouts of the men as the last grain sack was hauled off the barge, and they started to load it with goods for the return trip. They heard barrels of French wine and sugar roll along the quayside. Still he said nothing, but his hand tugged at the rich lace collar at his throat. Still she said nothing, but kept her head turned away from him, as if she had no interest in his pain.

A great clatter and rumble of wheels on the cobbles outside the window made her turn in surprise.

"Is that a carriage? Here?" he asked.

She said nothing, but stood listening, blank-faced, as a carriage rolled noisily up the cobbled quay to the warehouse and stopped outside the front door which gave on to the street.

"A gentleman's carriage?" he asked incredulously. "Here?"

They heard the clatter of the hooves as the horses were pulled up, and then the footman jumped down from the back, opened the carriage door, and turned to hammer on the front door of the warehouse.

Swiftly, Alys went past him, across the room, and lifted the bottom of the blind so that she could peep out onto the quay. She could only see the open door of the carriage, a billowing dark silk skirt, a tiny silk shoe with a black rose pinned on the toe. Then they heard the maid, stamping up the hall to open the shabby front door and recoil at the magnificence of the footman from the carriage.

"The Nobildonna," he announced, and Alys watched the hem of the gown sweep down the carriage steps, across the cobbles, and into the hall. Behind the rich gown came a plain hem, a maid of some sort, and Alys turned to James Avery.

"You have to go," she said rapidly. "I was not expecting . . . You will have to . . ."

"I'm not going without an answer."

"You have to!" She started towards him as if she would physically push him through the narrow doorway, but it was too late. The stunned housemaid had already thrown open the parlor door, there was a rustle of silk, and the veiled stranger had entered the room, paused on the threshold, taking in the wealthy gentleman and the plainly dressed woman in one swift glance. She crossed the room and took Alys in her arms and kissed her on both cheeks.

"You allow me? You forgive me? But I had nowhere else to come!" she said swiftly in a ripple of speech with an Italian accent.

James saw Alys, so furiously icy just a moment before, flush brightly, her blush staining her neck and her cheeks, saw her eyes fill with tears, as she said: "Of course you should have come! I didn't think . . ."

"And this is my baby," the lady said simply, beckoning to the maid behind her who carried a sleeping baby draped in the finest Venetian lace. "This is his son. This is your nephew. We called him Matteo."

Alys gave a little cry and held out her arms for the baby, looking down into the perfect face, tears coming to her eyes.

"Your nephew?" James Avery said, stepping forward to see the little face framed in ribboned lace. "Then this is Rob's boy?"

A furious glance from Alys did not prevent the lady from sweeping him a curtsey and throwing her dark veil back to show a vivacious beautiful face, her lips rosy with rouge, enhanced with a dark crescent patch beside her mouth.

"I'm honored, Lady . . . ?"

Alys did not volunteer the lady's name, nor did she mention his. She stood, awkward and angry, looking at them both, as if she could deny the courtesy of an introduction and ensure that they would never meet.

"I am Sir James Avery, of Northside Manor, Northallerton in York-shire." James bowed over the lady's hand.

"Nobildonna da Ricci," she replied. And then she turned to Alys. "That is how you say it? Da Ricci? I am right?"

"I suppose so," Alys said. "But you must be very tired." She glanced out of the window. "The carriage?"

"Ah, it is rented. They will unload my trunks, if you would pay them?"

Alys looked horrified. "I don't know if I have—"

"Please allow me," Sir James interrupted smoothly. "As a friend of the family."

"I shall pay them!" Alys insisted. "I can find it." She flung open the door and shouted an order to the maid and turned to the widow, who had followed every word of this exchange. "You'll want to rest. Let me show you upstairs and I'll get some tea."

"*Allora!* It is always tea with the English!" she exclaimed, throwing up her hands. "But I am not tired, and I don't want tea. And I am afraid I am interrupting you. Were you here on business, Sir James? Please stay! Please continue!"

"You are not interrupting, and he is going," Alys said firmly.

"I will come back tomorrow, when you have had time to think," Sir James said quickly. He turned to the lady: "Is Robert with you, Lady da Ricci? I should so like to see him again. He was my pupil and . . ."

The shocked look on both their faces told him that he had said something terrible. Alys shook her head as if she wished she had not heard the words and something in her face told James that the ostentatious mourning wear of the Italian lady was for Rob, little Rob Reekie who twenty-one years ago had been a brilliant boy of twelve and now was gone.

The widow's mouth quivered; she dropped into a seat and covered her face with her black-mittened hands.

"I am so sorry, so sorry." He was horrified at his blunder. He bowed to the lady. He turned to Alys. "I am sorry for your loss. I had no idea. If you had told me, I would not have been so clumsy. I am so sorry, Alys, Mrs. Stoney."

She held the baby, the fatherless boy, in her arms. "Why should I tell you anything?" she demanded fiercely. "Just go! And don't come back."

But the lady, with her face hidden, blindly stretched out her hand to him, as if for comfort. He could not help but take the warm hand in the tight black lace mitten.

"But he spoke of you!" she whispered. "I remember now. I know who you are. You were his tutor and he said you taught him Latin and were patient with him when he was just a little boy. He was grateful to you for that. He told me so."

James patted her hand. "I am so sorry for your loss," he said. "Forgive my clumsiness."

Mistily, she smiled up at him, blinking away tears from her dark eyes. "Forgiven," she said. "And forgotten at once. How should you guess such a tragedy? But call on me when you come again, and you can tell me what he was like when he was a boy. You must tell me all about his childhood. Promise me that you will?"

"I will," James said quickly before Alys could retract the invitation. "I will come tomorrow, after breakfast. And I'll leave you now." He bowed to both the women and nodded to the nursemaid and went quickly from the room before Alys could say another word. They heard him ask the maid for his horse and then they heard the front door slam. They sat in silence as they heard the horse coming around from the yard and stand, as he mounted up, and then clattered away.

"I thought his name was something else," the widow remarked.

"It was then."

"I did not know that he was a nobleman?"

"He was not, then."

"And wealthy?"

"Now, I suppose so."

"Ah," the lady considered her sister-in-law. "Is it all right that I came? Roberto told me to come to you if anything ever . . . if anything ever . . . if anything ever happened to him." Her face was tearstained and flushed. She took out a tiny handkerchief trimmed with black ribbon and put it to her eyes.

"Of course," Alys said. "Of course. And this is your home for as long as you want to stay."

The sleeping baby gave a gurgle and Alys shifted him from her shoulder to hold him in her arms, so she could look into the little pursed face for any sign of Rob.

"I think he is very like your brother," the widow said quietly. "It is a great comfort to me. When I first lost my love, my dearest Roberto, I thought I would die of the pain. It was only this little—this little angel—that kept me alive at all."

Alys put her lips to the warm head, where the pulse bumped so strongly. "He smells so sweet," she said wonderingly.

Her ladyship nodded. "My savior. May I show him to his grandmother?"

"I shall take you to see her," Alys said. "This has been a terrible shock for her, for us all. We only had your letter telling of his death last week, and then your letter from Greenwich three days ago. We're not even in mourning. I am so sorry."

The young woman looked up, her eyelashes drenched with tears. "It is nothing, it is nothing. What matters is the heart."

"You know that she is an invalid? But she will want to welcome you here at once. I'll just go up and tell her that you have come to us. Can

I have them bring you anything? If not tea, then perhaps a drink of chocolate? Or a glass of wine?"

"Just a glass of wine and water," the lady said. "And please tell your lady-mother that I wish to be no trouble to her. I can see her tomorrow, if she is resting now."

"I'll ask." Alys gave the baby to the nursemaid and went from the room, across the hall, and up the narrow stairs.

Alinor was bent over her letter, seated at a round table set in the glazed turret, struggling to write to her brother to tell him such bad news that she could not make herself believe it. The warm breeze coming in with the tide lifted a stray lock of white hair from her frowning face. She was surrounded by the tools of her trade: herbalism, posies of herbs drying on strings over her head, stirring in the air from the window, little bottles of oils and essences were ranked on the shelves on the far side of the room, and on the floor beneath them were big corked jars of oils. She was not yet fifty, her strikingly beautiful face honed by pain and loss, her eyes a darker gray than her modest gown, a white apron around her narrow waist, a white collar at her neck.

"Was that her? So soon?"

"You saw the carriage?"

"Yes—I was writing to Ned. To tell him."

"Ma—it's Rob's . . . it is . . ."

"Rob's widow?" Alinor asked without hesitation. "I thought it must be, when I saw the nursemaid, carrying the baby. It is Rob's baby boy?"

"Yes. He's so tiny, to come such a long way! Shall I bring her up?"

"Has she come to stay? I saw trunks on the coach?"

"I don't know how long . . ."

"I doubt this'll be good enough for her."

"I'll get Sarah's room ready for the maid and the baby, and I'll offer her Johnnie's room in the attic. I should have done it earlier but

I never dreamed she'd get here so soon. She hired her own carriage from Greenwich."

"Rob wrote that she was a wealthy widow. Poor child, she must feel that her old life is lost."

"Just like us," Alys remarked. "Homeless, and with the babies."

"Except we didn't have a hired carriage and a maid," Alinor pointed out. "Who was the gentleman? I couldn't see more than the top of his hat."

Alys hesitated, unsure what she should say. "Nobody," she lied. "A gentleman factor. He was selling a share in a slaver ship to the Guinea coast. Promised a hundredfold return, but the risk is too much for us."

"Ned wouldn't like it." Alinor glanced down at her inadequate letter to her brother, far away in New England, escaping his country that had chosen servitude under a king. "Ned would never trade in slaves."

"Ma . . ." Alys hesitated, not knowing how to speak to her mother. "You know that there can be no doubt?"

"Of my son's death?" Alinor named the loss she could not believe.

"His widow is here now. She can tell you herself."

"I know. I will believe it when she tells me, I am sure."

"D'you want to lie on your sofa when I bring her up? It's not too much for you?"

Alinor rose to her feet and took the half-dozen steps to the sofa and then seated herself as Alys lifted her legs and tucked her gown around her ankles.

"Comfortable? Can you breathe, Ma?"

"Aye, I'm well enough. Let her come up now."

JUNE 1670, HADLEY, NEW ENGLAND

Ned was in a land without kings, but not without authorities. A select-man from the town council of Hadley banged through the north gate from the town and clambered up the embankment of the river and down the other side to the rickety wooden pier, so he could clang the dangling old horseshoe on a rusty iron bar to summon the ferryman from wherever he was. Ned mounted the bank from the back yard of the little two-room house, wiping the earth from his hands, and paused at the summit to look down on him.

"There's no need to raise the dead. I was in my garden."

"Edward Ferryman?"

"Aye. As you know well enough. D'you want the ferry?"

"No, I thought you might be in the woods, so I clanged for the ferry to fetch you."

Ned silently raised his eyebrows, as if to imply that the man might call for the ferry but not the ferryman.

The man gestured to the paper in his hand. "This is official. You're wanted in town."

"Well, I can't leave the Quinnehtukqut." Ned gestured to the slow-moving river in its summer shallows.

"What?"

"The river. That's its name. How come you don't know that?"

"We call it the Connecticut."

"Same thing. It means long river, a long river with tides. I can't leave the ferry in daylight hours without someone to man the boat. You should know that. It's the town's own regulation."

"Is that French?" he asked curiously. "The Quin . . . whatever you called it? D'you call it by a French name?"

"The native tongue. The People of the Dawnlands."

"We don't call them that."

Ned shrugged. "Maybe you do or you don't; but it's their name. Because they're first to see the sun rise. All these lands are called Dawnlands."

"New England," the man corrected him.

"Did you come all this way to teach me how to talk?"

"They said in the town that you speak native. The elders say you must come to explain a deed to one of the natives."

Ned sighed. "I only speak a little; not enough to be of any use."

"We need a translator. We want to buy some more land, over the river, farther north, over there." He waved to where the huge trees came down and leaned curving boughs into the glassy water. "You'd want land there yourself, I suppose, you'd want land around your ferry pier?"

"How much land?" Ned asked curiously.

"Not much, another couple of hundred acres or so."

Ned shook his head, rubbed earth from his hands like a man brushing off sin. "I'm not the man for you. I left the old country to get away from all the moneymaking and grabbing from each other. When the king came back it was like rats in a malthouse. I don't want to start all over again here." He turned to go back to the garden behind his house.

The man looked at him, uncomprehending. "You talk like a Leveler!" He climbed up the little embankment to stand beside Ned.

Ned flinched a little at the memory of old battles, lost long ago. "Maybe I do. But I'd rather be left in peace, on my own plantation, than make a fortune."

"But why?" the selectman demanded. "Everyone's come here to make their fortune. God rewards his disciples. I came to make a better living than I could in the old country. Same as everyone. This is a new world. More and more people arriving, more and more being born. We want a better life! For ourselves and our families. It's God's will that we prosper here, His will that we came here and live according to His laws."

"Aye, but some people hoped for a new world without greed," Ned pointed out. "Me among them. Maybe it's God's will that we make a land without masters and men, sharing the garden like Eden." He turned and made his way down the rough steps back to his garden.

"We do share it!" the man insisted. "Share it among the godly. You have your own share here by the minister's goodwill."

"The elders'd do better to ask one of the native people." Ned undid the twine at his garden gate and went in. "Dozens of 'em speak good-enough English. Some of them Christian. What about John Sassamon? The schoolteacher? Him that's preaching to King Philip? He's in town, I brought him over this morning. He'll translate for you, as he does for the Council. He's been educated, he's been to Harvard College! I wouldn't know where to begin."

Ned fastened the little handmade gate behind him, and ordered his dog to sit. "Don't come any farther," he said firmly to the unwelcome visitor. "I've got seedlings in here that don't need treading."

"We don't want a native. Truth be told: we don't trust one to translate a deed to buy land. We don't want to find out in ten years' time that they called it a loan rather than a sale. We want one of our own."

"He is one of our own," Ned insisted. "Raised as an Englishman, at college with Englishmen. Crossed on my ferry this morning, wearing boots and breeches, with a hat on his head."

The man leaned over the garden fence, as if he feared the deep river might be listening to them, or the long grassy banks might overhear. "Nay, we don't trust any of 'em," he said. "It's not like it was. They're not like they were. They've gone sour. They're not like they were in their old king's time, welcoming us and wanting to trade, when they were simple savages."

"Simple? Was it truly all so sweethearted then?"

"My father said it was so," the man said. "They gave us land, wanted our trade. Welcomed us, wanted help against their enemies— against the Mohawks. Everyone knows that they invited us in. So here we are! They gave us land then, and now they have to give us more. And we'd pay a fair price."

"In what?" Ned asked skeptically.

"What?"

"What would you pay your fair price in?"

"Oh! Whatever they asked. Wampum. Or hats, or coats, whatever they wanted."

Ned shook his head at the exchange of acres of land for shell beads. "Wampum's lost its value," he pointed out. "And coats? You'd pay a couple of coats for a hundred acres of fields that they've planted and cleared and forest that they've managed for their hunting, and call it fair?" He hawked and spat on the ground, as if to get the taste of fraud from his mouth.

"They like coats," the man said sulkily.

Ned turned from the gate to end the argument, dropped to his knees, and picked up his hoeing stick, to weed around his vines of golden squash.

"What's that stink you're spreading there?"

"Fish guts," Ned said, ignoring the smell. "Shad. I plant one in each hillock."

"That's what natives do!"

"Aye, it was one of them taught me."

"And what's that you're using?"

Ned glanced at the old hoeing stick which had been rubbed with fat and roasted in ashes till it was hard, sharpened till it was as good as hammered iron. "This? What's wrong with it?"

"Native work," the man said contemptuously.

"It was traded to me for fair payment, and it does the job. I don't mind who made it, as long as it's good work."

"You use native tricks and tools, you'll become like them." He spoke as if it was a curse. "You be careful, or you'll be a savage yourself, and you'll answer for it. You know what happened to Edward Ashley?"

"Forty years ago," Ned said wearily.

"Sent back to England for living like a native," the selectman said triumphantly. "You start like this, with a hoeing stick, and next you're in moccasins and you're lost."

"I'm English, born and bred, and I'll die English." Ned reined in his irritation. "But I don't have to despise anyone else." He sat back on his heels. "I didn't come here to be a king looking down on subjects, forcing my ways on them in blood. I came here to live at peace, with my neighbors. All my neighbors: English and Indian."

The man glanced to the east, upriver where low-lying water meadows on the other side of the river became deep thick forest. "Even the ones you can't see? The ones that howl like wolves in the night and watch you from the swamp all the day?"

"Them too," Ned said equably. "The godly and ungodly, and those whose gods I don't know." He bent over his plants to show that the conversation was over; but still the messenger did not leave.

"We'll send for you again, you know." The man turned away from Ned's garden gate and headed back to the town. "Everyone has to serve. Even if you don't come now, you'll have to come to militia training. You can't just be English sitting on the riverside. You have to prove yourself English. You have to be English against our enemies. That's how we know you're English. That's how you know yourself. We're going to have to teach them a lesson!"

"I should think we've already taught them a lesson," Ned remarked to the earth beneath his knees. "Better not invite us in, better not welcome us."

JUNE 1670, LONDON

The Italian lady had to take off her hat and the dark veil, her black lace mittens, and wash her face and hands in the little attic bedroom before she could visit her mother-in-law. The baby was still sleeping but she took him in her arms and came into the room, strikingly beautiful, like a sorrowful Madonna. Alinor took in the dark gown cut low over her breasts, the creamy skin veiled by black lace, the pile of dark curling hair under the black trimmed cap, and the wide tragic eyes; but her attention was on the sleeping baby.

"Rob's boy," was all she said.

"Your grandson," Lady da Ricci whispered, and put the baby into Alinor's arms. "Doesn't he look like Roberto?"

Alinor received the baby with the confidence of a midwife who has attended hundreds of births, but she did not embrace him. She held him on her lap so that she could look down at the sleeping face, round as a moon with red lips that showed a rosy little sucking blister. She did not exclaim with instant love; strangely she said nothing for long moments as if she were interrogating the dark eyelashes on the creamy cheeks and the snub little nose, and when she looked up at the widow kneeling beside her sofa, her pale face was grave: "How old is he?"

"Ah, he is just five months old, God bless him, to lose his father when he was newborn."

"And his eyes?"

"Dark, dark blue, you will see when he wakes. Dark as the deep sea."

The Italian lady felt, rather than saw, the little shudder that Alinor could not suppress.

"He is so like his father," she asserted louder. "Every day I see it more."

"Do you?" Alinor asked neutrally.

"He is Matteo Roberto, but you must call him Matthew of course. And Robert, for his father. Matthew Robert da Ricci."

"Da Ricci?"

"My title, and my married name."

The widow saw her mother-in-law's hand tighten on the beautiful lace trim of the white gown. "I'll call him Matteo, like you," was all that the older woman said.

"I hope it will comfort you, that though you have lost a son, I have brought your grandson to you?"

"I don't think . . ."

"You don't think . . . ?" the Italian woman repeated, almost as if she were daring Alinor to finish her thought. "What don't you think, Nonna? I shall call you dearest grandmother, you are his only grandmother!"

"I don't think that one child can take the place of another. Nor would I wish it."

"Oh! But to watch him grow up! An English boy in his father's country? Won't that joy take away the pain of your loss? Of our loss?"

Alinor said nothing, and the widow sensed that her lilting voice was somehow off key. "I must not tire you with my baby, and my sorrows."

"You don't tire me," Alinor said gently, giving the baby back to her. "And I'm glad that you have come and brought your son. I'm sorry we're not made ready for you. We only just got your letters. But you must have a home here as long as you want. Rob wrote that you have no family of your own?"

"No one," she said swiftly. "I have no one. I am an orphan. I have no one but you!"

"Then you shall stay as long as you wish, I'm only sorry that we don't have more to offer you."

The widow did not allow herself to glance around the room which was obviously a workplace, a sitting room, and a bedroom in one. "I want only to be with you. Is this your only house? What about your home in the country?"

"This is all we have."

"All I want is here," she breathed. "All I want is to live with you and with my sister, Alys."

Alinor nodded; but said nothing.

"Will you bless me?" her daughter-in-law prompted. "And call me Livia? And may I call you Mamma? May I call you *Mia Suocera,* my mother-in-law?"

Alinor's face paled as she closed her lips on a refusal. "Yes," she said. "Of course. God bless you, daughter."

The two young women dined alone in the parlor while the maid took a tray up the narrow stairs for Alinor. The nursemaid ate in the kitchen, sulking that there was no servants' hall. She took the baby under one arm and her candle in her hand and went up the narrow wooden stairs, to the first-floor bedroom, opposite the big front room that Alinor seldom left.

"Your mother is ill?" Livia asked Alys. "Roberto never told me she was so very ill."

"She had an accident," Alys replied.

Livia shook her head. "Ah, how sad. Just recently?"

"No, it was many years ago."

"But she will recover?"

"She can walk out in fine weather, but she gets very tired. She prefers to rest in her room."

"Oh, so sad! And she must have been a beautiful woman! To be struck down so!"

"Yes," said Alys shortly.

"Roberto never told me! He should have told me!"

"It was—" Alys broke off. She thought she could not answer for her brother to this exotic bride he had chosen. "It was a great shock to us all. We never spoke of it. We never speak of it at all."

The Nobildonna considered this for a moment. "An accident too terrible to discuss?"

"Exactly."

"You are silent?"

"Yes."

The pretty young woman considered this. "Was it your fault?" she asked baldly. "Since you have made a silence of an accident?"

Alys's face was stricken in the candlelight. "Yes, exactly. It was my fault. And I never speak of it, and nor does Ma."

The younger woman nodded as if secrets came naturally to her. "Very well. I shall say nothing also. So, tell me about the rest of your family. You have an uncle, do you not? Rob's uncle Ned?"

"Yes, but he is not in London. He would not live here, under a king. He writes every season from New England, and he sends us goods. Mostly herbs, he sends us rare herbs that we can sell to the apothecaries . . ."

"He leaves his home because he does not like the new king? But why should he care?" She laughed. "It's not as if they are likely to meet?"

"He's very staunch," Alys tried to explain. "He believed in the parliament, he fought in the New Model Army, he hates the rule of kings. When his leader Oliver Cromwell died, and they brought

Prince Charles back, my uncle left the country with others who think like him—great men, some of them. They would not live under a king and he would have executed them."

"He is wealthy in the New World?" she inquired. "He has a plantation? He has many slaves? He makes a fortune?"

"No, he has half a plot and the rights to the ferry. No slaves. He would never own a slave. He went with almost nothing, he had to leave our home."

"But it still belongs to the family?"

"No, it's lost. We were only ever tenants."

"I thought it was a great house, with servants and its own chapel?" she demanded.

"That was the Priory, where Rob stayed as a companion to the lord's son. My uncle Ned just had the ferry-house, and Ma and Rob and me lived in a little fisherman's cottage nearby."

Livia's pretty mouth pursed. "I thought you were a greater family than this!" she complained.

Alys gritted her teeth on her shame. "I'm afraid not."

But Livia was pursuing the family history. "Ah well, but you have children! Are they doing well? I so long to meet them! Where are they?"

"They are twins. My son, John, is at work, apprenticed to a merchant in the City. My daughter, Sarah, works as an apprentice milliner, she's nearly finished her time at the shop. She's very skillful, she takes after her grandmother—not me. They come home on Saturday after work."

"Heavens! You let her live away from home? In Venice we would never allow a girl such freedom."

Alys shrugged. "She's had to earn her own living, she has to have a trade. She's a sensible girl, I trust her."

Livia's laughter grated on Alys. "*Allora!* It is the young men I do not trust!"

Alys managed a smile; but said nothing.

"You do not arrange for her marriage to a wealthy gentleman?"

Alys shook her head. "No. It is better for her that she has her own trade, we think. And we don't know any wealthy gentlemen."

"But what about your visitor? Is he not wealthy?"

"We don't really know him." Alys ended this inquiry. "You must be very tired from your journey? But tomorrow I would be glad if you could tell me about your life with Rob. And . . . and . . . how he died."

"You surely had our letters?"

"We had letters from him when he first took up his post in Venice, and then he wrote that you would marry. He told us of little Matteo's birth and your happiness. But then we heard nothing until you wrote that he had drowned. We only got that letter last week. And then three days ago we had your letter from Greenwich telling of your arrival."

"Ah, I am so sorry! So sorry! I wrote from Venice at once, after my loss, and sent it at once. I did not think it would be so slow! I wrote again the moment that I landed. How good you are to welcome me when I bring such bad news!"

The maid came into the room and cleared the dishes. Nobildonna da Ricci looked around as if she were expecting more than the single plate of fruit and pastries.

"May I call you Livia?" Alys asked her. "You shall call me Sister Alys, if you wish."

"Roberto used to call me Lizzie, which made me laugh. He said he would make me into a real Englishwoman."

"You speak English so beautifully."

"Ah, my mother was an Englishwoman."

"Really? And your title?"

"It is my family title," she said. "An ancient name. So when I married, I added it to Ricci. That's the correct thing to do, isn't it?"

"I don't know," Alys said. "We've not got a title, we're not like that. Just a small family with nothing but this warehouse and two horses and the cart."

"But Roberto told me that Sir William Peachey was his patron, and James Summer was his great friend and tutor. He promised that when we came home we would have a great house in London, that he would be a famous physician."

"Rob was always ambitious," Alys conceded awkwardly. "But there's no great house. Just here." She looked around the small room and the cold grate. "This is an achievement for us . . . when I think where we came from . . ."

"Where did you come from?" Livia was curious. "For Roberto told me of land like the Venice lagoon—half land and half water, changing every tide, with the birds calling between sky and sea."

"It was like that," Alys agreed. "We were always on the edge, between poverty and surviving, between friends and enemies, in the tidelands between water and fields. We were on the edge of everything. At least here we are in a world with a firm footing. At least Uncle Ned is making a new life in a new land as he wants."

"But I want nothing more." Livia clasped Alys's hands, as if to swear a promise. "Nothing more than to enter the world with a firm footing. Nothing more than to make a new life, a better life. And we shall call each other sister and love each other as sisters should."

JUNE 1670, LONDON

The first morning after her arrival, Alinor invited Livia to take breakfast with her, and Alys helped the maid carry the heavy trays up the winding stairs. A small round table was laid with plain cutlery in the turret window and Alinor sat with her back to the river, with the glazed door open on the latch behind her, so that the ribbons of her cap stirred a little in the breeze. She could hear the gulls calling. It was a slack tide and the skiffs went quickly upstream, the sunlight shone on the water, and the ceiling of the room was dappled with the reflected ripples of light. "Tell me about your life in Venice," she invited Livia. "When did you meet my son?"

"We met in Venice. Italian families are very strict, you know? I was married very young to a much older man, a friend of my grandfather's. When the Conte, my husband, was taken ill, I had to call in a doctor; and everyone said that the young English doctor was the best in the world for my husband's condition."

"He trained at the university in Padua," Alinor said proudly.

"He came every day, he was so very kind. My husband had always been—" She broke off and looked at the older woman as if she could trust her to understand. "My husband was very . . . harsh with me. To tell you the truth: he was cruel, and Roberto was so kind. I fell in love with him." She looked from the older woman to the younger one. "I tried not to. I knew it was wrong, but I could not help myself."

Neither mother nor daughter exchanged the smallest glance. Alys fixed her eyes on the table as her mother watched Livia. "It is sometimes hard for a woman," Alinor agreed quietly. "Did Rob love you?"

"Not at first," she said. "He was always so careful, so correct. So English! You know what I mean?" She looked at their closed faces. "No, I suppose not! He used to come to the house wearing"—she broke off with a pretty little laugh—"such great boots! For going out on the marshes, you know? He used to walk on the sandbanks and islands, at low tide, where there were no paths or even tracks, he used to walk out and pick herbs and reeds. He would take a boat across the lagoon and then find his own way around the little islands. He knew his way as well as the fishermen that live on the lagoon. He would come into our old shuttered palace that was always so dark and so cool and I could smell the salt air, the open air on his jacket, in his hair—" She looked from one woman to the other. "It was like he was free, free as the birds of the lagoon and the salt marshes."

Alys glanced at her mother, who was leaning forward, drinking in the news of her son. "It sounds like our old home," she said.

"He was walking the tidelands," her mother agreed. "Like at Foulmire. He was walking in the paths between sea and land."

"He was!" Livia agreed. "There he was, living in the richest city in the world, but every afternoon he turned his back on it and went out into the lagoon and walked and listened to the cry of the birds. He liked our white birds, egrets, you know? He liked to watch them. He liked the waterside paths better than the gold markets and streets! He was so funny! Not like anyone else. He caught his own fish, imagine it! And he was not ashamed of being a countryman; he told people that he felt at home on the water and walking on the sandbanks and islands. And when my old husband became more and more ill, Roberto came to stay in the house to help to care for him, and when he died, Roberto was a great comfort."

Alys examined the bread rolls, not looking at her mother.

"I turned to him in my grief, and that was when I told him that I loved him," Livia whispered. "I should not have spoken, I know. But I was so lonely and so afraid in the great palace on the canal. It was so cold and so quiet, and when the family came for the funeral, I knew that they would throw me out and put the heir in my home. I knew they hated me: my husband had married me because I was young and beautiful." She gave a little laugh. "I was very beautiful when I was young."

Neither of her listeners assured her she was beautiful still, so Livia went on: "I only had one friend in the world." She looked imploringly at Alinor and reached out to clasp her hand. "Your son, Roberto."

Alys saw her mother withdraw her hand from the young woman's touch and wondered at her irritability. "Are you tired, Ma?" she asked her in an undertone.

"No, no," Alinor replied. She clasped her hands together in her lap, out of reach. "You must forgive me," she said to Livia. "I am an invalid. And Alys worries about me. Go on. Did Rob know you were in love with him?"

"Not at first," Livia said with a rueful little smile. "It's not how it should be at all. I know that in England it is the gentleman that speaks first? Isn't it so?"

Neither woman replied.

"I truly think that he was just sorry for me. He is—he was—so tenderhearted. Isn't he?"

"Yes," Alys said when her mother said nothing. "Yes, he was."

"When I had to leave Venice and go back to my family house in the hills outside Florence I thought I would never see him again. But he followed me." She put her hand to her heart. "He came to my family house and he told my cousin, the Signor, the head of my family, a very great family, that he loved me. It was the happiest moment of my life. The happiest ever."

"He wrote to us that he had met you, and that he admired you," Alys confirmed.

"Yes, he did," Alinor said. "And when he wrote to us that he would marry, we sent you some lace to trim your gown. Did you get it?"

"Oh yes, it was so beautiful! And I wrote in reply with my thanks. Did you receive that letter?"

Alys shook her head.

"I'm so sorry! I would not want you to think I was not grateful, and so glad of your good wishes. I wrote you a long letter. I sent it by a merchant. But who knows what happens to these ships! Such a long voyage and such dangerous seas!"

"Yes," Alinor agreed. "We've always lived on the edge of deep waters."

"So, we married quietly in Venice and we defended ourselves against my first husband's family."

"Against what?" Alys asked.

"Oh, they were jealous! And they said all sorts of things against me. Then, I found I was with child, and we were so glad. When little Matteo was born we knew that we had found true happiness. Then—ah, but you know the rest—"

"No, I don't," Alinor interrupted. "You have told me nothing!"

"You only wrote that he had drowned," Alys reminded her.

Livia took a sobbing breath. Clearly, it was an ordeal for the widow to speak. "Roberto was called out to one of the islands on a stormy night. I went with him, I often went with him. There was a terrible wind and our ship overturned. They pulled me out of the water at dawn, it was a miracle that I survived." She turned her face from the brightness of the window and hid it in her little black-trimmed handkerchief. "I wished that I had not survived," she whispered. "When they told me that he was dead . . . I told them to throw me back into the waters."

Alys looked at her mother, waiting for her to speak with her usual compassion; but the older woman said nothing, just watched, her gray eyes slightly narrowed, as if she were waiting to hear something more.

"So terrible," Alys whispered.

Livia nodded, dried her eyes, and managed a trembling smile. "I wrote to you of his death—I am sure I made no sense at all, I was so grieved! I knew I should come to you, I knew Roberto would have wanted it. So, though I was quite alone in the world, I packed up our little house, I spent all our savings on my passage on the ship, and here we are. I wrote to you as soon as we landed, and then I hired the coach and came. I have brought my English boy to his home."

There was a silence.

"And we're so glad you've come," said Alys too loudly into the quiet room. "Aren't we? Aren't we? Ma?"

"Yes," Alinor said. "Did they find the body?"

The question was so coldly abrupt that both young women stared at her.

"The body?" Livia repeated.

"Yes. Rob's drowned body. Did they find it? Drag it from the water, bury him with the proper rites? As a Protestant?"

"Ma!" Alys exclaimed.

"No," Livia said, the tears welling up again. "They didn't. It's so deep, and there are currents. They did not expect to find it—him—not after he had . . . sunk."

"Sunk," Alinor repeated slowly. "You tell me that my son—sunk?"

Alys put out her hand as if to stop the words but neither woman noticed her.

"We held a service of memorial at the place that he was lost," Livia said, her musical voice very low. "When the sea was calm, I went out on a little rowing boat; it was halfway between Venice and the island of Torcello. I put flowers on the water for you: white lilies on the dark tides."

"Oh really," Alinor said indifferently. She turned her head and looked down to the quayside. "There's that ship factor again," she said.

Livia leaned towards the window and glimpsed James Avery on the doorstep, being admitted to the house. "Oh, that is not a ship's factor," she said. "That's Sir James Avery, Roberto's tutor and friend. I met him yesterday."

The room froze. Nobody spoke. Alys could hear the maid slowly laboring up the stairs from the hall and then the creak as she opened the door. "Am I to clear the crocks?" she asked into the stunned silence.

"Yes, yes," Livia said, when no one else answered. She looked from Alinor's white face to Alys's fixed grimace. "Have I said something wrong? What is wrong?"

"James Avery is here? That was the visitor: James Avery?" Alinor demanded.

"Yes," Alys said tightly. "I didn't even know if you would recognize his real name?"

"Yes. It was to be my name. Of course I recognize it."

"He is Sir James. Turns out he has a title. Did you think it would be yours?" Alys demanded.

"Yes. He came here to see me?"

Alys silently nodded.

Mother and daughter looked at each other as if they were blind to the maid clattering around the table and Livia's avid face.

"Alys, when were you going to tell me?"

"I was never going to tell you."

The maid took the heavily laden tray and walked out of the room, leaving the door open. They heard her slow progress down the stairs and then the knock of the whip handle on the front door. They could hear her sigh, and the rattle of crockery as she put the tray down on the hall table. They listened as she opened the front door and said impatiently: "Go in! Go in!" sending Sir James into the empty parlor as she hefted the tray again and went down the hall to the kitchen to yell from the back door for the wagoner to take the gentleman's horse again.

"Has he been before?"

"Not before yesterday. I swear he has not."

"Or written?"

Alys's silence was a confession.

"He wrote to me? He has written to me?"

The daughter said nothing.

"Did you think you were keeping him from me, for my own good?" Alinor asked gently.

"No." Alys was driven into honesty, the words spilling out with sudden tears. "It was for me. I could hardly bear to touch his letters. I'd never have let him in if I'd known who he was yesterday, I'd have slammed the door in his face. As it is, I told him not to come back. Not for you, because I don't know what you feel—now, after all this time. It was for me. Because I will never forgive him."

"After all this time? As you say? After all this time?"

"More. More every year that you sicken."

"But he was so good to Roberto!" Livia interrupted. "And so charming a gentleman. I don't understand! You are angry, Sister Alys? You are distressed? And you . . . *Mia Suocera*?"

They both ignored her.

"He wrote to me?" Alinor's voice was a thread.

"I dropped his first letter in the fire, and when the wax burned off, a gold coin fell through the bars of the grate into the ashes. I didn't even know what it was, only that it was gold. It was a French pistole. I kept it. It paid for your medicine, we'd never have afforded the doctor without it. Next year he sent again. This time I lifted the seal and took the coin and burned the letter. I never wanted to know what he wrote. I never wanted to see his writing. I never wanted to see him again."

"But Roberto said he was so good . . ." Livia remarked. "And he is such a gentleman! His clothes . . ."

"He wasn't good to us," Alys said with quiet bitterness. "He was no gentleman then."

Her words drove Alinor to her feet, leaning on the breakfast table for support. At once, Alys jumped up to help her.

"No, I can walk. I'm just going to my chair." She took the three steps, leaning on the table and then the back of the chair, and when she was seated she was breathless, her face pale.

"Let me tell him to leave?" Alys asked her. "Ma? Please can I tell him to go?"

"Leave?"

"And come back in another twenty-one years?"

Alinor shook her head, fanning her face with her hand as if she would summon air. "I can't see him now."

"Oh, why not?" Livia's face was bright with curiosity. "Since he has come twice to see you? And before that, he sent money?"

"You don't have to see him, ever," Alys said fiercely.

"Ask him to come back tomorrow." Alinor struggled to speak. "I'll see him tomorrow, in the afternoon."

"I don't want him here again."

Alinor nodded. "I know, my dear, I know. Just this once."

Livia looked from one to the other, her dark gaze sharp. "But why not?"

"Not Saturday afternoon, not Sunday," Alys specified.

Alinor took a shuddering breath. "Oh? Is it the children he wants? Did he not come for me, but for them?"

"I don't know what he wants," Alys said stubbornly. "But he shan't have it."

Her mother looked at her with a long level stare. "I expect you do know," she said, her voice very low. "I expect he told you."

"I hate him."

"I know." She took a breath and closed her eyes, leaning her head back against the high chair. "Best tell him to come back this afternoon then. Not tomorrow so he can't see the children."

"Shall I tell him?" Livia offered helpfully. "Shall I run down and tell him to come back this afternoon?"

Alys nodded, and the young woman whisked from the room. They heard her high-heeled shoes clatter down the stairs to the parlor, and then they heard the door close behind her. In the sunlit bedroom Alinor reached out her hand silently to her daughter, and Alys gripped it.

James Avery was looking out of the window over the busy quayside; the grinding of the pulleys and the rolling of the barrels was a constant nagging din.

"Sir James." Livia entered and swept a deep curtsey to him.

He turned and bowed. "Nobildonna da Ricci."

"Madam Ricci will see you this afternoon," she said simply. "It is too early now. She is unwell, you understand. And of course, old people do not like to meet their friends early in the day."

He hesitated as if he could not understand what she was saying.

She gave him a mischievous smile. "You must not surprise us

ladies in the morning!" she said. "The older you are, the more there is to do!"

James flushed and looked awkward. "I did not think . . . I'll come back this afternoon then." He picked up his hat and whip from the table. "Would three o'clock be the right time?"

"Why not say four o'clock, and you can stay for dinner," she offered.

"She invited me for dinner?" He was astounded.

Her gleeful smile told him the truth. "No! It is my invitation; but I hope that they will agree."

"You are kind to me, Nobildonna da Ricci," he said, carefully hiding his disappointment. "But I think I had better wait for an invitation from Mrs. Stoney."

"From Sister Alys? She'll never make you welcome! Why does she dislike you so much?"

"I didn't know that she did?"

She laughed irrepressibly, and then clapped her hand over her pink lips and the little white teeth. "Ah, this house! Nobody laughs here!"

"They don't?"

"No, it is very grave. Roberto was such a happy young man. I thought everyone would be merry."

He started to speak and then checked himself, as if there was too much to say. "It all happened a long time ago."

"When the twins were born?"

"There are twins?"

She widened her dark eyes. "Did you not know? But I thought you came to see them?"

"I did not know there were twins," he said, carefully choosing his words. "I must speak to Mrs. Reekie. I might be able to . . . I could assist the boy. I have been blessed in my good fortune, and I would want to be of assistance to her, if I can."

"You have no family of your own?"

"My wife and I were childless. It was a great sorrow to us."

"But of course. It is a sorrow for any man and wife. Especially if there is property."

He smiled at her frankness. "You are a Venetian indeed. Yes, it is a great pity, especially if there is property."

"I am not a Venetian," she corrected him. "My family home is in the hills outside Florence. We are a very old family, a noble family. That is why I know the importance of a son and heir. And now I am an English lady. With an English boy. Would you have made Roberto your heir if he had lived?"

She could see him shift on his feet and look awkward. "I have a particular interest in the boy . . . in the twins."

"But Roberto is their uncle? Then my baby must be their cousin?"

"Yes, of course."

"So you must love my boy too," she insisted. "Let me show him to you."

"Perhaps I should go now and come back this afternoon?" he suggested, but she had already opened the parlor door and called out before he could speak, and then the nursemaid came from the kitchen with the baby in her arms.

Quickly Livia took the baby from the nursemaid and turned to James with her cheek against the little dark head. The baby was awake, and as she held him out to James, he fixed the man's face with a dark blue wondering gaze.

"Is he not beautiful?" she demanded, her hands still on him as she put him into James's arms, so they held him together.

"Yes," James said truly, struck with tenderness at the thought of this child, another child, growing up fatherless in this poor little house.

"See, how he likes you," she remarked, moving away so that James held the baby on his own, and felt his grip tighten with anxiety.

"I have no experience of babies," he said, holding him for only a moment and then trying to hand him back to her. "I don't know how to manage them. I don't know what they . . . prefer."

She laughed at that, but she took the child and held him against her shoulder, turning sideways so that James could see the exquisite baby face against the darkness of his mother's glossy hair and her profile, as clear-cut as a cameo. "Ah, you would learn in no time," she assured him. "You would be a wonderful father. I know you would be. Every man should raise his son. It is his legacy. How else can he leave a name in the world?"

The door opened behind her and Alys stood in the doorway. She looked in silence from her sister-in-law to James and back again. James flushed with embarrassment.

"My mother will see you this afternoon," Alys said icily to James. "Not now. Lady da Ricci was telling you to leave now."

"Indeed yes," the lady said, her dark eyes wide. "Forgive me, I was distracted."

James bowed. "At what time shall I come?" he asked, picking up his hat and riding whip.

"At four?" Livia suggested brightly. "And stay for dinner?"

"At three," Alys ruled. "For an hour."

JUNE 1670, HADLEY, NEW ENGLAND

Ned had pulled his ferry to the north side of the river and left it grounded where the shallow pebble beach made a dry landing place for passengers even when the river was in flood. He picked up his basket and walked up the narrow trail to Norwottuck village, his dog Red—named in memory of his old English dog—following at his heels.

He paused while he was still half a mile out and, self-consciously, cupped his hands to his mouth and made the "urr urr whoo hoo" call of the native owl, and waited till he heard the cry back. This was his permission to come to the village. He started on down the path and saw an old woman walking easily towards him. She must have been more than sixty but her hair, worn long on one side, was still black and her stride was confident. Only the deep wrinkles on her face and neck showed she was an elder of the village, a person of wisdom and experience.

"Quiet Squirrel," Ned said making a little nod to her. "Friend."

"*Nippe Sannup*," she said pleasantly, in her own language. "*Netop*."

Ned struggled to reply in the native tongue. "*Netop*, Quiet Squirrel. Want candlewood, want sassafras," he said. "Me come look-find?"

She had to hide a smile at the big man talking like a child. "Take what you need from the forest," she said generously. "And I have something to show you. I don't know if you Coatmen like this?"

She unbuttoned a satchel at her side and proffered a lump of rock. Ned took it from her hands, turned it over to examine it, and saw that the pebble had been cut in two and each half was hollow, but inside a tiny cave of diamonds sparkled with purple and blue crystals.

He looked from the jagged gems to Quiet Squirrel's face.

"What this?" he asked.

"Thunderstone," she told him. "It protects from lightning strike." When he frowned, uncomprehendingly, she raised her hands to the sky, and made a rumbling noise in her throat and then a "crick! crick!" noise. She brought her hands down, making a jagged gesture. "Lightning," she told him. She lifted the stone above her head and smiled. "Safe. This is a thunderstone: it protects from thunderstorms."

Ned nodded. "Lightning! Safe—I understand."

He thought at once that this would be something his sister in London could sell to merchants whose high wooden roofs left them vulnerable to lightning strike, whose terror was fire, who had sworn their city must never burn again. She could sell it to the new builders in London who were putting up church spires with brass weathercocks, and bell towers with bronze bells. "You got lots?" he asked. "Many? Many?"

She laughed at him, showing her teeth ground down from a diet of hard vegetable and grit. "Coatman!" she exclaimed. "You always want more. Show you one thing, you want a hundred."

Ruefully he spread his hands. "But I can sell this," he admitted in English, and then tried her language again: "Trade. Good trade. You want wampum?"

She shook her head. "Not wampum, not between you and me, not between friends." She took his hand to try to explain to him. "Wampum is a sacred thing, *Nippe Sannup*. Wampum is a holy thing. You should give it as a gift, to one you love to show them that you value them. It's not a coin. We should never have let your people use it for coin. It is not for sale. It shows love and respect. Respect is not for sale."

Ned grasped one word in ten of this but knew he had somehow offended. "Sorry," he said. "Sorry. Big feet—" He mimed trampling on her feelings. "Sorry. Big feet."

"What on earth are you doing now?" she asked him as he marched around the clearing trying to mime the idea of clumsiness. "You Coatmen are all quite mad."

Ned returned to her. "Sorry. You have more? This? Fair price?" He dipped his head. "Not wampum—not you to me wampum. We are friends."

She put her head on one side as if she were calculating. "I can get more," she said. "But you will pay me in musket parts, and small iron rods."

Ned recognized the English word "muskets." "Not guns," he objected. "No guns. No thundersticks. Not for People of Dawnlands. Very bad!"

"Not guns," she agreed pleasantly. "But hammer, mainspring, frizzen." She knew the English words for the parts of a musket, and showed him that she meant little parts of guns with her fingers.

"Why?" Ned asked uneasily. "Why want? Why want parts of guns?"

She smiled into his honest anxious face. "For hunting, of course," she lied. "For hunting deer, *Nippe Sannup*. What else?"

He was troubled. He did not have the words to ask her why she wanted parts to renovate muskets, if her people were arming, perhaps for a foray against another tribe which would disturb the balance of the whole region—English settlements as well as native peace treaties. "But all happy?" he asked, feeling like a fool under her steady dark gaze. "All good friends? *Netop*, yes? You like Coatmen?" He could not mask the note of pleading in his voice. "Friends with us? Us Englishmen? Friends with me?"

JUNE 1670, LONDON

The front door closed behind James, and the two young women stood in silence to listen to the clatter of the horseshoes on the cobbles as he rode down the quay.

"And where does he go? Sir James? Does he have a town house?" Livia asked.

"I have no idea."

"You don't ask him? You don't know if he stays at an inn or if he is so rich that he has a house of his own in London?"

"No."

"I would ask him," the younger woman asserted.

"I'd prefer you don't," Alys said, her awkwardness making her Sussex accent stronger. "He's no friend to the family, he never was. You need not be more than . . ."

"Polite?" Livia suggested with a little gleam. "Polite and cold? Like you?"

"Yes."

"Of course, I will always be polite to your guests."

There was a little silence in the small, stuffy room.

"And what do you do now?" Livia asked. "For the rest of the day? Do you, perhaps, walk out to look at shops? Do we go out to visit friends?"

"No!" Alys exclaimed. "I work. I have goods coming in on the coastal trading ships, and I store them in the warehouse. I break them into smaller loads and send them to the London markets and shops and inns. I order the return load, and I pack the goods and send them out for their return journey. We trade along the coast, Kent and Sussex and Hampshire."

"No society?" Livia asked.

"We are a working wharf," Alys explained. "In the coastal trade. There's no time for society."

"But why only the little ships?"

"Sometimes we have big ships. But mostly they have to go to the legal quays to pay their taxes. Only the untaxed loads can come here. Sometimes, when the wait for the Excise officers is too long, the big ships will come here to declare their tax and unload. We're called a sufferance wharf—we're allowed to take the overspill from the legal quays. Some mornings I go to the coffeehouses to meet the captains and the shipowners and bid for their business."

"They are pleasant places? For ladies? Could I come with you?"

Alys laughed at the thought of it. "No. You wouldn't like it. They're for business."

The younger woman widened her dark eyes and rested her lips against her baby's head. "You are a workingwoman—what do you call yourself? A storeman?"

"I'm a wharfinger."

"You do it all?"

Alys flushed. "It's how we live."

"Roberto told me that he was raised in the country, on the side of marshes that stretched to the sea and you never knew where the dry paths were and only people who lived there could find their way through the waters."

"That was more than twenty years ago," Alys said unwillingly. "Rob was telling you of our childhood home. But, after the accident, we had to leave Foulmire and come here. At first, we worked for the woman that owned this quay, and we did her deliveries with our cart and horse, and then we were able to buy her out. Ma went out as a midwife to our neighbors, and made herbal teas and possets. She still has a good trade with the apothecaries and Uncle Ned sends us goods from New England, especially herbs."

"You don't have a warehouse in the City? You don't own a ship?"

"This is all," Alys confirmed.

"But why does your husband not do all this work for you? Where is Mr. Stoney?"

Alys flushed deeply. "Surely Rob told you? I've got no husband. I had to bear the twins and raise them on my own."

"Ah, I am so sorry. No, he didn't tell me. I begin to think he was not honest with me. He made me think that you were a grander family by far, related to the Peachey family, and he was brought up with the lord's son, a friend of the family."

Again, Alys shook her head, her mouth folded into a severe line. "No," she said. "There's no family anymore. Rob was just a companion to Sir William Peachey's son; but only for one summer. Walter Peachey died years ago, his father too. Sir James Avery was their tutor. We're not related to any lords, and we're not friends with Sir James. And we never will be." She hesitated, her face flamed red. "Maybe Rob was ashamed to tell you. Perhaps he was ashamed of us."

"But Sir James comes to see your mother this afternoon?" Livia pursued. "There must be a friendship here, an acquaintance?"

"No," Alys said flatly. "He's coming just this once, and it makes no difference."

As Alys went into her counting room, in the corner of the warehouse, and Alinor rested upstairs, Livia left the baby with the nursemaid, put on her hat, and walked out on the quayside where the incoming tide was running fast, slapping against the walls and sweeping away the rubbish upstream. Laborers fell back from her path with exaggerated respect, lounging sailors tipped their caps to her face and whistled behind her back. She ignored them all, walking through them as if she were deaf to the shouted suggestions and catcalls. She did not turn her head, she did not flush with embarrassment. Only once did she stop, when a tall broad man blocked her path and seized her hands.

"Gi' us a kiss," he said, bending down and breathing a warm gust of beer into her face. To his surprise, instead of shrinking back she instantly gripped him tightly and pulled him closer, so that she could kick him, hard, just under the kneecap with her pointed shoe. He let out a yelp of surprise and pain and jumped back.

"*Vaffanculo!*" she spat at him. "If you lay one finger on me, you'll be sorry."

He bent and rubbed his knee. "God's blood, missis . . . I just . . ."

She turned her head and walked away before he could answer.

"Oy! Oy!" came the shout from his mates. "No luck, Jonas?"

He straightened up and made an obscene gesture, but he let Livia walk on, upriver. She turned inland from the quay along the little road that ran, potholed and muddy, behind the warehouses. She turned again, onto a cart track leading south, lined with small cottages with vegetable gardens. Behind them were green fields, and beyond them, a slow rise of green hills trimmed with darker hedges, capped with the soft billows of midsummer woods. Livia shaded her eyes and looked towards the horizon: nothing.

Nothing.

Livia, who had lived most of her life among the crowded squares and busy markets of Venice, saw nothing but emptiness: a waste of green, a few cows, a child watching them from the shade of an ash tree, and in the distance, the smoke from the chimney of an isolated farmhouse. Nothing.

"*Dio!*" she said horrified. "What a place!"

She gave a little "tut" of disapproval at the absence of activity, of shops, or diversion; she sighed irritably at the silence broken only by the cry of the seagulls over the river and the aspiring trill, high above her, of a lark. There was nothing here to give her any pleasure, and she turned her back on the fields, and went back the way she had come. The birds were singing in the hedges as she walked; she did not hear them.

"Where is she?" Alinor asked the maid who brought her some warm broth.

"Walking."

"Where has she gone walking?" she asked Alys, who came in, still wearing her baize apron from the counting house, with an ink stain on her finger.

"I don't know. I didn't even know she was out," Alys said indifferently. "Perhaps she's walked over Horsleydown."

"Wouldn't she have taken the nursemaid? Wouldn't she have taken the baby for fresh air?"

"I don't know," Alys said again. "Ma, this afternoon . . ."

"Yes?"

"Are you sure you want to see him? You don't have to see him at all, of course. I can just tell him . . ."

"What's he coming for?"

"I don't know."

"For his child?"

"He doesn't have a child," the younger woman replied stubbornly. "He'll never learn it from me."

"Nor me," Alinor promised, and when her daughter looked at her she smiled, with her old confidence. "Truly."

"He knew you were with child back then?"

Alinor turned her head away.

"Ma, did you tell him?"

"He knew I was carrying his child; but he did not claim me, nor own it."

"He may claim you now," Alys warned her; and was surprised by the luminous clarity of her mother's smile as she raised her head.

"Then he's a bit late," she said.

Livia returned from her walk just as Sir James stepped ashore from a little wherry boat at Horsleydown Stairs. Sir James paid his fare and climbed the greasy steps as she waited at the top. She smiled, as if surprised at their meeting, and gave him her hand. He bowed and kissed it.

"You have been out?" he asked, glancing around at the wharf and the idle men who were openly staring.

"I have to walk, for my health," she said. "Behind these houses and these warehouses are some beautiful fields, so green! Rob always told me that England is so green all year round."

"You should not walk alone," he said.

"Who is there to walk with me?" she asked. "My sister-in-law works all day long, she has no time for me! And my mamma-in-law is delicate."

"Your maid," he said. "Or their maid."

She gave a little giggle. "You have seen their maid?"

She let the silence lengthen, until the thought came to him that he could walk with her.

"Shall we go in?" he asked.

"Of course!" she said. "Forgive me, I have forgotten my Italian manners in this rough place! Please come in."

She preceded him into the little hall and took off her bonnet, keeping on a little cap deliciously trimmed with black ribbons. She led the way into the parlor that overlooked the quayside and dropped the blinds on the noise and the heat with a sigh, as if they were unbearable. In the shaded room, she turned back to him. "May I offer you some tea? I suppose you want tea? Or do gentlemen take wine in the afternoon in England?"

"Nothing, I thank you," he said. "I am here to visit Mrs. Reekie. Would you be so kind as to ask the maid to tell her I am here?"

"I will tell her myself," she said sweetly. "She's not the sort of maid who announces visitors. I had better do it. What business shall I say?"

His grip on his hat tightened. "Nothing . . . nothing . . . Just . . . she will know."

"A personal matter?" she suggested helpfully.

"Exactly so."

"I will tell her at once. May I plead on your behalf? Is there anything I can say to help you?"

He loosened his collar under her dark, sympathetic gaze. "No. I had better . . . I believe she will . . . at any rate. It is about the child. But she knows that, she will know that."

"Her grandchildren? Is there some way I can help you?"

He let out an exclamation and turned from her. "I am afraid you cannot help me," he said. "I am afraid nobody can. These are old troubles, and in my case, old sorrows."

"Is the boy yours?" she asked very quietly, coming to stand close to him, her face filled with compassion at his distress. "Do you think he is your own son?"

He turned and she saw his mouth tremble. "Yes," he said. "I believe so. I think he is mine. I think I have a son."

"Then he should know his father," she whispered gravely. "And you should know him."

Livia led Sir James up the narrow stairs, tapped on the door, and swung it open. He had to squeeze past her to enter the room but he was unaware of her perfume or the swish of her silk skirts as she drew them back; he saw nothing but Alinor, leaning on her high-backed chair, waiting for him, as she had waited for him in the meadow, as she had waited for him on the rickety pier.

"We were almost always out of doors," he blurted out, and he closed the door behind him.

"We were," she agreed. "There was never anywhere that we could go."

They both fell silent, looking at each other. He thought he would have known her anywhere, her gray eyes were the same, the direct gaze and the slight lift to her lips. Her hair, smoothed under her cap, was not the rich gold he had loved but bleached into a pale beauty. Her face was white, even her lips were cream; but she was the same woman he had loved and betrayed, the set of her shoulders and the turn of her head was instantly recognizable as the woman who lived, indomitably, on the edge of the mire and defied ill luck or high tides to wash her away.

She regarded him carefully, looking past the gloss of his prosperity, the fine clothes, the thickened body, to the troubled young man she had loved with such a reckless desire.

"You are ill," he said, his voice filled with pity.

She gave a little grimace at his tone. "I never recovered."

"You have a consumption?"

"Something like drowning," she said. "I drowned then, and I go on drowning. The water sits in my lungs."

He shut his eyes on the memory of the green water pouring from her mouth when they turned her limp body on her side. "I failed you." He found that he was on one knee before her, his head bowed. "I failed you terribly. I have never forgiven myself."

"Aye," she said indifferently. "But I forgave you almost at once. There was no need for you to set your own penance."

"I have served a hard penance." He looked eagerly upwards, wanting her to know that he too had suffered. "I was restored to my home, to the lands that I loved, and I married, but my wife took no pleasure in our life, and she never conceived a child. I am a widower now. I am alone with no one to continue my name."

"And so now you come to me?" She sat down and gestured that he should rise and take a seat.

"Now I am free to do what I should have done that day. I am free to claim you for my wife, my beloved wife, and to name your child as my child, and to give you both the home you should have had, and the future you should have had."

She said nothing for a long moment and the silence made him realize for the first time how arrogant he sounded. Outside the seagulls wheeled and cried. He heard the clatter of the sheets against the masts, and at that sound, which had always meant leaving and loss to him, his heart sank and he knew that she would refuse him.

"I'm sorry, James, but you're too late," she said quietly. "This is my home, and there is no child of yours here."

"I'm not too late. I am not too late, Alinor. I never ceased to love you, I wrote to you every year on Midsummer Eve, I never forgot you. Not even when I was married did I ever forget you. I swore I would come for you as soon as I was free."

Her dark gray eyes gleamed with inner laughter. "Then you cannot be surprised that your wife took no pleasure in her life with you," she observed.

He gasped at the sharpness of her wit. "Yes, I failed her too," he admitted. "I am a failure: as a lover to you, and as a husband to her. I have been wrong since the day I denied you. I was like Saint Peter: I did not own you when I should have done. The cock crowed and I did not hear."

She made a little tutting noise. "It was not the Garden of

Gethsemane! I was not crucified! My heart broke; but now it's healed. Go and live your life, James. You owe me nothing."

"But the king is restored," he tried to explain. "I want to be restored too! I want our victory. It won't be a victory for me until I am back in my house with you at my side."

She shook her head. "It's no victory for us, remember? Not for people like us. Ned left England rather than be subject to this king. He left his home rather than live with my shame. And Rob went too, and now his widow comes to my door to tell me he's drowned, and I can't even make myself believe her. I can't get back to my home. My brother can't return, my son never will."

He hesitated, driven to honesty. "Alinor—I must have my son. I have no one to continue my name, I have no one to inherit my house, my land. I can't bear to have a son raised in poverty when I should endow him."

"We're not poor," she snapped.

"I own hundreds of acres."

She was silent.

"They are rightfully his."

She sighed as if she were very weary. "You've imagined this boy," she said gently. "All these years. You've got no son, no more have I. There's no one here to inherit your fortune nor continue your name. You didn't want the baby when he was in the womb, you denied him then. He was lost to you the very day that you said that you didn't want him. Those words can't be unsaid. You didn't want him then, and now you don't have him. You are, as you wanted to be: childless." She put her hand to her throat. "I can't say more."

He leapt to his feet and reached for her. "Can I help you? Shall I call someone?"

She leaned back against the hard leather padding of the high-backed chair, her face as white as ice. She shook her head and closed her eyes. "Just go."

He dropped to his knees beside her chair, he took up her still hand and put the cold fingers to his lips; but when she did not open her eyes or even stir, he realized that he could say nothing, do nothing but obey her. "I'll go," he whispered. "Please do not be distressed.

Forgive me—love. I'll speak to Alys on my way out. Forgive me . . . forgive me."

He glanced back at her ashen face as he took two steps to reach the door, closed it behind him, and all but stumbled down the stairs. Tabs, the maid, was arduously climbing up with a tray of small ale.

"D'you not want it now?" she demanded with a sigh.

He brushed past her without an answer. Alys was waiting at the foot of the stairs, standing like a statue, her face like stone. The door to the parlor was ajar; he guessed that Livia was inside, eavesdropping.

"She's ill," he exclaimed.

Alys nodded. "I know it."

"She refuses me," he said.

"What else?"

"I will come back," he said. "I can't leave it like this."

She said nothing but gestured to the front door and he could do nothing but bow to her, his face flushed and angry. He had to open the front door himself, and step out onto the wharf, ignoring the stevedores loading another cargo into a ship bobbing at midtide, and walk beside the river to Horsleydown Stairs to hail a wherry to take him back to the north side, to his beautiful London house on the Strand.

He thought for a wild moment that he should plunge into the muddy tide and drown before her house, that nothing else would wash his honor clean, that nothing else would free him from this pain. He heard the clink of chains from the bones hanging at the gibbet at the edge of the River Neckinger and thought how hateful this place was. He hated Alys with a hot murderous fury, and for a moment, he even hated Alinor too. She had been his inferior in every way, his for the taking, but somehow she had slipped away from him, like a mermaid in dark tides, and his son had gone too, like a changeling stolen by faeries. He wheeled and looked back at the house. The shabby little door was tight closed.

He looked up at her window and thought he could see the pale outline of her gown as she looked down at him. At once, his hand went to his hat; he swept it from his head and stood looking up, at her, bareheaded. "Alinor!" he whispered, as if she would throw open the window and call down to him.

He bowed with what dignity he could find, put his hat on his head, and turned to walk to the water stairs to hail a waterman, but there were no craft plying the incoming tide and he stood for a lifetime, looking at the dazzle of the sunlight on the dancing ripples, wondering if he could have said anything that would have persuaded her. The day was hot and exhausting, and he felt old and defeated, marooned among the poor on the wrong side of the river.

"Sir James?"

It was the widow, with a black lace shawl over her head, as if she had run down the stairs to bring him a message. At once he turned from the edge of the quay and went towards her.

"Tomorrow is Saturday," she said briefly. "The children come home after they have finished their work in the afternoon. If you were to come to take me for a walk at, say, four o'clock, we could come back at five. You would see the grandchildren. And perhaps they will invite you for dinner."

"She refuses to see me ever again."

"But you will see your boy, despite them both, if you meet me at four."

"He's my boy?" he said with a surge of longing. "He is?"

She spread her hands. "Only she can say. But you can at least see him."

"You are kind to me . . ." he said awkwardly.

"I have no friend in England but these . . ." She gestured at the mean little warehouse. "And perhaps you?"

JUNE 1670, HADLEY, NEW ENGLAND

Ned walked up the broad grazing lane that ran through the center of Hadley village with a big basket loaded with the fat red strawberries grown in his garden on one arm, and on the other a basket of wild leeks and mushrooms that he had gathered from the forest. Horses, cows, sheep, and even pigs cropped the wide track that ran through the center of town. Later in summer the cows would be released to graze with a cowherd to watch over them, the pigs would run freely in the forest to root for nuts and mushrooms, tearing up the earth with their sharp little hooves and their rooting tusks, and the horses would be released to run free and only brought in to work.

The weave of the basket on Ned's arm was the signature of the maker, a woman from the Pocumtuc who lived a few miles upriver of Ned's ferry and had given him a basket in return for free crossings. He had taught her some English words earlier in spring, when he was digging his plot, and the women used to call his ferry over to the north bank to bring them into the little town. She had come into his garden one evening at dusk and shown him the Seven Sister stars, just visible in the evening sky, and told him that their coming was a sign that it was time to plant beneath them.

"My name," she told him. "Plant-time Star."

"My name Ned," he replied.

Plant-time Star showed him how to heap the earth into hillocks, how to plant the seeds with a fish to feed them, how the three seeds—squash, beans, and maize—should grow together to feed the earth and should be eaten together to feed the body. "The three sisters," she said, as if there was something holy about planting. "Given to us: the People."

He had thought she would come back to see how the crops had grown but he had not seen her after an argument about fish traps set in the river. Someone going downriver to the sawmill at Northampton, steering a raft of felled logs, had grounded the boat on half a dozen of the exquisitely made basket traps. The women had complained to the elders at Hadley who had said, reasonably enough, that it was no one from the town, and that they must go for compensation to the sawmill, or to the logger himself—whoever he was. Now the women crossed the river in their own dugouts, as if they did not trust the raft ferry nor the broad green common that ran through the center of the town, where every house stared at them as they went by.

Ned missed their cheerful chatter, and the little goods they paid him as fees. He even spoke up for them at the town meeting, but no one could agree how long a native fish trap took to make, and what one of the fish traps would be worth. No Englishman had the knack of making them so no one could say, and many declared that native time was worthless anyway, and the traps were made from twigs that were worthless too.

Without the native women traders to walk with him, Ned went alone, calling at one house and then another down the street, exchanging his goods for a small tub of butter at one house, a whip of an apple tree at another, and setting some new-laid eggs against his slate at the third. He sold to households whose gardens were not as productive as his, and to those who would not spend time in the woods looking for food. The debts he paid with his produce were part of the constant exchange of the town. When Ned had first arrived he had hired other settlers to help him build his house, roof it, and set up his stock-proof fence.

"I don't dare go into the forest," one woman said, standing on her doorstep and looking at his basket of mushrooms. "I'd be afraid of getting lost."

"No fish today, Mr. Ferryman?" a woman called over the stock fence, irritated at the shortage.

"Not today," he said. "Probably next week." He did not tell her that he had set his fish traps as usual but someone had pulled up the stakes that held them to the riverbed and released all the fish but two or three, as if to leave enough for Ned to eat, but not enough for him to sell.

"You won't get my business if you can't be relied on," she said sharply.

"Why? Who else are you going to buy from?"

She looked around at the empty lane. The women who usually brought fish and food to trade walked past in silence, their creels dangling empty from their hands, their faces closed and unfriendly.

"I don't want to buy from them," she said, walking away, her expression sour.

"By the looks of it, they don't want to sell to you," Ned said under his voice.

Ned went on to the blacksmiths', where Samuel and Philip Smith worked at the forge in the double lot behind their clapboard houses. Ned swapped some leeks for a bag of new nails to fix the shingles on his house walls against the coming winter.

"Heard you refused to come into town," Samuel Smith said with a slow smile at Ned. "Thought it was odd."

"I didn't refuse!" Ned exclaimed. "I'll come when I'm needed. But I can't leave the ferry without warning. I've got to get someone to man it. Like now, Joel's lad is minding it for me. I'll come when I've something to sell or to buy, or when I can serve my neighbors or the Lord. Not because some selectman, in his place five minutes, comes and tells me I'm to take orders from him."

"All you old roundheads will only take orders from your own," Philip joked, and saw Ned's slow smile.

"Thing is," Sam interjected, "you don't know, living that far out and ferrying the savages as you do, friendly like, that there's rumors that the French are sending messages to them, stirring up trouble against us. Telling them we can't be trusted."

Ned gave him a rueful look. "Oh, can we be trusted?" he asked. "For I heard that the Massasoit—their chief—swore that he would sell no more of his people's land, and we swore he should keep his own; and yet we go on buying. I heard it was the Plymouth governor's own son: Josiah Winslow himself! Taking up mortgages on Indian lands and making them sell when they're caught in debt."

"But why not? Mr. Pynchon is buying land at Woronoco and Norwottuck. These lands are empty!" Philip protested. "The plague killed them before we arrived. It's God's own will that we take the land."

"Was London empty, after the great plague killed a family in every street?" Ned demanded.

The man hesitated, leaning on the bellows so the forge glowed red with the hiss of air: "What d'you mean?"

"Would it have been right for French families to move into the London houses that had a big red cross on the door, and the owners dead inside?"

"No, of course not."

"Then why call the lands empty, when you can see they were farmed, and worked for years? When you use their well-worn paths and trails through the forest and can see their fields well worked and the forest they've cleared of undergrowth for hunting? Just because they were sick, don't mean they don't own their fields as much as ever."

The two men looked at Ned, as if they were disappointed in him. The town of Hadley clung together with a common purpose, survived by a common will. Dissent in anything—from religious tradition to politics—was not welcome. "Nay, Ned, don't talk so daft," the older man counseled him. "You'll make no friends here talking like that. We've all got to stick together. Don't you want more land to master?"

"No," Ned said bluntly. "I had enough of masters in the old country, I don't want to breed more here. And I don't want to be one myself. I came because I thought we would all be equal, simple men together starting a new life among other simple men without masters. All I want is enough of a garden to farm and feed myself."

Philip Smith laughed and clapped Ned on the shoulder. "You're a rarity, Ned Ferryman!" he told him, despising his simplicity. "The last of the Levelers."

JUNE 1670, LONDON

James was waiting at the far end of the quay beside a stack of barrels, hidden from the blank windows of the house where every blind was drawn down, except the ones in the turret—Alinor's eyrie. The front door opened and the Italian widow stepped out, opened a black silk parasol against the glare, and tripped lightly in her little silk shoes over the cobbles towards him.

"We will walk towards the City," was the first thing she said.

"Not to the fields?"

"No."

He offered his arm and she took it, resting her hand on the crook of his elbow. "Is this very shocking?" she asked him, peeping upwards. "Should we have a chaperone?"

"Not since I am a friend of the family," he answered her seriously. "I hope you have told them you are meeting me?"

"I must make sure you are always on friendly terms!" She avoided the question. "For I want you to take me to London, even perhaps to visit your friends at court."

"The court is no place for a lady," he corrected her. "Nobody attends court but for gambling and vice. I only go for essential meetings of business."

"But I have business there," she surprised him.

"You do?"

The black ribbons on her hat trembled at her determined nod. "I do," she confirmed. "I am not quite a pauper. My first husband left me his antiquities, some beautiful sculptures from days long ago. I was told in Venice that the best prices are paid in London. Is that not true?"

"I wouldn't know," he said gloomily. "Certainly, they seem to be mad for spending."

"You do not collect art like the king? You have no taste for beautiful things yourself?"

"I suppose I like the new buildings, the classical taste . . ."

"Exactly so," she agreed. "And this is why I have come here. I have a small collection of the finest pieces, Greek and Ancient Roman sculptures for sale. I will have them shipped here. Perhaps Alys will send a ship for my goods. My first husband was a great collector, a most artistic man. His steward has maintained his collection for me. I was hoping to use my mother-in-law's warehouse as a saleroom for my goods. But I can see no one comes here—nobody would. So how am I going to meet the noblemen who love beautiful things unless you will introduce me?"

"Not at the court. It is no place for a lady," he repeated.

"I shall take your word for it," she assured him. "But perhaps you will direct me to the collectors, the gentlemen of taste and wealth, perhaps you will introduce me?"

"Really, I wouldn't know where to begin."

"Ah!" she said. "Beginning is always the hardest. But look! Here we are—you and I—beginning."

They walked in silence along the quiet quayside. "It is very different when there is no unloading," she remarked. "Even worse."

"It is still busy in the City," he said. "Even on a Saturday evening, even on a Sunday. Upriver."

"Yes," she said. "I can see that is where the warehouse should be. I wish they had not settled for being so small. And so dirty, and so far away from everything of interest. Is your house in the City, Sir James?"

"Not in the business quarter."

She admired the disdain in his voice.

"Avery House is more to the west, on the Strand. It was untouched by the fire, thanks be to God. That was all to the east of us. A terrible time. We escaped; but all our hangings and curtains were ruined by the smoke and had to be washed and some thrown away."

Apparently, she was not much interested in his hangings and curtains; she gazed across the river to the other side where the fields and rows of little riverside buildings were giving way to grand quays and warehouses.

"Some beautiful brocades." He remembered them when they were new, and the dead king was on his throne. "Chosen by my mother, some of them woven for her, to her own pattern. I remember her drawing them up, she had a wonderful eye . . ."

"Yes, yes," she said. "Very sad." Ahead of her, she could see the blunt outline of the White Tower and the high walls around it. "And so that is the famous Tower of London?"

"Yes," he said. "Perhaps, one day, Mrs. Stoney will take you to see the animals."

"I doubt it! Does she ever take a holiday?"

"I don't know," he said, thinking of the girl she had been, and her love of dancing and play, the summer when she had been queen of the harvest and had run faster than all the girls into the arms of the young man that she loved. "They were always a hardworking family."

"Roberto also," Livia said with a little sigh. "Many times I would beg him to stay home and rest. But he was always going out for poor sick people, or on his boat or walking on the marshes. A good wife should make a haven for her husband, don't you think? A wife is honor-bound to make her husband happy."

"I suppose so."

"And you have a house in the north of England too?"

"A country house," he said. "With land."

"It is very cold there?" She was interested. "Do you think I would be able to bear it?"

"No colder than the north of Italy, I believe. We have snow in winter and the winds are very cold. But it is very beautiful, and very peaceful."

"I love the peaceful countryside," she assured him. "Far more than the town! But I think you did not prosper in your proposal? I think your house will have no mistress? *La Suocera* does not consent?"

"*La Suocera?*"

"The mother-in-law, Mrs. Reekie. She does not accept your very generous proposal?"

"No, she does not agree with me yet, but I think she will come to see that I have much to offer her, and the children."

She gave a little laugh. "And so now you want both children? The girl Sarah and the boy Johnnie?"

His hurt showed on his face. "I don't know what to want," he admitted. "I should want her to come to me and bring her child with her."

She could not conceal her avid curiosity. "But why do you say this? The boy is Alys's son! You cannot want Alys? She is so cross with everyone!"

He withdrew from her eagerness. "It's not for me to say."

She paused in their walk and turned to him. "I am one of the family, their secrets are my secrets."

He bowed his head. "But they are not my secrets to tell," he said carefully. "Did Rob tell you nothing about them?"

She made a little pout. "He misled me. I thought it was a greater house and a noble family. He did not tell me that it was a little warehouse and two poor women scratching for a living and two children sent out to work."

"One child is mine, I am sure of it," he was driven to say.

She stopped in her path, grasped both his hands, and looked into his face, her dark eyes intent through her black lacy veil. "But you were not dishonorable, Milord. I am sure you would not be dishonorable."

"No," he said quickly. "No, I was not. I was young, and foolish, and mistaken. I was very mistaken. Sinfully wrong. But now I want to put things right."

"You made a baby with Alys?" she whispered. "You made a child on her?"

The shake of his head in denial was enough for her quick wits.

"*Dio!* With Mamma Reekie?"

His silence was as good as a confession. She recovered at once. "I shall help you," she assured him. "And you shall help me."

He took a breath. "It is not my secret to tell."

"I shall help you," she repeated. "And then you will help me."

He was about to say that he had no help to offer her when she turned and pointed to the bridge. "Ah! That is a fine sight! Even bigger than the Rialto in Venice but just as busy."

The huge bridge, heavy with buildings and shops, crowded with people crossing even now, cast a deep shadow along the quayside.

"It can take hours to get across," he said. "It is the only bridge, the only crossing. Really, another should be built but the watermen won't allow it . . ."

"So many shops," she said longingly. "And is that a church right in the middle?"

"The chapel of Saint Thomas á Becket. People used to say that you should go in and give thanks to God just for getting to the middle of the bridge because it takes so long to get through the crowds. But it is closed now."

"And is your house on the other side?"

"Oh no! Those are all merchants' houses and tradesmen. My house is farther west."

"Why, how far is it? Can we walk to it?"

"It's a good hour's walk," he said dampeningly. "And, no lady would cross the bridge on foot. You should take a wherry."

Prompted by the hundreds of bells chiming the three-quarter hour she turned their walk. "I wanted to see the City. We will go farther another day."

"The quays are not suitable for a lady," he said. "Not unaccompanied. And not during working hours."

"But how am I to get anywhere?" Impatiently she gestured to the looming bridge. "How am I to get to London if that is the only way to the City?"

In silence, they went quickly back along the quay, the way they had come.

"It is not what I hoped for at all," Livia told him, as they walked past the row of poor warehouses. Ahead was a young man and woman walking arm in arm.

Livia hurried forwards, all smiles. "Now, you must be Johnnie and Sarah!" she exclaimed, putting back her veil and stretching her hands to the young woman. "I am so glad! And how lucky that we should meet here! I am your aunt! Is it not ridiculous? That you should have an aunt such as I? But, indeed, I am the widow of my dear Roberto, and he is your uncle, so I must be your aunt, come to England to live with your mother and grandmother."

The girl, dark-haired and dark-eyed, crowned with an exquisite bonnet of navy blue with a dark blue veil, took the widow's outstretched hands and kissed her in welcome. "Mama wrote that you'd come, I'm honored to meet you, Nobildonna. And this is my brother, Johnnie."

Her brother snatched his hat off his fair head and bowed low.

"Ah, but you may kiss my hand." The Italian widow sparkled at him. "I am your aunt after all! I believe you could even kiss me on the cheek."

Shyly, he took her hand and bent and kissed it, then he turned and met James Avery's intent gaze.

"Sir?" he said.

"And this is my good friend and an old friend of your family," the Nobildonna said blithely. "Roberto's tutor when he was a boy, you know. A friend of the Peachey family. Come to visit your mother and grandmother."

The young man hesitated as his sister stepped forward and curtseyed. "We never have guests," he said simply.

James felt his throat tighten as he stared at the young man. The youth and he were matching heights, the boy had inherited Alinor's fair hair and dark gray eyes but there was something about his forehead and brow that was an echo of the Avery family, that could be seen in a dozen dark oil portraits hanging in Northside Manor. His straight honest gaze was that of a Yorkshireman; James found himself looking at his own self-deprecating, crooked smile. "My son," James said silently to himself. "This is my son. I meet him at last." Aloud he could say nothing but "Good day," to the pretty girl before him, and offer his hand for the young man to shake.

Johnnie Stoney was a polite young man; he shook hands with a little bow of his head to the well-dressed stranger and offered his arm to his newly arrived aunt. With Sarah and James Avery following, he opened the front door and ushered them in.

Alys came out of the counting house and saw the four of them together. At once the smile of welcome froze on her pale face.

"Look who I met on my walk!" Livia exclaimed delightedly. "Your beautiful children and Milord Avery! I have brought them all home with me. See how lucky I am! My second walk out, and I am surrounded with friends."

Alys recovered herself. "I didn't expect . . ."

Sarah gave her mother a hug. "It's five. Didn't you hear the bells?"

Johnnie bent to kiss his mother's cheek. "We all met on the doorstep."

"Let's sit! Go in! Go in!" the Nobildonna said happily. "I'll go and take off my hat. Shall I tell Tabs to bring tea?" She turned a laughing look on them all. "I suppose you all want tea? The English always want tea."

Johnnie glanced from his silent mother to the stranger. "We usually have a glass of small ale," he said awkwardly.

"Oh! So much better! I will be only a moment."

Even when she had left the room her presence lingered like a hint of perfume. They were silent, and took seats in silence, but for James, who remained standing, passing his hat from one hand to another. Johnnie was puzzled and looked at his mother, sensing her hostility; Sarah was watching James.

"Ma was going to come down for dinner," Alys said pointedly.

"I won't stay," James tried to reassure her. "But may I see her before I go?"

Before her children, Alys could not refuse him outright. "I think she's too tired."

A light footstep in the hall, the door opened, and Livia came in, the maid following with a tray of glasses and a jug of small ale.

"Do you still brew your own ale?" James asked Alys. She did not even look at him, let alone reply. Johnnie watched his mother, puzzled at her rudeness to a guest.

"Did you drink it before? In Sussex?" Sarah asked. "Did you know us then?"

"Yes. Long ago. Before you were born," he told her, taking a sip of his glass. "It was the best I had ever tasted then and this is still as good."

"We have our own malthouse in the yard," Johnnie told him. "It's brewed to my grandmother's recipe. She chooses the herbs for it, and she watches the malt being chitted. Sometimes she even turns it herself."

James nodded. "I would know it anywhere."

"I had such a lovely walk," Livia remarked. "And it was such a pleasure to meet you all just there on the quayside." Smilingly, she turned to Alys. "I put my head around the door of *Mia Suocera* when I went upstairs to take off my hat, and she said she would see Milord. Shall I take him up?"

Before Alys could refuse, James rose to his feet and followed Livia from the room.

"Don't be long!" Alys called. "She must not be overtired. I don't . . ."

Johnnie rose to his feet too. "Is everything all right, Ma?" he asked in an undertone, as the two left the room. "Is anything wrong?"

His mother glanced up at him as if she would beg him for help but could find no words. "She doesn't realize," was all she said. "She does not understand that your grandma should not have visitors."

"But Grandma said that they could go up?" Sarah pointed out. "And if she's well enough to come down for dinner with us, why shouldn't she have a visitor from the old days?"

Alinor was sitting at the table in the airy room with the glazed door open to the little balcony. Before her, on the table, was a bouquet of fresh lavender; she was stripping the violet seed heads from the stalks. She looked up as the two of them entered and Livia closed the door behind her, and stood in front of it, her hands held before her, as if she were a lady-in-waiting.

"You are staying?" Alinor asked her directly.

"As a chaperone," the young woman replied gravely. "As it is a matter of honor."

Alinor turned her attention to Sir James. "You're back again?"

"I have to come again and again until you will tell me how I can be of service to you. Until I can speak openly . . ." He glanced at Livia and fell silent.

"I need nothing," Alinor said steadily. "You can't be of service to me."

"A doctor?"

"I've seen doctors."

"A specialist doctor, Italian trained . . ."

"My son was a specialist doctor, Italian trained," she pointed out.

"But can I not find someone to consult?"

"I'm drowned," she said simply. "They pulled me out; but the water's still in my body. I'm a drowned woman, James. You're wasting your time on a drowned woman."

"I didn't know," he said miserably.

"You were there!" she exclaimed brutally. "It was you pulled me out! You know well enough."

"Alinor, come to my house where you can breathe the clean air," he urged her. "It's high, near the moorland, there is a beautiful garden, I have always thought of you in my herb garden. You should have it just as you wish. You shall come as my honored guest, even if you will not accept anything more."

In the doorway Livia froze, waiting for Alinor's reply.

"I am a wealthy man now, my beautiful house would be yours to command. And a carriage, and a parlor all your own. Your children could come too. I would never trouble you. Everything should be as you wish."

"I live as I wish here," she replied steadily.

If they had been alone together James would have dropped to his knees and pressed his hot face into her lap; as it was, he clenched his hat and fought to find his voice. "Alinor, I have so much to give you," he whispered. "My fortune, my houses—it's a burden to me if it is not yours. And I so want . . . my child."

"I've told you," she said to him. "I know you're a man in the habit of having your own way, and you royalists have won, in everything else you've triumphed! But in this one matter: you must fail. You didn't want the child then, you didn't want me then, that was your decision then—it's too late to change it now."

In the doorway Livia clasped her hands together, the image of a praying Madonna, and was perfectly still.

"Am I to be punished forever, for one mistake?"

"Am I?"

"We have both been punished enough!" he exclaimed. "But now I am restored, and I can restore you."

She shook her head. "I don't need your restoration. I'm not like your king. I was not expelled from my home. I just moved from a forlorn mire to a dirty river. I've made my own life here, as if I sieved it from the mud of the harbor and built it from sea wrack. I didn't think I'd live; but when I could breathe again I had lost the fear of death—the fear of anything. I can't be destroyed, I just change. The water didn't drown me, it flows through me. I am my own tidelands, I carry the water in my own lungs." She paused for a breath, her hand to her throat. "You find your own life, James. I can tell you: it's not here."

"There is no life for me, without you, and without my child!"

She nodded, her eyes never leaving his face. "That was your own choice," she said. "Freely made, and knowingly made. You did not want a child and now you have none. It's like a spell. It was your wish. You can't take it back, and it can't be unsaid."

"Is this your last word?"

Wearily she turned her head away from him and caught Livia's dark intent gaze on her. The younger woman's eyes were filled with tears; Livia was following every word, moved to deep emotion. "She said so," Livia spoke gently from the doorway. "She has given you her last word. You can ask for nothing more from her."

He looked at Alinor, as Livia opened the door in silence, and there was nothing he could do but leave. Livia followed him out and closed the door quietly behind them.

On the narrow landing, he caught her sleeve and she turned her beautiful face up to his.

"You don't understand," he said. "I love her, and together we have a child. I promised her marriage and now I need a wife, and I need my child to inherit."

Gently she put her warm hand over his. "But I do understand," she said surprisingly. "And I will help you. Come tomorrow and walk with me."

"On a Sunday?" he asked.

She had been raised as a Roman Catholic, and had never observed the Sabbath like a puritan. She shrugged. "Meet me tomorrow after dinner, and we can decide what is best to do."

JUNE 1670, HADLEY, NEW ENGLAND

Ned, planning to send a barrel of goods and herbs to England at the end of summer, traded a whole freshly caught salmon for a pair of barrels from the cooper. The minister's housekeeper was there, ordering a barrel for the manse.

"Good morning, Mr. Ferryman, I'll take some fresh fish for the minister, if you've got anything nice," she said.

"Of course," Ned said. "I've set my traps again and I've got some beautiful fat trout. Shall I carry it to your door?"

"I'd be grateful," she said.

"May I carry your basket for you? Are you finished here, Mrs. Rose?"

She put her initials in the cooper's book for the minister's order, and then gave Ned her basket as they walked around the cooper's house, out of his gate, and back into the broad street, past the meetinghouse, to where the minister's house was set at the junction. The wide green common grazing land ran north to south past his front door and at the side of his house was the west-to-east lane called the Middle Highway running out of town to the woods. The town fence protected his land and house from the grazing animals; his own gate led to a path to his front door, fastened with ironwork—a handsome latch.

"Fair weather," Ned said shyly, casting about for something to say to her, knowing that the whole town had watched them walk up the lane together. Everyone expected them to marry. Single men were not

welcomed in these frontier plantations where a man could only survive with the work of his wife and children, and a woman had to have
the protection of a man. There were only two other bachelors in the
town and each had been given a plot in return for plying his trade, his
specialist skills; both of them would be expected to marry. The minister John Russell had invited Ned to join the community and given him
the riverside lot outside the town fence and the ferry beside it, for his
loyal service in Oliver Cromwell's army. Mr. Russell wanted a man he
could trust to watch the north road and guard his secret guests. If Ned
wanted to settle in Hadley and be granted more land, and a bigger
house, he must marry. Mrs. Rose was a widowed indentured servant
at the manse. When her contracted time was served, she would have
to find another post and work for another household or marry one of
the settlers to get a house and land.

"It's fine now but it'll soon be too hot to speak," she predicted.
"The summers here are as cruel as the winters. I miss an English
summer day!"

"We all do, I think. But I like this warm weather."

The minister lived in a well-built house; handsome wooden steps
led up to a double front door. The housekeeper led Ned around to
the back, where the grassy lot stretched away east to the start of the
forest. Near the house a black slave chopped a tree into firewood,
another stacked it. Mrs. Rose led Ned up the two steps to the kitchen
door. They went in together, and Ned put down the baskets on the
scrubbed table.

"You can go down," Mrs. Rose said quietly. "They thought they'd
keep out of sight today in the cool, while there are messengers coming
and going."

She nodded him towards the main part of the house. Ned opened
the door and stepped into the wooden-floored hall. A long-case clock
ticked loudly, as if to proclaim the wealth of the master of the house.
Ned glanced into the empty study where the minister wrote his im-
passioned sermons. No one was there, so he rolled back the rug that
covered the trapdoor to the cellar. He tapped on the hatch door, the
old familiar rat-tat-tat-tatta-tatta-tat, and opened the hatch. A ladder extended below him into darkness. Ned climbed down into the

pitch-black and only when the hatch above him thudded back into place and he heard the shuffle of Mrs. Rose rolling back the rug, was there the sharp click of a flint, a spark, and the flare of a flame.

Ned felt his way to the bottom of the ladder and there, faces illuminated by the bright flame of candlewood, were his former commanders, both men in their sixties, exiles from the English Civil War which had finally turned against them: Edward Whalley and his son-in-law William Goffe, regicides, men who had signed the death sentence for their own king and were now hiding from a warrant of arrest from his son, the restored king. The three shook hands in silence and went from the foot of the ladder to the end of the storeroom where a window set high in the stone walls admitted a greenish light and fresh air to the cellar.

"No strangers in town? No one asking for us?" Edward asked of Ned, who had served them and guarded them for the five and a half years they had been living in Hadley.

"No one that I saw, no one came in on my ferry," Ned told him. "But you're wise to stay down here, there's another town meeting this afternoon and messengers expected from Boston. They're warning about the Pokanoket—if they're planning something? People out of town are fortifying their houses. I had one of the selectmen at my house telling me to come and translate for the town council, and that next I'd be mustered."

"Of course you'll serve," William told him. "There's not one of them has ever seen warfare. Half of them can't light a matchlock. The town needs you."

"There's not one of 'em I'd trust with a weapon," Ned said scathingly.

"Aye, but they're our people," Edward agreed with his son-in-law. "And they can be trained. Don't you remember the early days of the New Model Army? You can make a great army from ordinary men if their cause is just and you have time to train them."

"I was proud to serve then," Ned said quietly. "But that was my first and last cause. I served a great general to free my people from a tyrant. It was an honor to serve the Lord Protector against the tyrant King Charles. And when we won, and you two sat in judgment on him, I was there! I was in court for every day of his trial and I knew it was justice. I watched him step out of the Banqueting House that morning and put his head on the block. I swore then that I'd finished soldiering. I'd never take arms again. I swore I'd live in peace to the end of my days. I'd never make war on innocent people."

"Aye, but savages are not innocent people, Ned! These are not comrades like us in the New Model Army. They're not Christian, half of them are pagans. They don't think like we do. And mark my words, you'll have to choose a side sooner or later. Josiah Winslow himself said to me that there will come a time when it's us against them."

"His father would never have said that," Ned pointed out. "Everyone says his father and the Massasoit were true friends."

"That was then," Edward said. "When we first arrived there was real friendship, I know. This is now: it's changed. They've changed."

"The savages won't spare you if it comes to a fight of English against Indians," William said. "They're cruel enemies, Ned."

Ned nodded, reluctant to argue with men who had been his officers, and served in the highest council in England. "I really think it was us who were cruel," he volunteered quietly. "At Mystic Fort we fired the village with old people and women and children inside, and shot those that ran out. Even the Indians who served with us, the Narragansett, cried that it was too much! Too much—those were their very words. They couldn't believe that we would burn children and women alive."

"That was thirty years ago," William said. "Ancient history. And worse things happened in Ireland."

"And anyway, they make war like that now," Edward said grimly. "They've been quick to learn, they burn now, and they scalp too."

Ned threw up his hands. "Sirs, I'll not argue with you," he said. "I came to see that you're well and pay my respects."

William patted him on the back. "And we'd be fools to fall out with you," he said. "I don't forget that it was you that brought us here, two days' trail through the woods and up the river never setting a foot wrong. We were glad then that you were friendly with savages and knew their trails. We'd never have got here without them to guide us and you to command them. You're a good friend, Ned, we don't forget it."

"I thank you, sir."

"But their leader is a king, isn't he?" Edward could never let an argument go. "The Pokanoket call him King Philip? Never tell me that you'd serve a king rather than your brothers, Ned!"

Ned smiled. "He's not a king like Charles Stuart: a tyrant. He's their leader, but they consent to him leading them. They don't call him a king, that's the name we gave him. They call him Massasoit. His real name is Po Metacom. They don't call him Philip. It was us gave him the name Philip, and the title King, out of respect to his father, who truly was our savior the first winter we got here."

"That old story?" Edward queried.

"They'll never forget it. The English would all have died that first winter, but the Pokanoket built them shelters and gave them food. When the English robbed native corn stores, the Pokanoket gave them more, freely. That's part of their religion, to give to someone who has nothing. But you know, we even dug up their graves for the treasures that they had buried with their dead?"

Edward grimaced. "I hadn't heard that."

"It doesn't reflect very well on us, so it's not often told," Ned said wryly. "But we were like greedy beasts that first winter, and they were forgiving. We promised them then that we'd only come to trade: us on the coast, wanting no more than trading posts on the coast, and all the land should always be theirs. That's how people thought it would be. D'you remember, before our war, when King Charles was still on the throne, nobody ever thought we'd live here? Everyone thought the New World would be just for fishing and a few trading posts?"

"It's true," William Goffe ruled. "It never looked like a country for settling, it was like Africa or the East. Somewhere that you'd visit to make a fortune and be glad to get home alive. All the early settlements died or gave up."

"Aye, just so. But now this pickthank comes to my door and tells me that the land is empty—empty! So the English have the right to everything, that he wants to be a master. Doesn't even know how much land there is. Doesn't know beyond Hatfield, won't ever go upriver for fear of not getting back before dark. Doesn't even know how many natives there are. Thinks he's a hero to get as far north as Hadley. Thinks he's deep in an empty wilderness when he comes through the town gate to my lot. Doesn't know nowt!"

William Goffe laughed at Ned's indignation and poured a glass of small ale for him from a jug on the table. "He's got you rattled," he remarked, and waited for the rueful warmth of Ned's reluctant smile.

"He's the sort of man who decides what side he's on, when he sees who's winning," Ned warned them. "The sort that welcomed you as heroes, like they did in Boston when you got here, but then as soon as they heard the death sentence from the English courts, decided that they'd rather send you back to England for trial. No heart for one side or another. No heart at all."

"I suppose so," William agreed. There was a pause as he poured more small ale. "Who's like us?" he asked in the old drinking oath they had picked up from the Battle of Dunbar when they had defeated the royalist Scots and won a victory for the common men of England and the Commonwealth.

"Damn few, and they're all dead," Ned replied.

They clinked glasses and then fell silent for a moment.

"No free-born Englishmen would ever send us back," Edward said. "I know they didn't dare to defy the king's proclamation openly; but they passed us hand to hand in secret till we were safe here."

"I don't know how they can bear a king in England," William said. "After living in freedom! After godly rule!"

"Would you go back to fight against Charles the Second?" Ned asked curiously.

"I'd sail tomorrow. Wouldn't you? I wait for the call, I expect it, any day now."

William laughed shortly. "Well, it's a feud now! What with naming me as unforgivable, putting a price on my head, and hunting me down through the old world and the new, spying on my wife and daughter! Executing my brothers-in-arms! I'll never forget hiding in the cave from his spies. I won't forgive living here, hidden by friends, ducking into the cellar at the first hint of strangers, putting all of you in danger as well as myself."

The men were silent, thinking of the old battles they had won and the final battle they had lost, that had driven them into exile.

"I suppose I'd fight against him if I had to," Ned said slowly. "If I was called. But I'd hoped to leave the old country and the wars of the old country, and live in peace. It's not that England was ever a kindly mother to me or to mine."

"No wife?" Edward asked, missing his own wife, Mary, in distant England.

"No wife," Ned confirmed.

"No family at all?"

"I have a sister and her children. Poorly treated and poorly lodged. A sinner, like us all, but God knows more sinned against."

The men fell silent.

"Anyway," Ned said more cheerfully. "You're safe now. The minister keeps his faith, Mr. Russell will never betray you."

"He's a good man," William confirmed. "But I think we'll take to the woods for the summer season; it's weary work staying out of sight, living in a town but not being part of it. Hearing them practice the drills against attack and knowing they don't know the first thing to do. They've not even built palisades! An enemy troop could march right in."

"You can hide in the woods near me and I'll keep you supplied," Ned offered.

"Near you, or deeper into the forest," William said. "Maybe even back to the coast. Anywhere that King Charles can't send men to find us."

"It's been more than twenty years since we beheaded his father," Ned said. "Surely there must come a time when the king offers pardons."

"Not him!" Edward exclaimed. "This is a man who dug up his dead enemies and hanged their corpses. Cromwell himself! Our commander and the greatest men that ever served their country? Dug out of his grave and executed for spite. What good does he think that does? Raising the dead to slight them? It's superstition like a fool, it's little more than witchcraft."

"Stupid," Ned replied, whose sister had once been swum as a witch. "I can't abide that sort of thinking."

JUNE 1670, LONDON

As soon as James had gone, Sarah ran upstairs and brought her grandmother down to the parlor. Tabs laid the table and brought in the dinner—a venison pie from the nearby bakehouse, and a plate of oysters.

The family bowed their heads as Alinor gave thanks for the food. "And may my brother have as good a dinner and be as light of heart as we are tonight, in the new land that is his home."

"Amen," everyone said. Alys glanced at her mother. They had always named Rob when they said grace, but now Rob was gone and his widow took up her fork and waited to be served.

"Are they starving you at Mr. Watson's?" Alys asked her son as he sliced the pie and gave himself a good portion, oozing with dark rich gravy.

"No, they set a good-enough table, and us counting house lads eat with the family, but there is nothing in the world like your small ale and shell bread, Ma."

"Madame Piercy takes nothing but tea and bread and butter at dinnertime," Sarah volunteered. "She says true ladies have no appetite. We girls go out to the pie shop every day."

"Then how will you ever save your wages?" her mother demanded.

"Ma, I can't. Between ribbons and dinners, I can't make it stretch."

"When I was your age, I only bought ribbons from the Chichester fair and that never more than once a quarter."

Sarah rolled her eyes. "But I'm surrounded by shops, Ma! It's like poaching was for you. Everywhere I turn, there is something to pick up."

Alinor smiled. "Don't you believe her! Your mother would have sold her soul for cherry ribbons," she said. "And surely you'll earn more when you're a senior milliner, Sarah?"

"Yes," the girl confirmed. "And I'll bring it home, I promise."

Alinor turned to Johnnie. "And is Mr. Watson pleased with you?"

"He's pleased with nothing," Johnnie answered. "With the court so much in debt and the king such a spendthrift, all he can see, all anyone can see, is more taxes ahead. Taxes for all the City merchants to pay for luxuries at the court." He turned to his mother. "D'you want me to look at the books with you tomorrow?"

"I'd be glad of it," she said. "If you're not too tired. You do look pale, my boy."

"Ah, don't fuss," he said, grinning at her. "I was out drinking with the other lads last night and I have a headache from bad wine."

"So, does he not get scolded for spending his wages on drink?" Sarah demanded. "Ribbons are forbidden, but drink is all right?"

"He's a boy," her grandmother teased her. "He can do as he wishes."

"You'll never get a husband if you're such a shrew." Johnnie winked at her.

Sarah kicked his chair with her foot under the table. "Don't want one!"

"Now stop, you two," Alys said quietly. "What will your aunt be thinking?"

"I think they are adorable!" Livia said warmly. "But tell me—am I trespassing in someone's bedroom? I am in the attic room next to Tabs?"

"That's my room," Johnnie said.

"I thought it must be, with the books and the charts. My nursemaid and baby have taken the bedroom downstairs."

"That was mine," Sarah said.

"Could you sleep with your baby and the nursemaid for tonight?" Alys asked Livia.

The young woman spread her hands in apology. "Alas, I cannot! If I sleep near Matteo he cries for me, and it wakes me and I can never sleep again. He seems to know that I am in the room, and he calls for me! It is so sweet! But if Miss Sarah would condescend to sleep with my nursemaid, Carlotta, and the baby, I know the baby would be quiet as a little mouse? Would you agree? You don't object?"

"All right," Sarah said. "Since it's my bed anyway. But where is Johnnie to sleep?"

"I can bed down here," he offered.

"I would never dream of it. He must have his room and I will share with your mamma if she permits."

"Me?" Alys demanded.

Livia smiled. "Of course," she said blandly. "There is nowhere else. You don't object to sharing with me? I don't snore at all."

"No," said Alys. "Of course."

Alinor went up to her room early; but the rest of the little family sat at the table playing Game of Goose and talking about their week. Livia's bright assessing gaze went from one young face to another looking for the resemblance to Sir James, wondering if it was possible that the handsome youth and the pretty girl were not twin brother and sister. Raised together and always in each other's company, they knew what the other was thinking and often finished each other's sentences, their expressions mirrored each other. Livia thought they could well be twins—only a mother could have known the truth. Only a father seeking an heir could have dreamed of separating them, could have wanted one, without the other.

At midnight Alys said, "Come, you two. You've got to be up in the morning for church. It's time for bed now."

In the hall their nighttime candles were each in a candlestick. Alys went to the kitchen to check that the back door was locked, and the fire banked down for the night.

"All safe?" Johnnie asked, his foot on the bottom stair, his candle lit.

"All safe," she confirmed.

"D'you still draw the runes against house fire in the ashes?" Sarah asked.

Alys smiled. "Of course! Think what your grandma would say if she found me letting the house burn down for want of a mark to keep the fire in the grate."

"Good night." Sarah kissed her mother and then, when Livia opened her arms, she kissed her aunt too.

"Good night," Johnnie said from the cramped landing.

"You don't kiss me good night?" Livia teased, and laughed to see him blush, and hurriedly go up to his attic room.

Alys turned into her mother's room to say good night, as Livia went into Alys's bedroom. She set down the candle on a washstand and looked around the room. It was sparsely furnished with a large wooden chest at the foot of the bed. She lifted the lid and found thick jackets and winter cloaks, and—she rummaged into each corner—a metal box which might hold money or perhaps jewelry. She flicked open the catch and lifted the lid. On the top was writing paper and a stick of old sealing wax, and underneath it were white ribbons, now brown with age, and a posy of dried herbs tied in with some dry and wrinkled berries. Livia glanced at them: a bridal buttonhole—a winter bridal buttonhole—but who had worn it? And where was he now?

She took off her black trimmed cap and put it beside the small silvered mirror on the little table. She unbelted her overdress and laid it carefully in the top of the chest. Underneath she had her silk underdress which she hung to air on the back of the door. By the time Alys came in, Livia was in her beautiful linen nightshift, trimmed with the finest lace, her hairbrush in her hand.

"Would you?" she asked familiarly, and sat on the end of the bed and tossed her mane of dark glossy hair over her shoulders.

"D'you like it plaited for the night?" Alys stumbled.

"Please. I usually ask Carlotta to do it, but I don't want to disturb them."

"Of course."

Gently, and then with more confidence, Alys swept the brush through the thick mass of black hair. "It is beautiful," she said.

"Roberto used to brush it for me. He said that your mother had hair like a wheat field, yours was the color of barley, and I had hair the color of night."

Alys finished the plait with a neat bow of white ribbon, and turned to undress herself, as Livia went to the bed. "Which side do you like?"

Alys kept her face turned away. "I never slept in the same bed as my husband. I don't have a side. I don't know which."

"Ah," Livia said quietly. "I will go this side, then, near the door in case I have to go to little Matteo in the night, and you shall sleep by the window, unless the sunlight is too bright for you when it rises?"

"No, no," Alys said. "The shutters are closed, and anyway, I'm an early riser." She coiled her hair into a loose knot, pulled on a cap, dragged a nightgown over her clothes, and then blew out their candle. In the dark she shuffled out of her gown and petticoats under her nightgown before shaking them out and laying them on the chest and getting into bed. It occurred to her, for the first time, that though she had lain with a man she had passionately loved, they had never had even one night together, parting on their wedding day.

She lay rigid, stiff as a bolster, her head on the pillow pointing south, her feet due north, like a locked compass. She did not dare to stretch or slump.

"Are you cold?" came a whisper out of the darkness.

"A little." She did not know what she felt.

A warm hand reached under her shoulders and drew her close. "Rest your head here," Livia invited. "We are both lonely, we are both alone. Rest your head here, and we can sleep together."

Through the thin nightgown Alys could feel the warmth of the young woman, she could smell her perfume of roses. Slowly she relaxed, and they fell asleep lulled by the quiet lapping of the low tide.

JUNE 1670, LONDON

In the morning Livia was still sleeping, dark eyelashes swept down over the soft curve of her cheek, as Alys got up, dressed in silence, and tiptoed from the room for fear of waking the young woman who slept through the noise of the stirring house as if she were the princess in the story, and would wake only to the kiss of a prince.

Alys plaited her hair and put on her cap in the counting house before going into the kitchen where Tabs was blowing the embers into life. "Give me a small ale, please," she said.

"Thirsty?" Tabs demanded cheerfully. "I'm thirsty. It's that hot in my attic you'd never think it."

"Yes," Alys said repressively. "Can you lay the table for breakfast, Tabs? We'll just be us four. Mrs. Alinor won't be down. I'll take up her tray."

"Getting it done now," the young woman confirmed. "Will you take her a small ale now?"

Alys took a cup and went up the stairs, although she did not turn to the right to her mother's door but went to her own bedroom.

Livia was sitting up, leaning against the plain pillows, her embroidered cap framing her dark beautiful face, her nightgown pulled low to show her olive-skinned shoulders. She smiled as Alys came in.

"Ah, there you are!" she said. "I was lonely the moment that I woke, and found you gone."

"Here I am," Alys agreed uncertainly, proffering the drink. "I brought you this."

The family attended St. Olave's Church and there were special prayers for Rob. They all walked back with the minister who came to pray with Alinor. He wore a smart dark suit, but no vestments and no outward sign of his calling. Alinor had raised Alys during the puritan years of the Commonwealth and they still preferred their religion plain, with nothing of church ritual, even though times had changed. The new king was restoring the surplices and ceremonies at every altar, decking them with gold and silver. His papist wife had her own chapel and half of London genuflected behind her and dizzily inhaled incense at Mass. Alys, and all the old reformers, now had to accept the new rules which had once been called heresy. Anyone who could not stomach it had no choice but to leave the country, as Alinor's brother Ned had done.

"Will you stay for your dinner, Mr. Forth?" Alys asked politely, as he came down the narrow stairs after his visit to Alinor's room.

"I have to make other visits," he replied. "I cannot be seen to fail in my duties for a moment. The previous minister wants his parish back, his rectory, and especially his tithes. The communion expelled him for being a monarchist and half-papist and now the fashion is for monarchy and papistry again. He will return and all my work here will be overset."

"What will you do?" Sarah asked him.

"If I am forced out, I will sail to the Americas," he told her. "If I cannot serve the Lord here, I will go where the Saved want to hear my word."

"My uncle Ned is in the town of Hadley in New England," Alys remarked. "It's a new settlement, led into the wilderness by the minister, so they are a godly town with much preaching. He thinks as you do."

"Does he trade in furs?" he asked. "He could make a fortune."

"He wants to make a sufficiency, not to be the bane of any other."

"I pray that a godly man can do that," he agreed. "But I fear that one man's wealth is always another man's loss."

"Here, yes, but perhaps not in a new world?" Alys challenged. "Where land is free? It was his hope that he could live of his own, without hurting another."

"I pray that it does not come to it for me; but if I am forced to leave, I will come to you and ask for his direction."

"He'd be glad to see you." Alys bowed and Johnnie opened the front door and let the preacher out into the glaring light of the quay. Sarah was alone with her mother in the parlor.

"Did Uncle Ned know that man—Sir James?"

"No!" Alys lied at once. "Why d'you ask?"

"So how did Sir James know you and Grandma at Foulmire? How did he not meet Uncle Ned?"

"I meant that they were not friends," Alys corrected herself. "Your uncle Ned was the ferryman, of course he knew everyone."

"Before we were born."

"Yes, as you know."

"So did we all leave at once? Great-Uncle Ned, and Sir James and Grandma and you? Were we all in the wagon altogether?"

"No, it was just your grandma and me," Alys said unwillingly. "I must have told you a dozen times. Just you babies and Grandma and me—after a quarrel with the Millers at the tide mill over my wages. Ned didn't come till long after that. And then when the king was restored, he left for the Americas. Surely you remember! Now, I have to see what Tab is doing. I can smell burning."

"So why did they leave? Uncle Ned and Sir James?" Johnnie echoed his sister, coming in at the end of this conversation. "Together? But not with us? It can't have been about your wages, surely?"

"Oh really!" Alys hurried away. "What does it matter? It's so long ago! We left because we wanted a better life for you than we could have had on the mire, Uncle Ned left for conscience, when the king came in; and Sir James was only ever passing through. We weren't friends, we hardly knew him."

"Then why does he come here every day and see Grandma?" Johnnie joined with his sister.

"He doesn't come every day. He's only seen her twice," Alys said irritably.

"But why?" Johnnie asked.

"What?"

"Why does he come?"

"I don't know!" Alys blustered, breaking away from the two of them and opening the kitchen door. A haze of fatty smoke rolled into the hall. "Tabs! What are you doing in there?"

"Surely you must know," Johnnie said reasonably.

"I know that it's none of my business nor yours. And I don't want either of you talking to him. D'you hear?"

Alys closed the kitchen door on them. Sarah and Johnnie exchanged brief glances of complete understanding. "Something's not right," Sarah said.

"I know. I feel it."

"We'll find out," she decided.

After dinner Sarah sat with her grandmother upstairs in her room, sewing black ribbons for Alinor and Alys's mourning caps.

"Not for me, I won't wear it," Alinor said.

The girl hesitated. "Grandma, why not?"

"Sarah, I don't believe it, I can't feel that he's dead. I won't wear black for him."

The girl laid down her work. "Grandma, you wouldn't want to be disrespectful?"

"I won't lie."

"What does Ma say?"

"Nothing. I've not said anything to her."

Sarah scrutinized her grandmother. "You cannot doubt the word of his widow. It's not just a letter now, she has come all that long way, with her son, and now you know what happened?"

Alinor looked out of the window where a mist was uncoiling along the incoming tide. Sarah felt a chill in the room as if the hairs on the nape of her neck were standing up, one by one. She shivered.

Alinor glanced at her. "Yes," she said, as if it were a commonplace. "Something's not right. You feel it too."

Sarah got up to close the half door to the balcony outside.

"It's not the mist," Alinor told her granddaughter. "You know as well as I do that it's the sight."

"I don't see anything," the girl complained. "I just feel a chill."

"That's how it feels," Alinor confirmed. "I know something, but I don't know what. I felt it when she said that poor little baby would be a comfort to me. That he would replace Rob!"

"Nobody could replace Rob."

"It's not that . . . It's because . . ."

"What?" the girl prompted.

"I don't know." Alinor shook her head. "I can't see anything clear. But I just know that something's out of true."

"D'you know what is true, Grandma?"

"Yes," she said swiftly. "Always. As if the truth had a scent. I recognize it. And if you and me both feel the mist on the back of our necks—then there's a warning."

"A warning for who?"

"I don't know for sure." Alinor smiled at the girl and let the spell slip away. "But here's a lesson down the years, from my grandmother to my mother, from her to me and from me to you: mind that chill when you feel it . . . something's wrong."

"Can we put it right?" the girl whispered.

Alinor looked at her granddaughter, at the bright courage in her dark eyes, at the strength in her face. "Maybe you can," she said.

"How? How could I put it right? I don't even know what's wrong?"

"I don't know either. But I believe it will be you who finds the truth in this. And in the meantime, I won't wear black."

Sarah said nothing more but picked up her grandmother's cap and started to unpick the black ribbon. "What will you say?" she asked.

Alinor smiled ruefully. "I won't have to say anything," she said. "Everyone will just assume that I am a stupid old woman and I can't accept the truth."

"You don't care if people say that?"

She smiled. "I've been called worse."

Downstairs, Johnnie joined his mother in the counting house and they went through the transactions for the previous week, balancing the cash taken and spent against the stock held. They had to file the licenses to show that ships with foreign goods for the legal quays had been permitted to unload at the little wharf. They had to file the double-stamped dockets that showed that duty had been paid. Johnnie was meticulous with the documents: the smallest question against any one of the sufferance wharves would lose them the permission to bring cargoes onshore and pay the dues.

Livia put her head around the door and, seeing them both hard at work, laughed at their industry, and said that if she was to be neglected, she would take the baby and the nursemaid on her afternoon walk. They left the house together, and at the corner of Shad Thames the maid was surprised to see Sir James was waiting.

"I brought Matteo with me for some good country air," Livia explained to him as she strolled up. "It is not good for him to be indoors all the time. A baby should be in the fresh air, in the country. If only we could visit a house in the country!" She beckoned Carlotta to her side and lifted the white lace shawl from the baby's face. "See him smile? He knows you!"

"He's very small," Sir James said, looking at the tiny body in the trailing white gown.

"Oh yes, for he's so young! But you will see. He will grow. He will grow to be a little English boy, a strong, brave little English boy."

She turned away from her son and took Sir James's arm. "Shall we walk together into the fields? I so love the country."

"Of course, if you wish."

He let her take his arm and was relieved that the nursemaid followed them with the baby, like a chaperone, as they walked towards Horsleydown Fields.

"I understand now what it is you want from the warehouse," she said in an intimate whisper.

He did not like the way she said "the warehouse," as if they were a commodity that he might order on the wharf, and not the woman and her son that he loved.

"But Mrs. Reekie is of stone! And she is very ill, you don't know how very ill. There was a terrible accident. I think at sea. And then for her son Roberto to drown too!"

He could taste cowardice in his mouth like brine. "A very . . . tragic . . . coincidence."

"But here is another coincidence," she said, speaking quickly, her accent getting stronger in her excitement. "You come to the warehouse, wanting a wife and a son—and I come to the warehouse: a widow with a son!"

"The cases are hardly—"

"Don't you see?" she demanded. "The very things that you need: I have here. You hoped that Mrs. Reekie, a widow, had your child, and that she would marry you. But *ecco!* She denies you. But I have her son's child, and I am a widow. Do you see?"

He thought he could see nothing but the enchanting dimple at the side of her mouth where the fashionable black patch set off the creamy pink of her cheek.

"I must be very stupid . . ."

She laughed. "No! No! You are too modest. An Italian man would catch my meaning at once. But I don't care for Italian men, don't think that of me! If I had wanted to marry an Italian I had only to stay in Venice where I was much admired. But I need to have a friend in England, a man of property, someone who will introduce me to the people who will buy my antiquities. I need a protector in England, someone to care for me and my son. And my son needs a father, someone to keep us and educate him, bring him up as an English boy." She looked at him inquiringly. "Now do you see?"

"Are you proposing that I should help you? And be a father to your boy?" he asked, feeling his face grow hot at her immodesty.

"Of course!" she said limpidly, as if it were the most obvious of solutions. "You want a son?"

"I want my own son!" he said, as if it were wrenched from him.

She beckoned the nursemaid, who stepped forward again and showed the little face, the hands like tiny roses, the face like a flower in the lace cap. "Have this one!" she urged him. "And marry me."

JUNE 1670, HADLEY, NEW ENGLAND

Ned attended the town meeting about the defense of the country after the Sunday afternoon prayer service, standing at the back alongside the other single men of the town. There were only three of them; the other two were tradesmen: a glazier and a carpenter, invited by the minister and the elders to bring their skills and scrape a living on a half lot. Ned was not called on to speak, though he knew the native people better than any of them, meeting them daily on the river and in the forests, and ferrying them in and out of town. But a friendship with the native peoples was no longer seen as an advantage, it put a question mark over a man's loyalty; a knowledge of their language was not a useful skill unless it was put at the service of the settlers.

The messenger from Mr. John Pynchon, son of the founder of Springfield, commander of the militia, deputy to the general council and the greatest man in the valley, brought a stern warning: every town militia must be mustered, drilled, armed, and prepared to defend their own areas. Every town must report what the neighboring savages were doing, if they were friendly or complaining, if they were trading or refusing to service the settlers. There were reports that the leader of the Pokanoket tribe, King Philip, had invited the king of the Niantic people to his fort at Mount Hope. Ned listened as one speaker after another warned of the danger if the old rivalry between the Niantic and Pokanoket were ended, if the Niantic were to join with the disloyal Pokanoket, if they were to refuse land sales to the settlers, to deny trade, to deny service. Once or twice one of the elders glanced towards Ned, one of the few men from Hadley who used the many paths that criss-crossed New England, who met Niantic people on the river and in the forest. Ned kept his head down and said nothing.

Minister John Russell prayed for calm and careful judgment as the meeting ended and stood at the back of the meetinghouse with the elders to say good-bye to each neighbor. Ned was one of the last out and waited by the minister as he locked the door, pocketed the key, and they walked together to his house. The minister's wife and children and Mrs. Rose, the housekeeper, followed the men.

"You weren't at prayers earlier today, Ned Ferryman?"

"No, Minister, many of the Hatfield people like to hear your sermon and I ferried them across the river and home again."

"Who's keeping the ferry for you now?"

"John Sassamon. He said you had given permission."

"Yes. He's a good man, a Harvard man like me. He brought the message from Mr. Pynchon."

"Aye."

"Is it all quiet in the town, Ferryman? No natives coming and going on the ferry? No dugouts on the river, no more than usual?"

"Nothing out of the ordinary," Ned said. "They're still unhappy about the fish traps."

Minister Russell nodded. "Tell them if they bring in fish again, we'll pay a little extra," he said. "Let's get things back to normal. No ill will, no rumors."

"You'll be hard-pressed to silence the town, they'll be bound to worry about this news of the Pokanoket. I'm surprised Mr. Pynchon sent a public message, it's sure to frighten people."

"Yes, I know. But he had to put us on our guard. I wish people would realize that the Pokanoket, all savages, are given to us as our pupils. We must guide them—not fear them. We should be praying with them, teaching them the word. That's John Sassamon's godly work with King Philip. This land has been given to us by God, for us to lead His children out of pagan darkness to salvation. We are to be a light to nations. It's a mission, Ned. We're called to do God's work here."

"Amen," Ned said. John Russell was a fervent puritan minister with enough conviction in congregationalism to move his church into unbroken land; so loyal to the old cause of parliament to hide two of Cromwell's generals in his cellar and give Ned the job of ferryman and watchman at the gate. "I know it's God's will that we are here. It's just that some of us are careless. The fish traps—"

John Russell laughed. "Not the fish traps again!" he exclaimed. "As I said—tell the women we will pay extra for fish for the next two weeks. They can't blame us for traffic on the river; clearing the forests and making timber is good for us all. They should be grateful!"

The two men arrived at the handsome gate and walked up the path to the front door. "I led the people into the wilderness, to make this new town of saints," John Russell said honestly. "God called me to find new land for new houses, to lead the children of God out of bondage. It's His will that has brought us here to make a city on a hill. No savages are going to stand in our way for the price of half a dozen fish traps. No savages are going to threaten us for the sake of half a dozen acres."

"Agreed." Ned tipped his hat; but the minister called to him before he turned to walk back to his house.

"Come into the kitchen and see Mrs. Rose," Mr. Russell said, opening his front door and greeting his housekeeper. "She wants to settle up with you. I think we're in your debt."

"It's nothing," Ned said, but he followed the housekeeper across the hall and into the kitchen at the back of the house.

"What price did you want for the trout?" the housekeeper asked, taking off her tall black hat and putting it carefully in a cupboard, straightening the flaps on her white cap.

Ned thought of the men hidden in the cellar and the cost to the household, secretly borne for nearly six years. "Have them with my thanks," he said. "And I'll bring some more asparagus, when it's ready."

She nodded. "Will you take a glass of sassafras beer before you go?"

"Thank you," he said.

He stood awkwardly as she went into the cool larder and poured them both a small glass. When she came out, she gestured to the two hard chairs either side of the cold grate. "You can sit," she said.

He raised his glass to her and drank. "I shall have this and go," he said. "I've got to get back to the ferry before dark."

She hesitated. "I hope you're safe out there, on the riverside, Mr. Ferryman? Outside the fence?"

"I'm safe enough. And the fence only stops cows. I'm only as undefended as the rest of the town. You know, I'm not very far out, Mrs. Rose. Perhaps one day you will walk out and visit me. I should like to show you my garden, and the asparagus beds."

She darted him the quick fugitive glance of a woman unaccustomed to smiling. "Perhaps I will," she half promised. "But not while people say the savages are unsafe."

"The Pokanoket are miles away, at the coast," he protested, "and I doubt they are any danger to us at all. I'm just at the end of the lane. You could probably see my roof from your upstairs window."

"I can see the river," she agreed.

"Then you can almost see me. I'm on the very edge where the land meets water."

"But beyond you is the river and the woods beyond that . . ." She shuddered. "And they are people of the water and of the trees. You can't see them in the forests and they are silent on the river. I wouldn't dare to come until we hear they've done with visiting around and complaining of us. They have to submit to our rules."

"After harvest, all this talk will die down," he reassured her. "There's no need for them to submit to anything. We've all sworn to treaties. It's probably nothing more than the tribes gathering for a celebration, there's nothing to fear."

"I'll come later in the summer then," she said. She allowed herself a quick glance at his face, to see that he was still looking at her. "I should like to visit you."

JUNE 1670, LONDON

Tabs had cleared away the dinner things and gone out for her Sunday afternoon off, so the family gathered in the kitchen. Alinor sat in a chair at the hearth where the embers of the Newcastle coal still radiated heat. Sarah stood on a stool to string up fresh herbs to dry. "How long will you leave these, Grandma?"

"You can see them for yourself next Sunday. They have to be so dry that they don't rot, and yet not to have lost all their essence. See when you think they are ready."

Johnnie came through the door to the yard with a basket of fresh-cut mint. "D'you have room for any more?"

His sister made a space on the big kitchen table. "I'll make some more strings. Is this the last of it?"

"I cut a lot, it was spilling over and choking the eyebright."

"I need a bigger garden," Alinor said. "But there's no room in the yard. Perhaps we could take a little field over the road?"

"Who'd dig it?" Sarah demanded. "Johnnie and I are town children. We've got soft hands! And we're only here on Sundays. Ma is too busy and Tabs wouldn't thank you for more work."

"It's a pity that the skills should be lost. Our family have been herbalists and midwives for generations. And with your uncle Ned sending us herbs from abroad—who knows what he might find, and what properties they might have? Your uncle Rob started as an apprentice to an apothecary."

"And we were fishermen," Johnnie pointed out. "And farmers," he added, thinking of his own missing father, a Sussex farmer who abandoned his pregnant wife on their wedding day. "And scoundrels," he added.

"Some trades are worth forgetting," Alinor ruled. "We've not been so lucky with fathers."

"So, what did Sir James want with you?" Sarah asked casually, twisting stems of mint into a posy. "What did he want with us?"

"He was a friend many years ago," Alinor said, choosing her words with care. "He wanted to offer us a refuge at his house."

"A refuge?" Sarah demanded skeptically. "What sort of refuge?"

"We couldn't go," Johnnie spoke at once with his sister.

"No, of course not," Alinor agreed. "It's in the far north, I've never been, though I dreamed of it once . . ."

"Did he love you?" The thought struck Sarah and she turned to her grandmother. "Before your accident, did he want to marry you?"

Alinor answered at once, not pausing for a moment. "Oh no, my dear! And besides, I was married to Alys's father! It's such a long time ago—he was Rob's tutor and very kind to him. And now he thinks to be kind to us. But we could never go. However would we run the business? And I'd never leave you two, and your indentures not up yet. It's not to be thought of."

"He's thinking of it though," Johnnie remarked.

"He'll think of it no more," Alinor said with quiet dignity.

"He's very particular with Johnnie," Sarah remarked. "He couldn't take his eyes off him."

"It'd be the resemblance to his uncle Rob," Alinor replied without hesitation.

"I thought I looked like Uncle Rob?" Sarah challenged.

Alys came into the kitchen carrying a tray of things from the parlor. She put them on the sideboard for want of space on the table which was heaped with sweet-scented leaves as Alinor stripped the bottom leaves and Sarah tied them in posies. "Whispering secrets?" she asked lightly.

"No secrets," Alinor said smoothly. "But Johnnie'll have to dig out some of the mint. We've got too much."

On Horsleydown, the poor houses gave way to little fields and then to wide green rolling hills, with beechwoods crowning the hills on either side of the road. Carlotta, the nursemaid, dawdled behind the couple who walked, arm in arm, their heads together. Beside a fallen tree Livia hesitated. "May I sit here?"

"Of course, of course!" James brushed the trunk with the gloves that he held in his hand and spread a silk handkerchief from his pocket. He helped her to sit, and remained standing before her. Carlotta plumped down on the grass and put the baby on her shawl so he could look up at the sky and the crisscrossing birds.

"You don't answer me?" Livia spoke lightly, as if she were remarking on the view behind them, the silvery river snaking into the heart of the City hazed with smoke from a thousand hearths. "Few men would hesitate."

"Of course," he hurried. "But my circumstances are peculiar. My long affection for your family, my relationship to Rob . . . And it is my own son that I want. If they say he is not here, have they sent him away? If Johnnie is truly Mrs. Stoney's son, what has become of my boy?"

"But if you find your son—how old would he be now?" she asked, looking up at him.

"Twenty-one," he said, knowing at once, without calculating.

"Twenty-one this summer. I swore I would find him when he was twenty-one if they did not send for me before."

"*Allora!*" she said, waving away the longing in his voice. "This is very old history! Say you find him and he does not want to come to you? Perhaps he ran away from the warehouse? I know I would! Perhaps he was a bad son and that is why they have forgotten him? Perhaps he has another life of his own, married to a woman you could not countenance, with a disagreeable family? Perhaps they are in want, perhaps he has a dozen ugly bastards? There are many reasons for you not wanting to own him. Many good reasons not to find him."

"I never thought—"

"Of course not! Why should you? Because you were trusting that they would keep and raise your child! But they have not done so! He is not the young man you dreamed of, just as *La Suocera* is not the loving mamma that I imagined, and the rich wharf with a beautiful house is not as it should be. Are we trapped by our plans? No! I thought they would be wealthy and living in a beautiful London house. I thought they would take me in to a great family and I would be able to sell my antiquities and make my fortune. But no! It is not as Rob told me at all, and I have to change my plans. Just as you do."

"You are very . . . ." He could not find the word for her bright determination which was at once so gratingly unfeminine and yet so charmingly bold.

"Yes I am!" She took his unspoken word as a compliment. "And you too should see that things are not as you have dreamed but that you can make something of them. Isn't that what this whole city is about? Rebuilding from the ruins? What the new king is like? A restored mistake? Not as you thought; but something can be done with him. Isn't that what you would call the spirit of the age?"

"You think the spirit of the age is to seize whatever there is, even if it is not true to your vision?" he asked bitterly. "To give up your ideal for what you can win?"

She stood and gestured at the view behind her, towards London where she knew there was wealth and opportunity, and decadence too. "Oh yes!" she declared. "If it was exiled: let it return. If it burns down: rebuild it. If it was robbed: restore it. If it is free—let us take it.

I shall be an English lady in a beautiful grand house with a thriving business in antiquities, a storehouse in Venice and a gallery in London because I have set my heart on it—one way or another—why not? You should have a wife and a baby son, because that is what you desire. Why should you not restore yourself? Why should you not come into your own again? Why should we not take what we want and go where we are not invited? Why should we not be happy?"

They walked home together without him giving her an answer, but she was content that she had put a swirl of ideas in his head. At the front door she put her hand on the latch and said carelessly over her shoulder: "Come for me tomorrow, and I will have discovered where your son is. I will tell you."

"I'm grateful." He stumbled on the words. "I would not have you spy on them . . . but I have to know . . ."

She shrugged. "Of course you must." She smiled. "Good day."

She opened the door, waved the nursemaid and the baby inside, and gave him her hand. He bowed over it and she leaned towards him. "But think of me," she whispered. "Why not?"

He had no answer for her, but she did not wait for one. In a moment, she was gone and only her rose-petal perfume was left on the heavy summer air.

Sarah and Johnnie took supper in the kitchen with their mother, then walked down the quay to London Bridge and crossed to the north side of the river. They walked together arm in arm, their steps matching, to Sarah's millinery workshop.

"That was odd, that Sir James," Johnnie remarked. "What d'you think he wanted? What d'you think he really said to Grandma?"

"I've never seen Ma so flustered," Sarah agreed.

"But why would he turn up? And why speak to Grandma about a refuge? What can he mean: a refuge?"

"Perhaps he's something to do with our Lady Aunt?" Sarah suggested.

"Odd that they should have just met on her walk?"

"D'you think they're working together? I'll ask at the milliner's if anyone has ever heard of him."

"In a milliner's?" Johnnie asked skeptically.

"If he's ever bought a hat for a woman in this town, they'll know."

"I suppose so. I'll ask at Mr. Watson's if they know his name, if his credit is good."

"He looks like a wealthy man. That collar alone was worth ten shillings."

They paused at a bow window, the shop front of Sarah's workplace. "That's one of mine." Sarah pointed to a wisp of golden net and some glass flowers.

"How much?" Her brother strained to see. "Two pounds for what? Some beads and some wire?"

"It's not the beads and wire, it's the art of putting it together," she said with assumed dignity, then she giggled. "It's the name on the hatbox to tell the truth," she admitted. "I'd give the world to be able to open my own shop and have my own name on the hatbox, and not to have to work for someone else."

"When Uncle Ned's ship comes in," her brother replied. "From America. Filled with Indian gold."

At bedtime in the warehouse, Livia paused on the stairs and asked Alys: "May I stay in your room again? The attic room is so stuffy and hot."

"Of course," Alys replied a little awkwardly. "I was going to ask if you . . . but then I thought . . ."

"I sleep so much better with someone in the bed," Livia confided. "I miss your brother so much in my sleep. I wake and wonder where he is. But beside you, I am at peace."

The two women went into Alys's bedroom. "Don't undress under your gown like that," Livia told her. "We are just women, the same as each other. There's no need for shame. Here—let me help you."

Gently, hands on her shoulders, she turned Alys around, and undid the fastenings at the back of her gown and lowered it for her to step out. "And you can be my maid in return."

"All right," Alys said, blushing furiously as she stood in her under-dress and undid Livia's gown and helped her slide it from her shoulders over her slim hips till it lay in a pool of black silk at her feet. Livia stepped out of it, and let Alys pick it up and spread it gently in the chest.

"So pretty!" Alys exclaimed as she turned and saw Livia in her shift of silk trimmed with black lace.

"Roberto always liked me to have the best." Livia took the hem in her hands and pulled it over her head. She stood before her sister-in-law, quite naked. Alys took the shift, shook it out, and laid it flat in the chest, her hands trembling. When she turned back, Livia was pulling her nightshift over her head, and then she turned and sat on the edge of the bed. "Will you do my hair?"

Alys pulled the ivory pins from the thick black hair and it tumbled over Livia's bare shoulders. "It's a pity to plait it up," she remarked.

"Perhaps tomorrow you will help me wash it?" Livia asked. "Roberto used to help me wash and dry it."

"Of course," Alys said. "If you want."

She turned her back and whipped off her own dayshift and pulled on her nightgown as quickly as she could. But when she turned back to the bed there was no need for self-consciousness, Livia was not watching her. She had climbed into the big soft bed and was lying back on the pillows. She reached out her arms. "Come and hold me! Hold me and let me sleep like a little girl in your arms."

Shyly, Alys climbed in beside her, and felt the warm lithe body slide against her own. "Isn't this better than being alone?" Livia asked as her head dropped to Alys's shoulder. "I hate sleeping alone."

JUNE 1670, HADLEY, NEW ENGLAND

The morning after the town meeting the iron bar clanged on the far side of the bank and Ned left his breakfast to climb the embankment and look at the other side. Quiet Squirrel was standing there with her fishing creel in her hands, her daughter and two other women beside her.

He raised a hand to them, stepped onto his ferry, and hauled the raft across, going hand over hand on the damp rope. He ran it to the pebble shore and the Norwottuck women stepped on board, saying *"Netop, Netop"* one after another. Last on board was Quiet Squirrel. *"Netop, Nippe Sannup,"* she said.

"Netop, Quiet Squirrel, you're selling fish today?"

"Is it true they will pay more?"

"How you know that?" Ned asked, smiling. "Quick!"

"We listened at the meetinghouse window," she said, matter-of-factly. "We're not such fools as to be deaf to our neighbors. Especially when they talk about us—at the tops of their voices."

Ned understood only some of this. But he smiled. "Glad see you. We want friends with Norwottuck."

Her smile crinkled the skin around her dark eyes. "Didn't sound like it," she said cynically. But when she could tell from his trusting face that he did not understand her, she spoke more slowly. "You Coatmen want land," she said flatly. "You want servants. You want people to feed you and hunt for you. I don't think you really want friendship."

Ned understood most of this; he spread his hands. "I'm friendly," he said. "Hopeful. We're all good people. Try harder. Why not?"

"Why not?" she agreed. "You can be hopeful."

JUNE 1670, LONDON

The three women took breakfast together in Alinor's room, the noise of the Monday morning quayside below them, the brightness of the sunshine muted by the linen curtains, the seabirds outside calling over the high tide and diving for fish into the water.

"May I speak of a little matter of business?" Livia asked when Tabs had cleared the plates and the jug of small ale.

"Business?" Alinor asked.

"Indeed yes," she replied. "I hope to be a help to you here, and not a burden. If I had known that it was so small a house and so mean a business, I would not have thrown myself on your kindness—but Roberto did not tell me."

"I'm sorry if that's so," Alinor said a little stiffly. "We've never pretended to be more than we are."

"No, it is I that am sorry that I have no fortune to bring you! But I have prospects. This is what I want to discuss."

Alys glanced at her mother and opened the curtain halfway so she could look down at the quayside below. "I'm expecting a cargo," she remarked. "I'll have to go when the ship comes in."

"Of course," Livia said politely. "I know that the little ships come before everything! I will be quick. It is this: my first husband was a wealthy and noble man. His family had a large collection of antiquities—marble busts, statues, columns, and friezes—beautiful things from the old days of Greece and Rome. You know the sort of things I mean?"

The two women nodded.

"He taught me how to identify the beautiful things, you know they are become so fashionable now? He taught me their value and how to know a real antiquity from one newly made and sold as counterfeit."

"People do that?" Alys asked, curious.

"They do. It is a crime of course. But our collection was all good. He made me the keeper, and I acquired pieces, and I sold some that did not suit our taste, especially to the visitors from France and the Germans too. They love the old beautiful things, but the greatest collectors, and those with the most money to spend, are the English." She paused, looking from one face to another. "You can see what I am thinking!" she asked with a charming smile.

Clearly, they could not. "When my husband died, his family claimed our palazzo—our palace, our beautiful house on the Grand Canal. The palace and everything in it, the tapestries on the walls and even the beautiful pastellone of the floor, they valued everything and took it all from me. They went through my trunks of clothes as I left, to see that I took nothing, as if I were a thief! They checked the smallest cameo, the tiniest coin. Even the things that he had given me as a wife were taken from me as a widow. The family jewels, the family fine linen . . . Roberto was most shocked."

"Roberto was there?" Alinor asked.

"Of course, as my husband's doctor, he was there all through his last illness, and at the end. But what they did not know, and I did not tell them, was that not all the antiquities were in the house. Many of them were in my store, guarded by my husband's steward, being restored and cleaned. I did not tell my late husband's cruel family about them! They were my treasures, I thought, not theirs. So I kept them safe, Roberto and I planned to send them to you by ship—here to your warehouse—and to sell them to your friends in the City."

"Rob thought of this?" Alinor asked blankly.

"Oh yes!" Livia responded. "It was all his idea. The best prices for the antiquities are paid by the English lords building their houses and making their collections. Is that not true?"

"It might be true," Alys conceded. "But we don't move in those circles."

"I know that now!" Livia said with a hint of impatience. "But still it is my hope that I might bring my collection from Venice and sell here. Sir James knows these people, and I think he will introduce me, so that I can sell the treasures. Roberto's treasures, his inheritance to his son. And I hope you will ship them for me and store them here, so that I can sell them with Sir James?"

"Not Sir James," Alinor said at once.

"Do you know another nobleman?"

"We don't know him," Alinor corrected her.

"Forgive me," Livia said rapidly. "Of course, I know that you refused him, but I thought that you held him . . . in some esteem?"

Alinor rested her hand at the base of her throat and gestured to Alys to open the top half of the door to the balcony. The wind was coming from the east, and the stink of the tallow and burning fat from the tanneries on the Neckinger billowed in like a cloud of grease.

"If we sold the antiquities, we could buy a better warehouse further upriver where the air is cleaner," Livia observed.

Alinor sat back in her chair. "Forgive me," she said, clearing her throat with a cough.

"You are distressed that Sir James helps me?" Livia asked. "May I not ask him? When it is Roberto's legacy to his son? What objection do you have to him when he offers you so much, so freely? How has he offended you?"

Alys closed the window as if she did not want even the seagulls, wheeling over the high tide, to hear what her mother was going to say.

"I was carrying his child when there was an accident," Alinor admitted.

Livia nodded gravely, alert to every quiet word.

"My mother was nearly drowned."

"And I lost the baby."

"She nearly died herself," Alys said quietly. "We came away—we could not live there after that. My husband's family would not have me in their house, and we found a refuge here. I gave birth to my twins here. My uncle Ned left our home too, and Rob went to train at Padua as soon as he finished his apprenticeship in Chichester. We've none of us ever been back."

"How you must have suffered!" Livia exclaimed.

"At first we did. Not now."

Livia wrinkled her forehead as if she were puzzled. "You were expecting babies together? Both at the same time? But you had twins, Alys? And my *Cara Suocera* miscarried her baby?"

"Yes."

"How very unlucky!"

"Yes," Alinor confirmed without a tremor.

"But you made your living from what you had?"

"Yes. We have done."

"But that is all that I want to do," she said simply. "My son's inheritance and my dower are in carved marble and bronze in my store in Venice. I want to sell them in London. I want to make a living out of what I have. You, of all people, would not tell me that is wrong."

"No," Alinor agreed. "If they're yours, I am sure you're right."

"It was Roberto's own plan. He said that you would send a ship for the antiquities and you would sell them for us."

"We could try," Alys said. "I suppose we could advertise that we have these goods? But people would not come down here to see them, we would have to find an agent who sells them?" She hesitated. "Do you have money for the rent of a gallery or a saleroom?"

Livia spread her little hands. "I have nothing. Roberto spent all his time on poor patients who could not pay. He left me and his son penniless."

"That's not like him," Alinor observed quietly.

"Oh no! For I have my treasures," the widow assured her. "But I have to sell them! Surely I may ask Sir James to show them for me, to the people that he knows. If you would only allow me to use him for our good? You need never meet him again. I would manage him. I would never bring him here."

Alys looked at her mother for refusal. "We can do it without him," she said stubbornly. "We don't need him."

"He will keep coming here, and keep coming here, until he knows about his son," Livia warned her. "Why should I not meet him for you and tell him? You owe him nothing! Let me tell him there is no son, and no hope; but that I will work with him."

"I think you've made your mind up to do this?" Alinor asked, and was rewarded by a gleam of Livia's impertinent little smile.

"Ah, you understand me," she frankly admitted. "You see the sort of woman I am—like you, like you both. I am determined to survive this terrible loss, and I hope I am brave as you were. Yes, indeed, I am determined; but I have not spoken to him. If you allow me to do business with him you will never meet him again; but he can be of service to me, and to Roberto's son."

Again, Alys looked at her mother for a refusal.

"Very well." Alinor turned to her daughter. "She's right, Sir James knows these people and this is his world." A twist of her mouth showed what she thought of Sir James's world. "Let him introduce her—we can't."

"You permit?" Livia turned to Alys. "You will let me share with you in this business? You will send a ship for my treasures and let me keep Sir James from you and your mother and the dear children?"

The swift grimace that came and went on Alys's face told Livia that she had guessed correctly that, more than anything, Alys wanted the wealthy nobleman kept away from her son.

"I shall keep him from the children and from your mother," Livia promised. "I will tell him that his own child died in the accident, and that the two children are yours. I will convince him of it. He will believe me, I shall persuade him. I am good at persuading people."

"Are you?" Alinor asked.

"When it is the right thing."

"It's such a great expense," Alys said awkwardly. "It's not the sort of thing we usually do. We're not merchants, Livia. We just load and unload for the merchants and the captains."

Livia widened her eyes. "Do you not have enough money?" she asked. "Not for one voyage going only one way?"

Alys flushed. "I could find it, I suppose. I could borrow some of it. But we've never borrowed. We've never put all our money in one venture."

"Shall I ask Sir James if he will pay for the shipping?" Livia asked. "I am sure that he would."

"No!" Alys said abruptly. "Don't do that."

"Then what?" Livia asked helplessly. "What shall we do?"

Alys exchanged a glance with her mother. "I'll find the money," she said. "Just this once."

JUNE 1670, LONDON

That afternoon, Sir James, waiting at the bridge over the canal, saw Livia come out of the warehouse front door, put up a black-trimmed parasol against the bright sunshine, and then beckon the nursemaid and baby to follow her. He was relieved to be chaperoned; but he feared that the presence of the maid would not prevent Livia from saying anything that she liked.

"You don't have a parasol for the baby?" he asked.

"He is Italian," she replied. "The sun is good for him."

"Half Italian," he corrected her.

"Of course, half Italian, half English, and perhaps he will be a—what do you say?—a York-shire-man."

The matter was too serious for him to return her smile. "Your ladyship, I don't think that can be. I must say—"

"No, no, don't say a word!" she interrupted him. "Let us walk in the beautiful fields and I will tell you something that you should know. I have permission from *La Suocera* to tell you, and from her daughter too. I think the daughter is the strictest of the two, don't you? But a mother of twins must be obeyed."

"Alys? You say twins? Both children are Alys's children? You know that for sure?"

She walked beside him, her hand lightly on his arm. "I will tell you it all," she promised him. "When I am on my little seat."

He forced himself to speak of the weather and of the flock of sheep in the distance. She asked how far it was to the warehouse from his home, and how long it took him by boat, or by horse.

"About half an hour by boat. If the tide is with me," he said.

"And if you wanted to send something from the warehouse to the City?" she said. "Some big, bulky things? Would you send them by boat or by wagon?"

He guessed she was speaking of her antique objects. "I think they would have to go to the Custom House near Queenhithe," he said. "To pay duties."

"I have to pay duties before they are sold?" she asked. "I pay duties on the value of them before I sell them? They think I can afford to pay duties before I have made any money?"

"I don't know." He felt very tired. "It's not something I've ever gone into."

As if she sensed his mood, she glanced up at him and smiled. "Ah, business!" she said with a wave of her gloved hand. "We will not talk about business. It is beneath us."

They had reached the fallen tree where she had sat before. Again, he spread a fresh silk handkerchief and she perched on the trunk of the tree while he stood before her, and the nursemaid put a shawl on the grass and laid the baby down, bending over to see his smile. She gave him a leaf and took it from him when he put it in his mouth. She showed him a twig. She tickled his round cheeks with a buttercup, smiling at his rich chuckle.

Livia held her parasol over her head and peeped up at Sir James. "I have found out about your child," she said. "As I promised I would."

Now that he was about to know, he found that he almost wanted to be left in ignorance. "Tell me," he forced himself to say.

"They trusted me with the truth, so that I might tell you."

"Yes," he said. "And?"

"You know that Mrs. Reekie was carrying your child before the accident?"

The drop of his head told her that he had known this, and that still he had failed to save her.

"After the accident she nearly died."

"The child? What happened to the child?" he whispered.

"She miscarried the baby. It died. There is no child. You have no son."

He gave a little stagger, as if a blow had finally fallen. "You are sure? There is no doubt? No . . . deceit?"

"I am sure. They would not lie on a matter so sacred."

"But Johnnie? I was so sure he . . ."

"He is Alys's boy. Sarah is hers too. Alys was carrying twins when she left her husband." She paused. "I don't know about him," she said. "I'll ask if you want."

"No, it doesn't matter. It was their wedding day. I'm not interested in him."

She was shocked. "Their wedding day? Heavens! What happened?"

"It was their wedding day—the day it . . . all happened."

"A winter wedding?" she asked, thinking of the ribbon and the dried berries in Alys's cupboard. "How sad. Very sad and tragic."

"Are you sure of this?" he asked her. "It is not a lie they have made up together?"

"Why would they lie about something like this, against their own interests? They would be far more likely to say Johnnie is your child and claim your fortune!"

He tried to speak; he turned away. "So I have no son," he said, almost to himself. "All these years when I have been hoping . . . and I sent money. But there was no child. There never was."

She gave him a moment to walk up and down, he went past Matteo, who crowed to see him and waved a blade of grass; but James was blind to everything. He came back to stand before Livia. "Forgive me," he said. "It's a blow."

"But you are free perhaps now? From your sorrow?" She lifted her parasol so he could see her encouraging smile. "You are free to make a new life again."

"I would not blame her if she had given the child away, or hidden him from me," he spoke half to himself. "I wouldn't blame her if she had found a family to take him and he had been adopted. I would forgive her even if I could never see him."

"Yes, but she did not." Livia had to nip her plump lower lip to contain her irritation. "She told me. Alys heard her tell me. Just as I said. He died, and she buried him."

"I can see his grave?"

"At sea," she said quietly. "They would not have received him in the churchyard. A miscarried bastard."

That silenced him. He bowed his head. "God forgive me."

"I swear this, on the life of my own son," she said earnestly. "You have no child. He died. You are free."

He took a little step away from the beautiful young woman seated, as if posed for a portrait, on the fallen tree with the midsummer green meadow all around her, and a flock of sheep in the middle distance. She turned and beckoned to the nursemaid, who picked up Matteo and gave him to his mother. When Sir James turned back to look at her, she was smiling down at her son. She looked up, and when she saw he was watching her, she kissed Matteo's little head.

"And so, I told him," Livia told Alys, seated on the bed as Alys brushed her black hair that night. "He took it very calmly."

"He will leave us alone now?"

"I need his help to sell the antiquities; but he will never trouble you or *Mia Suocera* again. He may come to see me; but he will leave without seeing either of you."

Alys finished plaiting Livia's hair and got into bed, ready to insist that Sir James was never to come to the warehouse, that was their agreement. Slowly, Livia loosened her gown and stepped out of it, pulled her dayshift over her head and laid them both in the chest. Naked, she stood before the bed, as the candlelight played on her olive skin, made shadows between her breasts, between her legs, as beautiful as a statue and as alluring as a nymph. She unfolded her nightshift and tossed it high in the air, so for a moment she stood, arms raised, her head up, then she caught her shift over her head and pulled it down.

"You agree?"

Alys, stunned by Livia's shameless beauty, could not speak.

Livia turned back the bedsheets and slid into Alys's arms. She repeated the words she had said to Sir James. "It was very sad and surely very tragic. But we can be happy now. Sir James is forgiven and will not see your mother, you and your children are safe, and I"—she caught a little breath of anticipation—"I shall make my son's fortune. Roberto's son will be brought up as a gentleman."

Alys could not speak, could not even think with the image of the upflung nightgown and the upreaching curved brown body, feeling the warmth of the beautiful young woman slowly enfolding her.

"You say nothing?" Livia whispered, her breath against Alys's neck. "But I think we will all be happy."

JUNE 1670, HADLEY, NEW ENGLAND

At dusk Ned shut up the hens in their little coop, a lean-to beside the house, led the cow and calf to their pen and closed the gate on them, brought the two sheep into their little enclosure beside the cows, and threw them a shared armful of hay. The river chuckled and lapped in the darkness and a great flock of wild pigeons flew over Ned's head, going to their roost in the forest, thousands of them darkening the sky like a storm cloud.

He tied his dog on a long rope in his kennel between the front door and the animals, to warn of foxes in the night, or any other predator— the settlers did not know for sure what animals hid in the forest and might threaten their stock. The dog gave a low growl and Ned felt the warm ruff of fur at his neck as his hackles went up.

"What's up, Red? Something out there?" Ned asked quietly.

Quickly, he stepped into the house and lifted his gun down from the hooks over the front door, tapped a small measure of black powder into the pan so that it was ready to fire. Ned had been an infantryman for Oliver Cromwell in the New Model Army; they had all despised the old-fashioned musket, which needed the musketeer to blow a lit fuse into fiery redness and hold it to the pan for the gun to fire. Ned had bought a new flintlock that sparked its own fire and was ready in a moment. Now he swung open his front door, held his gun before him, pointed towards the silent darkness of the fields, his dog poised beside him, and said quietly: "Who's there?"

If it were any of the People of the Dawnlands or any of the Indian nations, he knew they need not answer; they could be at the back of the house, coming silently up the riverbank as he peered, blind as a mole, out of the front door. They could be on the roof and only the dog would sense them. But Ned had traded with many men and women, talked with them, broken bread, shared salt, and trusted that nobody would come against him without warning. "Who's there?" he repeated.

The clatter of shoes on the track told him that it was white men. "Halt! Who goes there?" Ned shouted. "I'm armed." He held the gun in his right hand and stretched his left hand to the dog's stout leather collar, ready to let him off the chain.

"Pax quaeritur bello," came the whisper.

Ned put up his gun and clipped the chain back on the dog. It was the motto of Oliver Cromwell: "Peace comes through war."

"Come forward," he said. "I'm alone."

William Goffe and Edward Whalley stepped forwards out of the darkness and, without a word, Ned lowered the cock on the gun, pushed open his front door, and they all went inside.

"No spies?" was all he asked. "No one see you pass?"

The two men shook their heads.

"Did you come up the common way?"

"Round the long way: out east to the forest, and then back along the riverbank."

Ned opened the door and listened intently. He heard his dog settling down, turning round and round in his kennel and lying down, the call of hunting owls, and the noises of the forest at nighttime, familiar to him now after many nights alone. Beyond his door the voice of the river chattered softly in the darkness, there was no splash of an oar. Any white man following the two exiles around the margins of the town would have brushed against shrubs and low swinging branches, disturbed roosting birds, broken twigs, scattered stones on the path under heavy boots. Only an Indian could move in silence through the grasslands, brush, and swamp. Ned closed the door and the shutters so that there was no crack for any spy.

"We won't stay," William said.

"You can . . ."

"No, we're going to live off the land for the summer. We're tired of battening on old comrades."

"It's not battening," Ned objected. "It's what any of us would do for the other."

"Aye, I know," William agreed. "But this season we can live off our own, in the open, like free men, not like hibernating mice."

"Where'll you go?" Ned asked. "Stay near, and I can bring you some blankets and ale and the like. There's a Norwottuck village just upriver, I know them—they'd shelter you."

"I wouldn't feel safe among them," Edward ruled. "We're going south to the coast, near where we were before. Can you take us back there for the summer? And bring us back here for the winter?"

"Aye," Ned said. "I'll have to get someone to mind the ferry."

"Won't people ask where you've gone?" William queried.

"Some of them'll probably guess," Ned said. "But if the ferry's manned and I tell everyone I'm going hunting and gathering herbs for a few days, nobody'll say anything. I'll come with you for a day's march, and I'll hand you on to a native guide who can show you the rest of the way."

Edward and William exchanged a glance. "I haven't come this far to be beheaded by a savage and have my scalp sent to England for the reward," Edward said sourly.

"Nay, you'll be safe enough with a guide. They've got nothing against those of us that live modest and farm a few acres. It's the others that have turned them sour: them that can't be satisfied with a hundred acres, them that foul the rivers, them that run hogs through the cornfields. They who insult them, and get them into debt and then say the debt must be paid in land. But they won't hurt two men traveling in peace."

Neither man looked wholly reassured. "But will they know there's a reward on our heads?" Edward asked.

"They know everything! But they'd think it dishonorable to betray a guest for money," Ned assured him. "But you—in return—" He broke off, trying to find the words to explain. "When you meet them—you have to treat them like equals," he said awkwardly. "Not like servants. They're proud—proud as a cavalier lord in their own way—they have their own ideas as to how things should be, they have their own masters and ministers. They have their own God and their own prayers. And more than anything, they hate to be disrespected."

William clapped him on the back. "You're a good man, Ned! You've a kind word for everyone, even savages. We'll leave in the morning, yes?"

Ned nodded. "As soon as I've got someone to man my ferry. You can sleep in my bed," he offered. "It'll be a while before you have a bed again. I'll roll up before the fire."

Before he slept Ned took a sheet of rough paper and with his home-made quill pen and a little jar of ink made from crushed soot and an addled egg yolk, scratched a note for his sister, Alinor, and pinned it with one of his new shingle nails to his rough table, for anyone to find in case he did not come home from his hunting trip.

If you find this and I, Ned Ferryman, have not returned from the forest please to send it to Mrs. Alinor Reekie / Reekie Wharf / Savoury Dock / Southwark Village / London.

Sister Alinor

God bless you. I am writing this in case of mischance before I go into the woods hunting with my dog. If it should go amiss for me then someone will have found it and sent it to you. This is farewell and God bless you, Sister.

You should collect my goods. I have some beasts that should be sold and the value sent to you. I would think about £10. My land and cabin would be worth about £40. You could ask the minister at Hadley Mr. John Russell to forward you the value. Tell him pelts or goods not wampum.

Or you could keep the house and ferry and Johnnie might do worse than to come here himself if he's not too grand to keep a ferry. It's no harder than making a living on Foulmire, and sometimes, when the mist comes off the river and all the birds are flying low, I think it is very like our old home. Sometimes the river comes over its banks into the swamp and the only way through is the little paths that the savages know—that I am learning. I see Foulmire again every dawn here.

I don't regret coming here though I was driven by your shame and the defeat of my cause. I still think that his lordship was not fit to judge you and no man is fit to rule me. I like this land without kings or rulers but men who walk quietly in hidden ways.

God bless you, Sister—and if I don't return know that you were always loved by your brother—

NED FERRYMAN

JUNE 1670, LONDON

Johnnie walked around to Sarah's workshop in the early morning, breakfasting on a warm roll that he bought from a passing baker's boy, so that he could see his sister before work started.

"No Followers," said the cook as he knocked on the kitchen door. "No gentlemen callers. And who comes courting at dawn?"

"I'm Sarah's brother," Johnnie said humbly. "May I see her for a moment?"

The cook swung open the door and the millinery assistants and senior girls, sitting at their breakfast at the big kitchen table, all turned around and stared at the handsome young man on the doorstep, and then, like a flock of startled pigeons in the corn, flew out of the room, abandoning their plates.

"I didn't mean to disturb . . ." Johnnie said, weakly.

Only Sarah stayed and she came to the back door. "They're man-mad," she told him. "They'll all be running off to pull out their curl papers and get properly dressed. If you stay long enough they'll all be back."

"But it's only me, why bother?" he asked as she came out and closed the kitchen door behind her. The two of them sat companionably on the stone doorstep, looking over the tidy yard, the delivery horse nodding over the half door, the groom filling a bucket at the pump.

"Thruppence a day for a junior, tenpence a day for a senior," she said. "The only hope for any of us is that a man sees us and proposes marriage and takes us away from here. There's no way to make a living out of feathers and glass and straw unless you own the shop."

"You don't want to train for another trade?" he demanded anxiously. "You know Ma can't afford new indentures."

"No," she said. "Though I'd rather be in a real business and not women's trade. For some reason they're always paid cheap. But I won't get stuck here, hoping for a man to rescue me. I'll find a way to set up on my own, or I'll find a patron and make headdresses and hats just for her. The court is full of women who want their own look. All the new actresses want to stand out. I don't have to marry some fool to save me from this." She thought for a moment. "If I could do exactly what I want, I'd go and buy the silks and lace where they're made, off the loom. Think of that!"

He was troubled. "But where's that? Constantinople? India?"

She shrugged. "Just a dream, a milliner's dream. Anyway, why're you here so early?"

"I came to see if you've learned anything more about Sir James? His credit's good, I asked Mr. Watson last night. Sir James is well known as a man of means, he's an investor in the East India Company, you can't do that without a fortune behind you, and his credit's solid. Owns half of Yorkshire, and a good property in London, and he has money with the goldsmith's too."

"Was he in exile with the king? Was he a royalist?"

"Aye, he'll have paid a huge fine to settle with the parliament commissioners so he could get his lands back. Then when the king came in, he'll have got it all back again, rewarded for loyalty. He's a wealthy man: clever enough to be on the right side at the right time. He was a royalist until the last minute, turned his collar, and then turned it again."

"So how does he know our ma?" she asked. "And what did he have to do with our grandma?"

"He was Uncle Rob's tutor," he reminded her. "But that doesn't explain why he's so close to the widow. Walking out with her on a Saturday afternoon? They looked like they were courting when we met them on the quay."

"No, he just looked awkward," Sarah said astutely. "I bet she looks like she's courting with every man she meets, she'd look like that with a bargee. She's just one of those women who always look as if everyone's in love with her. I don't think he's running after her; I think boot's on t'other foot: she's got her eye on him."

"You can't know that! What d'you think she wants?"

"I can't tell. She's so pretty mannered all the time, I can't tell where the real woman starts and stops."

"She's very . . ." Johnnie had no words for Livia's relentless allure. "She makes me feel . . . There's something about her."

"Something expensive."

"She makes my toes curl," he confessed. "She looks at me and I can't think what to say."

"She makes my claws curl," Sarah replied acidly. "I know exactly what I'd say."

He laughed at her. "I'd like to hear it!"

"What d'you think she came here for, if not to marry someone rich?" Sarah demanded.

"Well, she's got a catch if she can net Sir James. Do the milliners know anything against him?"

She shook her head. "No mistress. They'd know that in the sewing room the moment he ordered a lace collar. You know, he might be what he says he is: an old friend of Uncle Rob's and a country gentleman."

"Then what does he want with us?" Johnnie asked. "For we are neither."

"Can't we ask Ma?"

Johnnie looked awkward. "I s'pose so—but I always feel when we ask her things it's as if we're missing a father," he said. "As if we're saying she isn't enough. Like we're blaming her for what happened. Like we want a father instead of her."

"We're twenty-one!" his sister exclaimed. "Aren't we old enough to ask yet?"

They were silent for a moment as they realized they were still not old enough to challenge their mother.

"I couldn't hurt her, just for curiosity," Johnnie said, and Sarah nodded in agreement.

"See you next Saturday?" he asked, and she rose to her feet to go in the kitchen door.

"I get my afternoon off tomorrow," she said. "You?"

"Not this week," he said. "But if you come by the warehouse at six I'll take you out for a lamb chop when we finish."

"Dinner on you? I'll be there."

He gripped her shoulders, they rubbed cheeks rather than kissed, with the easy familiarity of loving siblings, then he watched her bound up the steps to the door and heard the gale of laughter that greeted her from the millinery girls demanding why she had not brought her handsome brother to breakfast.

JUNE 1670, HADLEY, NEW ENGLAND

As soon as it was light, Ned pulled his ferry, hand over hand on the rope, to the west side of the river and made an interrogative owl's hoot into the darkness of the forest. He sat down at the foot of a tree and waited, his eyes towards the shadows of the forest, so that they would remain sharp and not be dazzled by the gray sheen of the quietly moving river. A little while later a female owl answered "whoo whoo."

"Come," Ned whispered, and without a sound a woman stepped from the shelter of the trees.

"*Nippe Sannup*?" she said. "You are early? This is our time: it's us who are named the People of the Dawn."

"Quiet Squirrel, I thank you for coming," Ned said formally in English. She squatted beside him and he took in her lined face, the cracked and worn skin of her hands. He smelled the scent of her: red cedar wood, sassafras, and the soft clean smell of her buckskin cape.

"What do you want, *Netop*?"

"Mind ferry?" he asked, attempting her language. "Me walk with friends to sea."

She smiled at his attempt at her speech. "They are weary of being men of the twilight?"

He frowned, trying to understand. "Want to go. Want walk."

"They walk in the forest and by the river when at dusk, thinking they are hidden by the shadows." She smiled. "Of course we see them."

"They are good men. Safe? Safe with Dawnland People?"

"They're safe with us. It is your rulers who say where people can and cannot go. We know that a man can walk anywhere. But your friends had better not go back to where they hid before. Won't your king send his men to look there?"

He frowned at the ripple of words. "Somewhere else?"

She nodded. "Somewhere better. I will ask someone to take you. He knows the lands here and at the coast. He will know a good place."

"He come now? Quick quick?"

She thought that the white men were like children, not just in speech but in thought, in the impatience of their demands.

"You can start the journey, he will find you on the way," she said. "He has his own business before he travels."

Ned shifted awkwardly, feeling his knees stiffening up. "What doing . . . ? What he doing?"

No child of the People would be so rude as to ask a direct question. Especially when asking for a favor.

"He does his own business, Ferryman. We do not answer to you."

"No trouble?" Ned asked, awkwardly conscious of his lack of fluency. "He friendly?"

"I don't know his business. I don't ask him. Do I keep the fees for the ferry?"

"Take fees, I give nails too." Ned knew she would get little profit from the ferry, she would not charge a crossing fee to any of her people, nor any of the neighboring people. They lived in a world of gifting and favors to show power and to strengthen family bonds. They would never charge money for a favor as the settlers did; they thought it beneath them to make little profits off each other. And there was no point paying her in food—she was a better gardener, fisher, and gatherer than he would ever be. But all the native people loved anything made of metal, to hammer into their own use. He knew she would be glad of nails.

"And little iron rods," she specified.

He knew that the Indian craftsmen could repair muskets if they had metal. But he had no choice but to pay her the fee she wanted.

"Nails and rods."

"Very well." She got to her feet in one sinuous motion as Ned pushed himself upwards, giving a little grunt at the effort.

"That's your shoes," she told him. "Those shoes make your bones ache."

"It's age," Ned told her. "I am more than fifty."

She laughed and her dark eyes gleamed at him. "I am far older than you," she told him. "Many winters older, and I can still outrun you. It's those shoes you wear." She patted his shoulder. "And your ridiculous hat," she said affectionately, knowing he could not understand her words.

Ned was still smiling at her condemnation of his shoes, as he pulled the two of them over the river on the ferry. The pale light of the dawn summer sky reflected on the sleek water. "I'll wait here," she said, her hand on the ferry rope. "Will you bring the Coatmen now?"

"Yes," he said. "We come quick."

She smiled at him, knowing that Englishmen would take a long time to start a journey, they always fussed about a thousand things, they always carried far too much.

In the house, William and Edward were up and dressed, eating cornmeal biscuits. "Where have you been?" Edward asked.

"I've got us a guide," Ned said. "He's going to find us on the way."

He filled his birch-bark bottle with water from the earthenware jar and wiped his face and neck with sassafras oil. "Want some of this?" He offered them the oil.

"What is it?" Edward asked.

"Sassafras oil, keeps the flies off."

"Nothing keeps the flies off," Edward said pessimistically, and William laughed.

Ned did not pull on the jacket that he wore to go to town but swung a cape of knotted reeds over his shirt.

"You look like a savage," Edward remarked. "Will you wear a feather in your hair?"

"Keeps the flies off," Ned claimed.

"Nothing keeps the flies off," Edward repeated.

The three men came silently out of the house, climbed the riverbank, and looked back to the grazed wide way to the sleeping town, then they turned towards the river.

"Who's that on the ferry?" William demanded.

"A woman of the Norwottuck," Ned said. "My neighbor. She minds the ferry when I go into the woods."

"An old lady?" Edward asked.

"She's the elder of the village. She knows everything that happens that side of the river, and everything that happens in Hadley too."

"Is she trustworthy?" William asked. "Does she know of us?"

"Aye," Ned replied. "I said. She knows everything that goes on within fifty miles. She minds the ferry for me, she sells me sassafras and all sorts of things from the forest. Things I didn't even know when I first got here."

Ned snapped his fingers and his dog Red bounded down the bank and jumped neatly onto the ferry. Ned and the men followed and climbed on board as Quiet Squirrel wordlessly pulled on the rope to haul them across to the opposite bank. The ferry grounded on the pebble beach, William and Edward took up their little sacks, and went at once into the shelter of the woods. Ned turned to say good-bye to Quiet Squirrel.

"Tomorrow night I come back," he said, and raised a hand.

"Tomorrow night, Ned."

"Guide meets us?"

She smiled at him. "Quick! Quick!" she mocked him. "He will find you. You start—if you can walk at all in those shoes."

Ned chuckled at the insult, threw her a salute, and turned, his dog at his heels, his musket slung over his back, to lead the way south.

JUNE 1670, LONDON

"It is quite ridiculous that we meet like this," Livia said sharply to Sir James the next afternoon. "Like a maidservant creeping out to meet a footman! You must write down for me the address of your London house and then I can write to you and suggest a time and place to meet when we need to talk."

He felt himself flinch at her bluntness. "Of course, I am honored," he said quietly.

"Because we have much to do together."

"We do?"

They were taking their usual path, along Savoury Dock, as St. Saviour's Dock was ironically known to its neighbors who were sickened by the stink of the industries pouring their waste into the river. They turned right into Five Foot Lane, ignoring the catcalls of street urchins and the occasional appeal of vendors of small goods, and they wound their way through the line of little cottages to the fields where the sheep grazed in the distance and she could sit on the tree that he now thought of as "theirs."

"We do," she confirmed smartly. "And this is not a place of business."

"I am not a businessman," he said gently. "I have no place of business."

She peeped up at him in her charming way. "I know," she agreed. "You are above all this. But I have to toil and sow and reap for my boy, you know. For his inheritance. And his family, this family that I find myself among, these are working people and I cannot be idle. They need my help and I am going to help them."

"But I . . ." he started.

"You can just leave, of course," she offered him. "You need never see any of them again. You have been forgiven for your sins and no doubt you forgive them theirs. You tried to reenter their lives and you have been shut out. There is nothing more for you here. You could go now and never come back, arrange another marriage and hope for a son of your own."

He blinked. "I could," he said cautiously.

"Or you could help me save them," she said, her voice a little lower, beguiling. "You could help this poor family to make a living, better than it is now. You abandoned them in poverty, and they cannot rise without our help. You can have no contact with Mrs. Reekie, you know, but her grandson should grow up as a prosperous English boy. You will tell me where he should go to school? I am sure that he should go to your school? At what age does he have to start? Should you introduce him?"

He flushed with embarrassment. "I didn't go to an English school," he said. "I was tutored at home and then I went to a seminary. I was intended for the priesthood."

"*Dio!*" she exclaimed. "You? An English Milord?"

"There are many English Roman Catholics," he said awkwardly. "But I lost my vocation, I had . . . I had a crisis of faith . . . and, like many, I converted to the Protestant Church and took up my title and my lands."

She had no interest in his religion. "Oh! So! Where should Matteo go to school?"

"Perhaps Westminster?" he recovered. "I could assist you with that."

She clasped her hands. "I ask for nothing from you but a little help. I was impulsive before, you understand that I am Italian? I see a happy outcome and I long for it all at once. You will find me passionate! You will forgive me that. But I will never trouble you with my dreams again. I thought that I could be a wife to you and give you a son—I thought it like a miracle that we should meet when I am the very thing that you want. But I see I was too quick for you! From now on we shall be nothing more than friends and partners."

He was flushed with embarrassment at her frankness, but stirred by her words. "I could not engage myself to do more than make introductions for you, to gentlemen who are buying antiquities, and their agents," he said stiffly.

"Nothing more than that," she agreed. "Alys will arrange the shipping, I shall order the antiquities, you shall do nothing more than invite people to your house and make the introductions, and I shall sell the things."

"At my house?" His refusal was immediate; but she laughed gaily and put her hands on his. "Not your beautiful house in the country," she assured him. "I don't ask for that. No, no, all I want is to be allowed to place some of my best and most beautiful pieces in your London house so that your friends and acquaintances may come and admire them, in your salon. That is how they should be seen." She paused as a thought struck her. "Oh, but you do have a salon? This is not two rooms over a coffeehouse? In some shabby corner? You do have a proper house?"

He was stung. "It is Avery House, madam, on the Strand."

She jumped to her feet in delight and kissed him on both cheeks. "That will do splendidly!" she exclaimed, as if he had agreed. "I will come tomorrow."

JUNE 1670, HADLEY, NEW ENGLAND

The three men walked for hours on the track that wound through the forest of tall strong trees, the fallen leaves from last year rustling beneath their feet. Ned kept up a brisk pace but both William and Edward were men in their sixties, they had been indoors for months, only walking at dawn and dusk, hoping to be unseen. The hot sun beat down, the flies rose like a thick mist from the brackish water on either side of the narrow path, and swarmed around their faces, constantly biting. Ned called a halt, and they all drank from his bottle.

"How d'you ever find your way?" Edward gasped, taking a sip of water. "This whole forest goes on forever and it all looks the same."

"I've been out this way a few times," Ned said. "And I was raised on a mire, I learned as a boy how to find little tracks and remember them."

"You hunt here?"

"No. We've got no land rights here and the People like to keep it for themselves, they don't want boot prints on their paths and guns banging off in their forests and frightening the animals. This is their lands, not ours. Though some of the townsfolk are trying to buy here."

"You don't come here for beaver pelts?"

Ned shook his head. "It's been trapped out," he said. "Long before I got here. They say that when we first came here there was a dam in every stream: thousands of beavers. Now they're all gone. The dams are breaking, the lakes behind them are draining away. If you take all the beavers you lose the dam, you lose the lake and that changes the rivers, and so you get no beaver. That's why they call us stupid."

"It's got to be farmed," William insisted. "Anything else is wasteland."

"Maybe some land ought to be wasteland?" Ned suggested. "Maybe God made it like that for a reason?"

"'Increase ye, and be ye multiplied, and fill ye the earth, and make ye it subject; and be ye lords to the fishes of the sea, and to volatiles of heaven, and to all living beasts that be moved on earth and be ye lords, or rule ye,'" William quoted Genesis.

"Amen," said Edward.

Ned nodded. "Amen. Are we ready to go on?"

"When will we meet with the savages?" Edward asked.

"When they want," Ned said with a smile. "They'll have been watching us ever since we started on this trail."

Edward hunched his shoulders. "How could they?" he said. "We've gone in silence."

Ned laughed shortly. "Not to them," he said. "To them we've sounded like a fife-and-drum band marching through the woods."

"We've barely spoken," William protested.

"The deer know, don't they?" Ned said. "The deer heard us from the first step? The People know the woods as well as the deer."

"Can't you order them to show themselves?" Edward said irritably.

"Nay, they're free men on their own lands."

They said nothing more as Ned led the way on a path which was no wider than his shoulders, putting one foot before the other, his English boots making clear marks in the mud where moccasins had left no trace.

They went past a deep hole, like a posthole, and Ned paused for a moment, cleared a vine which was trailing across it, and turned to go on.

"Just give me a moment to catch my breath," William said.

As they waited, Edward idly poked a stick in the side of the hole; the sandy gray soil spilled inwards.

"Don't do that," Ned warned him. "It's important to them. They keep it clear and open. You saw me weed the vine."

"What is it? A posthole? Out here?"

"It's a story hole," Ned replied. "And a signpost."

"Which?"

"Both. Something happened here, someone was injured during a hunt, or a man asked his wife to marry him, or a woman gave birth, or there was an accident or a meeting or something. So they make this hole at the side of the track so that everyone remembers what took place here. Then, when they're telling someone where to go, which track to follow, they tell them to turn at that story."

William was puzzled. "It's like a way marker, but a register as well?"

"Yes. It's easy to remember, and to teach the children: their lives are mapped on the land, going back hundreds of years. The Lord only knows how long they've walked these trails. The story of their lives is on the land. Their history is their geography."

Edward shook his head. "They're strange folks."

"Strange to us," Ned said. "But I find my way round here better with the story holes than I ever did with milestones in England."

"What story does this hole tell?" William asked.

Ned hesitated, curiously reluctant to share with them.

"What does it matter anyway?" Edward demanded, tired and in pain, his face swollen with bites.

Ned led the way on, at a steady walk, on the long twisting path, through wet ground where the moss sucked at their boots, over higher ground where the lighter soil under the pine trees shifted under their feet and made them labor for every step, steadily south, and always behind him he heard the rasping breaths of the two men.

They walked until the burning sun went down behind the hills on their right, and slowly the sky grew milky and then gray and then a dark indigo blue. Ned handed out cornmeal biscuits and some dried meat, and showed them a raised patch of land, sheltered by a few boulders, so that the ground was dry beneath their blankets and they rolled themselves up.

"When will he meet us?" William asked again. "The savage guide?"

Ned shrugged. "When he's ready."

"I'm bitten to death," Edward said, ducking his face under his blanket. "Don't the bugs trouble you, Ned?"

"Here." Ned offered a small bottle made from sassafras bark and corked with a piece of the root. "Try it. It works. The Indian woman who minds my ferry traded me the bottle and the oil for some sugar."

"Does it really stop the biting?"

"Well, I'm seasoned," Ned said, looking through the canopy of trees at the stars over his head, piercingly silver in the completely black night sky. "I grew up with quatrain fever. I spent my childhood on a mire in Sussex."

"You owned land in England?" William asked curiously.

Ned thought he had not words to describe Foulmire to an outsider: the moonlight on the hidden paths, the grind and thunder of the tide mill, the strange lonely beauty of the sea flowing through and overspilling the land for miles in every direction, the call of the oystercatchers in their wheeling flight and the setting sun on their white arched wings.

"Nay, we never owned anything much," he said. "I had the right to work the ferry and my sister was the village midwife. Nobody troubled us as long as we stayed at the water's edge, poor as water voles. There's no profit in the tidal lands, there's no interest in them."

The dog raised his head and growled, looking into the darkness.

"Peace," Ned spoke half to the dog, half to the shadows of the rocks.

Then one of the shadows moved. Ned was up and reaching for his gun in a moment, as William and Edward struggled to their feet and stared around them.

"*Nippe Sannup?*" came a voice from the shadows.

"Aye, it's me," Ned answered in English, lowering the gun and calling Red to heel.

"What did he say? Who's there?" William demanded, rising to his feet and reaching for his hand ax.

"Peace. He asked if it was me. I know him."

"What did he call you?"

"*Nippe Sannup.* It means something like Waterman."

The dark shadow of a tree moved and materialized into a man of about fifty years. A tall Pokanoket, wearing an apron of deer leather, and several strands of beads, some of them deep purple wampum, a sheaf of arrows slung over one shoulder, his bow in his hand. He stepped forward and greeted Ned with the dip of his dark head. His long hair was tied to one side, his face unsmiling. He scrutinized the other two men and then turned to Ned with a quiet question in Pokanoket. Ned answered, and, apparently satisfied, the man patted the dog on the head and sat down on a boulder.

"What does he want?" William asked. "Beads?"

Ned hid a smile. "Nothing. We have nothing that he wants. He's come to guide you."

"Ask him if he knows somewhere we won't be found."

"I'll ask him. He'll know. He knows his own lands round here, and he knows ours too."

An exchange of halting questions and fluent answers left William and Edward waiting for a translation. Then Ned turned to them. "He says too many people know where you hid last time: West Rock Ridge, and it is better to go somewhere new. He knows some caves by the sea. No one but Po Metacom—the new Massasoit—and his councillors will know you're there. It's Pokanoket land and can't be sold, so settlers never go there. He says the sea is rich in shellfish, and lobster and crab and fish, you will eat well. There are fruits in the forest, wild strawberries and vines. Also, there are many birds and you can take their eggs. He says take only two from every nest. One of the

Pokanoket will visit often to see that you are well, and this man will bring you home at the end of the summer."

"He'd do that for us?"

Ned nodded. "If he says he will, he will."

William took Ned by the elbow and turned him away from the silent guide so he could mutter: "Po Metacom? The new Massasoit? So he's the son of the old one who first welcomed settlers?"

"That's the one."

"But isn't he the one who's complaining about us buying land? Who's complaining of us to others, the French? To Rhode Island?"

"Yes. That's the one," Ned repeated.

"But why?" Edward muttered to Ned. "If he's a troublemaker, why would he help us? When he's complaining about us? Complaining about Plymouth?"

Ned hesitated. "They have a tradition of helping people in need, it shows their power—so that's one reason. In his mind, if he guides you to safety and brings you back again you will owe him a debt. They hope you'll be grateful and remember them in future. They know you know the great men in Plymouth and Boston and they'll expect you to speak for them to the Commission." Ned paused. "Their way with us, with all the settlers—the French, the Dutch, all the newcomers— is to make alliances, and hope that we protect them from each other. Really, he's offering you an alliance."

"We can't be beholden!" Edward objected.

"We are already," Ned pointed out. "We wouldn't have survived if his father hadn't given us land and fed us when we were starving."

William leaned towards Ned. "He won't turn us in to King Charles's men? That's all that really matters?"

"No, this man works for the Massasoit Po Metacom, he's a go-between for the Massasoit and the United Colonies. He'll be hoping that you speak for them to the Commission. He's not interested in the new king in England."

"We can only bear witness that he is living at peace if we see it," Edward bargained. "He'd have to prove to us that they are not arming or gathering."

"You'll only see what he lets you see," Ned warned. "He's not a fool. And I don't think you can barter with him, if he's offering you a safe haven?"

"And he won't just . . ." Under the dark unsmiling gaze of the Pokanoket, Edward did not dare to name his real fear of murder.

"You're safe enough," Ned assured him. "If he gives you his word—that's his bond." Ned hesitated. "He's a man I know and I'd trust him. Josiah Winslow himself employs him, and—to be honest—we've got no other choice. We can go on without him—but we can't cross Pokanoket lands without a guide."

There was a silence then the two older men nodded. "We've little choice," Edward said.

"None," Ned said simply. "We're all strangers here, these are their lands, we're here by their leave."

William put out a hand which was not quite steady. "We are agreed?" he asked tentatively to the Indian.

"I'm very pleased to meet you," he said in perfect English.

JUNE 1670, LONDON

Livia left the baby with Alys, so that she could take Carlotta as a chaperone on her visit to Avery House. She used the last of her money to hire a wherry to cross the river from Horsleydown Stairs and a hackney carriage to the imposing gates that faced onto the Strand. She wished very much that she had a footman to walk with her up the steps and to hammer the big bronze knocker on the door. But Sir James opened his own front door to her, which made her feel at home, until she had an adverse thought: "Do you not want your servants to see me?"

"No!" he said, genuinely surprised. "I thought you would like it better if I greeted you myself."

He liked how her face, which had been a little pinched with anxiety, warmed under his attention.

"I do like it. That was kind of you," she said. "I would have preferred my own carriage to bring me here."

"Perhaps when you have sold your antiquities," he said, and was rewarded by a sudden smile. "I'll pay the hackney," he said when he saw that the driver was waiting and that she had not pulled a purse from her pocket. He gave the man a few coins and came back up the steps to lead her into his house.

"You don't have a carriage?" she asked.

"I don't need one in London. And I am here very seldom."

"Then I shall have to buy my own, when I have made my fortune. Now." She took his arm. "My antiquities! Where do you think we should show them? They need to be in good light, and a big space."

He hardly noticed that his help was now an accepted part of the plan as her maid took a seat in the hall and he guided Livia up the stairs.

"And where is your baby?" he asked.

"He is with Alys. She quite dotes on him. I would not be distracted by him while I am visiting you," she said. She gave him a quick promising smile. "You shall have my full attention!"

He said nothing as they reached the top of the stairs but gestured to the gallery that ran the length of the building, along the wide front, where the portraits of his ancestors took up only half of the walls. "Here," he said.

"There is room for busts, and heads, and columns," she said, delighted. "And these wonderful high windows for light. Why do you have so few things?"

"Some pieces were sold," he said. "The house was commandeered during the Cromwell years, and some things went missing. Stolen, by common soldiers. They didn't even know what they were taking. Probably hanging on some merchant's wall right now. I doubt we'll ever get them back."

"Why can't you get them back?" she demanded.

"It would be a hard claim to prove."

"Why don't you steal them back?"

He gave a shocked laugh. "I couldn't! Of course not!"

Quickly, she agreed with him. "No, of course not. So you must buy some new. I can give you an excellent price on some Caesars. Quite original, in historical order, on their own marble columns. They would be perfect here."

He laughed. "You would offer them to me at a good price?"

"At ten percent under the market price if you keep them here, in this gallery, and show them to your friends."

"I was joking . . ." he said.

"I never joke about money," she said seriously. "You can have ten percent under market price for anything you like if you will show them to people. Now, is there anywhere else that my antiquities could be shown? Do you have any space outside, for the big statues?"

"There is the garden," he said unwillingly, for the garden was his private haven in London, a long run of wide green space, down to the river, planted with apple trees and plum trees, dancing with blossom in early summer, bright with scarlet and bronze leaves in autumn when the boughs were laden with fruit. It had been his mother's favorite place, where she had held midsummer balls when the old king had been on his throne and everyone thought that nothing would ever change.

"Show me!" Livia demanded, and he gave her his hand and led her through the great glazed doors to the terrace at the back of the house, and then down the steps to the garden that led to the river.

"This is what I thought London would be like," she breathed. "Not a dirty little warehouse, run by two sad women, but this! A big English garden, and a river like silver."

"Are they sad? Would you call them sad?"

"No, they're where they want to be, it suits them—but this is like another world! High tide, and no wharves and noisy unloading, just the birds singing in the trees, and the fruit forming on the bough, and the grass under my feet! This is the England I dreamed of!"

He was exhilarated by her joy in his garden. "You like it? I love it here—but you should see my lands at Northallerton."

"I should love to come!" She took it swiftly, as a direct invitation. "For this is a paradise!"

"This is a pleasure garden, but at Northside Manor I have or-chards, and herb gardens, and vegetable gardens and a dairy and a bakehouse and . . . it is a manor that can keep itself. It can feed and house and manage itself. I can live off my own."

"When I was a little girl that's how we lived," she told him. "In the vineyards, outside Florence. We kept hens and cows and ducks and bees. I kept the hens, we had twenty eggs a day. I have always longed to live in the country again. Matteo should be brought up in the country."

"And yet your home was Venice," he observed.

Her dark eyelashes veiled her bright eyes. "You know that a young woman cannot choose," she said quietly. "My parents married me to Signor Fiori. He took me far from my home, and the countryside that I loved. I came to Venice like an exiled child. Do you know how that feels?"

"Yes," he said, the exiled child whose home had been stolen by the parliamentarians before he could inherit it from his royalist father. "I know what loss feels like."

She put her hand in his with her quick sympathy. "Ah, let us make each other happy again? I am bold with you because I understand your feelings so well. We are one and the same."

He flushed, but he did not drop her hand. "I should not mislead you; you know I am a new widower. I am not ready for another marriage."

She bowed her head. "I will wait for you to speak," she promised him. She looked up; he thought her lips were so warm and red that she must rouge them. "You must take as long as you like. I will wait for you to say the words that I long to hear."

JUNE 1670, HADLEY, NEW ENGLAND

Ned walked a little way with the two Englishmen and the Indian, until they came to a story hole at the side of the path where he stopped. "I'll leave you here," he said. "This was where a woman from the Pequot people, far from her home, picked up a baby muskrat, and she made it into a pet. She washed it clean so it didn't stink, and it followed her like a dog." He looked at the bewildered Englishmen. "The Pequots think the world was made when a woman fell from the skies and a muskrat brought her earth from the floor of the sea. She made the first land from the seabed, and gave birth to the People. So muskrats are an important animal for them. The Pequot woman was honoring her stories while with a strange people."

William and Edward exchanged a glance. "Paganism," William condemned in one word.

Ned shrugged. "Isn't it like us telling the gospel to Indians? That you keep telling your stories because they are part of who you are?"

Edward slapped him on the back. "Ned, soldier, first you spoke paganism—now heresy! It's just getting worse, not better. We're going to have to burn you for a heretic!"

Ned laughed at himself. "Well, it's the story for the hole," he said, "so perhaps you will remember it, for it's important. It marks where the Bay path, an Indian trail, crosses the Connecticut path, a way that the settlers use. We drive our beef down it all the way to Boston, see how rutted and muddy it is? And how wide? It's too busy for you: the settlers are fearful of the forest and travel in big groups, you'd be seen if you walked here. So you'll cross the drover road here, and Wussausmon will show you the hidden ways to the shore, he'll take you past the villages, the Nipmuc and the Narragansett homes. This is where I say good-bye. He'll bring you back to Hadley at the end of summer."

William took Ned's arm and drew him to one side. "Who is he? And how does a savage speak English as if he came from the University of Oxford?" he whispered.

"Because he attended Harvard College!" Ned told him. "He's a minister in one of the praying towns, he was brought up in an English household, his English name is John Sassamon. He advises the governor and the Council at Plymouth on Indian affairs."

"Well, he doesn't look like an Englishman," William said flatly.

"Not now—he's in his buckskins now, and goes by his tribal name Wussausmon," Ned tried to explain. "He serves Po Metacom, the Massasoit of the Pokanoket. He serves as a go-between for him and the governor at Plymouth. He serves Josiah Winslow. He's like an ambassador."

"No ambassador that I've ever seen," William persisted.

"He's one of the many that have worked to keep the peace between the Pokanoket and the settlers," Ned explained. "Fifty years we lived alongside each other—with complaints but no wars. Now, with more English coming, and the People feeling the pressure, it's harder for the leaders to keep the peace. Po Metacom—him that we call King Philip—depends upon advisors that can speak both languages, that can live in both worlds. Governor Prence trusts him too."

"You'd trust him?"

"He's a Christian and understands us. He's a Pokanoket and understands them. I'll tell him to guide you safely and bring you back at the end of summer and I know you'll be safe."

Ned turned to Wussausmon, and spoke quietly. "They can't go too fast," he said.

"They were soldiers, and yet so slow?" the man asked incredulously.

"Not like your braves," Ned shook his head. "They were great men in the English army against the English king. They rode horses into battle. They didn't run on a warpath like you. And now they're old. So take them slowly and bring them back to Hadley at the end of summer?"

The man nodded in silence.

"Did Quiet Squirrel send you to follow us from Hadley?" Ned asked curiously. "Did you come behind us all the way?"

Wussausmon grinned. "It wasn't hard. You went through the trees as quietly as a team of oxen plowing a field."

"Quiet Squirrel says it's my shoes," Ned admitted.

"She told me it was the stupid hat."

Ned laughed out loud. "She has no respect for me," he said.

Wussausmon laughed too. "We're just men. She has no high regard for any of us."

"Did she tell you that Hadley is mustering?"

"We knew that already."

"Have you told Po Metacom?"

Wussausmon bowed his head and said nothing. Ned felt reproved for rudeness.

"It's just that the Coatmen are anxious," Ned explained. "We know that your king is sending out messages. We hear he's even talking to the French, as far north as Canada—and they're our sworn enemies. It would be as if we talked to your enemies—the Mohawks. You'd feel betrayed."

"But you do talk to the Mohawks," Wussausmon pointed out.

Ned ignored the truth. "It makes the English anxious."

"You should be anxious, if you make laws, put them on us, and then break them," Wussausmon said.

Ned sighed and gave up on the interrogation. "I'll tell Minister Russell that you've been a good friend to us today. Are you coming back to Hadley this season?"

"I am going upriver."

There were no English settlements north of Hadley; if Wussausmon was going further north it could only be to meet with other tribes, and to invite them to join in a land freeze against the settlers—or worse.

Ned could not hide his unease. "If the Massasoit is unhappy with the governor and the Council at Plymouth, or the governor of the Massachusetts Bay Colony Council at Boston, he should speak to them. Better to deal with them direct. We don't like to see you talking among yourselves—joining together."

"For sure you don't!" Wussausmon smiled. "And I often speak with the English governors. The Massasoit is trying to get everyone to agree to stop selling land. He wants us to work as one power. Like you do."

"But he can't order them?"

"No," Wussausmon said. "He can't. He would not. That is why I go north and west for him, to get agreement with the tribes on your borders. Our leaders have to agree with their people, they are not tyrants like your king."

"Well, I'd say he's a better man for that." Ned was conscious of his divided loyalties. "But you don't ever want to quarrel with us."

"I have no quarrel with anyone," Wussausmon said quietly. "I live under your laws in your town; but when I am in the forest I live under our laws. I have to serve Po Metacom as he asks, I am his man."

"But converted," Ned suggested. "You are sworn to God. You're attending him at our request: as his tutor, as our ambassador. You were raised in an English home. You're our man too."

He nodded. "I am of two worlds," he said.

"That's can't be easy," Ned said, thinking of the divided loyalties of his home, of his sense of not belonging here, in the world that he thought would be his own.

"It is not."

JUNE 1670, LONDON

Alinor was well enough to dine with Alys and Livia in the parlor and was curious where Livia had been all day.

"I am making progress," Livia said happily. "I have seen the gallery and his garden where we can show the antiquities. They are suitable. So, you can send a ship for my things from Venice."

"But who will load them?" Alinor asked.

Livia spoke to Alys. "My first husband's steward still runs his workshop in Venice, as he did when my husband was alive. He still stores our goods, for loyalty. I have no money to pay him since my dear Roberto died. But he will do whatever I ask. I will write to him and tell him to pack the pieces that are stored."

"You must trust him," Alinor remarked.

"Oh yes! He was very good to me when my husband died and the family tried to take everything."

"He helped you to hide the treasures?" Alinor suggested.

"He knew they were mine. It was his workshop where they cleaned and repaired the treasures. He knows I will repay him, when the pieces are sold."

"He was your husband's steward; but he served you?" Alinor inquired. "And took your side against his master's family?"

Livia showed a tremulous smile. "I think he was sorry for me when they tried to steal from me."

"And Rob did not object to this partnership? This trusting partnership?"

Livia turned a laughing glance at her mother-in-law. "Ah! I see what you are saying. I must tell you that Maestro Russo is an old man, with a granddaughter of my age, and a wife who is a little old lady. His hair is white, he is stooped over a stick. He has been father and grandfather to me. He loved Roberto and thought of him as a grandson. And Roberto knew that he would do anything for us."

"You're very blessed in your friends," was all Alinor replied.

"How long will he need to pack and load?" Alys asked. "We could find a ship sailing for Venice and write to him. But then how long will he need to get the pieces ready?"

"He knows that I came here to sell my goods, he knows that I have no money until I sell my treasures," Livia replied. "It will take him no more than a few days to pack and get the permissions for them to leave the country."

"If he can pack them so quickly, I can commission a captain here to take your instructions and bring back goods."

Livia clapped her hands. "How clever you are! This is what it is to be a woman of business."

Alinor smiled and looked from one young woman to the other. "You can find the money?" she asked Alys.

Alys nodded. "How much space will they take in our store?" she asked.

"They'll be padded and crated, I should think they'll take the whole of the ground floor. But they won't be there for long, if you will send them on your wagon to Sir James's house."

Alys gave one of her rare smiles. "You're excited."

"This is going to make our fortune!" Livia exclaimed. "And your wharf will become known as a place to ship beautiful works of art and luxuries. You won't be heaving coal anymore." She caught Alys's hands and did a little dance on the spot; her joy was infectious.

"We've never heaved coal," Alinor said.

That night the two young women talked as they undressed, and brushed each other's hair.

"Thank you for looking after my darling Matteo today," Livia said. "Was he really very good for you?"

"I'd forgotten what it was like to spend time with a baby so young," Alys said. "He was perfect. He had the milk that Carlotta left for him and he slept for most of the time. I worked in the counting house, with him in the cradle at my side, and he and I sat with Ma for most of the afternoon. When he woke and cried, I walked him on the wharf and he watched the boats and the seagulls, I'm sure he was taking notice. He smiled and waved his little hands as if he was excited, and when he saw—"

"Yes, he is very clever," Livia said absentmindedly.

"And you? You are happy with the premises that you have found? His house is adequate?"

Livia noted that Sir James's name was apparently not to be mentioned. "Yes," she replied. "There's a big hall and an open gallery, and a garden. I can show about twenty pieces, I should think. I can use them as examples and take orders for more."

"You've got more than one load?"

"It was my husband's great passion," Livia said. "I hoped to make a business from it, buying and shipping and selling."

"I am surprised there are so many objects, so many people buying them."

Livia smoothed her pillow and got into bed. "People were making them for hundreds of years," she said. "So they are there, all round, if you know where to look, and you care to pick them up."

"You pick them up? For free?"

"My first husband started his collection from his own land. His quarry had been worked for years, and some pieces were just lying around, and there was a ruin of a house nearby with some beautiful urns—vases. Then all the little farmers who had ancient villas on their land or temples buried in their fields learned that people will pay more for the pieces of stone than for the olive crops! So now they dig them up and sell them to collectors and agents for collectors. You can go into the market in Venice and buy pieces of marble or old jewels and gold rings on the same stalls where they sell oil."

"There must be treasures in England too then," Alys remarked. "When my mother was a little girl she used to collect old coins—not gold or silver but the old clipped coins of base metal, just tokens."

"What would be the point of that?" Livia asked. "Nobody is going to buy chips of copper. It's not like gold. There's no profit."

Alys gave a superstitious shudder. "No, there was no real point," she agreed, getting into bed beside Livia. "She just liked them. She had a purse of them. It was . . ."

"What?"

"Just a purse, of dross."

"No point at all," the young woman said flatly, and leaned over and blew out the candle so the room was plunged into darkness.

JULY 1670, LONDON

Alys walked west along the quay to the merchants' coffeehouse where she did her morning business. As a woman wharfinger she was a rarity in the crowded meetinghouse. Most of the other women merchants, shipowners, ship wives, and carter widows sent an apprentice or a son into the coffeehouses to meet with customers and clients. But Alys had been a regular in two or three coffee shops for years and knew that Paton's in Harp Lane was the best place to meet shipowners for the Mediterranean and Adriatic trade.

She looked for Captain Shore, master of the *Sweet Hope,* who had taken Rob to Italy when he first went to study at Padua. The Captain usually met his customers at a table in a room at the rear of the warren of a building, and Alys glanced over the high-backed settles where a couple of captains were taking instructions and letters for their destinations. She approached a table where a broad man with thinning fair hair and a weather-beaten face was folding some papers into a wallet.

"Captain Shore," she said pleasantly.

At once, he rose to his feet and offered his hand. "Good day to you, Mrs. Stoney. It's good to see you."

Courteously, he waited for her to sit in the chair opposite him, before he dropped back down onto the settle. "I was sorry to hear of the loss of your brother," he said bluntly. "A fine young man . . . I got to know him on the way to Venice—Lord! It must have been ten years ago. But I remember him."

"Thank you," Alys said. "I need to send a letter of instruction to a storehouse in Venice about his goods. They belong to Rob's widow, her personal furniture. There is a steward who will pack the things and supervise the loading on your ship. You'll deliver to our wharf."

"Not going to the legal quay to pay the duty?" the Captain confirmed. "Direct to you, we don't need to report?"

"Yes, it's her personal goods."

"I won't be responsible for their condition," he warned her. "Furniture: never travels well."

"Very well," Alys agreed.

"Nothing dangerous?" the Captain specified. "No poisons or guns or cannon or anything I don't want on my ship. No wildlife," he added. "Nothing that needs looking after. No pets. No slaves. No vegetables or plants. Just goods."

"It's mostly stone," Alys assured him. "Statues and the like."

"Heavy then," he said pessimistically.

"Will you do it?"

"Aye."

"We'll pay half now and half on receipt."

He thought for a moment. "Five pounds a ton," he said. "D'you know the weight of her furniture?"

Alys grimaced. "I don't know for sure. But it can't be more than six tons. I'll pay you fifteen pounds now, and the rest, depending on weight, when you unload."

"Agreed."

"This is the storehouse." Alys slid Livia's letter of instruction to her steward across the table.

"Russo!" the Captain exclaimed, looking at the address. "Oh, I know him. I've shipped goods for him before. More than once." He shot her a look from under sandy eyebrows. "I never knew he was anyone's steward. I thought it was all his own business—sharp business at that."

"My sister-in-law trusts him," Alys replied. "He was her steward."

"If he suits her," the Captain conceded. "If you're sure, Mrs. Stoney? It's not your usual trade and he's not the sort of man you'd usually deal with?"

"He is my sister-in-law's steward," Alys repeated. "He's got her goods in his storehouse. She trusts him."

"As you wish," he nodded. "But if it all miscarries in Venice and

I have to leave empty-handed, I'll come back to you for a guinea for my time."

"Agreed," Alys said. "But I expect you to deliver the crates. There should be about twenty."

"I've got room," he said. "I'm carrying coffee."

"How long?" Alys asked the question that every merchant always asked, knowing that they would never get an answer.

"As long as it takes," he said. "What are we now? July? I sail this week, get there early August, then load, then come back. I'll stop at Lisbon going out and Cadiz coming back. I should be with you end of September." He rapped the table with his knuckles for luck. "God willing."

Alys rose to her feet and spat into her hand and extended it, the Captain did the same. She felt without distaste the warm squish of saliva and his roughened cracked palm. "Godspeed," she said.

"Aye," he said, taciturn, and tucked the order into his wallet and took a pull of small ale.

AUGUST 1670, HADLEY, NEW ENGLAND

Mrs. Rose, the minister's housekeeper, brought a letter for Ned out to the ferry-house as the burning sun cooled at the end of the day and there was finally some relief from the heat.

"I thank you for your trouble," Ned said, surprised to see her.

"Mr. Russell was going to send one of the slaves, but I thought I'd take a walk," she said, looking at the dog, and the garden, anywhere but Ned's face. "Now that the sun's going down and it's a little cooler. Is it from your sister?"

"Yes," he said, glancing at the handwriting. "Out of season. Usually she replies to my letter spring and autumn."

"You write by the tides?" she asked. "Though you're so far inland now?"

"The big moons," he said. "I see them, and they remind me to write."

"Well, I'll leave you to read it," she said, turning back towards town.

"No! Don't go at once," he invited her. "I'm so glad you came."

"Well, I thought I would," she said.

"Would you like a drink?" Ned indicated the path through the garden towards the river. "You could sit and take a drink? Sumach? Or milk? I've got milk?"

She hesitated, as if she would like to stay.

"Please," Ned said. "Take a seat, watch the river, you don't have to walk back straightaway, do you?"

"I can stay for a while," she said cautiously, and took a seat.

Ned went inside and reappeared with two wooden beakers, beautifully carved, and a jug of sumach berry water. "Here," he said, and poured her a cup.

She sipped. "Very good," she said. "How long do you leave the berries to steep?"

"Overnight," Ned replied.

"Are you not lonely out here?" she asked, watching the sudden turquoise flash of a kingfisher, low over the water, bright as a dragonfly.

"There's always someone wanting the ferry," he said. "Or with something to trade. And the dugouts pass by, quite often they stop to talk, or they have something to show me, or to sell, or a message they want me to tell someone coming after."

She gave an exaggerated shudder. "You mean natives? I don't know how you dare talk to them," she said. "What messages can you carry for them? I'd be afraid."

Ned found himself puffing up a little at her admiration. He checked himself. "We're neighbors," he said. "It's right to be neighborly."

"Not with them," she contradicted him. "I came here to make a new England; not live like a savage."

"I hoped for a new England too," he said. He found himself looking for a common ground with this woman who held such strong opinions; but had never expressed them to him before. "One without masters or lords or even a king."

Now she looked up at him with a smile. "You and me both know that you can get rid of a king, but there are always masters, and servants," she said. "And even though we were well rid of one king, his son came back."

"Pray he doesn't come over here," Ned said, hoping for a smile.

"We can trust the governor to keep us free of him, and his heresies. God's law is greater than man's—even a king's—and we have our charter."

"Amen," Ned said politely, well aware that New England was righteously devout and the minister's housekeeper more than most.

"But how do you cook here?" she demanded.

"As anyone does, over the fire. I've let it go out in this hot weather. I might light a little fire outside later, and roast a fish on a spit. I could catch another, if you'd like to stay."

She hesitated. "I have to get back to cook dinner. Perhaps another time."

Ned nodded.

"And how do you do your washing?"

"There you have me!" Ned admitted. "I pay one of the women to come and do my washing."

"Not savages?" she asked, a little shocked, and when he nodded she shook her head. "Savages won't get your linen white. You can bring your collars to the minister's house and I'll do them in our weekly wash."

"I'm obliged to you," Ned said politely. "But I won't impose. Not now that you have a little holiday, with your guests gone away for the summer."

"They're no trouble," she said. "Men of God, both of them, and exiles for a great cause."

"Have you always been in service?" Ned asked shyly.

"From when I was a girl in Devon. My master was called by God to come here and brought us, his household servants, with him. He died on the voyage, my husband too, and we that were left had to find new places. It wasn't hard—everyone wants a servant over here, and I chose to work for the minister as he promised me a plot of land in his new settlement, if I found a husband at the end of my time with him."

"You want your own land?" Ned asked.

"Of course," she said simply. "Everyone does."

"You would farm it yourself?"

She risked a glance at his face. "I hope to marry a good husband and we'll farm it together," she said bluntly.

Ned hesitated, not knowing how to answer her, and at once she finished her cup and rose to her feet.

"I'll leave you to read your letter."

"I would walk you back into town—"

"I know you can't leave the ferry," she said. She hesitated and then told him what she had been thinking from the very first day she had seen the ferry-house go up and Ned spreading reeds for thatch on the roof. "You could make it a good business here. You could build a bigger house and open it as an inn for travelers going north, you could hire men to farm your plot, and maids to serve. If you had a wife who knew her trade in the kitchen this could be the best house on the river."

Ned did not argue that he had no appetite for a good business and desire to be an innkeeper. He smiled down at her. "You're an enterprising woman," was all he said.

"That's why I came here," she agreed. "I was called by God to make a new life in this new world, and I thought it could be a better life than the old." She hesitated. "There's nothing wrong with that? Wanting a better life?"

"No," Ned said quickly. "And it's what I wanted. I wanted a better life too. Just not . . . not at anyone else's cost."

She put out her hand to shake, as if she were a man. "Good-bye."

He took her work-hardened hand in his own, and closed his other hand over it, so they were hand-clasped. "I'll see you the day after tomorrow," he promised her. "I'm picking fruit tomorrow. Shall I save anything for you? I'll have high bush blueberries and the first of the wild grapes."

"I'll take three pound of blueberries for bottling." She hesitated but she did not draw her hand away from his warm clasp. "I'll be glad to see you, Mr. Ferryman. The minister has no objection to you coming to the house to visit me."

Ned was very sure that John Russell had no objection to a visit, nor to a marriage. The whole village of Hadley was of the minister's making; he had moved his congregation here from the river settlements in Connecticut, he had measured out the plots himself and invited other settlers to come. Ned had been awarded the ferry to the north and a plot of land, for escorting and guarding William Goffe and Edward Whalley; but even Ned must be settled under the rule of the town and that meant attendance at church, a godly marriage, and a family for his plot. Mrs. Rose was an indentured servant, a widow; she too must settle and marry at the end of her service.

Ned followed his guest to the town gate and opened it for her; she passed through with a little smile.

"I'll see you, Mr. Ferryman," she said, and started to walk down the wide green common way.

It struck Ned that this was not the freedom that he had hoped for when he had crossed the ocean. He had dreamed of a life that they had passionately imagined, in the evening lectures of Cromwell's army—a land where every man would have his own plot, his own faith, and his own rights. Every man would have had his moment of blinding illuminating godliness that would guide him for the rest of his life, every man would have his own voice in government and every man of every color would be free and equal. But here in the land that he had thought would be free, there were still laws that put everyone in his place, there were still masters and men, landlords and servants. Ned was still pulling a ferry, and his wife would be a maid, an indentured servant whose greatest ambition was to make others serve her.

He thought he should have said something warmer, something more agreeable in reply to her plan of winning a husband, but he had not found the words. He thought he had always been a fool around women. His wife had died young, and the only woman he had ever understood had been his sister, and she had betrayed everything he had believed, and nearly died for her falseness. So he let Mrs. Rose go, and she walked on, her white bonnet visible all the way down the track.

Ned turned inside to open Alinor's letter and, at the first line, pulled the stool towards his rough table, to read and reread the words, holding the paper to the light from the open door to make out the scratched-out sentences. As soon as he understood that his nephew was drowned he dropped his head to his hands and prayed for the soul of Rob, the bright boy who had been the brightest hope of his family and who had been lost in deep waters. With a little groan Ned slid off his stool to his knees to pray for the boy's mother, Alinor, and that she survived this new blow, and learned to accept it, as yet another tragic loss.

"Amen," he said quietly. "Lord, You know the pain that this family has endured. Spare us any more. Let my sister come to understand that her son is lost to this world and gone to another. Let her find peace at her home, and me in mine."

AUGUST 1670, LONDON

The shipping on the Thames was at its peak in the fairer weather; the great galleons from the East Indies which had caught an early monsoon wind passed the little wharf as if they disdained it, heading to their own deep moorings, and their own great warehouses. Alys maintained her rounds of meeting merchants, drumming up business for the wharf, and seeing the goods in and out, and the Custom duties paid.

Reekie Wharf was the preferred quay for a Kentish hoy that brought broadcloth in winter, and wheat and fruits in harvest time. The master— an old comrade of Ned's—docked in August and Alys was able to climb the stairs to her mother's room, where she was tying herbal posies to prevent fever, and put a bowl with fresh plums in her lap.

"Sussex plums," she said. "Captain Billen brought them."

Alinor closed her eyes to taste them as if she could see the tree, and the wall around Ferry-house garden, and the little house on the edge of the mire.

"It must have been a good summer on Foulmire for these to be so sweet," was all she said.

The only idle person in the warehouse was Livia, who could think of nothing but the return of her ship from Venice carrying her goods; but could do nothing to make it come sooner. She hemmed her own exquisite linen, she played with her baby for a little while and then left him with Alys or Alinor for the whole afternoon as she walked in the fields and orchards to the south. She complained of boredom and of the heat, of the monotony of the warehouse life, of the likelihood of them all getting sick from the stinking River Neckinger that discharged into the Thames beside the warehouse. Her only interest was the design and ordering of some small elegant cards, like tradesman's cards but on thicker quality paper. They showed a drawing of a classical statue head and, beneath, the address of Avery House.

"But these make it look as if you own the place," Alys objected when Livia showed her the top face of the cards in their box.

"I can't give my address as Reekie Wharf, Savoury Dock, can I?" Livia replied sharply. "These are antiquities of great value. No man of fortune and taste would be interested in them if he knew they came from here."

"You are ashamed of us?" Alys asked levelly.

"Not at all! This is a matter of business. Not how things are, but how they look."

"And does he not object? To how things look? To your using his house, his name?" As usual, in conversation she left James nameless.

"He will have no objection," Livia ruled.

Alys gaped at the younger woman. "He will? You say: he will? He doesn't know?"

"He knows I am showing my antiquities at his house. Of course, I have to give out his address. How else will people know where to come?"

"I thought they were his friends, they'd know where he lives?"

"This will remind them to return."

"However did you pay for them?"

Livia turned her head away to hide a rush of tears. "They were not very expensive, and I had to have them, Alys."

Alys had a moment of dread. "You've never borrowed money from him?"

"No! I would not!"

"Then how?"

Livia's head drooped. "I sold my earrings."

"Oh! My dear!" Alys was shocked. "You shouldn't have done that. I could have lent you the money."

"I couldn't ask you," Livia said, putting her black trimmed handkerchief to her eyes. "How could I? Not after how you were about the shipping. I can't bear to be a burden to you . . ."

"Did you pawn them? Can we get them back?"

"They gave me three shillings for them."

Alys went at once into the counting house, opened the cashbox, and came back with the money in her hand. "There!" she said. "Money's tight, but it's always tight, and I'll never let you sell your jewelry. Get them back, and never do that again. Come to me for anything else you need. Rob wouldn't have wanted you to sell your little things."

"But he's not here!" Livia exclaimed, tears pouring down her face, her lower lip trembling. "I have to make my way in the world without him, and I just can't! I don't know how!"

"I'm here!" Alys exclaimed. "I'm here! I'll take care of you, and little Matteo too. I always will."

Livia flung herself into Alys's arms. "You're such a good sister," she breathed. "I shall come to you for everything, I won't do such a thing again. Roberto gave them to me on our betrothal, it broke my heart to sell them."

Alys held her close. "Of course you must come to me for anything you need. You're family, this is a family business, our fortune is yours."

Livia stepped away, dried her eyes, and tucked the coins in her pocket. Alys rubbed her face with her hands, smoothed down her apron, and her gaze fell on the cards again. "But I wish you hadn't had them printed like this."

"I can get them reprinted, but it would cost another three shillings? I won't allow the extravagance."

"It looks as if you live there."

"It does not look as if I live there," Livia ruled. "It looks as if you can visit Avery House to see my antiquities, and you may apply to Avery House by letter if you wish to purchase. Avery House is my shop window, just as Sarah has a shop window for her hats. Nobody thinks she lives in the window."

AUGUST 1670, LONDON

Sir James, when he saw the visiting card for Livia's antiquities giving Avery House as the address, merely raised his eyebrows.

"You're very organized," was all he said. "Do you hope that I will distribute these cards for you? As if we were hucksters and Avery House our stall? Are people to order antiques from me as if I were a grocer?"

"No, no," she said. "That would never do. I should never ask such a thing of you! I should never stoop to trade myself! See your name is not on here, nor mine. Just the address. These are for me to give to people who make an inquiry. All I want you to do is to invite people to a little party, to see our antiquities. I will show them the pieces, and then I will give them the cards, I will write on each card with a note of the piece they like and the price. So that they remember the antiquities are for sale and can be purchased from me."

"You want me to invite people?"

"Gentlemen and ladies that you know." She gave a little shake to her gown, as if dismissing everyone else in London. "No one commercial. We don't want dealers or tradesmen or people of that sort."

"I agree," he said hastily. "But I don't have a circle of friends like that. I lived in Yorkshire with my wife and my aunt at Northside Manor, and we seldom came to London. After my wife died, I closed Avery House. I only opened it this year for—" He broke off.

She felt a sting of jealousy as she realized he had opened it for Alinor; but she made sure that her smile never wavered. "You must have family friends?" she pursued. "Relations?"

"Of course I do."

"And people who were friends of your parents."

"Naturally. Though not everyone came home from exile." He shook his head, thinking of those who had never returned.

"But there must be some people who were on your side for the king who came back and who owe you favors?" Livia pursued. "Many people. People whose secrets you kept? Were you not a royalist? Are you not the winners now?"

He gave a little resigned shrug. "Very well. I shall send out cards for a breakfast party."

"If ladies are coming you will need a hostess," she reminded him.

He hesitated. "I suppose I can ask my aunt if she will come south from Northallerton . . ."

"I shall do it," Livia offered. "It is no trouble, and I have to be here anyway to speak of the antiquities. You can tell people that I am the widow of your former pupil Walter Peachey. They can think that we have been friends for years."

He was shocked. "I cannot give you another man's name!"

She smiled up at him. "It does not matter, does it, my dear Sir James? It gives you and I a provenance which we need. We can hardly say that we met at a dirty little warehouse, and that you were there to offer for a poor wharfinger's mother, to claim your bastard son; can we?"

"No, of course we can't say that, it would be a disgrace!" He was shocked.

"So we have to explain how we met," she pointed out. "And why you would provide me with a gallery to show my first collection? All I am saying is we need a little polish."

"Polish?" He examined the word.

"A little shine to deceive the eye." She smiled. "As we do in the workshop. To add luster. A little polish. I will call myself Nobildonna da Picci, do you see? No change at all, just one little letter; and then no one can doubt our friendship is anything but you kindly helping the widow of your late pupil Walter Robert Peachey, my late husband. It is a more elegant name anyway, I think. We preserve my reputation from comment, and we spare you any connection to the wharf. You don't want to expose me to gossip, do you?"

AUGUST 1670, LONDON

Sarah, home as usual for Saturday night, helped her grandmother to bed, straightening her bedding and smoothing the pillow and drawing the curtains against the night sky. A harvest moon lay low over the river and Alinor asked her to leave them open so that she could see the warm yellow light.

"You don't fear it'll give you bad dreams?" the girl teased.

"I like to dream. Sometimes I dream I am a girl again back on Foulmire, and the sound of the gulls are the cries of the birds on the mire. Sometimes I dream they are the birds that Rob loved on the lagoon at Venice and that he is listening to them now."

"You dream of him like a wish?" the girl asked with ready sympathy.

"No," Alinor said firmly. "I dream of him like a certainty."

Sarah drew up the little stool and sat beside the bed. "A certainty? What d'you mean?"

"He was sure-footed, my son: that's certain. He was a good swimmer: that's certain. What she told us—"

"What Livia said?"

"Aye. What she told us can't be true: that's certain. She told us he was always taking out a boat on the lagoon, and walking on the sandbanks and islands. So he wouldn't have drowned there. Not my Rob, not in water that came and went, that was sometimes land and sometimes sea."

Sarah listened, wide-eyed.

"If she'd told me he'd been killed in a fight or taken sick, I might've believed her. Sudden, and with no time for him to think of me. If she'd told us he was buried, I might've come to believe it. But I can't imagine him drowned and no gravestone in his name. Besides, if he'd drowned, I'd have known it. I'd have known the moment it happened. It's not possible that Rob drowned—and me in the yard on a sunny day, shredding lavender, picking thyme, singing . . . it just couldn't happen."

Sarah nodded.

"I see you sitting there, thinking that I am losing my wits." Alinor smiled at her granddaughter. "But I so nearly drowned once, myself. Could my son go beneath the water and me not feel it? In the water that's even now in my lungs?"

Sarah got to her feet and drew the curtain a little more open so they could both see the path of the moonlight on the river.

"I keep looking for him," Alinor confessed. "I see the sails and think one of these ships will bring him home. I think he'll come with her statues." She turned and smiled at her granddaughter. "For some people, this world is not quite . . . watertight. The other world comes in . . . sometimes we can reach out to it. It's like Foulmire—sometimes it's land and sometimes it's water. Sometimes I know this world, sometimes I glimpse the other. Don't you?"

"Oh, Grandma—I know you hope I do, I'd like to think that I did," she said quietly. "But I don't have the sight."

"I know you do," Alinor challenged her.

"Well it's not clear to me . . ."

"It's rarely clear," Alinor confessed. "And I've no proof of anything. Nothing to say to your mother. Nothing to ask anything of Livia."

"What would you ask her if you could?"

"I'd ask why she's dressed in black but spending every day with another man? Is her little heart broken but mending fast? And if she is no widow; then where is my boy?"

SEPTEMBER 1670, LONDON

The tide was on the ebb and the terns, hovering over the water, were dropping into the waves with a splash and coming up with tiny silver fish in their sharp beaks. Livia hesitated in the doorway of Alinor's bedroom, Matteo in her arms, and spoke to Alys, who was collecting a tray full of posset bags from her mother's worktable.

"Can you have him this morning?" she asked. "I need Carlotta to walk me over London Bridge."

"Not now," Alys answered. "I'm expecting a ship."

"He can spend the morning with me," Alinor offered. "He's no trouble."

"I'll take him for a walk when they've unloaded," Alys promised. "I'll be free at noon, but then I should have another cargo this afternoon . . ."

There was a shout from the quay below, where a lighterman stood up in his rocking boat. "Delivery for Reekie Warehouse," he yelled.

Alys opened the door and stepped out onto the little balcony. "Reekie Wharf! What've you got?" she shouted down.

He gestured to the crate in the prow of his boat. "From New England," he said. He pointed to the ship behind him, hove to, and taking on lines from a barge to go upriver.

"Wait there! I'll come down." Alys hurried from the room.

Livia raised her arched eyebrows at Alinor. "How she runs when someone shouts for her!"

"She has to pay for their time," Alinor said. "Of course she runs. I'll go down and see as well. It'll be something from Ned."

"More herbs?" Livia suggested limpidly as she followed Alinor downstairs, Matteo against her shoulder.

The lighterman and a couple of dockers carried the crate into the warehouse. Alys paid for the shipping and then fetched the hammer from the wall to open the lid.

"Tabs can do that," Livia said.

"I can do it." Alys pulled nails from the top of the crate till it was ready to open. She smiled at her mother. "I know you'll want to open it." Skillfully, she levered up the lid but left it resting on top.

Alinor cautiously lifted the lid and at once the rich strong smell of sassafras breathed into the room.

"There must be something else inside," Alys told her. "It was heavy."

Alinor scraped a little of the dried leaves aside and found the cool globe of rock. "It feels like pebbles."

"Could it be ore?" Livia asked, interested at once. She handed the baby to Alys and stepped forwards to see. "Gold-bearing ore?"

"He wouldn't send gold in a crate." Alinor drew it out and weighed it in her hand. It was a big stone, the size of a cobble, gray and uninteresting on the outside but it was split, it opened in her hands and she gave a little gasp.

It was a treasure, a sparkling sharp-toothed cave of jewels, purple as dark as indigo, and so white as to be translucent. "Will you look at this?"

"Are they diamonds?" Livia breathed. "Has he found diamonds? Purple diamonds?"

"He's written." Alys pulled out the sheet of paper packed in the crate. *"Dear Sister and Niece Alys,"* she read aloud. *"Here is a crate of sassafras leaves, which I know you can always use, and a stone that the Norwottuck people call 'thunderstones.' They say that a stone like this draws lightning away safely to the ground. I have not seen such a thing, but I thought it might be helpful in the spires and roofs of London. If you can sell them at a profit I can get more. It cost me 6d. in trade goods, so let me know if it's worthwhile. In haste to catch the boat—your loving brother, Ned."*

"He says nothing about me? Nor his nephew?" Livia asked.

"This will have crossed with my letter," Alinor told her. "It takes a long time for news to reach him—a month and a half—sometimes more?" She put the thunderstone together and then opened it up again. "This is beautiful." She turned to Alys. "Will you take it to the apothecary and see if he has any sale for it?" she asked her. "You can tell him we've got a new delivery of sassafras too. I'll keep some back to make bags and tisanes, but you might ask him what he'd pay by the pound?"

"I'll go this afternoon," Alys started, but then she clicked her tongue in irritation. "No, I can't, I'm expecting some fruit from Kent." She turned to Livia. "Could you go? You could go on from the Strand with Carlotta."

"I?" Livia asked, looking from one woman to another as if it were an extraordinary request that she could hardly understand.

"Why not?" Alinor asked quietly.

Livia just glanced at Alys, who answered for her. "Oh! No, Ma, of course she can't."

"Why not?" Alinor turned the question to her daughter.

Alys flushed. "She's a lady, she can't go selling things to a shop. It's not right. She can't go into a shop and haggle for something . . . in English . . . with Mr. Jenikins who's always so . . . It's not her language, it's not her place."

"Is this true?" Alinor asked Livia as if she were curious. "Our work is beneath you?"

"No! No! Of course I will go," Livia said gracefully. "If you ask me, I will go, *Mia Suocera*. Of course. I can't do it as well as darling Alys, but I can try. If you wish it, I will try. I want to help, I will do anything you ask me."

Alinor turned to her daughter: "You go when you're able. See if he wants more of these thunderstones and what he'll pay."

"But I will go if you want me?" Livia interposed.

Alinor did not even glance at her inquiring face. "Nay, you think no more of it," she said.

SEPTEMBER 1670, HADLEY, NEW ENGLAND

Ned's garden sprawled with green weeds at the end of the hot humid summer, the river broad and limpid green, the woods on the far side a wall of green, the meadows above them a yellowing green, and the pines above them a deep purple green. Even Ned's clothes in his box were green with mold, and every hole under his eaves and every corner of his root cellar was sprouting a little nest of green shoots. He spent hours every day hoeing his crop with his stone-blade hoe, and peeling back the leaves from the ripening heads of corn so they dried brown. As his crop of beans flourished, climbing around the corn stalks, and his squash vines trailed on the ground, more and more animals came from the forest on either side of his acreage to raid his harvest. Black flocks of crows darkened the sky and would have stripped the field bare if Red had not bounded barking from his kennel. Squirrels came scampering along the branches of the trees overhead, partridge hens led their fat chicks, ducking under his fence to pick and scratch in his precious seedbeds. Ned repaired his fence, sticking willow wands into watered earth, weaving them together, to mark out his half lot of four acres, trying to grow a tame little English hedge to keep out a wilderness of trees that stretched for miles, greater than all of England, perhaps greater than Christendom. Nobody knew how far the land extended, it could go on to the Indies for all anyone knew.

Wussausmon, walking up the broad common stretch from the south one evening, was unrecognizable, dressed as an Englishman in breeches, shoes, and a shirt and a jacket. He opened the north gate from the town, came to Ned's garden gate, and remarked: "You English, you cannot leave anything alone."

Ned looked up at the friendly voice, and looked again as he recognized the Pokanoket man under the English hat. "I didn't recognize you!"

"These are the clothes of my other world," he said. "And now my name is John Sassamon."

Ned rose to his feet. "Come in, whatever your name," he said, taking the loop of twine off the little gate.

"I won't interrupt your work."

"I'll go on with it. Sit here. I'll be finished in a moment."

Ned pinched the garden soil into a low wall of mud around the willow whip and puddled the water to its bare stalk. "Every beast from the forest thinks it can overrun my garden and eat my crops," he complained. "I wish I could build a wall against them! Or carve a moat from the river."

The man laughed. "Why not move the forest back?"

"The Dutch, in their country, hold back the sea," Ned told him.

"So I heard. Does the sea not push back? Do the rivers not mind?"

"Actually, the sea does push back," Ned conceded. "And perhaps the river does mind. I've never thought of what they might feel—the rivers and the seas—when we master them."

"Of course they mind—are we not the same being as them? The blood in my veins, the water in the river? We all flow. We all move with the moon."

Ned sat back on his heels. "When I was a lad I thought that it was the tide that pulled up the moon and turned my days into nights." He finished the watering in silence, his finger over the top of the stoneware bottle regulating the flow that dripped from the hole in the bottom. "My sister believes that women's moods and courses come and go with the moon, and with the tides."

"Of course they do," John said simply. "You've missed that one." He pointed to a willow whip. "And this is squaws' work. You should marry a woman to do this work for you."

"You think it's beneath a man to hoe and weed?"

John laughed. "No! No! Beyond us! It's a skill that we men lack.

Only the women have the skills to feed everyone. They learn from their mothers, and their mothers from the grandmothers, backwards and backwards to the day when Mother Earth taught women. All we men grow is tobacco. A white man like you'll never feed a family from your planting. You can't care for the earth like a woman can."

"I could take a plow to it," Ned pointed out. "A pair of ox and a man. Then you'd see a crop of wheat that no squaw could grow."

"It'd be a desert in four seasons. And the dust would blow around you like snow. This is no land for plowing, it has to rest; but you English will never let anything rest. You enslave everything."

"I don't," Ned objected. "I feed the land as Quiet Squirrel told me. Why—I'm half a Norwottuck already," he claimed, making the man laugh. "The people in Hadley accuse me of turning Indian. They say that I don't know what I am."

"Between two worlds, and unsteady in both," John suggested.

Ned looked up at the dark broad-planed face under the ugly English hat.

"Unsteady." Ned repeated the word, and shifted his feet in his uncomfortable shoes. "Anyway, no woman would live with me out here. She would say it's too far out of town, and too close to the forest."

"What about the one that you walk with?" John suggested. "Mrs. Rose? You carried her basket."

"You saw me? Where were you? I didn't see you?"

John shrugged. "I wasn't in my hat," he said, as if native dress made him invisible.

Ned was strangely disturbed. "I didn't know you were watching me."

"We watch all of you."

The two men moved to the rough bench that Ned had at the back of the house, facing the river. They could see the posts of the pier, the raft rocking at the side, the ropes looped to the opposite bank dipping and rising in the water with the flow.

"Because you don't trust us anymore?" Ned said gloomily.

John chuckled, distracted by the river. "You caught my cousin in your ferry rope the other night. He did not see the rope across the river and he forgot it was there. Nearly overturned him in his dugout. He was cursing you and your water-walker."

"I thought you all just ducked under the ropes, or paddled over them?"

"It was dark, he forgot."

"And where was he going downriver in the dark?" Ned asked.

John shifted his gaze, looked over at the hills, shrugged. "Taking a message . . . I don't know."

"The Massasoit is still unhappy with the Council at Plymouth?" Ned asked. "He's talking to other tribes? I spoke to the minister and he said he would warn the Council."

"Your Council speaks to him as if he were one of their servants. I translate their words, I hear them speak as if we are theirs to command. They snap out orders as if we are slaves, as if this land is not ours; though they know they are newcomers. It has been ours since the rising of the first sun shone first on us, long before Englishmen came."

Ned fetched two cups of root tea. John gave him a pinch of tobacco from the pouch at his belt and they both filled their pipes and smoked in silence. The aromatic cloud kept the insects away from their faces, and they were both aware that the smoke was sacred in the religion that neither practiced. Together they watched the sun set on their left behind the high terraces of the river, as the sky slowly turned from cream to darkness.

"Your friends will come back next moon," John said. "It's not been a good summer for them."

"What's wrong with them?"

John shrugged. "Who knows? They have discontent in their blood."

"Will you bring them?"

"As I promised."

"Thank you." Ned hesitated. "They're not happy?"

John shrugged. "They eat well enough and they are warm and dry. The women take them extra food sometimes. But they miss their homes. And they say they will never get home to England, not while this king is on your throne."

Ned nodded. "They were two of the judges that executed this king's father. He forgave those who fought—I was in that army—but he said the judges must die."

John nodded; it was part of his law that a life should be paid for a life, so that part of the story did not surprise him. But a rebellion against a leader was unknown. "You took up arms against your own king? And they killed him?"

"He was a tyrant," Ned tried to explain. "In my country we have an agreement about what kings may do. Even though they are kings. We had a parliament—like the General Court here. But he did not respect them, so we fought him and caught him and then we executed him."

"I have heard of this. Did your friends smash his head? With a club?"

Ned choked on shock at the picture John conjured up and laughed awkwardly. "No, no," he said. "We beheaded him. With an ax."

It still sounded barbaric. Ned wondered that he had never thought of this before. "We built a scaffold, outside his palace," he said, thinking that everything he said made the execution sound worse. "It was a proper trial. Before judges, many judges."

John looked incredulous. "We'd never kill a king." He shook his head, disbelieving. "You are a most violent people."

"I'm not explaining it well," Ned said. "Don't tell people—it's more complicated than I can say."

"But you crucified your God as well?"

Ned tried to laugh. "That wasn't us! That was years before!"

John shook his head. "You are a strange people to us," he said. "I was raised in an English family and studied at Harvard, but I don't think I will ever understand you. I translate between my people and the people of my raising—English—and I know the words, but the meaning!" He broke off.

"An Englishman's word is as good as an oath," Ned said stiffly.

John shook his head. "We both know that's not true," he said.

Ned felt anger rise and then he slapped his guest on the shoulder. "God forgive us," he said. "You're right. God help us, indeed. We speak falsely to you and to each other. We're sinners indeed." He got to his feet and fetched the jug of small ale; but he paused before he poured a cup. "I'm forbidden from giving you liquor," he said, "for fear that I cheat you while you're dead drunk. We are trying to be good neighbors, you know."

"Oh, get me drunk and buy my land." John held out his cup. "I've got an eight-acre plot in a praying town; it's only mine if I obey your laws and deny my people's faith. I go between my angry ruler and yours. Get me drunk, steal my land, and throw me onto the streets of Plymouth."

Ned poured the small ale. "They don't want your eight acres in Natick. You know what they want: the great lands near Boston. So the city can grow and spread."

John nodded. "I know it. We all know it. But this has been our land forever, tracked with our feet, the animals we hunt are the kin of the animals our ancestors hunted. They are kin to us. We belong here. We can't sell."

"Are you agreed?" Ned asked curiously. "Are you coming together as people say? To resist us?"

John raised his cup to the silent river. "You know I can't say. Would you not be bound to pass my words to your elders? Would they not tell the governor? And then they'll summon the Massasoit as if he were their servant, scold him and fine him and take more of our land and pretend it is a just punishment and not your greed? I warn you—I want to warn you; but I will not betray him."

"He mustn't gather the tribes together," Ned said flatly. "I warn you in return: it would be the end of all our hopes to live free and at peace here."

"But we are not free," John pointed out. "We are not at peace. When your king overstepped his rights you killed him. What should we do when you overstep? The Pokanoket are tired of you, and your broken promises. I translate nothing but insults. The Pokanoket are tired of me too."

"Are they? Is the Massasoit tired of you? Is it dangerous to go between two worlds? Should you stay in the praying town and be an Englishman, where we can keep you safe?"

"You can't keep me safe, you can't even keep yourselves safe. Your town is fenced with wood that wouldn't stop deer. You know we can make fire in a forest and tell it which way to go! If we told fire to come to Hadley, your roofs would burn in a moment, we could walk through the ashes. If we were all as one and we rose as one against you, you would not be able to resist us."

"We can," Ned said firmly. "Don't tell anyone that we can't."

"So now you're all Englishman? I thought you were half Norwottuck?"

Ned sighed. "I am a man at peace, in a peaceful country," he said. "Neither Indian nor English."

"We will all have to choose a side at the end of the peace."

"God forbid," Ned said sourly. "None of the militia know how to march." Then he remembered that he was speaking to a Pokanoket. "Don't tell anyone that either."

SEPTEMBER 1670, LONDON

Alinor, Livia, and Alys were breakfasting in Alinor's room. The glazed door was open and the warm air breathed into the room. For once it smelled only of salt and the sea, the stink of the river was washed away by the high tide. Livia, waiting for her ship to come in, was too nervous to eat anything; she drank her chocolate and nibbled at the edge of a roll of bread. Alys glanced at her. "Would you eat some pastries?" she asked. "I can send Tab out for something sweet?"

"No! No, I am eating this." She broke off a little crumb.

"What did the apothecary say about the thunderstone?" Alinor asked her daughter.

"He paid well for it. He'd never seen such a thing before. Three shillings a pound, and it was a pound and a half weight. When you write to Uncle Ned, tell him that we can sell more. And any curiosities—he told me the gentlemen of science are taking an interest in such things, especially from New England."

"And the sassafras?"

"He has it on sale at four shillings a pound and he offered to buy from me at two and six a pound. I think I could have got more but I said yes, because—" Alys broke off.

"Because we need the money now," her mother finished the sentence.

Livia ate a tiny crumb of bread, her eyes on the river.

"The cashbox is emptier than I'd like," Alys admitted. "But it'll come in." She smiled. "Perhaps today! On Livia's ship!"

Livia took a tiny sip of chocolate and said nothing.

"Well, I'll get started," said Alys, and rose to her feet, kissed her mother on the cheeks, and went out of the room. They could hear her heavy footsteps on the stairs and the closing of the door of the counting house.

"I am so anxious," Livia volunteered.

"You are?"

"See? I cannot eat, I cannot sleep. I even dream of my ship at night. I so much want this for all of us. I feel that I owe it to Roberto, to give his son my dowry as an inheritance, since his loving father could do nothing for him."

"You dream of it?" Alinor asked her.

"Yes! Yes!"

"D'you ever dream that Rob might come on it?"

Livia recovered rapidly from her shock at the question. "Alas no," she said. "No. It is not possible, *Mia Suocera*. I don't dream of it."

Alinor nodded. "It's due this week, I think?"

"Yes. But I suppose a ship can often be late?"

"It can be many days late," Alinor confirmed. "Many things can delay it."

"Like what?" Livia demanded in pretend alarm.

"Contrary winds, or a delay leaving port," Alinor listed. "Or—what is worse—it can be on time; but the cargo spoiled in a storm at sea or robbed."

Livia gave a little pretend moan into her hands and then raised her laughing face to her mother-in-law. "Ah, now you are teasing me! You are frightening me!" she said. "My antiquities are too heavy to be stolen at sea, and they will not spoil from salt water. As long as they have not sunk, I am a wealthy widow."

"Not until they sell," Alinor reminded her. "All that the ship brings you is your goods and costs."

Livia clattered her cup down on the table, staring out of the window, her hand to the lace at her throat. "Look! Isn't that it? There's the galleon. Is that our galleon? Captain Whatever-his-name-is galleon? That ship mooring in the channel? Isn't that our ship?"

Alinor leaned forwards to get a better look. "I can't see the name from here. But it looks like it might be yours."

Livia was halfway to the door. "May I?"

"Go!" Alinor said to her with a smile. "Go! I'll watch from here."

The young woman flew out of the room. Alinor could hear the patter of her rapid feet on the stairs, could hear her calling: "Alys! Alys! Come! Come! I think it is my ship."

Alys dashed out of the counting house, letting the door bang behind her, and Livia dragged her out to the wharf to see the galleon dropping her sails and letting down the anchor, as the young woman danced with impatience on the shore. Alys had to take hold of Livia round her waist to keep her from the edge of the wharf. Together they watched the lightermen gather around the galleon in their flat-bottomed rowing boats, bidding for the work. The Captain shouted that he was going upriver, to queue for the legal quays to unload his goods. All he had here, were some crates to deliver to a lady: her own furniture coming to her from Venice.

"But heavy!" he warned the men.

Three lightermen agreed a price and the division of the work, and the precious cargo was lowered, piece by piece, into the rocking craft.

"I can hardly bear to look," Livia moaned.

"They won't let it fall," Alys assured her. "They make their living on the water."

Arm in arm the two women watched as the lightermen brought their boats alongside the wharf, tied up, and then the dockers laid hold of the Reekie pulley rope and hauled one heavy crate after another from the rocking boats up to the wharf.

"Don't let it bang on the quay, don't let it knock!" Livia instructed frantically.

Again, Alys lay hold of her. "Let them work," she advised.

Behind them, the Captain climbed down into the ship's dinghy and was brought to the stone steps before the house.

"Have you got everything? Did you bring it all?" Livia demanded before he had stepped onto the cobbles.

He looked past her to Alys, who shook hands with him.

"Good day to you. Did you have a good voyage, Captain Shore?" she asked with careful courtesy.

"Fair, Mrs. Stoney. It was fair."

"Do you have all my antiquities?" Livia repeated, a little more shrill.

Now that he had been greeted, he turned to her. "In the heavy crates? Aye."

"Not dropped, not shaken. All safe?"

His narrowed eyes in the scarred face looked past Livia to Alys. "Aye, all safe," he said quietly.

"We'll put them in the bottom warehouse," Alys decided.

"You must take great care!" Livia said. "They must not be dropped, not even rolled along."

"Are you paying me extra for extra care?" he asked her.

"No!" Livia said at once. "Only what she agreed! And she's paying, not me!"

His chapped lips parted in a grim smile. "As I thought," he said. He turned his head and shouted an order. To Alys he gave the bill of lading, the export license from Venice, and his bill. "They were just over six tons," he said. "But I'll charge you for the six: fifteen pounds you owe me."

Alys gritted her teeth. "I've got it, I'll pay you tomorrow morning."

"And I shall send you a message if I need another load," Livia said blithely.

"You've got more furniture?" he asked, surprised.

"It is a very large collection," Livia said.

"Well, you know where to find me," the Captain said to Alys. "I'll be at Paton's every morning till I sail, probably next month. I'd be glad to see you there, Mrs. Stoney. I'll bid you good day."

"I'll settle up with you then," Alys promised him. Unconsciously, she fingered the shillings from the apothecary in her pocket as she walked with the Captain to Horsleydown Stairs where his dinghy was waiting to take him back to the ship.

"See how long you've got to wait at the legal quay with your load," she advised him. "I heard this morning, it was weeks. They're queuing all down the river to get in. You can bring the ship back here and we can unload you."

"I'm obliged, but I'm carrying coffee, I have to unload under the king's lock. Otherwise I'd come to you, Mrs. Stoney. I know your rates are fair and your warehouse secure." He bowed his head. "Always a pleasure to do business with you, ma'am."

"Next time," Alys said pleasantly, and watched him go down the steps into his boat. He raised a hand in farewell and Alys walked back to the warehouse. She paused for a moment and looked up at her mother's little tower. Alinor had come out onto the balcony to lean on the rail and look towards the ship. Her hand shaded her eyes, her gown billowed a little in the breeze from the river; she stood very still, strangely attentive as if she were waiting for someone.

"Ma?" Alys called up from the quay. "Are you all right?"

Alinor looked down at her daughter. "Yes," she said. "There were no passengers?"

"None that'd want to disembark here," Alys stated the obvious.

"No," Alinor said quietly, and went back through the glazed door to her room.

"Alys, come!" came Livia's impatient cry from inside the warehouse, and Alys went inside and bolted the double doors behind her.

Livia was still standing before her crated goods, one hand on the crate as if she could feel a heartbeat. "I can hardly believe they're here," she said breathlessly.

"When will you take them to his house?" Alys asked.

"As soon as you can lend me the wagon."

Alys nodded, knowing that the wagon would earn no money but would be gone all day.

"As soon as I have them there, I will confirm the date of the showing. I want them to be at their very best." She turned to Alys. "You will help me, won't you? You will lend me your wagon and two men, and let me take it to and from the house? You know I'm only doing this for Matteo, for Roberto's son? So that he can have his inheritance in gold at the goldsmith's, rather than in lumps of marble left behind in Venice? You know I want to help here? Bring some money in, so that you can move to a cleaner part of the town?"

"And then will you leave us?" Alys remarked, her voice carefully neutral.

There was a pause while Livia took in what her sister-in-law was saying. "Leave you?"

"After your sale?"

"I did not think it," she said quietly. "Do you want me to leave? I know it is crowded. I know that Matteo means extra work for everyone . . ."

"No," Alys stumbled. "Not at all . . . but I thought . . . I would want you to stay! I would want you . . ." She could not say what she wanted; she did not know what she wanted.

But Livia was quick. She clasped her sister-in-law's hands. "No! My darling! My dearest! Don't think of me leaving! Have you been thinking that? Don't dream of it. This is for all of us, for all of us that Roberto loved, even your children will benefit! If I can make a fortune, then we will all buy a new house together and all live together. You will ship my goods, we will have a house and a gallery of antiquities. We will never part. You are my sister, are you not? *Mia Suocera* is my mother-in-law! We are family, I want no one else! We will live together always. We shall never be parted!"

Alys, her hands tightly clutched, felt her eyes fill with unexpected tears. "Oh! I'm so glad. I thought you would . . . I didn't want . . ."

Livia drew her sister-in-law into her arms, so that her little lacy cap was against Alys's smooth golden braids. "We will never be parted," Livia breathed. "You are all the family that is left to me, and I and the baby are all that is left of your brother. Of course, we will always be together, and our fortunes will be as one. You will help me, and I will help you."

SEPTEMBER 1670, HADLEY, NEW ENGLAND

It was easy for Ned, a man who had been born and bred on the Saxon shore, the band of marshland between deep seas and flooded fields, to remember the times of the year for his letter to Alinor. He wrote in the autumn equinox, when the waters of the swamps rose high under a huge moon, that hung so close in the pearly sky that he could write by its yellow light.

Autumn tide

My dear sister,

I am sending 1 barrel of dried herbs and some labeled seeds which you can set. They like a light soil (like river silt) and goodness in the soil (any muck. We use fish). 1 box of dried sassafras leaves. 2 boxes of sassafras dried bark and roots and 1 barrel dried fruits and roots. I have put a maple leaf between each package so you can see they have not been disturbed or we robbed.

Thank you for yours which came safe to me though it brought such bad news. No doubt Rob has gone to the Life Eternal, and we who will follow him should not grieve. His ways are mysterious indeed. How we should lose Rob and not others I don't know. I give thanks to God that you and Alys and your children are well and that Rob's widow and baby have come to you.

Things go well for me. I have laid down a corn store this season. One of the women of the People showed me how to dig a great hole in a sandbank, line and seal it with clay, and wrap my dry corn cobs so that they don't spoil. I have dried my beans and stored the squash; I have smoked fish. My friends in the village will take me on a deer hunt with them for winter meat. I have saved seeds to plant in spring from my garden and gathered nuts and seeds from the woods. They have plants that were strange to me at first, but now I grow them and harvest them. The squashes are like our marrows, only strangely shaped and colored. The native women grow them alongside beans and maize and they call them the sisters and say you must grow and cook the three together. The apple tree whip that you sent me last year has taken, bore three little apples and I have saved the seeds to plant in spring. The forests are full of berries at this season, one called a cranberry grows in the swamps in the poorest of soil. It is sharper even than a red currant but makes a very good jam. When they're fully ripe I will fill all the jars that I own, which are not many as they're shipped from England. I mostly use galley pots made from clay by the native women that are so strong they can be set in the embers like an iron kettle. I seal them with parchment and string and beeswax when they cool. Yes! I have finally traded for a swarm of English bees. Very fierce—I only wish you were here to befriend them.

I need no candles! I use candlewood cut from pitch pines. The splinters burn like a candle and it yields turpentine. I am laying in firewood against the winter and repairing the cracks in the cabin with clay and sap from the trees mixed together. I have shielded one wall with shingles to keep out the cold. If there is time I shall put on an extra layer of thatch which the native people bring upriver from the coast. The natives tell me that I should

DOUBLE THE THICKNESS EVERY YEAR AS THE REEDS DRY OUT AND SETTLE AND THE WINTERS HERE ARE BITTER WITH SNOW FOR MONTHS. I AM BETTER PREPARED EVERY YEAR.

I WILL HAVE NO VISITORS FROM WINTER TILL THAW, EXCEPT THE NATIVE PEOPLE WHO WALK ALIKE THROUGH SNOW AND HEAT. ONE OR TWO OF THEM WILL COME TO ME WITH DRIED MEATS AND STORED CORN TO SHARE, AND I WILL GIVE THEM AN EGG OR TWO IF ANY OF THE HENS WILL LAY THROUGH THE COLD WEATHER. I HAVE TO BRING THEM INDOORS—JUST LIKE YOU HAD THEM AT YOUR OLD HOME. THEY WOULD DIE OF COLD OTHERWISE. THEY THINK IT RIGHT TO ROOST ON MY FEET ON MY BED, AND WHEN I TURN IN THE NIGHT THEY CLUCK AT ME FOR DISTURBING THEM.

I TRUST THE NEW KING IS NOT TURNING PAPIST OR TYRANT? WE GET SO LITTLE NEWS HERE AND MOST OF THE SETTLERS ARE INDIFFERENT TO HIM—PROVIDED HE STAYS AT A DISTANCE AND DOES NOT TRY TO RULE US! HERE WE ARE FREE OF EVERYTHING BUT THE RULE OF THE ELDERS, AND IF YOU DON'T LIKE THEM, YOU CAN TAKE YOUR MUSKET AND BED ROLL AND GO—THERE IS A WHOLE COUNTRY TO ROAM. THEY MAY TRY—BUT NOBODY CAN MUSTER OR ORDER ME—AND THIS IS WHAT I WANTED ALL THOSE YEARS AGO WHEN MY COMRADES IN THE ARMY SAID THAT WE MEN MIGHT RULE OURSELVES, OWN OUR OWN LAND, AND CALL NO MAN MASTER.

I THINK OF YOU AT FULL MOON. GOD BLESS YOU ALL,

YOUR LOVING BROTHER
NED.

SEPTEMBER 1670, LONDON

On Saturday, when Johnnie and Sarah came home, they demanded to see the wrapped crates and then set up such a clamor that at least one should be opened, that Livia said she could not resist them. "But they have been packed so carefully!" she laughingly complained.

"We'll repack them, Aunt Livia," Sarah assured her.

"This is seaworthy packing, so that they can be carried from ship to shore and in the wagon to their new home!"

"I know, I know!" Johnnie replied. "And we know how to do it! We were born and raised in a wharf! We'll repack them if you will just let us see one! Only one!"

"But you already know what they are like! You have seen such things at Whitehall Palace. You will have admired the king's collection. It is just marble busts and columns."

"We don't go to court!" Sarah said dismissively. "And anyway, these are your marble busts and columns! That you've been waiting for, that you've spoken of every Saturday, that you've prayed for every Sunday. I want to see them!"

"Do let us see what you have," Johnnie urged her. "And I can pack it up again. I can nail up the cases."

"Ah! I cannot resist you, Johnnie! I spoil you, and that is the truth."

"Very well, open them! I command it! We have to see!"

"If you command with that smile, I have to obey!"

Johnnie fetched a claw hammer from the tools hung at the side of the warehouse and levered the nails from the packing wood. With meticulous care, he laid one plank after another to the side, till all that stood before the rapt audience was a canvas padded with off-cuts from wool fleeces, too ripped and dirty for sale.

Sarah and Livia stood back while Johnnie and his mother unfurled the canvas and dropped it to the floor. They pulled the fleeces away to reveal the pillar that stood tall in the debris of packing. The scent of lanolin from the fleeces wafted into the warehouse and behind that a stranger smell: exotic, dusty and spicy: "Venice," Livia sighed. "That is the very scent of my home."

"Just this?" Johnnie asked. "Just a pillar? A stone pillar?"

"But carved," his mother pointed out.

"It's marble," Livia defended her antiquity, "and very old."

"I thought it would be a Caesar head!"

"I have Caesar heads. But you're not opening every package to find them," Livia countered.

Only Sarah had not spoken. Now she turned to Livia. "Can I touch?"

Livia laughed. "Yes. It was pulled down and buried in the ground and heaved up by a team of peasant farmers, before it was scraped clean and polished up. Of course you can touch."

Dazed, Sarah stepped closer over the canvas and fleeces, to put her fingers in the groove of the column. "It's smooth," she said. "Smooth as silk."

"The finest Carrara marble," Livia confirmed. "The most valuable. Look at the color, like snow."

Sarah ran her fingers across the grooves as if she were a blind woman and could only trace the shape. She stretched up and came to a tracery of foliage and stopped. "This is honeysuckle," she said. "It's a honeysuckle, look at the flower!"

"Yes," Livia agreed.

"It's like a flower that is frozen, like it froze into stone. It's like life. How old?"

Livia shrugged. "A thousand years?"

"There was honeysuckle growing in Italy a thousand years ago? And a craftsman looked at it so closely that he sculpted it into this stone? So that I, a thousand years later, can see honeysuckle?"

"At last one of you who admires my treasure!" Livia said with a sideways glance at Johnnie. "You were clamoring to see it, but you do not love it as Sarah and I."

"If we could only see them all . . ." Sarah hinted.

"No, no, no," Livia laughed. "When I unpack them for showing at the house, you may come and see them there. Not you," she twinkled to Johnnie, "not you, as you don't love my treasures. But Sarah, you may come when I am unpacking and we will look at them by ourselves. Not at the party," she added with a reassuring nod to Alys.

"I don't want to come to the party," Sarah said surprisingly. "It's not the people I want to see, but the statues. When can I come? My next afternoon off is Wednesday."

"Come on Wednesday," Livia assured her. "And I will show you everything."

"I love it," Sarah said, resting a lingering hand on the column. "It is like a hat, but bigger."

"A hat, but bigger?" Johnnie exclaimed, and they all laughed at the girl.

She flushed but she would not deny her feelings. "A hat, a really beautiful hat, is well made, and perfectly finished, and you can look at it from any side and it is a thing of beauty," she said. "You can't see the work that has been put in, it looks easy, not labored. And this stone is the same."

"It is a work of craft and of art," Livia agreed with her. "And— luckily for us, just like hats—in fashion right now. But I am glad that you see it, Sarah. You are my niece indeed." Sarah glowed at the praise but her aunt was looking past her, at Johnnie. "But you," she exclaimed to him flirtatiously, "you are nothing more than a barbarian!"

That night Alys went into her mother's room to say good night to her, and found her sitting in darkness in her chair, looking over the shining water of the river to where the moon was low on the horizon, a harvest moon, a golden moon with a shimmering yellow reflection in the water below.

"Ma?" she said uncertainly. "Are you all right?"

"Aye," the older woman said quietly. "Just looking. Just dreaming."

"Are you ready to go to bed?" her daughter asked. "It's late."

Gently Alys helped her mother to the bed, drew the curtains on the window, and turned back to the pale beautiful face on the white pillow.

"And so she has her treasures safe in our warehouse," Alinor said quietly in the dark.

"As we agreed."

"And she takes them to him, and shows them in his house, as if they were partners?"

"Yes. But she never mentions his name to me, and I believe she never speaks of us to him. She knows we will not see him, nor speak of him."

"Does he stay here for her, d'you think? When his home is in the north? Why does he not go back there?"

"We don't care, do we?" Alys burst out, troubled at her mother's dreamy voice. "We said he was to go, that we would never see him again. You don't want him back, do you?"

"No. But I can't help but wonder what she thinks of him, and he of her."

Alys was shocked. "She thinks nothing of him! She'll never recover from the loss of Rob. She still cries for him in the night. Her only comfort is to be with us, to be with me. She says that she'll stay with us for always. We're her family now. She does not think anything of . . . him."

"I'm glad of that," Alinor said calmly. "If that's what she says. I'm glad that we comfort her for her loss—if we do."

"Does it not comfort you?" Alys whispered. "To have Rob's wife and his baby under our roof?"

In the silence, Alinor shook her head.

"Why not?" Alys demanded. "Why does she not comfort you, Ma?"

"Ah," said Alinor. "That I can't say. I'm not yet sure enough to speak."

SEPTEMBER 1670, HADLEY, NEW ENGLAND

Ned was called to the ferry in the morning by a clang of a horseshoe on the far side, and when he went to the pier and looked across he could see Quiet Squirrel and some women from her village. One of them had a little girl, of about six, gripping her buckskin skirt.

"Coming!" Ned called, and stepped from the pier to the ferry and pulled it across the wide river.

Chattering among themselves, the women came down the shingle beach and stepped on board the grounded ferry. Quiet Squirrel was last on, taking one hand of the little girl while her mother held the other.

"*Netop,*" Ned said to the child, and all the women on the ferry replied: "*Netop, Nippe Sannup*! Hello, Ferryman."

The little girl looked up at the tall Englishman, her dark eyes taking in his friendly open smile, his white linen shirt, his thick trousers. Her dark gaze scanned him from his tall black hat to his heavy shoes. She turned to her mother: "He smells very strange," she said in their language. "And why does he stare at me?"

"He can understand some of our speech, you know," Quiet Squirrel told her. "Better not say he smells. Besides, he can't help it, they spend all their time wrapped up in thick clothes as if it were winter."

"I think you strange," Ned replied to the child. He did not know the word for "smell."

The little girl laughed. "Why does he speak like a baby?"

"He speaks like a child, but he is a man," Quiet Squirrel replied.

Ned took hold of the rope, rocked the raft gently to free it from the beach, and then pulled it steadily across the river.

"Can we pay in dried meat?" Quiet Squirrel asked. "You'll want dried meat for your winter stores, Ferryman."

"Yes-yes," Ned acknowledged. He smiled down at the little girl. "She too heavy! Pay twice!"

There was a chorus of laughter from the women. "Pay by weight!" they exclaimed. "Quiet Squirrel costs nothing!" The little girl squirmed near to her mother and hid her face in her skirts, she was laughing so much.

"You very fat!" Ned told her. "You sink my ferry."

The child had to sit on the planks as her legs buckled beneath her with laughter.

"*Nippe Sannup*, you're very funny," Quiet Squirrel told him. "This is my little granddaughter, Red Berries in Rain."

"Not little," the child said, her eyes on Ned's smiling face.

"Very big," Ned said in her language. "Married?"

The child rocked with laughter. "I'll marry you!"

All the women cried out and laughed together. "No! No! Sannup! You must marry me!" one of the bolder ones cried, leading a chorus of proposals. "Marry me! Marry me!"

"Aren't you marrying the thin one with no home? The one who never pays full price?" Quiet Squirrel asked.

"You know everything?" Ned demanded, easily recognizing Mrs. Rose from this description.

"Most things," Quiet Squirrel said with pleasure.

"Maybe marry," Ned said. "Maybe not. What you think?"

The ferry reached the other side and nudged against the pier. It rocked as the women climbed off and Quiet Squirrel and her daughter kept a gentle hand on the little girl.

"I think you would make a good husband," she told him seriously. "But if you married and had a family you would become a greedy farmer like all the rest. And you would not be your own man. And I think you want to be your own man, just as we want to be ourselves."

She spoke too fast and used too many strange words for Ned to understand, and without trying to explain she handed him some dried deer meat wrapped in woven cattail leaves. "Wrap it tight, keep it dry," she said, patting him on the shoulder. "And don't you marry."

SEPTEMBER 1670, LONDON

Sarah went down the newly washed steps to the kitchen door of Avery House and tapped on the panel.

"Who is it now?" came the irritable shout from inside.

"Sarah Stoney," she said inaudibly. She raised her voice and repeated: "Sarah Stoney."

"Never 'eard of 'er," came the discouraging reply.

Sarah stepped up and peered over the half door. "Sarah Stoney for Nobildonna da Ricci," she said. "I've come to see the antiquities. She said I might."

"Step in, step in," came the shout. "I can't leave this."

Sarah opened the door and came into the kitchen to see a brawny red-faced woman, floured to the elbows, kneading a huge mound of pastry at a stone-topped table in the middle of the kitchen. Copper pans gleamed over the closed stove in the yawning hearth, a pump over the sink ran icy water, a dog in the corner growled at the stranger and sat down again.

"Come in. For Lady Peachey, are you?"

Sarah, at a loss at the strange name, replied: "To see the statues."

"Glib will take you," the woman nodded. "Shout out of that door. It's just the backstairs. Shout for Glib."

Sarah, horribly embarrassed, crossed the kitchen and opened the door that the cook had indicated. "Glib!" she called.

A clatter of shoes on the wooden stairs preceded Glib, a gangling youth.

"Take the young lady to Lady Peachey, she's in the gallery," the cook ordered him. "And then come straight back here. I'll need you to fetch the fruit from the store." She turned to Sarah. "Follow him," she commanded. "You shouldn't have come in this door anyway, unless you're Trade. Which of course you may be. As might be her ladyship, Her Highness. For all anybody knows."

Sarah followed Glib's skinny shoulders in too-large livery up the short flight of stairs from the basement kitchen, through the green baize door into the startlingly high and bright hall. He crossed the black-and-white marble slabs and led the way up a stone staircase to the gallery at the top. It ran the length of the front of the house and, at the end, standing before a column of pure white marble, Sarah recognized the dark silhouette of the Italian widow.

"Aunt Livia!"

"Ah, Sarah," she said, turning around and offering her cool cheek for a kiss. "You found your way, then."

"It's very grand," Sarah whispered, turning to see that Glib was retreating back down the stairs. "I did not expect it to be so very—"

"Yes, I'm pleased," Livia interrupted her. "See, here is the column you liked so much, it looks very handsome here. I have put it here, and on either side of the gallery I have six, just six each side, heads of Caesars. That's all I am having up here—I don't want it to be crowded. It must not look like . . ."

But she had already lost the girl. Sarah had stepped back and was craning her head to see the statues. Twice as large as life, the blind bronze eyes stared into the gallery, unseeing. Each stone head stood on a fluted column of creamy marble, each one crowned with shining laurel leaves of bronze. The faces, rounded or beaky, indulgent or stern, seemed to look back at the girl who gazed up at them, rapt, going from one to another and stretching out her hand to touch the cool column.

"They are extraordinary," the girl whispered. "Are they real?"

The widow glanced quickly behind, as if afraid that Glib had heard. "Whatever d'you mean?" she demanded, her voice sharp. "What are you saying? Are they real? What a question!"

"Were they really like this? Was this one really so fat in life? Did he not mind being shown with such a pursy little mouth?"

"Oh! I misunderstood you. Well, I don't know. I think they were made later, not at the time. Perhaps from the coins, or perhaps from a drawing? They must have been made at the same time, for they were made as a set."

"Who made them?"

"Oh, it's too long ago for us to know that. But they were found all together in what had been a great hall so perhaps some wealthy man in ancient times wanted to dine with all the Caesars. And now, I hope, another wealthy man will see them and want to repeat the experience."

"They're not beautiful . . ." The girl struggled to understand her sense of awe.

"It hardly matters," Livia remarked, stepping back and looking not at the Caesars but at the upturned face of her niece. "It hardly matters."

"Beauty doesn't matter?"

Livia was astounded. "Have you understood nothing? What matters is that they sell! Have you understood nothing from working in a shop?"

"But your husband, your first husband?"

"What about him?"

"Did he not collect them for their beauty?"

Livia tossed her head, and then recollected herself. "It is him I am thinking about," she said very soberly. "He would not have wanted me to fall so far as a little wharf on the Thames. He would not want me to live in such a place. He would have wanted his collection to be my dower—for me to live as I should, as the Nobildonna da Picci."

"Reekie," Sarah corrected.

The widow shrugged her black satin shoulders and gave her pretty tinkling laugh. "I cannot say it, try as I might. Roberto always laughed at me. I will have to call it Picci. It is a pretty compliment to the Sussex family. Now, would you like to see the statues in the garden?"

"But wasn't Peachey the name of the lord at Foulmire? Uncle Rob's patron."

"Yes, as I say, a pretty compliment to him, don't you think? And amusing, that when I turn my name from Italian to English it sounds like his?"

"I don't know . . ."

"Do you want to see the statues in the garden? I can't waste my time."

"Yes, yes, I do, please."

The widow led the way down the grand staircase to the black-and-white paved hall, her black skirts hushing on the marble. Sarah thought how well she suited the classical beauty of this house; in the warehouse she always seemed too exotic, her color too vivid.

"Do you love coming here?" she asked as they passed through the high glazed doors to the terrace, and then she gasped at the garden laid out below them, studded with statues, and the silver of the river at the end of the garden. "Oh! This is beautiful!"

Livia ran down the steps and led Sarah from one statue to another, one just a fragment of a bigger piece—a water vase, a hydria that had once been held, thousands of years ago, by a marble hand, whose stone fingers and nails were still clasped on the handle.

"Oh!" Sarah breathed. "Look!"

Livia smiled and pointed farther down the garden where part of a frieze had been laid on the ground so that visitors could see the story of the horses riding out to battle, the riders stern and beautiful holding the rippling manes.

The girl knelt beside them as if she were praying. "May I touch?" she asked. Livia nodded, and Sarah bent over the figures, tracing nostril and nose, ears pricked, arching neck and the strong muscled torsos of the riders.

"You can look at them all," Livia said. "I will wait for you on the terrace."

She turned and went back up the steps to sit on a stone bench set back against the sun-warmed wall. Sir James stepped through the glazed door to his study and found her there. From the garden below, Sarah saw his polite bow, and the way that Livia rose at once and came so close that he stepped back. Livia shot a secretive little glance back towards the garden as if she did not want Sarah to see them. She slid her hand in his arm and drew him indoors, out of sight, as if they were lovers in hiding.

"A viewing?" James asked her, as she closed the door to the terrace behind them.

"Just the child from the warehouse. I would prefer if she did not see you. Or rather—her mother would prefer it, and I cannot cross her."

"I want nothing to do with her," he said gently. "I understand she is not mine. I see no resemblance. She is a pretty girl, with her dark hair and eyes, but I don't dream that she is mine."

"Hardly pretty," she amended. "They are both poor little things. She is a millinery girl without an education. But she has a sense of beauty that she has learned from lace and tinsel that I could make something of."

"Would you want to make something of her?" he asked curiously.

She looked up at him, her creamy skin flushed a little from the sunshine. "No," she said. "I have no time for a strange child of common stock from a warehouse. Why would I want a child such as that, when I can breed and raise a noble one?"

He bowed, hiding his agreement. "I have some replies to the invitations."

"Are people coming?" she asked eagerly.

He nodded. "About ten people have told me they will attend, and here—" He gestured to the desk. "There are more replies to open."

"Oh, let me open them!" she begged. "Nobody ever writes to me these days, I never break a seal on good paper. Do let me!"

He laughed, feeling tender towards her. "Come then." He drew back the chair so she might sit at his desk.

Sarah, mounting the steps to the terrace from the garden below, saw Livia brush against James, as she took her seat in his chair, at his desk, and took up his silver letter opener, as if she were the mistress of the house and his wife.

"Sarah was taken with your statues," Alys remarked to Livia as they got into bed the following Sunday night. "She couldn't speak of anything else this morning."

"She has an eye for beauty," Livia allowed, tying the ribbons at the front of her nightgown.

"She said she saw him."

"He was there, but I sent him away to his study," Livia said. "I knew you would not want her to see him."

"Thank you for that. You'll think me a fool but . . ."

Livia slid her arm around Alys and drew her close. "I don't think you're foolish," she said, brushing back a lock of hair from the woman's lined face. "I know he was your enemy. And I am not befriending him. I am using him to make our fortune. I ceased to be his friend from the moment that I understood how you felt. Your friends are my friends, your enemies mine. Your feelings are my feelings."

Alys could feel the warmth of Livia's body through the silky nightgown. "I hope you're safe with him. He's not a man I'd trust. He ruined us."

"It will go well," the younger woman said confidently. "It is he who should be anxious. I'm going to be the one who profits from this." She drew closer and put her head on Alys's shoulder. "I am not too heavy? I love it when you hold me and I can fall asleep in your arms. I feel beloved again. I need to feel beloved."

"You're not too heavy," Alys said quietly, letting Livia press her cheek against her neck and snuggle in. "Will you go to his house all day tomorrow as well?"

"Of course! I have so much to do!"

OCTOBER 1670, HADLEY, NEW ENGLAND

As the weather started to turn colder and the trees shed blazing leaves of gold, bronze, and red, swirling around in a blizzard of color, Ned rethatched his roof of reeds, knowing that the nights would get longer and colder until the snows came to make everything white and silent.

He was straddling his ridge pole, tying in the stacks that he had traded from the Nipmuc who brought great rafts of reeds upriver, towed behind their dugouts from the coastal marshes, when he heard the clang of the horseshoe from the far side of the river. Looking across, shading his eyes from the low red autumn sun, he could see the figure of an Indian man, the unmistakable profile of buckskin leggings and a bare chest half-covered with a leather cape. Ned grunted with irritation at having to interrupt his work, but went hand over hand down his roof ladder, and then scrambled down the rough wood ladder that leaned against his wall.

He went out of his garden gate, up the rough steps in the landward side of the bank, and stepped down to the frosty white pier on the river side. The water was colder every day. He rubbed his rough hands together as he stepped on the ferry, unhooked it, pulled on the cold damp rope, and saw, as the ferry bobbed and yawed across the river, that the Indian was Wussausmon, and behind him, shielded by the trees of the forest, were the puritan lords: William Goffe and Edward Whalley.

Ned jumped ashore with real pleasure, greeted Wussausmon, and turned to his comrades. "Good to see you! You're well? Safe? All well?"

The three men embraced. "God bless you, Ned, here we are back with you," said William.

"All quiet here?" Edward demanded, peering across the river to Ned's house.

"All quiet, all safe," Ned assured them. "I can take you across now, you can wait in my house till evening, and we'll walk round the forest way to the minister's house at dusk."

"I can tell him you're coming," Wussausmon volunteered. "I'm going into town."

"Like that?" Ned gestured to the buckskin leggings and cape.

"Like this," he confirmed. "No one notices me like this."

"Good, good," William agreed, walking down the beach and onto the grounded ferry, followed by Edward and Wussausmon. Ned pushed off, and rocked the ferry to get it into the flow of the water so that he could pull them over.

"You look well," he remarked.

They did. The summer at the shore had put a tan on their skin and flesh on their bones. They had walked and hunted, rested and gathered food. They had fished and swum. Their Pokanoket neighbors had loaned them a dugout and they had paddled up and down the coast and up the Kittacuck River. They had prayed with local people who listened to the gospel with courtesy but were not converted, and they had seen no English: not one settler, only a white sail, far away on the horizon.

"We've been desperate for news," William said. "Any news from England, Ned?"

"They say there'll be another war with the Dutch," Ned volunteered. "They're not allowing any Dutch shipping to take our goods."

Both men looked immediately disapproving. "A war against godly men?" William asked.

"The king'll probably join with the French against them," Ned suggested. "That's what they're saying."

The ferry nudged the pier and Ned tied it off.

"God help the country, fighting a godly realm in alliance with papists, with a king married to a heretic. God teach them a better way to go." William closed his eyes briefly in prayer. "And what will it mean to us here? Are we settlers supposed to fight the war too? In front of the savages in the New World? It's the worst thing we could do."

"Lord make him see sense," Edward joined the prayer.

Wussausmon looked from one man to another. "You pray against your king?" he asked.

"We've done far worse than that." William opened his eyes and smiled.

OCTOBER 1670, LONDON

Livia was seated in a high-backed chair in the black-and-white checkerboard hall of Avery House by half past nine on the day of the viewing breakfast. In the basement kitchen the servants prepared silver salvers of biscuits, pastries, and fruits. Bottles of wine chilled in buckets of cold well water. Great jugs of freshly squeezed lemonade were cooling in the sink. Everything was ready.

Sir James stood in his study door admiring Livia, seated in the hall. She was dwarfed by the thick wooden arms and the high back of the chair, but she radiated self-possession and a pretty dignity of her own. He knew that she was nervous; but she did not fidget or run from kitchen to garden to check that everything was ready. She contained her nerves behind a calm smile and only the rise and fall of her black lace bodice showed that her heart was pounding.

"They will come." He stepped into the hall to reassure her. "But they will come throughout the day. We can't expect anyone to come on the striking of the ten o'clock bell."

The face she tilted up towards him was serene. "I know," she said. "And besides, you have a beautiful house that anyone would be glad to visit, and I am showing genuine rare antiquities. I know that we are together offering the very best. People are bound to come, and if they come: they are bound to admire."

He thought she showed her quality in her self-control. That she was—just as she said of her antiquities—something rare and beautiful He was glad that he had opened his house for her, that his memories of his wife's awkward silences could be overlaid by this dainty little woman and the occasion she had single-handedly created. The ten o'clock church bell rang at St. Clement Danes and all over the house there were silvery chimes of ten from clocks in the study and in the drawing room, and loud pealing from all the neighborhood churches.

"Will you take a glass of lemonade?" he said. "We cannot expect people to be on the very dot—"

There was a hammer on the door and the noise of a carriage outside. With a triumphant smile at him she motioned Glib to open the door and the nominated maid to stand ready to take the hats and sticks. As the door opened, she rose to her feet and waited, like a queen, for her first guest.

Sir James recognized Lady Barton and her daughter, old friends of his mother, and, stepping forwards, made the introductions. Livia curtseyed to precisely the right level as he introduced her and gave her hand to her ladyship and led the two of them upstairs. She did not glance back at him and beam, as he had been afraid she would do. She was perfectly dignified. As she went up the stairs, her black silk skirt brushing the worked-iron bannister, there was another knock on the door and a well-known landowner, famous for his park and gardens, was there, hat and cane in hand, coming to visit the antiquities. Sir James realized that it was he who was beaming, like a schoolboy, up at Livia.

They closed the front doors on the last guest at three in the afternoon. "Come into the parlor," Sir James said. "You must be exhausted."

Livia dropped into a chair. "How many people?" was all she asked. "I lost count."

"As many as a hundred," he confirmed, taking a seat opposite hers. "Were there any actual orders?"

She showed him a little notebook that she had on a silver chain at her waist. "Three for sure, and two others who are going to measure their dining hall to make sure they have enough space. Most people said they would write within a few days. But three promised to buy."

He shook his head. "You were magnificent!" he said. "And so calm!"

"Because you were there," she assured him. "And because I was in Avery House. How could I be anything but calm when the house is so beautiful and there have been such wonderful women in this place before me? I thought of what you have told me of your mother, and I wanted her to be proud of the house . . . and even of me," she added.

"She would have been," he said. "She would have seen, as I have done, how hard you work and how easy you make it look."

She glowed with pleasure and came across the room to his chair. She bent quickly and put her lips to his cheek. "Thank you for saying that," she said. "That is the best of the day. It has been a wonderful day; but that is the best."

He could smell her perfume, sun-warmed roses, and for a moment he thought that he could put his hands on her slim waist and pull her down to sit on his lap and kiss her lips. He hesitated, half-afraid of his own desire, aware that this was a woman without protection in his house, and that she was the daughter-in-law of the woman that he had loved all his life.

"Forgive me . . ." he started, but she had already slipped away to the door.

"I shall leave you to dine in peace," she said, as if she did not want him at all. "I must get back to the warehouse and tell them how well we have done. I shall be able to help them to buy new premises, and have a better life, and I am glad of it. Wait till they hear!"

"Will you tell them I send my best wishes, that I am glad of your success for them, and happy that I have been able to help?"

She came back to him and put her hand on his arm. "No," she said tenderly. "Alas, they will not hear your name. They even warn me against trusting you." She paused, her pretty face looking up at him. "I hope I don't cause you pain when I tell you they have cut you out of their lives. You should think of yourself as free of them."

"I am forgotten?"

She showed him a tentative smile. "Is it not for the best? Since there is nothing that binds you to them?"

He knew it was. "Then I may forget too?" he asked her.

"You forget too," she assured him lightly. "It is the past. It was long ago. A boy's error. Nothing from the past shall haunt us. You are making a new England here, you can be free of the ghosts and sorrows of the past! The war is over, the plague has finished, the fire is out. All the old heartaches are healed. There is no need to feel old pain."

He knew she was right; she was inviting him to enter a new world that had been here all along, but he had not realized he could enter it. He raised her hand to his lips and kissed it. "At last, it's over."

He sent Glib the footman to walk her to the wherry and pay for it, to cross with her and escort her to the warehouse door. The lad waited, hoping for a tip, but she slipped inside without a word to him and closed the door and leaned her back against it, savoring the success of her day—with the antiquities, with the buyers, and with James himself.

Alys came out of the counting house, frowning. "You're very late," was all she said in her level tone. "Ma and I have eaten, but I saved some soup for you."

Livia's frustration at the dullness of the woman in her poky poor little hall, with her offers of boiled-up soup and her complaint of lateness, suddenly burst out. "I don't want soup. I've had the most wonderful day; I don't want to come home to soup!"

Alys's welcoming smile drained from her face. "Did you want something else? There might be—"

"Nothing! I've had the finest of food, a wonderful start. It was a wonderful day!"

"Your things sold well?"

"Beyond my dreams! James said—" She bit off his name. "It was a triumph. A hundred people came!"

"If you give me the money, I'll put it in the cashbox?" Alys held out her hand. "I'll take it to the goldsmith's in the morning."

Livia's rage at the poverty of her home and the contrast with her triumph at Avery House spilled out in a torrent of words. "Look at you with your hand held out! Like a beggar! Of course, I don't have the money now! D'you think I'm running a market stall? D'you think

I haggle and trade and spit on my hand and shake it? That's not how I do business."

Alys flushed a deep red as her hand dropped awkwardly to her side. "What other way is there? You sell something, and you take the money. How else do you do business? Have you taken no money at all?"

"Of course, you have no idea! I create an interest, I make a fashion, everyone in London is talking about my antiquities. I have sold nothing! I would be mad to do so! But I have spoken to everyone. Between now and next month the orders will pour in and compete with each other. Of course, no money changes hands today! Do you think I am some grubby shopkeeper? A poor workingwoman?"

Alys was stunned into silence. Livia took off her bonnet and handed it to her, as if she were a servant. "Oh, tell Tabs to bring my soup, if that's all there is?" she ordered. "And a little bread? And a glass of wine?"

"Of course," Alys said, her voice flatter than ever. She stalked down the hall to the kitchen door and put her head around it and gave the order to Tabs. She paused outside the parlor; she could not bring herself to go in, hurt by Livia's words but angry at the injustice. She opened the door, ready to speak but at once she saw that Livia's mood had changed. She was stretched in the chair, her head flung back, her eyelids closed, a smile on her lips.

"You ought to have a bell for Tabs," she remarked. "It is ridiculous to have to go to the kitchen for everything you want." When Alys did not answer, she opened her eyes. "It was the most wonderful day," she repeated dreamily.

"I don't see how; if you come home as poor as you went out," Alys returned.

Livia's sloe eyes showed a gleam. "I know you don't, my dear," she said. "Which is why a woman like you runs a sufferance wharf—under sufferance to trade, and under sufferance to live—but I am, tonight, the acknowledged provider of the best and most beautiful architectural antiquities in London."

"It is a sufferance wharf," Alys conceded, resentment making her Sussex accent stronger. "Honestly run, with steady trade. You're right we live in this world on sufferance. My mother was not suffered to be herself; but horribly pursued and punished. My husband's family would not suffer my presence; and I was driven from my home. I don't blame you for looking down on us; but Rob would never've done so. He never allowed anyone to say a word against his ma or me. Rob was proud of us, proud of our surviving: poor women though we are, unfashionable women though we are!"

She turned and went quietly upstairs, as Tabs brought in the soup and the fresh bread roll and the glass of wine.

Much later, Livia came into the darkened bedroom. "Alys," she said to the shadowy bed. There was no answer.

In the dark, she slipped off her beautiful gown and her silk under-gown. Alys could hear the whisper of the material but she lay still and closed her eyes, pretending sleep. Livia did not feel for her nightgown under her pillow, she lifted the sheets and slipped into bed naked. The ropes of the bed creaked beneath her weight. Alys was far away over her own side, a cold space between them.

Livia slid up to Alys's unresponsive back. She put a gentle hand on Alys's hunched shoulder: "Forgive me, Alys. My sister, my love. Forgive me. I spoke unkindly. I cannot help that I am not like you, nor like your mother or your daughter. I'm a woman unlike any you have met before. I cannot be diminished, Alys. I would die if I were diminished."

Alys said not a word; but Livia sensed she was holding her breath to listen.

"I could not bear to be like you, a woman driven down into work, driven out of her home. I wouldn't stoop to it. I would rather die than be poor, Alys."

Still, Alys said nothing,

"I'm not an honest woman, nor a straightforward woman, not in the way that you and your mother are. And I know I'm vain and flighty." Her voice quavered with emotion. "I was vain this evening. I was cruel to you. I am a beautiful liar, if you like. I am all twists and turns and misdirection. You cannot trust me. I recommend that you do not trust me. I am not actually evil; but I am not straightforward. I am not simple."

Alys breathed out and Livia continued: "You think that a woman should be honorable. I've seen you speak to the captains, to the warehousemen, even to the lumpers. You speak to them with respect and you demand that they respect you: a good trader. You think that a woman succeeds by being like a man. You think that if you act like a good honest man you will rise in a man's world. You think you will succeed on your merits. You think hard work and God's blessing will be rewarded."

"I am honest," Alys was driven into speech. "I learned it—the hardest way."

"I'm not," Livia replied quickly. "I am far more interesting than honest. I am far more successful than honesty could ever be. I am only ever honest to myself. My face in the mirror is the only one that I trust with my secrets. I never lie to myself, Alys, I know what I am doing when nobody else knows. And I don't do things by accident. I never do something and not know why, I'm never driven by an unknown desire, I never run in one direction while yearning for the other. I always know who I am, and what I want, and I go to my way in a roundabout fashion so that no one can refuse me. The only honest word I utter is to myself." She paused. "That is admirable, in a way. In its own way. I am admirable; in my own way."

"But what do you want here?" Alys cried out to her, sitting up and turning round so that her sister-in-law could see—even in the shadowy room—her eyes red from crying and her face twisted with distress. "What d'you want here, if you despise us so much? Why stay in our home when it's so poor? Why are you using our warehouse but going out to make money with our enemy? Why've you come here to distress us? Why d'you work with him? What d'you want? What were you planning, when you came here, all little and crushed and grieving? When you came so beautiful that a heart would break to see your face? And the first thing you did was reach out your hand to him? You held your handkerchief to your eyes and you reached for him! How can you boast of your pride when you flung yourself at him?"

Livia flung herself into Alys's arms, kissed her hot face, wet with tears, lay along the lean length of her. "I want you," she whispered in her ear. "That's what I want. I know it now, and the moment I met you. I want to be like you: simple and honorable and brave. I want you to love me as I am: curious and duplicitous as I am. I want to belong here with you. I want to be yours: heart and soul. I want you to own me as a sister, I want to be the great love of your life. I want you to see past the beautiful surface of me, past my luster, and see me for myself."

"Luster," Alys repeated the unusual word.

"The shine on a beautiful marble, the gleam on a skin of bronze. The glow of my perfect skin." She gave a low laugh.

"I can't bear lies," Alys whispered in reply. "You don't know what they cost me, what they cost my ma. You don't know how we both told lies until there was such a tangle of deceit that we were drowned under the weight of them. We weren't punished for our crime, my crime. It was the lies that destroyed us. I can't live with a pack of lies. I can't bear it."

"You must, you must bear me," Livia urged her, pressing her warm breasts against Alys's cool nightgown. "For you are the only person in the world that I speak the truth to. The only one in the world that I love and trust. I have to be with you. You have to love me in return. Please, Alys. Without you I have no one! I have nowhere to live, I have no friend. I am an orphan, alone in the world. I am a widow. How can you not love me? How can you not pity me? You are my sister: be a sister to me!"

Alys did not plunge into Livia's arms but hesitated, scrutinized the beautiful face in the stripes of moonlight. "Can I trust you not to lie to me?" she demanded. "Even if you lie to everyone else? Can you be honest to me, here, when we are alone together, in this room? Even if you lie all the day to everyone else?"

Two tears like pearls rolled down Livia's cheeks, her lips trembled. "Yes," she said. "I swear I will be true to you; if you will love me."

The two women looked at each other, unmoving for a long moment, and then Alys opened her arms and they kissed, deeply kissed, and fell asleep, enwrapped, Alys's face buried in Livia's dark hair, Livia's hands linked behind Alys's back, drawing her close and holding her close all night.

OCTOBER 1670, LONDON

Sarah and Johnnie walked back from church together, as Sarah described Avery House, and Livia's presence as the lady of the house, under the name of Lady Peachey.

"You think she'll catch him?" Johnnie muttered, one eye on his mother walking before him arm in arm with Livia.

"She's got him wrapped around her finger," Sarah said. "She walks in and out of the house as if it was her own."

"Then she'll be a wealthy woman, and she can pay her debts to us."

"There's plenty of money there," Sarah confirmed.

They followed Livia and Alys through the front door and parted in the little hall. Sarah went upstairs to sew with Alinor, while Johnnie went to the counting house with his mother.

As soon as he looked at the books he saw that the warehouse had carried the cost of loading, shipping, and unloading, that Livia paid nothing for the storage of her goods in the warehouse, and nothing for them to be delivered by the Reekie wagon to Avery House, crossing and recrossing the river on the expensive horse ferry. The warehouse books had never showed such debt before, the cashbox was almost empty.

"Has she promised payment when she sells?" he asked. He looked at the outlay and then asked more hopefully: "Or is she paying us a share of the profits, are we partners with her?"

Alys shook her head. "I didn't ask for a partnership," she said. "I just paid for the shipping, and then the wagon of course. She knows it's more than we can bear for very long. She'll repay us as soon as she makes her sale."

"I thought she'd done the sales?"

"That was the viewing. She's got orders, but she's taken no money yet."

"Don't they pay on ordering?" he asked.

Alys shrugged uncomfortably. "It's not a business we know, Johnnie. We have to trust her that she knows how it's done."

The young man was troubled. "I see that, Ma, but we've never carried costs like this before. And where's the certificate of tax for her goods? Did she pay it herself, and keep the certificate?"

"She doesn't owe tax as it's her private furniture, delivered to her home, here."

The young man looked up at his mother. "It's not really private furniture," he said. "And though it was delivered here, she's not kept it here, at home. We're not sitting on her chairs now! She should have declared it as antiquities for sale; for she's selling it, and she's selling it very publicly too."

"To gentlemen, to noblemen," his mother replied. "Nobody who's going to ask to see a tax receipt."

She had shocked him. "Ma, we always pay the Excise duty. What're you saying?"

"Just that she insisted, this is a way of doing business that we don't know—"

"I swear that we don't!" he interrupted her. "Because it's against the law, it's criminal, Ma! If the Customs were to take an interest, we're clearly in the wrong, we should've reported it as an import, and Captain Shore should've landed it at the legal quays or met the exciseman here. When I stood with you and she showed us the columns so proudly—I never knew! It's as good as contraband. How could you let her do it?"

He broke off as another thought, a worse thought, struck him. "What did Captain Shore say about it?"

"Same as you," she admitted, her voice very low.

"Why didn't he take the crates to the legal quays straightaway?"

"As a favor to me," she whispered. "I told him it was her furniture and he agreed to land it here."

"You lied to him?"

Reluctantly, she nodded. "But anyway, Johnnie, we couldn't have paid the Excise duties. You see for yourself how short we are this month."

The young man looked horrified. "You didn't declare because you knew you couldn't pay?"

Her silence told him that he was right. "Why didn't you make her pay for the shipping and the tax herself?" he asked more quietly. "They're her own goods?"

"How could a lady like her go to Paton's and hire a captain?" she demanded. "And anyway, she has no money till they're sold."

He stepped down from the high clerk's chair and faced his mother. "This goes round and round," he said flatly. "Down and down. If she can't afford to ship her goods and pay the tax on them, then she can't afford to be in business. You taught me that yourself. She should have borrowed the money from the goldsmith's against the sales. She could have done that with a proper deed and a repayment time. But instead she's just dipped her hand in the cashbox: our cashbox."

His mother was white-faced, twisting the corner of her Sunday apron. "Johnnie, I couldn't refuse her. Rob's wife! And his baby in our house? I had to commission and pay Captain Shore, I had to lend her our wagon to take the goods to Avery House."

The two of them were silent. Johnnie closed the ledger as if he could not bear to see the figures. He put his hand on it, as if it were a Bible and he might swear an oath.

"Ma, every single line in your books has always been right. You taught me yourself that everything's got to be correct, everything must balance. Everything's got to be accounted for and nothing, *nothing*, ever slipped under the table. No bribes, no backhanders, no tips, no cheats. No stone dust in the flour, no sand in the sugar, no water in the wine. No wine in the brandy. We load and we store and we ship—full measure. We pay our duties—full rate. That's how we have the reputation of the best small sufferance wharf on this side of the river."

Alys said nothing.

"That's how we stay in business. We're a tiny wharf but we're honest. People trust us. That's how you got into business with only thruppence to your name. That's how you've stayed in business for all these years, that's how you've built this up from nothing."

Alys nodded.

"So what's changed, Ma?" he asked with his usual directness. "Why would you cheat for her?"

"Because she's Rob's widow," his mother repeated. "With Rob's baby in her arms. She has to be able to sell her own goods, her widow's dower, to keep herself. Rob would've wanted us to help her. We've got no choice. And Johnnie . . . I feel so tender towards her."

"I don't remember my uncle very well," Johnnie replied thoughtfully. "But would he have asked you to cheat for him?"

There was a silence. Reluctantly, Alys told her son the truth: "No. He would not."

"So this is her way, and her idea."

Alys said nothing, thinking how Livia had confessed that she was a liar, and promised to tell the truth only in their bedroom, in darkness, to Alys.

"She is honest with me," she said quietly. "She does not lie to me."

"You trust her." It was an accusation and so he was surprised by the sudden illumination of his mother's smile.

"Yes, I trust her," she agreed. "I trust her."

Alinor was pounding dried herbs in a little pestle at the round table in her bedroom, the window open to the frosty air. Below the turret the tide was starting to ebb. On the other side of the table Sarah was sewing a measured scoop of the mixture into tiny cheesecloth bags to sell as a tea to cure sickness in the notorious Bight of Benin off the fever coast of Africa. A quarter of the crews of the slave ships would die of the sickness that breathed hotly off the marshy River Niger. Alinor's teas were a famous preventive.

Sarah was chatting as she worked, telling her grandmother of the week at the milliner's shop, the departure of one of the girls who had found a protector and was going to be set up in a little house in the

City with her own black slave servant, and would never have to sweep her own floor ever again.

"But it's not never again," Alinor observed. "Unless she saves her money and retires a lady."

"I know," Sarah said. "I know. But she's the same age as me—think of me having my own house and slave!"

"I'd rather not!" Alinor said with a smile. "Think of your keeper! Is the man old and fat and ugly?"

"Yes," Sarah conceded. "I suppose it's not worth it."

"It's a bad bargain for a woman," Alinor agreed. "Aside from the sin—if you have a baby or two, it's a bad start for them, poor little angels—and not their fault."

"No, I know. I am outstandingly virtuous, you know, Grandma?"

Alinor laughed. "Coming from a house like this and a mother like yours, you could hardly help it. There is no way you could be false."

"False?" the girl repeated.

"Counterfeit," her grandmother said. "Appearing as one thing but being another."

"You think Livia is false?" the girl said acutely.

"Quite the opposite! She never takes a false step, she never strikes a wrong note. She's never uncertain. It's as if everything is . . . practiced . . . like a performance. And every step is for her own good, whatever she promises your ma."

"People do strange things. How can we know? If you think she's up to something, shouldn't we ask her directly? Put it to her? In all honesty?"

The older woman shook her head. "Better to let her continue as she is—using this house as her home, launching her business and herself, making money from your ma's wharf, battening on a stranger. Going far from here, and yet coming back every night. Using us, and seeming to love us, promising everything; but taking, taking, taking, all the time."

Sarah gave a little hiss, and found that her hand was clenched in the old sign to ward off witchcraft, her thumb between her first two fingers. "You make her sound evil."

"I don't know what she is."

"So how will we find out?"

The old woman did not reply.

"How, Grandma? How shall we ever know?"

Slowly Alinor turned away from the window to Sarah, and her face was no longer haunted, but lit with a mischievous smile, as if she were still a wild girl on the edge of the mire, with gifts she dared not use, and a pocket full of valueless tokens. "I've been wondering how to answer these questions," she admitted, her gray eyes dancing. "And I've got an idea. I think it's a good idea. D'you really want to know?"

"Yes! Of course I do. I've mistrusted her from the first moment I saw her and now . . . even more."

"So, Sarah, why don't you go to Venice?"

"What?"

"Go to Venice, go to Livia's warehouse, find her steward, see if he is the trustworthy grandfather that she describes, who loved Rob like his own son? See where they lived, see what family Livia left in the great palace she speaks of. Speak to Rob's patients, ask what they thought of the young couple."

Sarah's lips parted. "Go to Venice?"

"Why not?"

"And find Livia's true past?"

"Don't you want to?"

"Yes! Yes I do. But I'm not freed from my apprenticeship."

"I know. Go when you're free!"

"I wouldn't know where . . ." Slowly her refusal trailed into silence as she thought of the adventure she might undertake. "Of course!" she said simply. "What a chance! What an adventure! Of course, I'll go!"

Alinor's smile was as sunny as the girl's joy. "For the adventure," she said. "Because there is more to life than hats."

Sarah laughed despite herself. "More to life than hats?"

"You know that there is."

"As soon as I complete my apprenticeship," the girl promised. "At the end of this month, when I get my apprentice papers. I'll go, and then we'll know."

OCTOBER 1670, HADLEY, NEW ENGLAND

Ned with a basket of produce foraged from the woods walked down the broad common lane into the village, shouting his goods as he walked: "Mushrooms! Groundnuts! Berries! Nuts of all kind!"

He stopped at every door where he was called until he reached the house at the junction of the middle way to the woods, and went through the minister's handsome gate and round to the back.

The kitchen door stood half-open. Ned tapped. "Come in!" Mrs. Rose shouted from the interior. Ned entered to find the kitchen smelling sweet and Mrs. Rose hot and flushed stirring a kettle of cranberry jam. "You can see, I can't show you in."

"I came to see you, as well as them," he said awkwardly. "I have some nuts for you, chestnuts and hickory."

"Thank you," she said, not stopping her work. "Just tip them there, on the side."

He obeyed her and stood awkwardly before her as she dropped a drip of jam on a cold plate to see if it would set.

"I won't be able to come to town very often when the snows come," he said.

She glanced up at him. "Of course," she said. "You'll stay in your ferry-house all through the winter?"

"Aye," Ned said. "I've made it weatherproof and winter-tight."

"Wouldn't suit me," she said bluntly. "Will you be snowed in?"

Ned nodded. "For some days," he said. "I'll dig a track round the house to feed the beasts, but I can't dig out as far as the common lane. I'll have to climb out through the snowdrifts when I want to come to town."

She returned the kettle to the heat. "I couldn't live out there," she told him. "Not all the year round. If the minister gives me a plot, as he's promised, at the end of my indentures, I'd tell him, I don't want one that far out. I'd rather be nearer the village center, near the meetinghouse so I can pray every Sunday, winter and summer. I'd be too afraid, on the very edge, halfway into the forest, with savages strolling past my door as if they owned it. I came here to live among my people, to make a new England; not live in the woods like an animal."

"I understand," Ned said. "You do get used to it, you know. I've never had neighbors. If you're a ferryman you're always on the water's edge. Your house is on the land but your living's on the water. It was like that for me in England too. And of course, back then, during the war, I was for the people, the common people, when everyone around me on the island or in the town of Chichester was for the king. I feel like I've always been out of step."

"You can't be for the People now!" she said jokingly, using the name that some of the tribes used for themselves.

Ned did not answer to the joke. "I don't know who I'm for anymore."

"For us," she told him, as if it were obvious. She looked up from her work, earnestly. "For the elect who make a new world here, for those who oppose the tyranny of the king, for this village, where we all have to do our work to keep the settlement safe, and strong, for Mr. Russell's congregation. For your wife if you get one, for your family if you have one, for yourself."

"Yes," Ned agreed. "Yes. Of course. Yes."

"You can't have doubts, Mr. Ferryman," she said flatly. "We can't build a new country without being sure that we are God's chosen people. I wouldn't marry a man who had doubts."

"Yes," Ned repeated. "Of course. Yes."

OCTOBER 1670, LONDON

Livia met Sir James in the black-and-white marble hall of Avery House.

"I was just going out," he said, hat in hand.

"I was just coming in to see if there were any letters for me," she said, turning to the gilt-framed ornate mirror and taking off her hat.

He could not help but think that hers must be the most beautiful face that the mirror had ever reflected. He paused for a moment to watch her as she regarded her own heart-shaped face with the dark wide eyes, removed the hatpin, stabbed it into the bonnet, and then her gaze turned to him and he looked away.

"Are there any letters?" he asked awkwardly.

"I don't know," she said with a smile. "I've only just arrived. I haven't looked for them yet."

"They leave them on that table for you," he said. "They don't bring them to me."

"I know." She was as self-possessed as if he were a visitor to her house and not the other way around. She moved with easy grace to the half table that he indicated, took the letters, and sat on the chair beside the table.

"If you need to write, you may use my study," he said. "There are pens, and paper."

At once she rose up and followed him into his study. He gestured that she might take the seat behind the great desk. It was tidy, but there was a closed ledger marked Avery House, and another marked Northside Manor, and a third marked Douai. Her quick glance flickered over all three but when she sat on the great chair and looked up at him, she was blandly uninterested.

"Pen," he offered. "Paper. If you leave anything that you want posted I can frank it for you."

"Frank it?"

"I'll sign the envelope and your letters go for free, under my frank, as I am a member of the House of Commons," he explained.

She inclined her head to hide her triumphant smile. "Thank you. If someone wants to see the antiquities again, may I invite them?"

"Of course," he said. "I can be here."

"I wouldn't take up your time," she said politely.

"It would be no trouble, and . . . if they were acquaintances of mine it would be wrong of me, it would be impolite—not to be at home."

"How right you are!" she exclaimed. "People would wonder what I was doing here without you. I should be taken up for a burglar!"

He did not laugh with her.

"And so, shall we say a week on Tuesday?" she went on smoothly.

He did not think she would suggest a day so near, but he bowed. "Certainly," he said. "Of course."

Her smile was very charming. "And may we give them—I don't know—tea? Or something?"

"Yes, of course. I'll tell the cook to be ready."

"Oh, please let me," she said. "You should not be worried about things like tea for the ladies."

"I do entertain." He was nettled. "This is not a complete bachelor den. I am not a barbarian."

She made a little apologetic gesture with her black-mittened hands and placed them on either side of her face so that he looked, despite himself, at her warm rosy mouth. "I never thought such a thing," she protested. "I wanted to spare you more trouble."

He nodded. "It is my wish to help you. Ordering tea is nothing."

She smiled and took up the three letters. "I am so pleased that we can do this together," she said. "The warehouse family would never accept help from you, but this way, they don't even know what you are doing for them. I am your gateway to helping them. We do it together. I have very high hopes that we might buy them a better warehouse upriver, in a cleaner part of town, and they might be happy."

"You're generous," he conceded, though there was something

about her tone that grated on him. "And knowing that the money is going to them makes all the difference for me." He looked out of the window at the garden that ran down to the river and then turned back to her. "I would like to buy the statue of the fawn. It looks so well out there."

She nodded, not at all eager. "Ah, you are the second person to admire it. Well, the third in truth. But I will sell it to you. At the discount we agreed."

"I don't want the discount," he said, a little irritated. "If you are going to buy a house for Mrs. Reekie, I want to contribute to that. Indeed, I should like you to let me know if I can help with the cost of the house, or the hire of the servants, or the cost of moving, or anything that she needs."

"You would have to give the money to me," she specified. "They would never accept it from you."

"I understand."

"So, you would have to trust me with a large sum of money," she pursued.

"I do trust you, of course. I know your plans for the ladies are nothing but generous and good. I know that you love them."

"Just as much as you do," she said quietly. "We can join together in our kindness to them. We will be partners."

He shifted his feet a little, as if he wanted to walk away from her talk of a partnership of charity.

She saw it at once. "I'll tell my buyers that it will be a week on Tuesday at three," she said, and he bowed and left the room.

When she heard Glib close the front door behind him, and the footman's lazy stroll back to the servants' stairs, she pulled the ledger marked Douai towards her and turned the pages. It seemed to be a list of donations credited to a religious house in France, a seminary for Roman Catholic priests. Livia guessed he was acting as a treasurer for his old school and she had no more interest in it. She put it precisely in its original position and opened the ledger marked Avery House. She widened her eyes at the cost of running a great house in London and pursed her lips in irritation that James should spend so much on candles while she had to scrape together shillings from the bottom of her traveling trunk and wheedle them from Alys.

The Northside Manor book was longer and more complicated, showing rent from the farms, profits from sales of animals and goods, rent from the mill, from the bakery, from the brewhouse, and wages, gifts, and purchases. She did not understand at first that one page was costs and one page was profits, and that there was a balancing figure at the bottom of each page. She had never seen an accounting book like this before, and she looked bewildered, able only to see that there were large sums involved, and that James was, genuinely, very wealthy.

A noise from the hall made her slam the book and push it away and bend over her own letters as Glib knocked on the door and asked if she wanted her messages delivered by hand.

"I'll leave them for Sir James to frank for me," she said.

Glib nodded. "That's what her ladyship used to do."

"I know," Livia said, waving him away. "That's why I do it."

On her return to the warehouse, walking through the hot dirty streets, Livia found Alys setting out to the coffeehouse for her regular noon meeting with captains and merchants who might use the wharf, as the wait for the legal quays was lengthening in these shorter days of autumn.

"Shall I come with you?" Livia asked, taking her arm.

Alys nearly laughed. "You're dressed far too fine," she said. "Nobody would talk with me if I walked in with you. They would think that I had risen in the world and was no longer interested in unloading apples for penny profits."

"I am too fine?" Livia asked, as surprised as if she had never considered her appearance before.

"Far too beautiful," Alys said, giving her a little push towards the front door. "Go and sit with Ma. She's planning a great feast for Sunday to celebrate Sarah's day of freedom. She will be a time-served milliner, and in December, Johnnie will be out of his apprenticeship too."

"Of course it is a pleasure to sit with your mother, but when will you be home?"

"When I have secured next month's business," Alys said. "However long it takes."

"Spending hours on apples?" Livia teased. "But shall you see the Captain again? The one who went to Venice?"

"Yes, he'll be there. He'll be going to Venice again."

"He is faithful?" Livia asked.

"He's always reliable."

"Ask him if he has room for some more antiquities," Livia said. "The same sort of load? Say twenty crates? At the same price and terms? I'll write out the directions again, he can go to my old steward and collect them."

Silently, Alys followed her into the warehouse as Livia helped herself to a pen and tore a page of paper from the back of the ledger to write her steward's address.

Alys did not take it, her face was flushed with embarrassment. She put her hands behind her back though Livia offered her the address. "I'm sorry, my dear, I am so sorry . . . but I can't commission him. I don't know how to say this . . ."

"Whatever is the matter?" Livia asked, smiling.

"I don't have the money to pay him. I can't commission him, until we earn."

Livia widened her eyes. "But surely, you don't have to pay him until he returns? You only pay a little now?"

"I have to pay half now, and we really don't . . ."

"Pay him his price now and when he returns I will have the money from the sale to pay him the second half. I will pay it myself. Don't worry."

Alys hesitated. "We've never run the warehouse like that," she said. "We've always had enough in the chest to pay for the whole bill, before commissioning anything."

"*Allora!*" Livia remarked gleefully. "And now you are living beyond your means, as you should, as we should, as I have always done. For we know that we are going to earn more than you have ever earned before! But we have to get the goods here before we can sell them! We cannot make money without spending money. We have to have more antiquities to sell and you have to pay the Captain to fetch them. What is the difficulty? Is there nothing in the cashbox at all?"

"It's pounds he wants, not shillings! I've got about fourteen pounds. I can just stretch to pay the first half, but I don't have the rest."

"But this doesn't matter!" Livia smiled and took Alys's anxious face in both hands and kissed her on the mouth. "Send him out with your little savings, and when he returns I will have sold the antiquities and I will pay him. Be happy!" she told her.

"It's just that we never . . ."

"You've never had such profitable trade before."

"It's such a risk!"

"No it is not," Livia ruled. "You are trusting me, as we agreed. You have to trust me."

Alinor, in her bright high room, was drawing up a list of Sarah's favorite dishes for the feast on Sunday. She had prepared her a gift, a soft shapeless pillow stuffed with lavender and rosemary for repelling moths, catnip and chamomile for repelling fleas. "You press it in a bonnet to help it keep shape." She showed Livia. "And it keeps out the moths. Her mother is getting her a hatbox, and we are going to hire a signwriter to paint her name on the outside in curly letters, like a proper milliner."

"But she can't open her own business, can she?" Livia confirmed. "She'll never have her own hatboxes?"

"Ah no, we couldn't afford to set her up in a millinery business. Rents are impossible, a millinery shop needs to be in the City. She will have to sign on as a senior milliner where she is now. She'll stay for a year, and only then perhaps look for another position."

"It's like slavery," Livia exclaimed, who had been married younger than Sarah was now. "All she can hope for is a kind master. And what about Johnnie? Is he to be cast into slavery too, poor handsome boy?"

"He completes his apprenticeship at Christmas, and then he'll be a senior clerk. His great ambition is to be a writer for the East India Company—but we can't introduce him."

"His merits are not enough? When he has served his time?"

"No. It's not merit—you have to know the right people and they propose you. Even the lowliest clerk has a patron. Johnnie will never get into the Company without a patron."

"What you need is a wealthy and well-positioned friend," Livia observed.

Alinor gave her a grave level look. "We don't have one," was all she said. "Johnnie and Sarah will have to make their own way in the world. Like their uncle Rob did."

"Ah yes," Livia said, her hand on her heart at once. "My Roberto earned his success because he studied so hard and learned so much."

"He would not have given one word to that man that you call a friend." Alinor was steely. "They parted in a silence that Rob would never have broken."

"He's no friend of mine," Livia said earnestly. She took Alinor's hand and held it in her own. "I use his house, I use his name only to make our fortune," she promised. "As soon as I can, I shall buy a house to show my goods and I will never see him again. You will never think of him again."

Alinor withdrew her hand. "I would not think of him now if you were not at his house every day," she said quietly.

Livia picked up the menu for Sunday. "But this is a feast!" she said.

Alinor let her turn the conversation. "We celebrate so seldom these days. When I was a girl there were feast days all the time. Harvest home and Christmas and Midsummer Day and Easter, and the quarter days as well, and the saints' days, Plough Monday and Beating the Bounds . . ."

"Are they not all restored now?" Livia asked. "Now that the king has come back to London and everyone is happy again?"

"They were country festivals. They can't happen in the town." Alinor looked out over the river as if she could see the long horizon of the mire and the procession of people going to the little church with flowers in their hats.

"Would you like to live in the country again?" Livia inquired. "Roberto was always speaking of his home, and the tide coming in over the land. It's what he loved about Venice—the marshes outside the city and the sandbanks and the reeds. He said it was like the country of his childhood, half sea and half water and never certain."

"He knew the lagoon?" Alinor asked. "He knew it well?"

"Oh yes. He could have found his way blindfolded. He was always out on it."

OCTOBER 1670, HADLEY, NEW ENGLAND

It was a bitterly cold morning and Ned thought it unlikely that anyone from Hatfield, on the opposite bank of the river, would risk the ferry journey on the icy water even to attend the Sunday church service at Hadley meetinghouse. He heaped the embers of the fire under an earthenware cover and, smiling at himself for folly, he drew the little signs in the ashes that his mother had always made, to keep the house safe from an accidental fire in her absence. She had taught them to him and Alinor, and Alinor had taught them to Alys and Rob. He had no doubt that Sarah and Johnnie knew them too, and he wondered how far back in time the tradition stretched among the Ferryman family, and how many children, yet unborn, would be told that they—like the Pokanoket—could teach fire when to blaze, and when to lie quiet.

He glanced round the sparse cottage, pulled on his thick winter coat, and gave his well-worn shoes a quick rub with his sleeve. He left his dog on the chain in the kennel. "No, you can't come," he told Red. "It's too cold for you to wait outside, and happen I'll visit Mrs. Rose after the service."

Red's ears drooped and he went back into his kennel.

"Back soon," Ned told him as he turned up his collar and pulled his hat down over his ears and strode through the north gate and down the common lane to the meetinghouse. From every front gate and front door men and women and their children were walking towards the church, greeting each other, and calling children to order, quieter and more thoughtful on the Sabbath.

Ned found himself alongside one of Hadley's other single men, Tom Carpenter.

"Good day to you," Ned said. "Cold."

"Aye," he returned.

They walked in silence for a moment. "Will you not take the ferry out till spring?" Tom Carpenter suggested. "You won't take a penny in fees."

"No," Ned agreed. "It's a fair-weather trade."

"Never going to make a fortune on that," the man observed.

"I know," Ned said. "But I don't need a fortune, I just want a living."

They were outside the meetinghouse; mothers were gathering their children. John Russell the minister came from his gate followed by his wife and children, Mrs. Rose, his housekeeper, behind them, and the three slaves behind her.

"She'll never have you with nothing to offer but a half plot and a half-year ferry," Tom Carpenter said, his gaze resting on Mrs. Rose. She nodded a greeting to them both, and her color rose slightly, as if she knew they were talking about her as she walked past them, following her master.

"How would you know?" Ned asked curiously.

Tom grinned at him. "This town!" he said. "Everyone knows everything. Everyone knows you visit her, that she walked down with your letter in the summer. And everyone knows that she wants a full plot, and a life as far from service as possible. She wants her own servants, that one. She wants her own slaves!"

"I know," Ned said. "But I can't see how to change my ways."

"That's the very thing we came here for!" Tom Carpenter exclaimed. "Came here to change our ways. To be in one communion, one people before God. To make a good living, not scrape a wage. To marry and found a family, to build a town and make a country. For me, this is the greatest chance at a new life, in a new country, and make it better than the old one!"

"God bless you," Ned said as they turned and followed the minister's family into the cold shade of the church, from the icy brightness outside. "It's a great ambition."

"But you don't share it?" his neighbor suggested, lowering his voice as the two of them took their place, as single men with only a half plot, at the back of the church, ahead of the servants and apprentices, but behind the masters and planters.

"I want a new life," Ned agreed, lowering his voice too. "I want a communion and a town and a new country just like you. I thought this would be an earthly Paradise, a place without sin. I didn't expect to jostle my neighbors for a living. I just don't know what I'd have to give up, if I wanted to truly belong here."

"What d'you give up?" Tom Carpenter whispered as John Russell took his place at the front of the congregation and opened his Prayer Book.

Ned shrugged. "Being a law to myself," he muttered. "Living of my own. Being no one's bane."

"Aye, Ned, you're a funny one," Tom said, and turned his attention to the service as John Russell started the opening prayers.

The service was winter-short; the meetinghouse, even with the little stove at one end, was too cold for a long sermon, and those whose homes were at the far end of the town were conscious that they would have a hard walk home with the cold wind against them. As soon as prayers were finished the congregation agreed the names of the selectman and the different town officers who would be appointed at the town meeting, and someone mentioned there was a cow in the town pound that must be claimed at once. A young father announced the birth of his child who would be baptized at home, with none of the papist trappings which had been reintroduced to the church in England.

As the congregation filed out, Ned fell into step beside Mrs. Rose.

"Is it cold enough for you?" she asked him, smiling. "Out on that cold riverbank beside that cold river?"

"It is," he said. "But I think it will be worse before it's better."

"You can be sure of that," she said. She hesitated. "Would you take a glass of mulled ale before you walk home?"

There was something about her self-consciousness as she invited him, something about the way that Tom Carpenter watched them, the way that the whole town seemed to pause as they spilled out of the meetinghouse into the lane, that turned Ned away.

"I have to get back to the Quinnehtukqut," he heard himself say.

"Connecticut," she corrected him, her voice hard, "Remember, we say Connecticut," and Ned bowed his head in farewell.

OCTOBER 1670, LONDON

Johnnie and Sarah followed their mother, Livia, and the two maidservants up the muddy lane to St. Olave's Church.

"Time served!" he congratulated her. "Senior milliner."

"A few pennies more a week," she pointed out. "Maybe a customer of my own if she's lowly and poor. A higher seat up the table at dinner and served after the older girls instead of at the very last. Nothing else. It's not much."

"Steady work," Johnnie advised. "A wage paid on time once a quarter, and your mistress makes no deductions, now that you don't have to live in. What would you rather do? Run the wharf?"

The girl put her hand on his arm. "I'll tell you what I'm going to do, but it's a secret," she said.

"What?" He glanced up the lane to where their mother, Livia, Carlotta, and Tabs were entering the church. "What? We can't be late for church."

She dropped her hand. "All right then. But don't complain later that I didn't tell you."

"You're planning something stupid," he predicted as she walked on. "You're never leaving the millinery shop? You're never leaving without another post to go to and some mad idea, like sewing herb tea bags with Grandma? Or the statues . . . oh God, Sarah . . . not the statues . . ."

She turned back to him, and he crowed with laughter. "I always know what you're thinking. You're going to go in with Aunt Livia and trade in statues!"

She snatched at his hands to silence him, though there was no one near them down the narrow street that led to the church. "Don't you say a word! Don't you dare say one word, Johnnie!"

"Tell me what you're going to do."

"This is a secret," she told him.

He made the little hangman gesture of their childhood oath which said that either would be hanged on the gibbet at Savoury Dock before betraying the other. She leaned so close that the feather on her bonnet tickled his face. He listened intently till she finished.

"You can't go," he said flatly.

"Grandma herself is sending me."

"It's not safe."

"Why not?"

"It's not safe for a girl," he amended.

"I'll be with Captain Shore," she pointed out. "And then I'll go straight to Livia's steward. She says he loved Uncle Rob like a grandson. He speaks English and I know a little Italian. He was her family steward. She says he has ten children. He'll probably take me in to stay with them. Why not?"

He made a face, took off his hat, and scratched his head. "I should go with you," he said.

"Really, Johnnie, you know you can't. You've got to finish your time and your master would rip up your indentures if you upped and left."

"I can't let you go on your own."

"Yes, you can. You know I'm no fool. I can look after myself. And if Grandma's happy, you can't object."

He nodded. "You can run faster than any girl I know. And fight like an alley cat. But Venice! All that way?"

She took his arm and they walked together towards the church. Over their heads, the first-story windows leaning towards each other made the street like a tunnel. Their footsteps echoed and Sarah lowered her voice. "If something were ever to go wrong for me, d'you think you'd know?" she asked. "Would you know without being told?"

"Oh yes," he said at once. "But that's being a twin, isn't it?"

"Grandma says she'd know if her son was dead. I believe her. I think she would."

That made him pause. "Grandma does not believe Livia that he drowned?"

She nodded.

"That's a terrible accusation," he said slowly. "That Aunt Livia is a fraud? Not Rob's widow? Perhaps not even our aunt?"

"I know," the girl said. "It's that important. That's why I'm going."

All through the service and the long sermon Johnnie wondered if he should tell his mother of Sarah's plan, but a lifetime of loyalty to his twin through all the little adventures of wharfinger life silenced him. By the time they filed out of the church and walked home with the minister, Johnnie's mind was made up. As Mr. Forth went upstairs to pray with Alinor, Johnnie turned into the counting house with his mother to balance the week's books, fully decided to say nothing.

As soon as he was seated on the high clerk's stool, he saw the address of Signor Russo, written in Livia's large dramatic scrawl. He knew at once it must be the directions to the steward's house in Venice, and without saying a word, silently palmed it as his mother came into the room and opened the ledgers.

One glance confirmed his fears. "I see she's started another debt, and still paid us nothing from her last voyage," he remarked. He did not say who it was, owing money to the warehouse. Only one debt had ever been left to run in the two decades that they had been in business.

"She's sending for more antiquities," his mother said tightly. "She's so sure of selling these that she wants more. We'll stand the charges again. She's doing it for us, for all of us. She wants to buy a bigger warehouse, somewhere better for your grandma, and we'll all live there together. It'll be a home for you, when you finish your apprenticeship, and for Sarah."

"We only need more bedrooms because she's here," he pointed out. "We never needed a bigger house than this before. It's been good enough for twenty years."

"She has plans for us . . ."

"How does she get to make plans for us?"

His mother flushed. "She's family, Johnnie. She's your aunt. She has a right to . . ."

"Not like family at all," he said gravely. "She brings in nothing. Nobody in the family is idle. Sarah brought home her pennies the day that she started work. You've always had my wages. Even Grandma grows herbs and makes her teas. Uncle Ned is on the other side of the world and yet he still sends us goods. Nobody takes money out. Nobody spends the family money. We never risk it. We've always earned, not speculated."

"Livia's not making pennies on lavender bags, she's on the way to a fortune." His mother bridled. "And as Rob's widow and our kin we should support her. She thinks we could get a bigger warehouse and sell the antiques direct from Venice."

"Is she going to put up the money for a bigger warehouse?"

"When she's paid . . ."

"Or does she mean that we should be her banker?"

"We'd be in partnership," Alys said defensively. "It would be a family venture. I trust her. I've come to love her as a sister indeed. I believe her word. I believe in her knowledge of the statues. She says she's going to make a fortune, she says she's going to buy a house and share it with us, she's going to live with us. When I think of living with her, for the rest of my life, at my side—" She broke off. "It would change my life completely," she said quietly.

"You want a bigger wharf?"

"A bigger wharf, a better house, somewhere with a garden for your grandma. And a companion, a friend for me. Someone to share the worry."

Johnnie had a painful sense of his mother's long years of loneliness. "I should do more."

"No, Son, you do all I ask of you. But to have someone at my side, as a sister, now that you two have left home. It would be—"

"But Ma, is she . . . reliable?" he asked, trying to find the right words. "She came so suddenly? With nothing but what she stood up in? We know nothing about her? All that we know is what she's told us."

"Yes," Alys said firmly. "We know she was Rob's wife and the mother of his child. What more do we need to know? She has a true heart, I know it, Johnnie. And she's found a family in us. We're not going to fail her."

The young man felt acutely torn between his sister's secret and his mother's trust. "I hope so," he said uncertainly.

Alinor came down for dinner after praying with Mr. Forth, and Tabs served the family in the parlor with several different dishes and a jug of wine from Paton's with their compliments to Miss Stoney on the day of her completing her apprenticeship. They had roasted oysters and roasted beef from the cookhouse, and Alinor had made Sussex pond pudding with a lump of sweet butter in the middle. After dinner they played at riddles, and then Johnnie and Sarah sang the rhythmic chants that the lightermen sung as they unloaded their boats, with much-amended lyrics to cover the usual obscenities. Alinor recited a country poem from Sussex that her mother had taught her, and Livia sang an Italian folk song with a swirling little dance that she did in the corner on the worn floorboards. It was late when they banked down the parlor fire and took their candles up the stairs to bed.

Johnnie stopped Sarah with a hand on her arm and slipped the scrap of paper with the address into her pocket without a word. Nobody noticed and the twins moved as one: Sarah to her bedroom that she shared with Carlotta and the baby, Johnnie up the narrow stairs to his attic room.

"Did you draw the runes?" Alinor confirmed with Alys as they went to her room.

"Of course, Ma." The younger woman helped her mother into bed and went to her own room.

Livia was already in bed with her candle blown out. "It's sad when a girl leaves her childhood," she said into the shadowy bedroom.

"Not sad for her! Sarah is glad to have completed her time."

"But now she will have to marry, and her life will be decided for her. Children and a husband, and she will never be able to do what she wants."

"Not in England," Alys said, lifting the sheet and sliding into bed.

Livia turned to her and put her head in the warm crook of Alys's neck. "Ah, that's good."

Alys drew the younger woman to her and stroked her smooth braided head, inhaling the warm perfume of roses. "You know, in England, a wife can have her own business, earn her own money, she can declare herself independent of her husband—a feme sole—and her money is hers, and her business is hers too."

"Is that so?" Livia asked, suddenly alert. "A husband does not take everything on marriage?"

"They have to agree, of course, she cannot do it without his agreement. She has to go to the City fathers and they have to give her a deed to say that she is a feme sole. But if she declares herself to be so, and everyone agrees, then she can own her own house, keep her own fortune, and run her own business. Ma is a widow, I am a feme sole, the business is our own."

"But the child of a marriage between a feme sole and a man with money still inherits his father's estate?"

"He would. And his mother can leave her fortune to him if she wishes. It is in her gift."

"And they are still married—she would get her widow's dower if the husband died?"

"Yes. Livia—why does this matter to you? What are you thinking?"

"Nothing! Not at all," the younger woman said rapidly. "It's just so unlike my home. In Venice, if you are a woman, your life is ended at the church door. I was a nothing. Nothing. Until Roberto saw me and then I came into the light again."

"His loss must have been terrible for you," Alys said sympathetically.

"It was the end of everything; but he showed me what I might be and now I am in England, with you, and with your family, and I can hope again."

"Do you hope?" Alys asked, a sense of something like desire rising up in her.

Livia slid a little closer. "I have more than hope," she whispered, her lips against Alys's shoulder. "I have found my heart and my home."

"My love." Alys drew the younger woman closer, so they touched, from lips down the long line of their bodies to their entwined feet.

"And does the husband of a feme sole have to pay her debts?" Livia whispered.

Alys sighed and released her embrace. "No, she is responsible for her own debts."

"Interesting," Livia remarked, and turned on her side and went to sleep.

OCTOBER 1670, LONDON

Johnnie was up early on Monday morning, to get to his City merchant house on time, and was surprised to find Sarah in the kitchen, heating his small ale and cutting the bread for his breakfast.

"No Tabs?" he asked.

"I said she could lie in," Sarah said. "Ma will be down in a minute. I wanted to see you. Before I go."

He looked directly at her and made a little grimace that she understood at once as anxiety for her, guilt that he was not going with her, and pain at their separation. She stepped towards him, gripped him, and they held each other tightly.

"Take care!" he said urgently. "Don't do anything stupid. For God's sake come home. We can't stand another loss. It would kill Grandma—especially as she sent you."

"Lord! I hadn't thought of that," she exclaimed. "I'll come back safe and sound. Don't worry!"

Their mother's step on the stair made them break apart and Sarah turned to the fire.

"You're up early, Sarah," Alys remarked.

Sarah turned and smiled. "I know. I couldn't sleep."

After Johnnie left, and Sarah and her mother cleared the dishes, Sarah kissed her mother good-bye, surprising her by the warmth of her embrace, and ran up the stairs to see her grandmother. The older woman pressed a guinea into her hand. "Keep it safe," she said. "If you need anything."

The girl hesitated. "How d'you have this?" she asked. "A whole guinea?"

"It's my burial money," Alinor said. "I saved it up over the years and kept it for myself. To pay for my burial at Foulmire, beside my ma, in the little churchyard at St. Wilfrid's."

"I shouldn't take your burial money, Grandma."

"You take it. I won't need it. I'm not going to die until I see my son again," Alinor said confidently. "You've told them at the milliner's that you're leaving?"

The girl nodded. "I told them I'd be away for a quarter. They weren't happy, but they'll take me back when I return. Ma thinks I'm going to work as usual."

"And you have the money for your passage?"

Sarah nodded. "I've got enough. It feels wrong not giving it to Ma. And Johnnie's given me some."

"You've told Johnnie?"

"I can trust him. But, Grandma, maybe don't tell Ma, for she'll only tell Livia."

Alinor nodded. "She tells her everything. I'll say you went to stay with a friend in the country, for a week. And, at the end of the week, I'll tell her then. That'll give you a start, so Livia can't send a message to warn them."

The girl frowned. "You think she has people working for her? But doing what?"

"I don't know. But I don't want her knowing that you've gone to find her out."

The girl was struck for the first time with the enormity of her task. "Grandma! If I find Uncle Rob, what am I to do?"

"Just tell him what's happening here," Alinor advised. "Tell him Livia's here, and what she's doing. Tell him she's got your mother wrapped around her little finger and she's running us into debt. He'll know what should be done. Once you find him, he can decide what is best."

"I don't have to bring him home?"

Alinor laughed. "A little thing like you? No. He's a grown man. He must decide what he wants to do. All you have to do is see him. So I know that he is alive. And take this . . ." She picked up a worn red leather purse from the table. "I don't know if it will be any use to you. But you should have it."

"What is it?" Sarah asked, thinking that it could not be more money, though coins chinked inside the red leather.

"Little tokens, tiny old coins that I used to find when I was a girl at Foulmire. Rob would know them at once. If he doubts you come from me, or doubts your word, show them to him."

The girl said nothing; she thought with pity that her grandmother's senses must be failing, to send her to the wealthiest city in the world with a purse of clippings to look for a drowned son, as if she could buy him back from the underworld. "And, Grandma, if I don't find him?" the girl suggested hesitantly. "If I find that it's true and that he's drowned?"

"Ah, if he's dead and buried at sea then bring something back that he owned, if you can," Alinor said, her face suddenly haggard. "I'll have it in my coffin when I'm buried so that something of his can be buried on land in Christian ground, so his soul doesn't wash around the world in dark tides. And if I've just been a foolish old woman who can't bear the truth and makes up a stupid story, then bring back that to me—as hard and true as it is, Sarah. I'd rather have a hard truth than a soft lie. If he's drowned, then take a boat out to where they say he went down, and throw some flowers on the water and say a prayer for him. Say his name. Tell him that I love him."

"I will," she whispered. "If I can do nothing else, I can do that. You can tell Ma and Livia that I've gone to honor his grave." She paused for a moment. "What flowers? Any flowers especially, Grandma?"

"Forget-me-nots."

Livia, with Carlotta, the nursemaid, trailing unhappily behind with the baby in her arms, walked the length of St. Olave's Street to London Bridge. She elbowed her way through the teeming crowds on the bridge, snapping over her shoulder that Carlotta should keep up. Porters carrying trays on their heads or sacks on their backs pushed into the two women, wagoners bellowed for people to make way, shopkeepers shouted bargains at them, and beggars plucked at their skirts. Often the press of people was so great that they could make no way at all but just had to stand, crushed in the crowd, and wait for everyone to move on.

"This is unbearable!" Livia exclaimed as Matteo wailed unhappily in Carlotta's arms; but there was no avoiding the queues of slowly moving people.

Halfway over the bridge the crowd thinned at the disused church; but then the way narrowed again and the women had to push along the drawbridge, and finally spill out onto Thames Street.

"Follow me!" Livia ordered, and led the way for a mile up Thames Street, struggled through the smoke-stained half-ruined City gate, over the Fleet Bridge into Fleet Street, and elbowed her way around the half-built Temple Bar to emerge with a sigh of relief into the paved way of the Strand.

It was a long way to carry a baby, stepping over the filth in the road, ignoring the stares of more fashionable people, avoiding the impertinent poor. Beggars had to be sidestepped, street sellers with everything from eels to posies of flowers and fruit from the country had to be refused. Carlotta was flustered and upset by the time they got to the steps of Avery House and Livia impatiently pulled the huge iron doorbell.

"Why did we not take a boat?" Carlotta hissed. "What do all these people want us to buy?"

"We have no money for a boat." Livia spat her reply, and then turned a smiling face to the door as Glib silently opened the double-height door to the two of them. "Is Sir James at home?" Livia asked coolly, walking past him to the mirror and taking off her hat, pausing briefly to see the reflection of her perfect face.

"In his study. Am I to show you in?"

"I'll go in," Livia said. She nodded to Carlotta to sit on the chair in the hall and rock the fretful baby. "Keep him quiet!" she snapped.

Glib did not warn her that Sir James had a visitor: but when he threw open the door for Livia she saw a stranger in the room. She hesitated on the threshold before stepping forwards with a charming smile. "Forgive me, I thought you were alone. I did not mean to intrude."

"No, come in, come in. I know this is your time to come for your letters." Sir James beckoned her in. "Indeed, this is someone who can advise us. I have shown him the statues in the gallery already, my brother-in-law, George Pakenham."

Livia extended her black-mittened hand, curtseyed, glanced up at the gentleman from under her dark eyelashes. "I will not disturb you. I will take my letters and leave you to your discussions."

"Not at all, please take a seat. We were just going to have a glass of claret, weren't we, George?"

George, a rotund man of about fifty, lifted a chair from the side of the room and placed it near to the table. "Please, won't you sit, ma'am?"

"Lady Peachey," she corrected quietly.

"Your ladyship."

"I will sit," she said, sinking into the chair and smoothing her black silk skirts. "But I will not delay you. I only came to make sure that we were all ready." She turned to George Pakenham to explain. "It is to be an exhibition tea, for those who want to see the statues again." She put her head to one side. "Do you like them? They are said to be among the most beautiful in Venice, in Italy."

"I've seen them," George said pleasantly. "And I must say I thought they were remarkable."

Livia clasped her hands together at his praise and smiled at Sir James.

"Some of them are modern copies, of course, and some original pieces cobbled together. But one or two are the real thing."

She froze. He saw the convulsive little tremor of her throat as she swallowed. Then she turned to Sir James. "They're not copies," was all she said, her voice unsteady.

"George is something of a connoisseur. He's a diplomat, he's been all over. He was in Venice and Florence, and he saw some wonderful statues at the Dutch courts and the German courts, didn't you? They're great collectors there, he tells me . . ." James blundered into silence.

"My antiquities are not copies," she repeated flatly. She turned to George. "You cannot have looked closely, sir. I have nothing but what is ancient and beautiful. This was my late husband's collection, and he was famous for his good taste. This is my dower. You do me a great disservice if you speak against them."

"I would as soon slander a lady's reputation, as speak against her antiquities—not that I have ever met with a lady selling antiquities before!" He gave her a knowing smile, he almost winked. "I well understand that it is a question of value."

Glib knocked at the door and came into the room with a dewy bottle of ratafia and a dusty one of claret and three glasses.

"Pour." Sir James, harassed, gestured him to get on with his task. "George—you didn't say, as we were looking round . . ."

"No, for what would you know, old fellow? I wanted to speak to the owner, of course, her ladyship here."

Livia said nothing until the cold glass of wine was in her hand and Glib was gone from the room. She took a sip. "Of course it is a question of value to me," she said quietly. "As a measure of the judgment of the Conte—my late husband, a famous patron of the arts. Value to me as my dower. And value to Sir James as a means to help a most deserving family, poor cousins of my husband's family. Poor but proud widowed women who will accept help from me, but from no other quarter. If you devalue my antiquities, sir, you damage many people. Including, I think, your brother-in-law, who houses them."

"Alas, madam. I have to speak, when I see my dear late sister's house being used as a shop for some goods that are most definitely—"

She rose to her feet, summoning all her courage. She did not glance to Sir James but knew his eyes were on her. "This is Avery House," she reminded Sir George icily. "Not Pakenham House—if there is such a place? It is Sir James's house; not yours. Your late sister is mistress here no longer. If Sir James admires the statues and they seem good to him, if he wants them to sell at a profit because he has a charitable ambition for the profits, then what do you do here, sir, but disturb Sir James, diminish the profits for a charitable cause, and distress me?"

She was magnificent, James was speechless. George put down his glass with a heavy hand and rose to his feet to go. "I'll see you at the coffeehouse," he said over his shoulder to Sir James. He took Livia's hand and bowed low over it. "You rebuke me, madam—" he started.

"Lady Peachey," she corrected him, unblinking.

"You rebuke me, your ladyship, and I apologize if I have offended you. I will not say another word against your antiquities. Not here or elsewhere. I wanted only to know what was your intention in bringing these . . . these objects here for sale? What is it that you hoped for? And now I think I have a very good idea!"

He walked to the double doors, threw them open himself, turned on the threshold, and bowed himself out.

Livia hardly dared to look at James. He came quickly round the desk to her and she had no clever words to turn the situation. She turned to him white-faced, her mouth working. Without a word, he reached out for her, drew her in to his embrace. "Forgive me, forgive me for letting him speak like that to you. I had no idea that was his opinion."

"Ohhh," Livia sighed, leaning against him, her mind racing.

"I should never have shown him . . . I should never have let him . . ."

Livia trembled a little, with unshed tears.

"I suppose he grieves for his sister, my late wife. But he has no right to say that you should not show your beautiful statues here! He has no command in my house, I shall do as I wish, and he shall never, never insult one of my guests again. He overreaches himself. I can only apologize."

"So unkind!" Livia breathed shuddered with relief. "I was so shocked!" Her tears brimming onto her cheeks were completely real. She was weak at the knees at the narrowness of her escape; he felt her yield to him and he tightened his grip on her to hold her up and then kissed the tears away, one and then another, and then a rain of kisses on her face, as he drew her close to him, one arm around her waist, his hand pressing her breast.

"I can never come here again." She trembled. "I can never be alone with you again. My honor . . . He said such things of me . . ."

"Marry me," he whispered. "This shall be your house and you will do what you damn well want. I won't hear a word against you! Marry me, Livia!"

"Yes!" she gasped. "Yes, Sir James, I will."

He hardly knew what he had said or what she had agreed as she broke from him, at once, called in the baby from the hall, told Carlotta—the only witness that she could summon—and proposed a toast to the betrothal in a glass of ratafia. Carlotta took a glass and drank to her new master. "We will be happy," Livia promised him. "I know it. We will be so happy."

Sir James took a seat behind his desk, his head whirling. "But what about the ladies at the warehouse?" He found that he had adopted Livia's way of speaking about the woman he had loved.

"I won't say anything there yet," Livia decided. "They don't like to be unsettled. We will wait until my statues have sold and I can give them the profits, and I will order another batch and they can sell them. I shall make them importers of fine art rather than wharfingers of corn and apples. We will buy them a house, a storehouse, in a better district—you will know where!—and they can sell my antiquities. We will get them established in a better trade, with a better house."

"You won't tell them now?"

"Not until they can manage without me." She remembered her plan for Johnnie. "But in the meantime, we can place their son in a good position."

"We can?"

"Ah yes, he wants to enter the Company, you know? The East India Company?"

"Yes, of course I know it, I am an investor."

"So you can give him a letter of introduction, and he can get a post?"

"I can write the letter. But I thought his mother would take nothing from me . . ."

"From me! It will come from me! I shall swear him to secrecy. And then, when I leave them to marry you, we will have provided for all of them, the girl in her shop, the boy in his post, and the two ladies with agreeable work. There can be no reproach. You know how Alys can be! So angry and sad! And Alinor so very weak, and so old. Let me set them up in a little business and then we will be free to be happy ourselves."

"My dear, of course. You know how I—"

"But we can marry in the meantime," she interrupted him, twinkling. "I don't ask you to wait! Married and as happy as swallows on the wing. And little Matteo will be your son and take your name. And soon—perhaps next year—we will have a child of our own together."

"You want to marry at once? And for Matteo to be—er—mine?" He felt his head spinning and he put down his glass of the strong wine, thinking that he had taken rather a lot for early morning. "I thought you meant to wait . . . Marry without telling them? Secretly? I mean—why?"

"Of course," she said limpidly. "We shall marry at once. You have swept me off my feet."

NOVEMBER 1670, LONDON

The second shipment from Venice was arranged between Alys and Captain Shore at his usual table in Paton's Coffee Shop.

"I had the address written out for you . . ." Alys opened her book but could not find the paper where Livia had written the address of her storehouse. "I am sorry, I thought I had it to hand . . ."

"Same place as before?"

"Yes, the lady's steward."

"Then I don't need directions. I know the man. I'll go to the same place as before." He hesitated. "Thing is, Mrs. Stoney . . . You're happy with him, are you? Because you're not his only customer. It's not just her furniture in his store. He does a lot of trade."

"He was her late husband's steward," Alys said coolly. "A position of great trust. She trusts him."

"Then I'll say nothing more. Same terms?"

"Yes, collect and ship another twenty crates. Five pounds a ton."

She took out a purse and counted out fifteen pounds in a promissory note from a merchant, and coins.

"Scraping the bottom of the cashbox?" the Captain guessed. He picked up the note. "Is this good?"

"Yes," she said shortly. "And you'll deliver another twenty crates?"

"How many has she got tucked away out there?" he asked curiously.

"It's her dower. Her personal goods."

The Captain scowled at her. "And that steward of hers is going to get an export license for another twenty crates of goods, personal goods? Not antiquities for export, his usual trade, which needs another license entirely, but 'personal goods'? And you want me to land them at your warehouse as personal goods? Paying no tax in London neither?"

"Yes," Alys confirmed.

"Was it a palace she owned, that she's emptying?"

"It was, actually," Alys replied.

He gave her a level gaze from under bushy salt-bleached eyebrows. "Never in all my dealing with you have I seen you put a false account in to Excise," he said. "Everyone else does it, all the time—but never you."

"This isn't false," Alys protested.

"False as whore's tears," he said roundly. "But it's not me risking my neck for a pair of dark eyes and a nasty temper."

"I'm not—" Alys started, and was surprised when he put a calloused hand on top of hers.

"I don't ask," he said kindly. "But when I come home, and this deal is done, I shall speak with you, Mrs. Stoney," he said. "And I shall put a question to you, and you'll tell me the truth. But not till then."

"I always tell the tr—" Alys was halted by the pressure of his warm hand over her own.

"I know," he said. "I know you were as straight as an arrow. You're not yourself now. But I'll put a question to you. When I come home."

NOVEMBER 1670, HADLEY, NEW ENGLAND

The winter was coming surely onward, Ned felt as if it were coming just for him, like a private enemy. Every day was shorter, every night was colder; he went into the woods at midday and gathered as many nuts as he could, peeling bark off the sassafras tree, picking the last growth of the moss, looking out for the edible mushrooms, rooting for groundnuts, knowing that the darkness was coming, knowing that the snow would come and hide everything. He sold the calf to one of the other settlers so that he did not have to feed him through the winter, and took cheeses and two smoked hams in trade. He stabled the cow and the sheep together, so that they could keep each other warm, and when he locked them up under a black sky, pierced with stars, the frozen cold of the metal bolt made his mittens stick to the iron.

The extra thatch on his house was all that stood between him and yawning arc of the icy sky. Ned, who had been exposed to the elements all his life, and had never feared an English winter, thought that this was a season that took a man to the edge of fear.

He was so dreading the solitary nights of winter that he was delighted to see Wussausmon's dugout nose to the pier, and the man clamber out and come up the steps to the bank.

"Lord! It's good to see you!" he said. "I am sick of my own company already, and it's only November."

Wussausmon showed his slow smile. "Why not go into the town for the winter? Would they not give you a bed at the minister's house?"

Ned shrugged. "I can't leave the beasts," he said. "And Mr. Russell's house is crowded as it is. I'll get used to it as the winter closes in—I'm just getting used to it now. Are you staying the night?"

The man shook his head. "I'm going downriver. I was at Norwottuck this morning and Quiet Squirrel sent these for you. She says you can have them for a cheese." He held out a bundle that looked like an armful of half-woven basketware.

"Come in out of the cold anyway," Ned said. "What are you doing at Norwottuck in this season? I'd have thought you'd be beside your fire at home in Natick?" He led the way indoors and pulled off his thick woolen jacket.

"Visiting," Wussausmon said nonchalantly.

"Pokanoket business?" Ned asked acutely.

"Colony business, actually," Wussausmon said. "The governor

and Council at Plymouth asked me to take messages to all the tribes that are not allied to the Pokanoket."

"Are there any?" Ned demanded. "Surely, those who aren't kin have sworn friendship?"

"Hardly any. I told them that. But the Council is determined to turn his own friends and kinsmen against the Massasoit."

Ned hesitated, wanting to ask more.

"See what she's sent you!" Wussausmon urged.

Ned sat on a stool as Wussausmon lowered himself in an easy crouch. Ned disentangled his gift. At first he thought it was a fish trap; he saw bended whips of supple sticks tied together with strings of hide, and woven with split withies. They looked like two great flat baskets. He looked at Wussausmon for an explanation.

"Snowshoes!" the man told him. "Quiet Squirrel made them for you, thinking that you would be able to walk into the woods when the snow comes. Have you got some already?"

"No!" Ned exclaimed. "I don't know anyone who has them. I've only seen a French trapper wear them. I've always dug out my path and struggled along. Isn't it hard to learn to walk on them?"

"It's just walking," Wussausmon smiled. "Coatmen can walk? Just keep your tips up."

"How do I fit them?" Ned asked.

"That's the other part of her gift to you," Wussausmon told him. "You'll have to give up your shoes, you'll have to wear moccasins like the People of the Dawnlands."

"She's always hated my shoes," Ned complained. "And my feet will freeze!"

"No, they won't. These are winter moccasins, they're made from moose fur; your feet will be warm. Far better than in your boots, and she's given you buckskin leggings to tuck into them."

Ned looked at the beautifully stitched moccasins, more like the bootees that an English child might wear in the cradle than shoes for a man, but he could see they were thickly lined with fur and were made with double skins, real native boots.

"Try them!" Wussausmon suggested.

Ned heeled off his heavy shoes and his cold damp hose and slid a bare foot into the fur-lined moccasin; the comfort and the warmth was instantaneous. Wussausmon laughed aloud at Ned's face.

"Shall I tell her you'll give her a cheese for them?"

"They're worth two!" Ned swore. "And tell her she is a good friend to think of me in these cold days."

NOVEMBER 1670, LONDON

Alys and Livia waved at the passing masts of Captain Shore's galleon as it went downriver at midday, under a darkening sky.

"Godspeed," Livia called after it. "God bless."

"I hope it's not going to be stormy," Alys said.

"God grant them good weather," Livia agreed. "Especially coming back with my goods."

"Amen," Alys said as the two women went into the warehouse front door and closed it behind them. "But before it returns we have to earn some money! I can't pay for the return voyage and the delivery. I've got next to nothing in the chest, after paying Captain Shore. I'm having to ask some creditors to wait."

The younger woman slipped her arm around Alys's waist and rested her smooth cheek and scented ringlet curls against Alys's shoulder. "Make them wait," she recommended. "Unless you want me to borrow from Sir James?"

"No! No, of course not. We don't need anything from him. We can stretch it. Tabs can wait for her wages. If the worst comes to the worst I can borrow at Paton's against the next cargo."

"Of course Tab can wait," Livia agreed. "You feed and house her, after all! And could you borrow enough to take another bigger warehouse?

Would it not make sense to get a bigger warehouse so that I don't have to sell at Sir James's house? So I never have to go to his house again?"

At once Alys looked anxious. "I'd rather you didn't go—but we couldn't raise such a sum, it would be far too much."

"If we sold this warehouse?"

"We can't sell here!"

"But my dear, how are we going to make more money unless we take our opportunities? You don't want me to be confined here forever, do you? Wouldn't it be wonderful to buy a new warehouse, somewhere more fashionable, somewhere that we could show the antiquities, and you could run the warehouse and I could sell the treasures in a gallery?" Livia took Alys by the waist and swayed with her as if they were dancing together. "It would be a real partnership, it would be our own business."

"I . . . I . . . don't think, I couldn't . . ." Alys floundered, torn between the beguiling picture of a thriving warehouse and a business that Livia could run alongside her, a partnership of work and love. "It sounds wonderful . . . but I couldn't raise such a sum. I couldn't risk our home . . . and Johnnie would never agree."

Livia's pretty laugh tinkled out. "Ah, Johnnie! We might as well ask Matteo for his permission. My love, we will not let our children rule us! We will think what we can do. Us together. And see! We have just seen our ship go out, we are going to see it come in. You don't know, you have no idea, what profit I am going to make. You don't know, you have no idea, what plans I have for us. Especially, you have no idea how happy we are going to be."

Sarah's bumboat hailed Captain Shore's galleon as it rolled at anchor, waiting for the tide. Passengers often joined ships at Greenwich, merchants often sent out a final load. Captain Shore himself helped her scramble aboard over the ship's rail.

"Whoa—a little lass?"

"I'm the maid at the Reekie warehouse," she said. "The Nobildonna has sent me to choose her goods in Venice and get them packed."

"I've already got the order from Mrs. Stoney," he protested.

"I'm to see they fulfill it," she said easily. "And then come home with them."

"Why?" he asked simply. "Why not let me fetch them like last time?"

Sarah shrugged. "You know what she's like," she said, confident that he did not. "She wants me to pick them out. I can't refuse. She just ordered me to come, and so here I am."

"She said nothing to me about sending a maid to do my work. I thought she trusted me, I've worked for her often enough!"

Sarah smiled at him. "Oh no no! Not Mrs. Stoney! She's fair enough—it's the other one. The Italian one. It's her that sent me."

"Ah," he said dourly. "Her." He showed Sarah into a small cabin and stowed her hatbox under the bunk. "We only stop at Lisbon," he warned her.

"That's fine," Sarah replied. "I didn't even want to come. I'm here to fetch her goods, and to meet my husband."

"What's he doing in Venice?" he asked, immediately suspicious.

"He's sick," Sarah improvised.

"How sick? For if they have sent him to the lazaretto we'll not even see him, you'll not be allowed to meet till the end of his quarantine, if he survives at all."

"No, nothing like that! It's a broken leg," she said glibly. "Nothing infectious. He's a trader . . . a trader in silks. I'm to choose her goods and bring him home."

He looked at her, his blue eyes acute under his sandy eyebrows. "I hope you're telling me the truth, young lady?"

"Oh yes," she lied cheerfully. "I am."

NOVEMBER 1670, LONDON

The next morning Alinor told Alys that Sarah had sent a message from the millinery shop to say that she had gone to the country for a visit and would be back within the week. The three women were sewing herb bags in Alinor's high room. Below the turret, the tide flowed in, a surge of rubbish on the incoming waves, creamy with foam from the tanneries and dye shops that had drained out to sea and were now washing in again. Seagulls cried and dived into the mess. Alinor watched for cormorants breasting the water and soaring gulls in the sky and spoke absentmindedly: "It was Ruth from the milliner's shop. Getting married from her village and she wanted Sarah to cook her wedding breakfast."

"And that takes a week?"

"Oh, my dear, she's worked without a holiday for seven years! She's served her time, let her take a holiday."

"Alys, don't be a hard mamma!" Livia interpolated, resting her work in her lap. "Let our pretty girl stretch her wings. She'll be clipped and cribbed soon enough."

In silence, Alinor observed Livia advising Alys on how to treat her own daughter.

"I've never even heard of this Ruth before," Alys complained.

"You think she has run off with a lover?" Livia challenged, laughing at her. "No, you don't! So, let her go. She'll be back in a few days, won't she?"

Alinor smiled. "I'm sure you know best," she said with a little edge in her voice. "And are you going to the Strand today, my dear?"

Livia preened. "For my exhibition tea," she said smugly. "To meet the buyers. And one sale agreed: I have sold my Caesar heads!"

"How much?" Alys asked eagerly. "Are they as valuable as you thought?"

"A hundred pounds," Livia said, halving the sum without hesitation.

"One hundred?" Alys repeated disbelievingly. "One hundred pounds?"

"I told you!" the younger woman triumphed. "And Sir James is taking nothing from me for using his house!"

Alys glanced at her mother at the mention of his name. Alinor was impassive, her eyes on the bright face of her daughter-in-law.

"You'll bring the money home tonight?" Alys pressed her. "You know how badly we need it in the warehouse."

"It's not for running the warehouse," Livia ruled. "It's for buying us a beautiful new home."

"We are buying a new home?" Alinor asked.

Alys glanced from her to Livia. "It's a plan of Livia's," she explained shortly. "And of course it would be wonderful to move to another house, out towards the country, with a garden. But, my dear, you owe for the warehousing, and for two voyages, and we cannot carry such a great debt."

Alinor watched the two young women as Livia spread her hands before her friend, like a magician, a trickster on a street corner, showing that he has nothing up his sleeves. "Don't nag me for money. For see? Nothing yet. But tonight, I will bring home a fortune."

Alys smiled, soothed at once.

"And we won't buy another poky little house far out of town," Livia declared. "You know what I have in mind."

"Does she?" Alinor remarked.

NOVEMBER 1670, HADLEY, NEW ENGLAND

Ned woke in the morning with bluish light filtering through his frosted window, and a memory from the night of the whisper of snow. He opened his door a crack and found a deep drift blown against the threshold, almost knee-high. It had been snowing all night again. Ned would have to dig himself out of his door. When the weather was bad, a howling wind and blizzard of snow, he tied a rope around his waist to the ring latch of his front door, and paid it out as he went to feed the cow and the sheep, huddled for warmth in their shared stall. He took an armful of logs on every return journey and followed his line back to his front door. Without the rope he would not have been able to find his way across his own yard, the battering of the snow was so blinding, the scream of the wind so deafening. Some days, in the middle of a storm, although he was standing no more than a few feet away, he could not see his own house. The world was a whirl of icy blindness; when he looked downward the snow was so thick around his knees that he could not see his own feet in the new moccasins.

But this day was so calm, and the sky so clear, that Ned had decided to try his new snowshoes and even go into town and sell some of his winter stores. He sat on his stool and tied his new moccasins and then worked his feet into the straps of the snowshoes. Feeling like a fool, he tramped clumsily to his door pulling on his heavy wool coat and his oiled cape on top. He had made his own fur hat out of rabbit skins and he pulled it down over his ears. He had no idea how he would manage with the basketwork boots like great hooves on his feet, and his first challenge was to step up from his threshold to the drift that had blown against his door. The snow was softest here and he sank and stumbled and fell headlong, and picked himself up again. He was panting and sweating with the effort, but once he had climbed onto the denser snow he found he could stand without sinking, and by adopting a slow laborious waddle, he found he could get along. When he looked back he saw that, though he was walking in snow that was feet deep, he was leaving a track of only a few inches.

It was exhilarating to walk on the top of snowdrifts instead of having to dig a path through them. It was still hard work, Ned was sweating and panting with the effort; but he could see that he could get to the town gate and even down the broad common road which was a snowfield of driven white. It was a beautiful day for his adventure with his new snowshoes, the sky a duck-egg blue, the shadows as dark blue as indigo on the dazzling snow. Ned lurched his way, a basket in each hand, to the north gate, half-buried in the drifts.

He swung his baskets over, and then climbed over himself. On the town side of the gate on more even ground, he found that the thick snow was smoother under his snowshoes, and he could stride forward, a little bowlegged, a little awkward, but definitely making progress.

As he went along he saw other houses of the town were snowed in. Most people had dug a narrow path from their doors to their byres or stables, most had cleared a narrow path to the common road, and Ned stood high on the snowdrifts as they came out, muffled up in furs, to buy anything they needed. Ned sold dried goods, berries, mushrooms, and some dried game meat, and corn kernels from his winter store.

People remarked on his strange snowshoes: some had never seen such a thing before. Ned explained that Quiet Squirrel had made them and traded them with him and that if anyone wanted a pair, he was sure that other trades could be made. But the men said that they would rather dig themselves paths to their stores and stables than stagger around like drunk Indians, and Ned would get frostbite and lose his feet, and the women said they could not wear them under skirts anyway.

John Russell was holding a prayer meeting, half a dozen people in his study and hall as he led them in prayer for guidance, for them as pilgrims in the cold land. Ned shed his snowshoes and his oiled cape, fur coat, and hat and bowed his head with the others. When the service was over the men and women exchanged news before opening the front door to the icy outer world. One of Ned's regular customers saw him and came forward.

"D'you have any fresh fish, Ned Ferryman?"

Ned ducked his head in apology. "It's been too cold to take from the weirs," he said. "Later in the season, perhaps I'll learn to fish through the ice."

"Would you dare?" she asked.

Ned swallowed, hiding his apprehension. "It's safe enough, I know."

She nodded and went away, and Ned looked around for Mrs. Rose, the minister's housekeeper. She came to his side. "I'll take some dried venison, Mr. Ferryman," she said. "And what are these?"

"Dried cranberries, and these are blueberries. I picked them myself. They're very good."

"I use them in pies," she said. "I'll have a quarter."

"I'll bring them through to the kitchen," he offered.

She inclined her head. "Will you take a seethed ale against this cold weather?"

"I should be glad of it."

She led the way to the kitchen at the back of the house.

"The nights are very long for our guests," she said quietly, speaking of the hidden men. "Too cold to go out, they stay upstairs and read. They barely see the sun."

"I'll visit them before I leave," Ned said. "They must feel imprisoned."

"If I were them, I'd go back to the old country and take my chance," she said.

"They'd be executed on the quay as soon as their ship arrived," he told her quietly. "There's no safe return for those that sentenced the old king to death. It's death for them there. Remember, they captured John Barkstead, John Okey, and Miles Corbet and executed them—hanged, drawn, and quartered them. And they were not even in England—the new King Charles had them traced and trapped in Holland, and dragged back to England to their deaths."

"Could just as well be death for them here," she pointed out. "No surety we all get through the winter—what with the savages and the weather and hunger? No doctor if you have an accident, no apothecary if you get sick. No surety at all."

"So why d'you stay here, Mrs. Rose?" Ned asked her. "Fearing it as you do? Why not go home when your indentures end?"

She turned her head away from him, so that her grim expression was hidden by the wings of her cap. "Same reason as everyone," she said tightly. "I came in the first place as I had hopes of a better life. God called me and my master ordered me. I didn't know it would be like this. I hoped for better, I still hope. And I don't have the money for my passage back home anyway."

NOVEMBER 1670, LONDON

Livia was determined to arrive at Avery House looking her best, and spent the shillings Alys had given her for her earrings on a waterman to take her to the private water stairs at Avery House. She tipped him to carry her up the green wet steps so that her black silk shoes would not get wet. "Oughter wear boots," he remarked sourly.

She gave him a penny without replying to him, and turned away to walk through the orchard, past the garden statues and the pretty marble fawn, and up the stone steps to the handsome terrace and the big glazed doors at the rear of the house.

Sir James was waiting to bow; but she slid into his arms and raised her face for his kiss, without even taking off her bonnet. He could not step back and kiss her hand, she was in his arms in a moment. The broad wings of the bonnet meant that he could not peck her on the cheek; there was nothing he could do but return her kiss and feel, with astounded desire, her warm lips part, as he tasted her mouth and the liquid softness of her tongue, which licked his. Raised as a celibate, and lately as a widower, he felt Livia's shameless sensuality like a physical shock. He felt an immediate burn of desire that drove all doubts from his mind. He tightened his grip on her and felt her lean back against his arm, as if he could have her, right there, on the terrace.

He forced himself to release her and step back from her, though he was breathless with desire, to find her eyes were bright, and she was laughing. *"Allora!"* she said delightedly. "I see that we must marry at once! We will shock the servants. Is this how you Englishmen greet your fiancées?"

"Forgive me!" At once, he was ashamed of his own need.

She laughed and untied her bonnet strings, the wide silk bow unfolding and tumbling down, reminding him of a petticoat opening on nakedness. He flushed at the thought and hoped that she did not guess it.

"No, there is nothing to forgive!" she assured him. She lifted the bonnet from her head and held it carelessly, swinging by the ribbons, so the black plume brushed the floor. "I am so glad to be an English wife again, you know we say in Italy that the only nation that loves their wives are the English? I cannot wait for our wedding day." She stepped a little closer so he could hear her whisper: "I cannot wait for our wedding night."

His desire for her drove any caution from his mind. "Oh, Livia . . . I . . ."

She turned and preceded him into the house without invitation, opening the glass door to his study and sitting in his own high-backed chair before his desk as if she were already his wife. She picked up the replies to the tea party and glanced through them. He seated himself on the visitor's chair, rather glad to have the desk between them. "Will you take some ale? Or wine and water? Or tea?" he asked.

"Shall we have ratafia again?" She smiled at him. "I think I will love the taste of it forever, as it will always remind me of last time I was here, when you told me you loved me and asked me to be your wife."

He served them both from the bottle on the sideboard and spoke as his back was turned. "My brother-in-law, George, wrote to me," he said. "He apologized for what he had said."

"As he should," she agreed smoothly. "I daresay we will forgive him, but never forget his rudeness to me."

He had to turn to hand her the glass. He was grave. "He did not repeat his challenge to the authenticity of the statues; but, my dear, I do fear . . ."

Her smile was warm but her eyes were very bright. "You fear?" She laughed. "I don't want a fearful husband!"

"Any doubt about their authenticity would be most embarrassing," he said, cautiously picking his words. He hardly knew what to say to her. He hoped that she understood at once that the thought of selling dubious goods, from his family home, to his own friends was unbearable to him. "I can't put it too strongly. If there is any doubt at all . . ."

"It's only one opinion," she said, as if that were the point. "And if he says he will not repeat it . . ."

"If there is any doubt about any one of the antiquities, they must all be withdrawn from sale," he said firmly. "I cannot be in the position that I am selling, at a profit, to my friends, something which might be—"

"Might be what?" She dared him to speak out.

"Uncertain?"

"What do you mean?" she demanded flatly.

He swallowed. "False."

The word dropped into the room like a stone into a deep well. She widened her eyes at him; but said nothing.

"In any way," he faltered. "Of course, without your knowing . . . nobody is saying that you . . ."

"You see yourself, that they are all things of supreme beauty," she pointed out.

"I do. But are they . . . ?"

"Lustrous," she said. "With the luster of beautiful age."

"They are surprisingly well polished. For things so old . . ."

"They were chosen by my first husband, a famed and most tasteful patron of the arts, out of all the things that he could have bought with his vast fortune. Each object you have here, he saw, and considered, and judged it to be worthy of his collection."

"Could he have been misled?"

"No."

"Could someone have substituted a false one for his good one, a copy of an original, perhaps after his death? Or when the goods were stored? Or when they were shipped here to you?"

"No," she stated flatly, though they both knew she could not possibly know.

"It's not likely that my brother-in-law is wrong," he said very quietly. "He is an authority. If he says that some of the Caesar heads are copies, even very good copies, then we must listen to him. My dear, he is certainly right."

"No, he is not," she said flatly. "It is not possible that my antiquities are not good. And anyway, we do not have to listen to him. I certainly am not going to listen to him. He speaks to you, not to me. It is you who are going to have to choose who you believe. The brother of your dead wife, who resents your new happiness? Or your promised wife? Your betrothed wife?"

She saw the dilemma he was in and tightened it a notch. "You have offered me your good name and your fortune and I bring you all of mine. These are your antiquities now, are you going to undermine your own honor? Are they to be false, and you to be false, when you have spent your life struggling to be true?"

"A matter of honor?" He could hardly follow her. "How is it a matter of my honor?"

"They are your antiquities!" she exclaimed impatiently. "You are my husband! What is mine is yours. Would you handle anything but a true thing? Have you become some sort of mountebank?"

"Of course not!" he exclaimed. "Of course I am not!"

"Well! There you are!" she said simply, as if the discussion was completely ended and he had agreed with her.

They finished their wine in silence, and he glanced at her face to see if she was as his first wife had been: silently, chillingly sulky; but she returned him a radiant smile, as if there were nothing wrong, and then she asked him to show her around the house. As the mistress-to-be she wanted to see it from attic bedrooms to cellars, and his spirits rose as he showed her the wine stocks in the cellar, each carefully racked and numbered. "Collected by my father and my grandfather and his father," he told her.

She had seen far greater cellars in the vineyards around her home where they had been making wine for centuries and keeping only the best; but she nodded as if she were hugely impressed. "And nobody tells you they are not good!" she said, as if it were a shared joke.

He showed her the imposing rooms on the ground floor that led off the grand marble hall: the dining room, the parlor, and the receiving room with the double doors that could be thrown open to the hall.

"But this is a perfect house for grand parties!" she exclaimed.

"My mother and father entertained the king here," he said. "The king and the whole court."

"Oh, we will do that," she said instantly.

"That was the old king," he corrected. "King Charles, not his son. I don't think the court is a suitable place for a lady now."

She looked up into his face and reached up and patted his cheek. "We will be grand," she said. "And we will entertain the king. There will be no impropriety in your house, but we will take our place where we belong."

He felt a leap of hope that she might make his house the place that it should be, that somehow the king and the country would be as they should be, that the old days would be truly restored to him, that he would not have to feel so many doubts about this shallow polished replica of his old life. He took her hand to lead her up the stairs to see the bedrooms. They were all shrouded in linen sheets to keep out the moths and the dust. Only in his own room, facing over the garden and the river, was the bed made up, and the shutters open to the sunshine.

"You sleep here?" she asked, leaning against the bed.

"I do."

"And not in the big bedroom with the four-poster bed?"

"That was the room I shared with my wife. It is too big for one man, and I don't come to London very often."

"But we shall use that one, the biggest bedroom?"

"Yes," he said. "When we visit London. And we must decide when our wedding should be. We shall marry at my home, Northside Manor in Yorkshire. I shall go to my home and send for you and we shall have the banns called in my parish church."

"I thought we would marry at once!" she said. "Didn't we agree at once?"

"We did, but I cannot," he started.

Her gaze was as sharp as a knife. "You promised me."

"I have to be married in my own parish," he said gently. "I cannot be married in secret, in a hurry, as if we had something to hide. I have to be married at the church where all my family have been baptized and married and buried."

"Then shall we go to your home at once?"

"I will have to make it ready . . ." He suddenly checked as a thought struck him. "You are Protestant? You are of the reformed religion?"

She had not thought of this. "I am Roman Catholic," she admitted. "But I have no objection . . ."

"I didn't think! Before we can be married, you will have to be instructed and confirmed in the English church," he said. "I will have to find you a minister here, in London, to instruct you. When he has seen you through baptism and confirmation, you shall come to Northside Manor, to me, and we will marry."

"There's no need . . ."

"My dear, it has to be done."

"I can take baptism at once. Surely I can be baptized tomorrow!"

"Not without instruction. The religion is one of understanding, not simply faith."

She could not hide her irritation. "But how long is all this going to take?" she demanded.

He thought for a moment. "Six months? No more than a year."

"We can't wait a year to be married!" she exclaimed shrilly.

"Why not? We are young."

"But we want a child at once!"

He took her hand and kissed it. "A true Avery, born of a Protestant father and mother and baptized into the church in Northallerton parish."

"But I thought you were a Roman Catholic anyway?"

"I was raised in the true—" He cut short the heretical phrase. "I told you I was raised as a Roman Catholic, but my parents and I had to surrender our faith to come home and reclaim our lands. It was an act that was very painful to me, very costly to my pride and my soul. It felt wrong, it still tears at me. But I will allow no doubt over my ownership of my lands, and over the inheritance of my son. As a Roman Catholic I would be barred from public office, but I was born to serve and lead my community. I am honor bound to take up my duties. So there can never be any question about my wife and my heir. You will have to convert immediately—even little Matteo will have to be baptized into the Church of England. I can have no doubt over the affiliation of anyone in my household."

She held up her hands. "Stop! Stop!" she said urgently. "Don't be so serious, my darling, so grave about a happy matter! We will marry in whatever church you like, and Matteo can be christened at the same time. He can take your name and be your son. But I cannot wait forever. We must marry this year, before Christmas. I cannot survive winter in that dreadful little warehouse—you have no idea how uncomfortable and crowded it is. I am sure I would be ill, it would make me ill, I have to be Lady Avery before the winter sets in."

"Can't you move?" he asked uneasily. "Move house, if it is so sickly? Why d'you need my name? Why would it make any difference? And surely, my dear, Matteo must keep his father's name. Wouldn't they think I was taking him from them?"

She saw at once that she had gone too fast for him, and she hid her impatience. She stepped closer and put her hands on the rich velvet of the lapels of his jacket. "I want your love and protection, I want to be somewhere warm," she whispered. "That's all I'm thinking. Somewhere warm with you. Do you not want me there, in your cold northern nights? When the wind howls outside and the snow drifts up to the door, will you not want me for company? For joy?"

She put her hands at the back of his neck and he felt a shiver all down his spine, as if she had touched the very core of his body; at once he lost his train of thought and all caution. She pulled his head towards her as if for a kiss; but as he bent forward she leaned back, pulling his mouth to her exposed throat, and let herself fall back on the bed and he, following her, was on top of her in a moment. His instinct was to rise, to apologize, but she kept her grip on him, wrapping her arms around him, opening her mouth and arching her back so she pressed against the length of him, until with a gasp he decided that he could not stop himself. Hungry to feel her, desperate to be inside her, he fumbled at his breeches as she pulled up her dark mourning silk gown, her silk petticoat, and he entered her with a groan of pleasure. At once she moved against him, urging him on.

"My God! Forgive me!" he said the moment he returned to awareness. "Forgive me! I should never! I did not mean . . ."

For a moment she was quite still and then she languidly turned her head towards him. As she opened her dark eyes she saw his troubled face and realized that she must reassure him. At once she found the right words: "Oh, I too am in the wrong," she said remorsefully. "For it was I who kissed you. I felt such a longing . . ."

He stood up at once, arranging his clothes, bitterly ashamed of himself. "And in my house! When you are my guest!" he said almost to himself. "In my care. Under my protection! God forgive me . . ."

"Ah well," she said, sitting up and rearranging her cap. "We are engaged to marry, after all. There is no great sin in it."

He could not understand her calmness at the assault on her honor. "No sin! But such a breach of . . . Forgive me, Livia. Did I hurt you?"

She realized that he was deeply shocked and that she must agree. She jumped up from the bed as if she were ashamed of lying back. She drooped her head so that all he could see was the enchanting line of her dark eyebrows and the dark eyelashes on her cheek. "Of course, you hurt me a little. It is only to be expected. A man such as you . . ." She turned her face to hide her blush.

"I'm a brute." He fell to his knees before her, and she leaned forward and gathered his head between her full breasts so he smelled her perfume of rose petals and the warmth of her skin, and desire for her rose up again.

"But we have to marry at once now," she whispered to him. "There can be no delaying."

"Yes, yes," he agreed, his lips at the smooth skin of her neck, as she guided his hand to her breast under the tight silk bodice.

"Just think! We might have conceived a child already!" she whispered with a lilt to her voice. "We will have to marry now."

"My God! Yes," he said. "Of course. Livia, trust me! Your name, your honor, is safe with me. Believe me! I shall go to Northallerton at once, and get the banns called. I shall send for you as soon as I can. And in the meantime I will get a minister to instruct you here in London, and tell him that you must convert at once. I need not say why: there are many people who convert to avoid the penalties. And Matteo can be christened as you say, when we are married . . ."

She rose to her feet and shook out her crumpled black gown. "Very well," she said, smiling. "Of course, it shall be just as you wish, my love. We shall do it just as you want. As long as it is at once. Before Christmas."

He took her hand and pressed kisses into it. "You forgive me?"

Sweetly, she brought her face to their clasped hands and kissed his fingers in reply. "You are my husband," she whispered. "I will always forgive you, everything."

All was ready for their guests to come. There were only half a dozen gentlemen, and they had no interest in the tea that Livia insisted on serving. Two of them took glasses of brandy with them as they walked in the garden and looked at the statues, at the apple trees bowing over rotting fallen fruits and the river beyond. The rest of them took cold Rhenish wine and talked to Livia in the gallery.

Nobody mentioned money, and Livia, glancing at James, realized that he was quite incapable of broaching the subject to these, his friends, even when they had come to his house to complete the purchase.

She tucked her hand in the arm of Sir Morris, an ugly middle-aged man in an elaborately expensive coat, and smiled up at him. "You must forgive my boldness," she said. "But these antiquities are my dower. I have to sell them for the benefit of my little son. I cannot leave it to anyone else, nobody in England but rare connoisseurs like you understands marble, nobody outside Italy would understand their value. So I must talk to you directly."

"Delighted," he said with a leer. "I never mind doing business with a lady. Though this is the first time I've discussed marble!"

"Indeed," she said coolly. "It is the Caesar heads you are interested in?"

"Got my steward to measure my dining room. They can all fit in, he tells me. If I want them. And I have a man who buys art for me, he'll come and look at them before I conclude."

She flicked out her black fan and looked at him over the top. "*Perdono!* I am not that bold!" she protested. "I cannot deal with agents and salesmen. You must excuse me."

She had surprised him. "I wouldn't buy a horse at this price without advice."

"These are Caesars, not horses."

"It's the question of provenance," he said.

"Exactly. They come from the collection of the Fiori family, my first husband's family. Their provenance is perfect."

"Yes, I suppose. But it's rare to have a full set, isn't it?"

"Extremely rare," she said unblinking. "That's why they are so expensive."

"You think they are expensive?"

"Would you rather they were cheap?"

He laughed, despite himself, at her contempt for the word "cheap."

"Nobildonna, you have mastered me. I shall buy them without asking for anyone else to look at them."

"But only if I will sell them to you . . ." she countered over her fan. "Perhaps I am not sure that you value them sufficiently?"

"If you will be so kind," he replied. "Am I begging you to fleece me now? Did we say two hundred pounds?"

"We said two hundred guineas."

He reached into a pocket in his jacket and brought out a folded piece of paper. "A promise to pay," he said. "On my goldsmith. Immediately."

She took it without looking at it, as if she disdained normal business practice.

"You don't check it?" he asked her.

She widened her eyes at him. "Do I need to? Would I question the words of a gentleman?"

He gave a little bow. "You are superb," he said, as if she were an actress in one of the new playhouses.

"Shall I send the antiquities to you, or will your people collect them?" she asked.

"I'll send my own people," he said. "I'm taking them to my country house. It's a pleasure to do business with you, Lady Peachey."

She inclined her head and stepped a little closer. "And I have more," she whispered. "I have a reclining female figure in the most beautiful marble, a creamy color marble just like skin. Completely naked, a Venus resting, with a dolphin under her feet, his head lying . . ." She turned aside and raised her fan to hide her blush. "Along her thighs. The contrast of the skin of the dolphin and her . . . her . . . it's very beautiful. The great classical artists put beauty before everything . . ." she recovered. "We moderns, we are bound to be limited by modesty. But not, I hope, blinded by it. This is a private piece, for a gentleman's study or his private gallery."

"I should like to see it," he said eagerly. "Quite naked, is she?"

"I would have to order it to be shipped from my late husband's store in Venice," she said. "I could show you a drawing and you could order it. I could not undertake to bring it into the country without a guaranteed purchaser. I would have to deliver it directly to you; I could not show it in Sir James's house, it is a piece so . . ."

He bent his head to hear her whisper.

"*Infiammando*," she breathed.

"Inflaming?" he confirmed.

Livia, sloe eyes turned down for modesty, only nodded.

"For sure, to a lady; but for a man of the world like me?"

"It's *indecente* to anyone," she assured him, turning her head away, embarrassed beyond words. "It would be *indecente* to the king himself, and we all know that he has an eye for art."

"How much?" he asked, breathing a little heavily.

"Ah, my Venus, my indecent Venus, would be five hundred."

"Guineas?"

She turned back and smiled. "Exactly."

James waited for Livia in his study, as the last guest left the house. She came in smiling and offered him Sir Morris's note of hand. "Will you take this for me?" she said. "I dare not take it to the warehouse. I am so afraid of thieves or fire!"

"I'll redeem it tomorrow," he said. "Shall I keep the gold at my goldsmith's for you?"

"Yes," she said. "That would be best, thank you."

He glanced at the amount. "You must be pleased," was all he said.

"I am," she agreed. "For the poor ladies."

He waited while she put on her bonnet and threw a little cape around her shoulders against the cold evening air, and then she took his arm and let him lead her through the garden towards the river. Glib went ahead of them to hail a skiff to come to the Avery pier.

"What a beautiful evening," she sighed. "What a wonderful day we have had."

She waited for him to reply, and when he was silent, she paused at the head of the steps to the pier. "Oh! I had quite forgotten! How foolish of me. Alys will be wanting to be paid for the shipping and the wagon."

"Immediately?" he asked, surprised.

"My dear, they are so hand to mouth, she has been dunning me for weeks. You have no idea! I have been quite uncomfortable . . ."

"I shall send your money from the goldsmith's tomorrow . . ." he suggested.

"No, no, I need it at once. She will be waiting up to empty my pocket. She'll be expecting it tonight."

"Surely she realizes that you would be paid in a promissory note?"

"My dear, they only deal in coins," she said. "She keeps everything she makes in a chest in the counting house. I doubt they've ever seen a note!"

"Of course . . ." He hesitated and reached into the deep pockets of his jacket. "Shall I give you some funds now?"

"That would be so kind," she said. "I should give my *Mia Suocera* something for housekeeping too."

He drew out a heavy purse and tipped out five gold guineas. "Would this be sufficient?"

She took it and breathed: "Thank you, you're very thoughtful. Perhaps ten? I would not want to embarrass myself in front of Alys, she's very grasping."

"She always was," he assured her, and handed over the entire purse, which disappeared into the placket sewn inside the waistband of her skirt. He bowed and kissed her hand and then helped her down the stair into the stern of the waiting skiff, as Glib scrambled into the seat in the prow. The boatman nodded to Sir James, pushed off, and started rowing.

The sun low on the river, the skiff went along its own shadow on the darkening water. The wind was coming in from the sea and the boat rocked gently on the little waves. Livia, a woman of Venice, took no notice of the birds skimming by her, going to roost for the night, or the beauty of the little moon rising before her. She looked back to the water stairs of Avery House and the tops of the trees beyond it in the orchard and the hidden garden, and thought only of the grand house behind that and the Avery fortune that had built and maintained it, and the ten guineas in her pocket.

The waterman drew up to the Horsleydown Stairs and Glib paid with Sir James's money, and got out of the boat first, to help Livia up the greasy steps. "You can go," she dismissed him when she reached the top.

He hesitated. His orders had been to see her into the warehouse, and he hoped she might pay for his return by boat.

She snapped her fingers in his face. "Did you not hear me? Go."

He bowed and set off on the walk back to Avery House, as Livia opened the mean front door and stepped into the dark little hall.

Alys was waiting for her. "I saved you dinner," she said eagerly. "I've been waiting for you!"

"I'm very tired," Livia said sulkily. "I don't want anything."

"Oh! Would you like some soup? Or a glass of—"

"I said: nothing! I think I'll go straight to bed."

"How was it?" Alys asked. "Did it go well? Did you . . . ?"

"I suppose you want money," Livia said unpleasantly.

"Well, of course I do! But I also hoped that you'd had a good day. I've been waiting for you. I've been thinking about you. I was worrying as it got dark that you wouldn't . . ."

"Wouldn't what?" Livia countered. "Bring home a pocket of shillings like your son and daughter have to do? Of course not! I have put my earnings into the care of Sir James who will deposit them at his goldsmith's! Did you think I would push a purse down my bodice like a thief?"

"I did hope you would bring money home, tonight," Alys admitted. "My dear, we need it! The warehouse has paid out for the shipping, and for the wagon, and for the lightermen. And we've commissioned a second voyage. I can't carry the debt! I did tell you? And you did say you would . . ."

Livia put her black silk shoe on the bottom stair. "I've earned a fortune today, more than you could have earned in a year, in ten years! I told you I would do so, and of course, I will pay my debts, but I shan't be paying out my money for your children's keep, nor for a maid who does not even come when she is called." She opened the purse from her pocket and pulled out five coins. "Here is five guineas and you'll have the rest later. I would have given you it at breakfast, there was no need for you to stay up and dun me on the doorstep."

"I just wanted to see you safe home!"

"You wanted to see the money safe home! All you care about is money. And don't wait up for me again, unless I ask you to."

NOVEMBER 1670, LONDON

Johnnie tidied his high desk in the merchant's counting house as the early dusk darkened the lofty dirty windows. The other clerks were putting on their jackets and hats, and leaving at the same time, but he did not walk with them to the bakehouse or coffeehouse. Instead he went down to the river and stood at a set of river stairs. The low tide lapped at his feet on the green weedy steps, a wash of rubbish, bits of cloth, the flat end of a bonnet, a sheet from a catalogue, some bits of wood, something stinking and dead; but he looked beyond the flotsam to the horizon. The river, even at dusk, was a forest of swaying masts, as ships—sails furled—were towed in by busy barges or moored in midchannel waiting for their turn to declare their duty and unload at the legal quays.

A child of the warehouse, Johnnie usually counted the queue of waiting ships and looked for the names of those that often came to the Reekie Wharf; but this evening he looked beyond them to the east where the thick gray clouds merged the sky into the sea on the dark horizon.

He was confident that Sarah would be safe on board Captain Shore's ship and that she would cope with whatever faced her in Venice. She was only twenty-one years old but the two of them had been raised on the streets, alleys, and wharves of St. Olave's, and he knew she was no fool. She had seen enough libertine men buying gewgaws for their mistresses at the milliner's not to be tricked or seduced by a few slick words, she had seen fellow apprentices leave the workshop in a carriage and come back barefoot. A child of the coastal trade, he was not fearful for her at sea; a firm believer in his grandmother's wisdom, he did not think she had been sent on a mission that she could not accomplish. But he believed himself to be half of a twin and, as she went farther and farther away, he felt as if half of himself was missing.

He walked along the wharf from one set of steps to another, not knowing where he was going in the gathering dusk, but understanding that he was undertaking a sort of vigil, a waiting for her, and that until she came home his family would be dispersed and he would have no comfort until he knew she was safe. Now he understood how it had been for his mother, when her brother, Rob, went away; for his grandmother when her brother, Ned, went to the New World. Now, as he tried to look through the dusk, as if he could see Sarah so far away at sea, he believed that his grandmother would know for sure if her own son was alive or dead.

NOVEMBER 1670, LONDON

Sarah had been away from her home for nearly a week when Alinor came down the narrow stairs to find Alys in the counting house, on the other side of the narrow hall.

"Alys, I need to talk to you."

At once, Alys slid down from her stool at the clerk's high desk where she worked. "Ma? Are you ill?"

"No," Alinor smiled. "No, I'm well. But I've something to say to you."

"Shall we go into the parlor?" Alys scattered a shaker of sand to dry the careful figures in the ledger, put a bookmark in her place, closed the ledger, and led the way across the hall. She settled her mother in a seat near the fireplace. "Shall I light the fire?"

"No, I'll go back upstairs again in a moment."

Neither woman would have lit a fire to burn in an empty room. It was one of the many grinding economies they had practiced all their lives.

"Balancing the books?" Alinor asked. "Are they right now? With Livia's payments?"

"Yes! Finally paying our debts," Alys said. "She paid us in the very nick of time, it was close." She closed the parlor door as if to shut out the threat of failure. "I've settled with Tabs and given her a little extra for her patience, and I'll be able to pay Captain Shore when he returns with the load. But we've got nothing to spare. It's close—too close," she confessed.

"And where's Livia now?" Alinor asked.

"At . . . with the statues," Alys replied. She never named Sir James to her mother.

"Again?" Alinor asked curiously. "I thought they were sold?"

"Now she's supervising their packing up and sending them off to the buyers."

"Will she pay us a share of the profits?" Alinor asked curiously.

Alys flushed slightly. "She's paid what she owed for shipping on the first voyage, she still owes for commissioning the second," she said. "I didn't ask for a share of her profits. After all, it's her widow's dower from her first marriage, we've no claim on it. And anyway, she plans to buy a house for us all to live in, she's saving up the money. We will be partners."

"Don't we have to buy the warehouse?" Alinor asked. "A new ware-house, for her to show her treasures?"

Alinor flushed. "As a partner, yes. I know she's ambitious, Ma, but this could take us to a better house and a better living than we've ever dreamed of."

There was a cold draft from the unshuttered windows. Alinor drew her shawl closer around her shoulders.

"You're cold. I'll light the fire for you." Alys rose to go to the kitchen for some embers.

"No, no, I'm not staying downstairs. I came down to tell you something.

Alys sat on a stool at her mother's feet and looked up into the worn and beautiful face. "Yes, Ma?"

"Sarah didn't go to see a friend. I sent her on an errand."

"You did?"

"A long errand, I'm afraid. I sent her to Venice, my dear. To find Rob."

For a moment Alys was silent as she could not believe what she had heard. "What?"

"I knew you wouldn't like it, so I told her to keep it secret. She was eager to go, I sent her with a little money—" She broke off and smiled. "And the old red purse of tokens. She sailed with Captain Shore, and she'll come home with him in the New Year."

Alys rose to her feet. "You sent Sarah to Venice? My daughter? Without telling me?"

"Aye, I'm sorry."

"Ma . . . I can't believe it . . . you sent Sarah?"

"Yes."

"But what for?"

Alinor folded her thin hands in her lap. "Because I don't think Rob is dead," she said very quietly. "I don't believe it. So I sent Sarah to see what she could find out. And if there's nothing, and he's dead, then I asked her to bring something back of his, that I might take in my coffin when I'm dead too."

Alys jumped to her feet, took two steps to the window, and then came back to her mother. "I can't begin to . . . Ma, what have you done?"

"Sarah feels as I do—both the children do. That there's more to Livia's story than she's told us. And I know—I know in my heart that Rob isn't dead. I just know it. He's not a young man to die in water, not when he could swim to shore, not when he could find his way home on hidden paths. Lord, Alys—think! He was raised on Foulmire, he'd never have drowned in shallow waters. If I'd been well enough I'd have gone myself. But Sarah leapt at the chance."

"How could you send her? Send my daughter in secret? Overseas? Ma, how could you!" Alys looked out of the window as if she expected the sails of Sarah's ship to appear, returning her home.

"My own daughter! And you made her keep it secret!"

"We only didn't tell you because we knew you wouldn't like it—"

"You were right!" Alys burst in.

"And because we don't trust Livia," Alinor said steadily. "She has you in her pocket."

Alys flushed red. "Ma!"

"She treats you as no one has ever done. She speaks to you with contempt, as if you were her servant, and then she gives you money, as if she could buy your pride."

"I've heard people speak worse to you," Alys rejoined.

"Yes. Many. But they never said they loved me in the next breath. They ordered me and I resented it. I didn't love them for it."

"She's Rob's widow . . . what's wrong with you? Why don't you trust her? She's paid her debt, she's going to give us a home! She's a true daughter to you. She'll find us a new house where there'll be room for us all, and a garden, and clean air! She's the savior of this family! She came here, when she could have gone anywhere! She's stayed here, though it's so poor and mean and so beneath her! And she's used our warehouse and our wharf to bring in her valuable dower and sold it to our benefit! She loves us! She loves me!"

Alinor said nothing but looked steadily at her daughter till Alys ran out of words and stood, furiously silent.

"Even if all this were true, I would still be a mother missing a son," Alinor said steadily. "Even if it were all true, I still would know in my heart, in my bones, Alys, that my son is alive. Even if it were all true, I would not believe that Rob is dead. None of this smells like truth to me, I don't feel it in my heart, I don't feel it in my bones."

"How should you know it?" Alys raged. "How should you feel it in your heart? In your bones? You were ducked for a witch—have you learned nothing? These are false gifts. You have no sight! These are nothing but the fancies of a sick woman. You were a fool once for love! Are you going to be a fool for spite?"

Alinor gave a little gasp, put her hand to her heart as if she would hold her breath in her body. For a moment she could say nothing. Then she raised herself from her chair and went to the door. One hand on the ring of the latch, she turned back and drew a shaky breath. "It's not witchcraft and never was. It's my ma's gift. I had it from her and gave it to my children. Rob had it and it guided him in his healing; you had it, but you put it from you. Now Sarah has it from me. And I tell you this—if my son were no longer in this world, I'd know it. Just as if Livia were a true daughter to me, I'd know it. Just as if her son was my grandson: I'd know it."

"These things are unknowable," Alys insisted, frightened at her mother's ashen certainty. "But money at the goldsmith's is real."

"It's not at your goldsmith's," Alinor said with the accuracy of a poor woman.

"Ma, sit down. Forgive me, I spoke in anger . . . I was . . ."

Alys pressed Alinor into the chair, and she sat still until she had gained her breath. Alys hurried to the kitchen and came back with a tot of brandy in a little glass and watched her drink till a little color came back to her drawn face.

"I shouldn't have spoken so," Alys whispered.

The older woman gave a wry smile. "Don't take it back just because I can't breathe. I'm not going to be one of those tyrants who faint to make people obey them."

Alys gave a shaky little laugh. "You're no tyrant, and I shouldn't have abused you. But you've done me very wrong, Ma."

"I haven't," Alinor said steadily. "I've done something I know to be right. And don't you go telling Livia where Sarah's gone. Nor what she's doing."

"I'd be ashamed to tell her!" Alys retorted, her voice low. "What could I tell her? That the mother-in-law that she loves doesn't believe her? That she's sent her granddaughter miles away, on a long sea voyage, to spy on her? Without telling me?"

A little smile twisted Alinor's mouth, but she was unrepentant. "Very well. We'll both of us say nothing. You can say, if she asks, that Sarah's staying in the country for a month. And in a month we'll find another excuse."

"You want me to lie to her," Alys accused. "The only person who has loved me since my husband abandoned me?"

Alinor nodded. "Do you think she doesn't lie to you?"

NOVEMBER 1670, HADLEY, NEW ENGLAND

One icy cold day in late November there was a gentle tap on Ned's door and Red lifted his head and gave a short welcoming bark. Ned opened the door to Wussausmon who was dressed in his thickest winter jacket, and grinning under a hat of muskrat fur.

"Come!" he said. "I'm going to take you fishing!"

"The river's full of ice," Ned protested.

"I know, I'm taking you to a lake. Have you ever been ice fishing?"

"No," Ned said with no eagerness. "Never."

Wussausmon hesitated. "What's wrong?"

"Nothing," Ned lied, putting on his big coat and tying his oiled cape on top.

"No—tell me?"

"No, no." Ned hid his embarrassment in irritation. "Nothing. Nothing, I tell you."

Wussausmon laughed at Ned's bad temper. "Ah, *Nippe Sannup!*" he said, putting his arm around Ned's shoulders. "Tell me what is the matter, for I can see you don't want to come fishing with me, though I thought it would be a great treat for you. And you could take a fish to your woman: Mrs. Rose."

"Don't speak of her like that," Ned warned him.

"Not a word! Not a word!" his irrepressible friend promised him. "But what is wrong, *Nippe Sannup?* Waterman? *Netop?* Friend?"

Ned sat to tie his moccasin boots, bending over them to hide his shame. "I'm not one of the People," he confessed. "I'm not one of you. I'm not used to such hard winters that the ice freezes so you can walk on it, dig a hole in it." His voice dropped lower. "It frightens me," he confessed. "We have frost fairs in London some winters, but you can see that it's frozen hard, and there are dozens of other people walking around. I can't stomach the thought of stepping on a deep lake all on my own, and hearing it crack below me. I can't bear to be all alone on the ice."

There was a silence and he glanced up, expecting more laughter, but Wussausmon's lively face was compassionate. "Of course," he said. "Why did you not tell me at once?"

Ned shrugged. "It's not the part of a man to be afraid," he said.

"Oh it is," Wussausmon assured him. "We teach our boys and girls to know their fear and step towards it as their friend. To use it as a warning. Far braver to face it than go away. Was that not the path of the Lord? In the wilderness? Facing His fear?"

"I don't know," he said. "That's for Mr. Russell. I don't know."

"Don't choose to be stupid," Wussausmon begged him. "What

else do you fear here, in this land which is not yours and is so strange to you?"

"The forest . . . the winter," Ned admitted. "God help me, I don't want to be a coward; but I keep thinking: what if I fell? Or a branch of a tree came down and pinned me down, or even something as little as I set my foot down wrong and turned my leg and couldn't get home? It could be the smallest of things and in this weather I would die before anyone knew I was missing." He took a breath. "They wouldn't find me till spring," he said. "They wouldn't even know I was out there."

Wussausmon put a gentle hand on Ned's shoulder. "Waterman, this is not cowardice, these are real fears of things that might really happen. It is true for me too: when I am sent all round the country on strange paths. Like you, I think: What if I were to make a mistake here and wander into country that I don't know? What if my enemies are waiting for me? What if someone somewhere has lost patience with a man who lives in two worlds but belongs to neither?"

"What d'you do?"

The man grasped Ned's hand and hauled him over the threshold and up the big bank of snow, helped him balance to put on his snowshoes. "Look around," he said. "That's what I do. I look around and I think all the time about what I am doing, not what I will do later or tomorrow, or any dream of tonight. I am here like a bird circling in the sky and always looking down, as the wolf going quietly through the woods, ears up, hackles up, scenting the wind, like the woods themselves always knowing. So I don't misstep or let a branch fall on me because I am watching all the time where I step, what the wind is doing in the trees, what is around me, every moment of the time."

"You watch for accidents as if they were enemies?" Ned asked.

"As if they were companions. They come with me everywhere I go, everything can always go wrong. I walk in a world where I am safe at this moment but who knows what happens next? I watch to see that accidents don't surprise me—but I know they are always there. I make sure they do not creep up on me while I am dreaming of something else." He looked into Ned's face. "You be the same. Don't be in a hurry, like Coatmen always are. Pause, watch, listen, smell, taste, hear, and use that other sense, wolf sense that tells you that something strange is happening even hundreds of miles away, bird sense that guides hundreds of them to move as one, turning at an invisible moment. You have to be dead to your wandering thoughts, never thinking of what has gone or what is coming next year, you have to forget the last step or the next, you have to be locked into here, now."

Ned thought. "Now? The wind now and the trees now?"

"Now, and now, and the next now after that. Where your feet are, and the snow under them, what is above your head and is anyone behind you?"

Ned nodded, thinking of awareness of the world around him, suddenly vivid and bright.

Wussausmon took his arm and looked into his face. "Now, can I teach you to fish?"

Ned grinned. "Yes, you can. And teach me how to watch all the time, as you do."

"You can try," the man promised. "But you are a people whose mind never stays on one thing at a time. Unless it is money."

"I will try," Ned promised.

"Follow me then," Wussausmon ordered. "And follow in my tracks, don't wander like a child."

Feeling the reproof, Ned followed exactly in his tracks through the deep snow, around trees, through clearings, crossing frozen swamp smoothed white under the drifts of snow until they came to a clearing in the forest and a small frozen lake.

"This is a good fishing lake," Wussausmon told him.

"I come here in summer," Ned said uneasily, thinking how deep and still the waters were, even in the heat of summertime.

"So in winter the fish are still here, under the ice."

Ned nodded. "I suppose so. I never thought."

"Of course. So watch: this is how we catch them."

Ned stood back as Wussausmon dropped his fishing pack, a buckskin bag, onto the snowy ice. He selected a tool like a long-handled hoe, showed Ned the bone blade on the end, and then scraped and stabbed. Ned flinched at the first blows, anxiously listening for a warning crack below his feet, but the ice was thick and silent, and as Wussausmon wore a hole through the ice he saw, disbelievingly, the black water slop into the hole inches below. The sides of the ice hole were clear and thick, little pieces of ice broke off and puddled in the bottom. Kneeling on his bag Wussausmon picked them out with a ladle.

"Pass me the decoy," he said over his shoulder, and Ned rooted in the open end of the bag till he found a piece of wood with twine twisted all around it and a little mock fish made of shells, wonderfully jointed so that it moved tail and fin. He handed it to Wussausmon who unwound the twine.

"Spear," he demanded.

Ned drew out a three-pronged spear, on a long pole, and put it into Wussausmon's hand.

"First you look," Wussausmon instructed, rising to his feet and stepping back so Ned could take his place, kneeling on the kit bag, peering into the wet darkness of the hole. He could see nothing; he felt the icy breath of the water frosting his hair, and blinked against the cold in his face. Then slowly, as his eyes made sense of shadows in darkness, he could see the outline of sleeping fish at the bottom of the lake, the pale flank of one, the outline of another. There was something extraordinarily beautiful in the silent sleep of the dormant creatures.

"There are fish!" he whispered, lifting his face to Wussausmon. "I see them."

"Indeed," the man confirmed with a smile. "Now, I am going to catch one, and then you are."

He took up his place leaning over the hole and released the decoy fish into the water, tweaking the twine up and down to make the fish move in the water as if it were swimming. Within moments the big fish had risen up from the depths, Wussausmon had the spear ready and in complete silence, barely even breathing, he made a steady thrust and plunged the spear into the water, brought it back, pulled it out, and laid it on the ice at Ned's feet, a fat writhing large-mouthed bass, speared through the middle.

"Give thanks and kill," he said shortly.

Ned, at a loss for an impromptu prayer, just said: "Thank you, fish, thank you, lake, thank you, Wussausmon," and feeling like a fool clubbed it on the head so it lay still.

"There," Wussausmon said smiling. "You have your first fish of winter. Now you can catch your own," and he stood up from the bag, gestured that Ned should kneel down, and waited, unmoving for a good hour, while Ned jiggled the decoy, speared into the darkness, cursed, got his hands wet, and tried all over again.

NOVEMBER 1670, AT SEA

Sarah had feared she would be seasick, and homesick, but she found that the movement of the boat lulled her to sleep and so the first night was quickly behind her, and when she woke in the morning she could walk easily on the moving deck, and she found the creak of the sails and the constant roll of the waves under the keel were exhilarating. Captain Shore allowed her to sit at the prow of the ship, as long as she did not distract the sailors from their work, and she spent days leaning over the side and watching the waves slide under the keel.

They ate well. Sarah was allowed to put out a line to fish. There were no vegetables or fruit after the first few days, but they took on extra stores in Lisbon. The seas were rough in the Atlantic and a buffeting wind drove the galleon through the water, making the sails strain and the sheets crack, but when they turned into the Mediterranean it grew calmer and even though it was winter in faraway England there were bright sunny days, and Sarah borrowed Captain Shore's big tropical hat when she leaned on the edge of the boat to see dolphin playing in the bow waves. She hardly thought what lay ahead of her, she avoided thinking about it. The enormity of the lie to her mother, the secret voyage, and the task ahead of her, was too much for her to imagine. Sarah let herself revel in the time at sea and not worry about the destination.

DECEMBER 1670, LONDON

Johnnie, coming out of his master's counting house with half a dozen other clerks for his weekly evening off, was astounded to find Livia waiting, the long-suffering Carlotta behind her, at the merchant's door.

"Aunt Livia!" he exclaimed.

"Ooo-er," shouted one of the clerks. "That's not like any aunt of mine."

Johnnie flushed to the roots of his fair hair but Livia laughed at the impertinence. For one horrified moment Johnnie thought she might shout back.

"Ignore them!" he said quickly. "Is Grandma ill? My mother?"

He could think of no reason that his exotic kinswoman should penetrate Bishopsgate, except to take him home for an emergency. "Have you heard from Sarah?" he demanded, suddenly fearful for his twin, so far away at sea.

"No." She laughed happily. "Would I have come across London to a street like this, filled with these dreadful young men, to carry a message from your sister? No, everything is well at home. Nothing has happened. Indeed, I believe that nothing ever happens at home but the turning of the smallest of pennies. I left them playing with Matteo. I came for you. I have a surprise for you."

"What is it?"

Confidently she took his arm and led him down the dark and dirty street, Carlotta trailing unhappily behind them. "Where are we going?"

"Just a little way, for I have some good news for you. But first, I must tell you the price of it."

He felt an immediate sense of caution, as if—however charming she was—any price she might set on anything would be impossibly high. "I have no money," he told her bluntly. "In my pocket I have enough for my dinner, but all my wages I give to Ma, to run the house and warehouse. And she's been very short recently, as I think you know."

"She's been paid," she said sweetly. "She has no complaint. And anyway, I don't want your pennies, darling boy, I want your friendship."

"Well, of course, you have that," he said cautiously.

"Let me explain," she said. "You know I have been engaged in an enterprise selling my antiquities at the house of our old family friend Sir James Avery?"

He nodded, saying nothing, keeping his gaze on her perfect profile as she watched her feet, stepping carefully, down the dirty street.

"Sir James is in my debt," she told him. "I have opened up his house and made it a center for those with an interest in ancient and beautiful things. He has been visited by some of the greatest men at court. I have restored his name to importance." They turned into Leadenhall Street. "You say nothing?"

He felt that she was too flirtatious and clever for him. "I don't know what to say."

"Ah, you are wise to stay silent then. *Allora*—he owes me a favor and I have allowed him to settle his debt to me in the form of an introduction."

"You have?"

"I have. I could have asked for anything, for myself, for Matteo, but I did not. Instead, I have this!" With a flourish she produced the letter from Sir James from under her cloak and pressed it into his hand. "An introduction for you, my dearest nephew."

"I don't want to be intro . . ." he began; but fell silent as she turned him around to face the gloriously ornate facade of the East India Company headquarters. The lower level, facing the street, was conventional enough, a double-height door set to the right of the building, but then on the next floor there were heavy full-height windows letting on to an ornate balcony of wooden carved balustrades, with a great portrait of one of the Company's famous ships in the center. A ship portrait was repeated on the next floor between high leaded windows, and the whole top-floor facade was a massive painting of a ship in full sail. Above that great boast, on the roof of the house, facing east, was a giant statue of a sailor, stick in one hand, hand on hip, as if to dominate the world.

"The East India Company," Johnnie whispered. "You've never got me an introduction into the East India Company?"

She put the letter into his hand. "The East India Company," she confirmed. "One of the writers will see you. That's his name on the letter. I have made you an appointment, it is now. Go in and tell him that Sir James Avery is your patron and supports your application for a place."

She gave him a little push. "Go on, I have done all this for you."

He took one step towards the overwhelming building. "And the price?" he remembered to ask.

She laughed. "A nothing. It is that you be a friend to me, Johnnie. There is no need to go through the books and worry your mother about my debts, there is no need to ask your mother if I should not pay Excise duty. I am sharing in the fortunes of your family—taking; but also giving—see what I am doing for you?"

He blushed red as he remembered that his grandmother thought her an imposter, and that Sarah was hoping to unmask her. "I don't speak against you . . ."

"There is nothing to say against me," she told him. "My reputation, as an honorable widow, has to be unblemished, perfect," she told him.

"I'm sure it is," he stumbled.

"And I have a plan which will be of great benefit to the whole family." She paused for a moment. "I am going to buy a warehouse, a very big warehouse in a good part of town. Your mother and grandmother will live above it, that will be their new home. And your mother and perhaps Sarah will sell the goods, beautiful antiquities which I will order from my store in Venice."

He was stunned. "We know nothing about that business," he said. "We're wharfingers, we ship small loads and—"

"I know what you do. This is completely different. You would work for me."

"I thought you were buying Grandma a house in the country?"

"A better house in clean air," she corrected him. "This will be better. Your mother can work downstairs and be close to her mother all day."

His head was whirling. "Are there enough customers for such things?"

"Yes," she said. "I could have sold my Caesar heads over and over. I am giving your family a great opportunity, Johnnie. I rely on you to advise them to take it."

"What d'you want me to do?" he asked her simply. "Would I still work here?" He glanced longingly at the building.

"Of course, and Sarah could stay at the millinery shop if she wants. This is to give your mother an easier, more profitable business, and your grandmother a more comfortable home. All I want from you is to advise when your mother speaks of it to you. Tell her that it is a good idea."

"But . . ."

"Don't you think it's a good idea? That your mother has a more profitable business and your grandmother a better home? That they trade in rare and valuable goods rather than cheap dirty stuff?"

"Yes, of course."

She extended her hand in the black lace mitten. "Then we have an agreement."

He had to take her hand and at once she drew him near, so close that he could smell the scent of roses from her bonnet, from her dark ringlets of hair. "We are partners," she said. "I will get you the one post that you want in all of London and you will help me to sell the wharf and buy the new house. You will give me your promise."

He blushed furiously, conscious of being an ungrateful fool, a young man, perhaps a stupid young man. "Of course, I can promise my support," he said, horribly embarrassed. "You're my aunt—though you don't look like one. And anything I can do to assist you . . . of course."

"Then we are agreed," she said, and finally released him. "Go and get your appointment. You should start at Easter. I have been very good to you, Johnnie."

"You have," he said fervently.

"And one thing more?"

"Yes?"

"Don't tell them any of this in the warehouse. Not any of it. Not our agreement, not your appointment, not till the day that you start work at Easter."

"But why?" He was bemused. "They will be so pleased!"

"I have my reasons," she said. "I have to make arrangements with Venice, I have to get my second shipment sold. I don't want your mother to feel that I am moving too fast. She has to sell the warehouse and borrow money. You know what she's like, so slow to see opportunity. Do you agree?"

He could not think why he should not agree, it was such a great benefit to him and there was no reason that he should tell his mother until he was about to start. But he was uncomfortably aware that there were secrets in the warehouse where there had never been any before. The unbalanced account books, Sarah's absence, the unpaid Excise duty, Livia's friendship with Sir James, this plan to sell and borrow, and—worst of all—his grandmother's suspicions of her.

"It will not hurt my mother or grandmother if we keep it secret?" he temporized, and she widened her dark eyes at him, the picture of innocence.

"How could it? No! And I would be the last person in the world to harm them," she said. "It is a little secret, just a delay. To spare me embarrassment." She paused. "You know that they do not like Sir James. They do not like my friendship with him. But it brings us wealth, and it brings you this opportunity. I don't want them to quarrel with me when I am trying to do good for them, and especially for you."

"Oh, I see!" he said.

"So we are agreed? I do you this great favor, you tell no one of it, and you remember you are obliged to me."

"I am!" he promised.

"So you can go," she told him. He did not see her raise her face for his kiss as he dashed across the road, dodging between carts, and entered the tall door of East India House at a run.

DECEMBER 1670, VENICE

At dawn, a cold dark December dawn, after more than a month at sea, Sarah heard the order to drop the sails and the ship slowed. Throwing a shawl around her shoulders she ran barefoot up the companionway to the upper deck in time to see a shallow boat rowed like a gondola by a standing oarsman come alongside, and the passenger climb nimbly up a lowered ladder. He greeted Captain Shore with a brief handshake and went to the wheel. The sails were raised again and the ship was underway with the stranger commanding.

"Who's that?" Sarah asked the ship's cook as he went past with two mugs of grog for the Captain and the steersman.

"Pilot," he said. "In his sandolo. Nobody knows the channels and the sandbanks like the *pedotti*. They have to live in Rovigno and guide the ships into the Custom quay."

"This is Venice?" Sarah asked, disappointed by the low-lying sandbars and scrubby islands. "I thought it was a grand city? I thought there were big houses, not just these farms? And some of these are not even islands, they're just sandbars."

The man laughed and went on to the wheel. "You keep watching," he advised her. "We're hours out."

Sarah went to the side and looked out through the gradually lightening mist. A succession of islands emerged, one after another, slowly changing into a landmass dim and purple. The marshy islands and little promontories became bigger, higher in the water, walled, with quays and piers, and then she started to see houses, at first built singly on little islands with a boat moored at the quay at the front, and then the islands were linked one to another, with little bridges and quays. The houses became bigger, more ornate, she could see the tossing heads of trees in beautiful gardens over the high walls, then there were fewer gardens and the houses ran side by side like a terrace with great water doors opening onto the lagoon, which was now narrowing ahead of them to become a broad beautiful canal, and she was no longer at sea but in a city, which looked, not as if it were built on water, but as if it had risen from it and was still dripping.

Sarah was astounded. A London child, she was not overawed by the crowds of people on the narrow quays running inland, nor the mass of water traffic in the broad waterway, but she could not believe the complete absence of horses and carriages and wagons: there were truly no roads, there was no grind of wheels or clatter of hooves, no smell of animals being driven to market. She found she was peering down the canal junctions assuming there must be lanes and fields and stables tucked behind the buildings; but where in London there might have been an alley, here there was the glassy shine of a canal with narrow dark quaysides running alongside it and dozens of low-slung bridges, some no more than a plank levered up on a rope that could be dropped for a pedestrian, and then raised for a passing boat.

On and on they went, the little craft before and behind them, traghetti crossing and recrossing from one side to another, gondolas spearing into the waters of the main channel and then swerving off into mysterious canals, barges loaded with enormous beams of wood, some of them with sharpened ends to be driven into the lagoon bed to form the piles for more new buildings and new quays; galleys, rowed by men bowed over the oars, skiffs, sandoli, wherries, boats of every sort and size.

Sarah's bare feet grew icy cold; but she could not tear herself from the side of the ship watching this extraordinary city unfold. They went past a palace, white as marble standing on a marble quay, blanched and priceless, its huge gates open wide. There were men in dark cloaks walking in the inner marble courtyard, the snowy walls around them pierced with a thousand windows looking down, looking out, missing nothing. Beside the palace was a high bell tower made of brick, set in a vast public square, lined on every side with more white buildings with more dark windows.

Captain Shore yelled an order to dip the standard as a sign of respect to the palace, as the ship went on, down the wide channel between beautiful buildings on each side, falling sheer into the glassy water.

Looking forward, Sarah could see a massive stone quay dividing the canal into two. At the sharply pointed prow of the quay was a high brick watchtower crowned with a four-sided roof and a swinging weathercock. The warehouse walls, crenellated like a castle, stretched back along the white marble quays; the warehouse doors stood in great ranks, on both sides, facing the water. Moored up on both sides of the quays were three or four oceangoing ships like their own, cargo hatches open, loading and unloading at the treble-height doors.

Captain Shore shouted the order to drop the sails, the *pedotti* let the ship nose slowly into her mooring place, and the crew threw lines to the waiting lumpers, who caught them and made them fast. The *pedotti* lashed the steering wheel and put his seal on it, to signify that the ship could not sail again without a pilot on board, threw a casual salute to Captain Shore, pocketed his fee, and was first down the gangplank to take a ship up the Grand Canal on the return journey. He disappeared among the crowd of dockers with sleds and carts for unloading, the officials, and the duty officers.

"Better stop gawping and get your boots on," Captain Shore advised, going past her. "They'll want to see you, an' all."

Sarah ducked down into her cabin, crammed her feet in her boots, packed her few things in her hatbox, slipped her money into her placket, tied her grandmother's red leather purse of tokens around her neck, and went up on deck. Captain Shore, busy with the mooring of his ship, waved her to wait.

"You can't go yet, they have to check you for disease." He nodded at the Venetian officials, dressed in the livery of the Doge, mounting the gangplank. "You have to have your papers before you can disembark."

Sarah stepped back as the two men came on board and took the ship's manifest and the crew list from Captain Shore.

"This passenger?" the first man demanded in perfect English.

"Mrs. Bathsheba Jolly," Sarah said, repeating the name of one of her workmates that she had told Captain Shore. "Of Kensington village, near London."

"In good health?" The official's hard gaze scanned her, looking for a feverish flush in her cheeks, or any trembling. "No swellings or sores?"

She shook her head.

"Have you kept company with the sick?"

"No," Sarah said. "There's no plague in London, thank God."

"You'd have been sent to the lazaretto if there was any chance of plague," he said grimly. "With the whole ship's crew. Left there for forty days' quarantine, however pretty."

"I don't have it," she assured him. "I don't know anyone who has had it. Really."

"Purpose of visit?"

"To collect some furniture belonging to my mistress from her store."

"Address?"

"Palazzo Russo," Sarah replied. "Ca' Garzoni."

"Occupation?"

"I am a milliner, serving Nobildonna da Ricci."

"The safety of the Republic of Venice is the responsibility of every citizen and visitor," the official told her sternly. "If you learn anything that would damage the Republic then you must report it at once. If you do not report it, you are regarded as party to the crime. Equally, if anyone believes that you are working against the Republic then you will be reported and taken up for questioning. Do you understand?"

Sarah swallowed down her unease, nodding obediently.

"The questioning is done inside the Palace of the Doge," the man said. "Everyone always answers. Punishment for wrongdoing is swift and very onerous."

"I understand," Sarah whispered. "But I assure you, I promise that I want no trouble with anyone. I'm a milliner!" She offered her occupation as if to claim that she was as unimportant as a wisp of silk on a bonnet. "Just a milliner! Running an errand."

"Even so, you are required to maintain the safety of the Republic," he repeated. "You are the eyes and ears of the Doge while you are his guest."

Sarah nodded again.

"You tell her how to make a report," the official ordered Captain Shore. "Then she can go ashore."

He produced a paper with a red seal in the corner, scribbled his signature, gave it to Sarah, and turned to start his inspection of the crew and goods.

Sarah showed the paper to Captain Shore. "I have to make a report?" she asked.

"That's your landing papers," he said. "It's called a permesso. They'll ask for your permesso. You show it to any official that asks for it. You have to carry it with you all the time. They know exactly who's here, in the city. This is your passport, you hand it back to them when you come on board to go home, you have to show it for them to let you leave. Keep it safe, you can't leave without it."

"What does he mean that I have to report?"

"If you see or hear anything that you think is a danger to the Republic, you write the name of the person on a slip of paper, and what they said or did, and you feed it to the lion."

"What?"

He smiled grimly at her increasing alarm. "See that lion's head on the dockside? Set into the wall?"

Sarah turned and saw, like a wall fountain, a lion's head carved in marble, its mouth gaping wide. "Yes?"

"It's a postbox. Shaped like a lion, or a wild man, or any kind of thing. You'll see them all over. You put your denunciation into the mouth of the lion—the Bocca di Leone—and one of the officials collects it, they collect every day, and they read everything, everything anyone says, and they arrest those they think might be guilty and take them away."

"But anyone could say anything!" Sarah protested.

"Oh, yes, they do."

"But they must arrest hundreds of people!"

Captain Shore smiled grimly. "That's the idea."

"Where do they take the prisoners?" Sarah asked nervously.

He pointed back down the Grand Canal.

"To the Doge's Palace. You saw that great palace that we came by?"
Sarah nodded.

"He lives there like a king; but he's not a king. He's one of the great
men of Venice, but he prides himself on being a servant of the people.
He works with the Council of Ten. Together, they rule the Republic,
the greatest power in Europe. Hundreds of men, thousands of men
work for him, like a court; but not a court. They don't dance or sing
or play or hunt like our court. They're not a court of fools. They
work, all day, all night, in absolute secret. They make trade treaties
and agreements with every country under the sun, they spy on every
country in the world, they sell to every country in the world, and they
watch their own people, night and day, and pick them up at the least
sign of trouble. The people of Venice have the wealthiest, safest city
in the world because they're watched, night and day, by themselves."

"A city of spies?"

"Exactly. You didn't mention meeting your husband to the officer?"

"He asked me what was the purpose of my visit—so I told him
about my work."

"As you wish. But if he asks me, I'm not going to lie for you."

"No," she said. "It's not a secret. I just didn't mention it."

He laughed shortly. "No such thing in this city." He took up a rope
and lashed the gangplank tighter to the stanchion on deck. "There,
you've got your papers, you're certified clean, I've told you how to report, you can go. Into a city of spies." He looked at the young woman.
"That steward—he'll bring your choice of goods to the quay here?
And do the paperwork like last time? He has to declare it at the Custom House. If he says it's private furniture, it's his own word on it,
not mine."

Sarah nodded. "Can you tell me how to find him?" she asked humbly. "I have his address, I thought it would be easy to find—but I
didn't expect it to be all water . . ."

He laughed shortly. "You have the address of his house?"

"I thought I'd walk down a road!"

He pointed to one of the idling children. "Get one of them to lead
you," he said.

"Are they safe?" Sarah asked doubtfully, looking at the crowd of begging children.

"This is Venice," he said again. "Nobody commits a crime unless they are unseen in complete darkness and probably working for the state. Nobody dares. Pay the lad a farthing. And pay the boatman what he asks. They don't cheat either."

"They don't cheat?" she asked incredulously.

"They don't dare. They'd be reported at once. And come back inside two weeks. We sail as soon as we are loaded, we're not allowed to stay beyond our time. Already they've issued our papers. If you're not here, I'll go without you. And get the goods here sooner rather than later; they'll want to inspect them."

"I will."

"And if you hope to bring your husband home with you, he'll have to have his papers in order."

"Yes, yes," she said.

"And take care," he warned her. "Everyone here is either a spy or a villain. Or both."

She hesitated at the top of the gangplank. "You make it sound like a nightmare."

"It is," he said dourly. "Your own husband will report you. If he's still alive."

DECEMBER 1670, LONDON

In the absence of Sarah and her neat stitches, Alys was sewing bags for sassafras tea with her mother. They worked at the round table in the glazed balcony of Alinor's room so they could catch the wintry light as the gray mist sighed against the windows and the low cloud billowed on the roof.

"Can you see to work?" Alys asked. "Shall I get candles?"

"We can't have candles in the middle of the day," Alinor replied. "I can see well enough." She took a pinch of herbs and laid them on a new square of cheesecloth. "Has she finished selling her goods? Are they all gone?"

Alys noted that now her mother never named Livia, just as she never named Sir James.

"Yes, they're all sold. I believe he's going to his home in the north, for the winter season. When he comes back to London, I suppose she'll put the new load up for sale in his house again."

"Has she given you the money she made?"

"No, it's at his goldsmith's for safekeeping," Alys said without a tremor.

"He's her partner? And you don't object?" her mother asked curiously.

"How can I object? I don't have a beautiful warehouse where she can show her things, I don't have an account at a goldsmith's where she can keep her money. I can't make demands of her or bring her down to our—"

"You're besotted with her," Alinor said quietly, and saw the deep blush spread across her daughter's face.

"I love her as a sister," Alys said stiffly.

"And does she love you?"

"Yes, when she's not at his house or chasing after his friends to buy her goods, I think she is happiest. When it is just her and me, she's at peace. In the future—if we can buy our own warehouse and run the business together—we'll be completely happy."

"You have to buy her a warehouse?"

"If I can, I will," Alys said. "It's our future."

"What if it turns out that she has deceived us?" Alinor named the worst fear.

"She hasn't," Alys said. "She wouldn't deceive me."

DECEMBER 1670, VENICE

The quay was bordered with hard white paving stones, the very pavements of Venice were priceless stone. Jostled by porters and gondoliers, passersby and street sellers, Sarah walked slowly, feeling unsteady after so long at sea, as if the ground was heaving like waves. She did not feel safe to linger before the Custom House, among the watching officials, so busy and stern. A guard on one of the bolted warehouse gates stared at her and she moved away, knowing that he was watching her go.

She rested her hatbox at the side of a stone bridge and looked inland, along a canal, marveling how the walls of the houses went sheer into the water, like brightly painted cliffs. Every great house had a water gate with an upright striped mooring pole for the private black gondola. One or two houses had left their water gates opened wide to the glassy canal, and she could see the shadowy interior, the water lapping gently against the marble stair as if the lagoon itself was a tenant.

Sarah felt in the pocket of her cape for the address of the house of Livia's old steward. When Johnnie had put it in her hand she thought it would be easy to find; but now, with streets of water and a spiderweb of narrow alleyways, she thought she was certain to get lost.

"Hey!" She beckoned one of the begging children and two little boys approached her. She showed them the piece of paper but neither of them could read. "Ca' Garzoni," she said. "Signor Russo. Russo!"

One boy turned to the other and spoke a stream of Venetian Italian, quite incomprehensible to Sarah. She tightened her grip on her hatbox and the little boy nodded to her and set off at a rapid pace, glancing back and beckoning that she should follow him. He went down to the quayside where a traghetto was taking on passengers to cross. The ferryman showed her an open palm, the international gesture for money, and she gave him an English halfpenny for herself and the two boys, and cautiously stepped from the wet steps into the rocking craft. The boatman poled them across, weaving around the canal traffic to the steps on the other side. The little boys sprang out and Sarah followed them, squeezing around women with baskets of shopping, market women with big panniers of goods, the watermaids with yokes on their shoulders loaded with slopping buckets of fresh water.

Sarah followed the boys down a narrow lane, houses on either side, some serving as little shops, a shutter propped over an open window, the windowsill serving as a counter for goods. Some were workshops, with a tailor seated cross-legged in the window for the light, or a cobbler bent over his last. She dawdled by the hat shop, marveling at the delicacy of the work and the richness of the fabrics, longing to go in and see the premises, the girls, and the exquisite patterns.

Every street led to water, every pavement ran alongside the smooth surface of a canal, or headed to a wooden bridge to connect one tiny lane to another. The canals were crowded with the little boats of traders going into the markets of the city carrying fruit and flowers and fish, local people ferrying their goods and delivering their products, and threading through it all, the sleek pitch-black gondolas with the gondoliers standing carelessly beautiful, high in the stern and propelling themselves and their passengers steadily forward, poling their craft through the canal traffic like needles through patchwork, calling a warning at every corner like the cry of a strange seabird: "Gondola! Gondola! Gondola!"

Every house had a tiny door on the narrow street for tradesmen or servants, but the grand door, the front door for visitors, residents, and guests, faced onto the water and opened to the lapping canal, so a boat could enter the house like a horse going into a stable and visitors could disembark on the private indoor quay. Sarah, peering through the open water gates, could see one or two gondoliers waiting for their masters, dressed in the house livery, straw hat in one hand, the other hand on the rearing prow of his craft, like a groom holding a horse. Someone jostled Sarah and she stopped staring and walked on.

The boys went through lane after lane and up and down over bridges and finally came to a great square with a central domed stone well in the center, caged in a heavy iron grating, surrounded by tall buildings. The little boys pointed to one with a small dark doorway and RUSSO carved in the stone over the arched door.

The boys closed on her, hands out again, Sarah gave them each another farthing, and made a shooing gesture that they should leave her. They did not argue as London urchins would have argued, they each made a little bow and disappeared in a moment down an alleyway. Sarah straightened her bonnet and strode to the door, knocked, stood back, and waited. There was a long silence and she knocked again, wondering what she should do if Livia had misled them all, and this was the house of a stranger, or an empty house. Then she heard the sound of bolts being shot back inside, the door creaked open, and a handsome man in his early thirties waited silently in the doorway. Sarah, with her keen judgment of men, honed by her apprenticeship in the millinery shop, scanned him from his expensive shoes, up his well-made suit of velvet, to his dark handsome face. She took in the gold signet ring on his finger and the slight scent of bay and vanilla. She noted the dark eyes and the slow, almost unwilling smile, which seemed to warm as he saw her, as if he were glad to find her on his doorstep. She found she could not stop herself smiling in return.

"Well, signorina!" he exclaimed, opening his door wide, speaking English. "I am Signor Russo at your service, and how may I help you?"

Sarah, dropping a little curtsey, realized that this was certainly not the elderly steward who had loved Rob like a grandson.

"Forgive me," she said. "I am looking for Signor Russo."

He bowed. "You have found him."

"I am looking for Signor Russo the elder."

"I am the oldest of my line," he said. "Who are you?"

"I am Bathsheba Jolly, from London," she said. "Nobildonna da Reekie's maid. How did you know I am English?"

He shrugged. "Your hat," he said. Sarah sensed this was not a compliment to English style. "Your perfect skin."

Now, she blushed. "I have brought a message from her ladyship."

He hesitated for a moment as if he were thinking rapidly, and then he opened the door. "Forgive my surprise. You come with a message from the Nobildonna? Of course you do! Then you must come in, come in. Forgive the state of the entrance, mostly my guests come by gondola to the water gate. Only the English would walk in Venice. Nobody else uses the street door."

"Of course, I am too English," Sarah said, speaking at random. "My lady laughs at me for it."

"She is well?" he asked, leading the way across the hall, which was floored with red-and-white pavers set diagonally, empty but for two giant statues one either side of the hall, glaring at each other with sightless eyes. He led the way up a set of wide marble stairs. Sarah followed and they came out to a first-floor salon where the grand windows looked over the greenish lapping canal.

"She is very well, extremely well," Sarah enthused, taking in the marble floor and the large marble table surrounded with weighty dining chairs of mahogany upholstered in golden velvet. The room was lined with statues, and hanging behind each one, on the silk-lined walls, were beautiful gold-framed mirrors to show every side of the polished marble figures. Sarah blinked at the opulence and looked up to see a magnificently painted ceiling and a glass chandelier reflected in the shine of the table, the glass blown into flower-like shapes in radiant colors. "Oh! What a beautiful room."

He bowed in acknowledgment. "May I take your box? Your cape, Miss Jolly?" He hesitated. "A handsome hatbox. 'Sarah' is the name of your milliner?"

She let him take her cape from her shoulders and felt the light touch of his hands. "Yes, I mean, no!" she said. "That is—I don't have a milliner—that's where I used to work."

"It is your first time in Venice? You must find it all very strange."

"I cannot stop staring. Every way I look there is something more lovely."

"The English love our city," he agreed. "Some for its houses, some for its people. But you have an eye for beauty."

She made a little gesture at the statues that lined the room. "You have beautiful things in your sight all the time."

"But I never take them for granted," he assured her. "It is an art to

learn—don't you think? To be surrounded by beauty and never become blind to it. The art of a good husband? To never become dulled
to something precious?"

"Oh, yes," said Sarah. "Of course, you must get used to it, but
sometimes it strikes you anew."

"And what do you love most?" he asked, as if her reply mattered to
him. "I have a warehouse, you know, of beautiful things. What should
I show you to strike you anew?"

She laughed and thought to herself that she sounded affected. She
tried to be more sober, but his intense attention made her feel giddy.
"I worked as a milliner," she confided. "I was surrounded by lovely
fabrics. But the thing I loved best were the feathers."

He laughed aloud. "You love feathers?" he said. "*Allora!* I shall take
you to the feather warehouse and you shall see every feather of every
bird under the sun."

"You have feather markets here?"

"In Venice, you can buy anything in the world as long as it is expensive and beautiful," he told her, and smiled at the brightness in
her face. "I will take you to the feather market and to the velvet warehouse, also to the silks markets. There is a lace market and some beautiful cloth from India for saris. But I am wasting your time, forgive
me. You will be here to work. Did the Nobildonna send you to me?"

"Yes." Sarah felt the scrutiny of his dark eyes on her face as she
lied. "She needs more sculptures. They have sold so well, that she
needs more."

He raised his dark eyebrows. "Why did she not send the Captain?"

"She wanted me to pick them out with you," Sarah had prepared
for this question. "I sailed with her captain, and she wants me to
travel home with them, to make sure that they are kept safe, and arrive safely."

"She does not trust him? He sold her short last time?"

"No! No! She has no complaint; but she is afraid of accidents, if you
send more delicate pieces."

He scrutinized her for a moment. "And you were her choice of
courier? Being so strong to lift them? And so fierce to defend them?"

Sarah tried to laugh but knew that she sounded nervous. "I am her only choice, for she has no money to pay wages for anyone else, you know? I am employed as a maid at the house where she lives, Mrs. Reekie's house. I am maid to Mrs. Reekie. So they lent me to her for free, and she said that I must help you pack the things and bring them home."

"She trusts you with me?" he suggested.

"Yes," Sarah stumbled, feeling there was something behind the question that she could not guess.

"And she trusts me with you?"

"Why not?" she said boldly, her heart beating in her ears.

"You have a letter of authorization?"

Sarah clutched her box and looked distressed. "In my other bag, with my money," she said remorsefully. "But I was robbed on the way to the ship in London! I am so sorry. It was a sealed letter so I don't even know what she said to you."

"Did you lose your money too?"

She nodded. "I have enough for my keep here, that I had in my placket, but a wicked child snatched my bag and ran."

He smiled at her. "Poor Miss Jolly," he said. "So if you could not defend your own bag, how shall you rescue the treasures from pirates?"

"I am sure that the Captain will defend his ship," she said, feeling that every smiling comment was a trap.

"For sure he will. And I see you are . . . intrepid. I shall call you Brave Miss Jolie, for you are."

"Brave?" she asked.

"And Jolie."

"Pretty?" she confirmed.

"Very," he said.

There was a silence while she absorbed this, and thought she had nothing to say in reply.

"Never tell me that I am the first man to tell you?"

Her blush told him that he was the first man that she had heard.

"*Allora!* Then I am a lucky man!" he said. "Now, what may I do for you? Shall you dine? Where are you staying?"

"I came straight here from the ship," she replied. "I will find an inn tonight and tomorrow come back at your convenience? And shall we go to your warehouse?"

"You are here already," he said. "This is my workshop, and my palazzo. We Venetians all work, we are not like your English lords. My dining room is where I show my antiquities. Everything you see here is for sale." He gestured out of the window. "Everything in Venice is for sale: from a whisper, to a mountain of gold."

Sarah nodded, trying not to look overwhelmed.

"You shall stay here," Signor Russo decided. "I will not hear a word against it. You shall sleep with my little sister in her bedroom. My mother will greet you and show you to your room. And then you and I shall go out for dinner, it's just around the corner and perfectly good. We dine early like the Doge. And after dinner I will show you the pieces I have here, and you will make your choice of what La Nobildonna would like. If you agree?"

Sarah smiled. "Of course," she said. "Thank you. But I can easily find an inn and come back here."

"My mother would never forgive me," he assured her.

He opened the door and called up the stairs. "In Venice we have our kitchens under the roof, it is better in case of fire, you know? And here she is."

A broad smiling woman came down the stairs, was told Sarah's assumed name, and kissed her warmly on both cheeks. Her son instructed her in rapid Italian that Sarah could not follow, and the woman took the hatbox and led Sarah into a room overlooking the canal furnished with a curtained bed, and—even here—a great many marble figures.

"Yes, these too are for sale!" Signor Russo said from the doorway. "You shall examine them when you are rested. But we will leave you to make yourself at home and I will come for you in an hour or so. Rest now."

"I can go to dine alone," Sarah protested. "I don't want to be any trouble."

"No, I shall come with you. It is the greatest city in the world, but unsuitable for a beautiful young woman."

"There are thieves?" she asked, glancing towards her box, safe on the bed.

"Of every legal sort, and lechers," he said. "Gamblers and spies. I am sorry to say we are decadent, Miss Jolie. We are all sinners in this most angelic of cities. You will find yourself much desired."

Sarah tried to laugh carelessly, like a woman of the world, but found she giggled. He smiled at her and ushered his mother from the room and closed the door and there was silence.

DECEMBER 1670, HADLEY, NEW ENGLAND

Darkness held the sky from afternoon till midmorning, ice held the lakes and ponds, snow held Ned's door closed so that every morning he had to break out like a man under siege. The path to the animals in their stall had to be dug out almost every day as the snow fell without ceasing; he did not even attempt to clean their pen, he just piled straw on straw so they were deep-littered on a thick bed.

Ned's food stores were covered with a drift of snow and had to be dug out, but the maize was keeping well and the jars of dried berries. He had enough to trade when he made his weekly trek into Hadley for extra supplies. Ned forced himself to struggle down the common grazing lane, now a snowy plain of white, supplying dried goods to his customers, demonstrating his faith at the meetinghouse, and his loyalty to the men in hiding.

They had no need for a guard at the ferry in this weather. No Englishman would brave the woods in winter, no Englishman would dare put a boat on the river in this weather. The settlers were uncertain canoeists in the shallow rivers of summer, none of them would take to the icy water in winter floods when floes of ice came tumbling down on the deep waters and a fall into the river would mean almost certain death. In midwinter the rivers would freeze solid, the icy current moving darkly under a treacherous sheet of ice. Any accident in this weather, indoors or out, was sure to be fatal. Ned woke every morning with a sense of relief that his fire had kept in, that he had survived another night. He spent his days in wearying anxiety—fearing a fall as if he were an old man, fearing the cold as if he were a girl, fearing the dark and the howl of the wolves on the other side of the bank as if he were a superstitious townsman.

One morning he was amazed to hear the clang of the iron on the bar beside the pier, as if someone wanted to summon him, a ferryman, to a frozen river. He had to put on his fur hat, his buckskin cape, his buckskin leggings, his thick mittens, his moccasins, and his oiled cape before he could open his door, kick aside the snowdrift, and step into his basketwork shoes onto the high bank of snow. He tramped around to the side of his house, thinking that he must have imagined the summons, but there, strolling towards him on the top of the bank, coming from the forest, light-footed as a winter hare on his snow-shoes, was Wussausmon, dressed in native winter clothes. Ned peered from under the brim of his thick fur hat at his friend, who seemed half-naked. "Good God, man! Are you not freezing?"

"I'm wrapped up warm enough," Wussausmon said cheerfully. "You beware that someone doesn't mistake you for a bear and shoot you. Where did you get that hat?"

"Made it myself," Ned said. It was a pair of cured rabbit skins, stitched clumsily together, covering his head and the back of his neck. He had a scarf sent by Alinor from London, knitted wool, wrapped around his mouth which was rapidly growing a beard of freezing ice from his breath.

Wussausmon suppressed a laugh. "I've brought you some fresh meat," he said. "I was hunting in the woods outside Norwottuck and Quiet Squirrel said you'd be glad of it."

"I am," Ned said, the juices rushing into his mouth at the thought of it. "I haven't shot a thing for weeks."

"They said you'd not been out for days."

Ned glanced away from Wussausmon's bright gaze. "I don't like to hunt alone," Ned said shortly.

"Why not?"

Ned hesitated to explain his fear. "If the weather closed in . . ."

Wussausmon was genuinely uncomprehending. "What?" he asked. "What would happen if the weather closed in?"

Ned ducked his head, awkward in his shame, lowered his voice though there was no one around the two men but the bare black trees, their trunks striped with snow. "I wouldn't be able to find my way home."

"Find your way home? In your own woods? To your own home? Why ever not?"

Ned shook his head, feeling embarrassed. "I get snow blind," he said. "I can't tell which way I am facing. If it snows heavily—I'm lost."

"How can you not know where you are on your own land? It's so strange."

Ned could not argue that it was strange not to know the way to your own door. He shrugged, embarrassed. "Aye; but I don't."

"D'you want to come over to Norwottuck with me? We're roasting venison."

Ned hesitated, longing for company, a warm fire, a good dinner, and the sound of other voices. But he looked at the gray skim of ice and the banked-up ice floes frozen in the river. "How would we get there?"

"We'll walk."

Ned tasted fear in his throat. "On the river? How d'you know it's safe?"

Wussausmon held out his hand. "I just do. Come on. I won't drop you through it."

Ned gripped the outstretched hand. "You'd better not." He tried to smile. "I'd sink like a stone in these coats."

Wussausmon led the way on the snow-topped pier, and then sat at the end, swung his legs round, and stepped down to the snowy river. He took half a dozen steps away into the middle of the river. "See?" he said to Ned. "It bears my weight. It will hold you."

Ned clenched his teeth on his fear and followed his friend, putting his feet exactly in Wussausmon's tracks. There was a creak from the ice and he froze, imagining at once the long snaking crack and his plunge down into deadly black water.

"It's nothing," Wussausmon assured him. "That's nothing. That's just it yielding to you. The warning noise is when it splinters, lots of little cracks at once."

Ned could not answer, he slid as gently as he could towards the other man. "Go on, go on," he said. "I don't want to come too close. I daren't stand still."

Wussausmon turned and led the way, stepping over Ned's ferry rope, frozen stiff with dripping icicles, passing the ferry's snow-capped landing place, upstream, to where the white drifted snow of the bank met the white drifted snow on the river. There was no way of knowing when they were on the shore until Wussausmon beamed at Ned. "And here you are!" he exclaimed. "Dry land. We're on the other side."

Ned grinned and gave a little chuckle at his own fear. "Thanks be to God! You'll think me a coward."

"No," Wussausmon said. "I don't blame you for fearing it." He led the way up the bank and away from the river, at a steady sliding pace, deeper into the woods, following a trail that was invisible to Ned, only stopping once, when they had to cross a strange rut, like a wagon wheel track, carved half a foot deep into the snow, curving through the forest from the south, running north towards the village. Beside it was a log tied to a rope and as they went past, Wussausmon picked up the rope, dropped the log into the rut, and towed it along, clearing it of drifted snow.

"What's this? This track?" Ned asked. "What is it?"

Wussausmon glanced behind him, still towing the log, which slid easily on the bed of packed snow. "It's for a snowsnake," he said.

Ned recoiled. "A snowsnake?" he repeated. "You have snakes here? In the snow?"

Wussausmon laughed. "No. No, Coatman! Coatman! Are you mad? All the real snakes are sleeping; they would die of the cold. This is our track, we make it as the snow starts to fall. It's how we send mes-sages in winter. We make a deep icy narrow track from one village to another, like this—this is one. And then if we have a message which is urgent, we throw a spear with the message into the entrance of the track. It goes fast, sliding along, and someone picks it up and throws it onward. Like your letters that you send to one another."

He saw Ned's amazed expression. "Only our messages can go through snowy woods and yours cannot."

Ned peered at the narrow rut, icy at the bottom, and imagined a spear whistling along it. "It goes fast?"

"As fast as a man can throw at the beginning—killing speed—and it rattles along, writhing like a snake as it slows down. Then when anyone sees it, they pick it up, read the message, and throw it again. Village to village." Wussausmon laughed at Ned's astonished face. "We're not as savage as you think."

"So even in winter, when us settlers are snowed in, you can send messages one to another, all around the country," Ned said slowly.

Wussausmon nodded. "And smoke signals," he pointed out. "We can send messages with smoke. On a calm day you can make a fire on Montaup and the signal will be seen at Accomack."

"Montaup? Accomack?"

"You call it Mount Hope. Accomack you call Plymouth."

"And you can travel in winter too," Ned went on. "When we can't go on the river or into the forests."

"It's not your home in winter, is it?" Wussausmon pointed out. "In winter it's ours again, as if the land and the people had never been parted, as if you had never come."

Wussausmon turned and went on and Ned labored to keep up with the steady shush-shush of his pace. The village came into sight ahead of them, a cluster of long low huts, walled with reed mats, roofed with thicker mats, the snow cleared all around them, a central fireplace with a huge fire and a whole deer roasting on a spit, a frame to the side where the hide was being cleaned, a big bowl of seething succotash in the embers. Fighting men were sorting spears and weapons in a corner of the village, a man, stripped to the waist because of the heat of the fire, was putting small metal bolts into the heart of red hot embers, drawing them out and hammering. Ned saw, with a pang of dread, that he was making pieces for a musket.

"See that?" Wussausmon indicated the half-built rearing wooden wall of a huge palisade.

"You're walling the village, you're building a fort here," Ned accused him.

"Yes," Wussausmon said. "So that no one can take this village and burn us out."

"You mean like the English did at Mystic Fort? But that was years ago. Nobody would burn you out of here."

"Then what is the Hadley militia drilling for?"

"They're not drilling now," Ned said.

"Just because you can do nothing in winter does not mean that our lives have to stop too."

"So this winter, while we hibernate like bears, you're preparing for war," Ned accused him. "You send messages in ways that we can't understand, we don't even know! You're bringing the tribes together: against us. You're walling the village, you're collecting weapons—I saw what he was making! You're getting ready for a war."

"Yes," Wussausmon confirmed. "That's why I brought you here—so you should see for yourself. We're getting ready—here, and at Montaup, all round the country, all the other tribes are getting ready too. I've warned the governor over and over again but he won't make a new peace treaty with the Pokanoket, he won't listen to our complaints. But if you, a settler, a soldier, tell him you have seen this, you have seen us armed and ready, he will believe you. I can't make him listen to me."

Quiet Squirrel came out of one of the houses and stood beside Wussausmon, her dark eyes on Ned.

"Come for dinner with us, take home gifts, you are welcome," Wussausmon said. "And tell them at Plymouth and Boston that they cannot go on like this. They have to stop at our boundaries, they have to respect our limits. I am showing you this so you can tell them, Ned."

"Tell them, Coatman," Quiet Squirrel said to him. "Be a peace bringer. Make them understand."

DECEMBER 1670, LONDON

Sir James was leaving for Northallerton, anxious to get to his home before the winter weather grew any worse. Avery House was to be shut up for the season. Livia shouldered Glib out of the way as he opened the front door and marched into the hall, hoping to persuade James to postpone the journey.

"I am sorry, everything is wrapped up here," James said to her. "I did not expect you today." He met her in the black-and-white checkered hall, as Glib labored up the stairs and slowly carried boxes down and out of the front door to strap them on the back of the hired carriage. The last of the statues were labeled and ready for collection in the hall beside them. Livia could see through the open door to the parlor that the furniture was draped with holland wraps.

"But I have a new consignment of antiquities coming," she said, putting her hand on his arm. "How am I to show them?"

"My dear!" He looked genuinely perturbed. "Why are they sending more? You know I cannot show them again. That was a first and last experience!" He tried to smile, but her grip on his arm tightened.

"They are my dower, the very last few things!" she said. "I thought you would allow me. In this house, which is to be my home?"

"I can't sell another collection," he said firmly. "One was bad enough. The people who came, Livia, and their belief that they could come time and again until they had decided, the way you had to barter and haggle with them! It was intolerable to me—to you too, I would have thought? The future Lady Avery will not hawk goods like a pedlar."

"It is my dower!" she whispered stubbornly, her lower lip trembling. "It is all I have in the world."

He hesitated and then found a solution. "I know! What is left of your dower shall come with you. You can put the pieces in the house and in the garden, here and at Northallerton. It can be the fortune that you bring me, my dearest. Not your widow's dower but your bridal dowry! How would that be? You shall make me into a collector, like your first husband! How is that?"

"Generous!" she said, trying to smile. "And so like you! Thank you, my darling. So will you give me the keys to the house so I can bring in my little things and make it ready for your return?"

James shook his head, his mind already on his journey. "Store them at the warehouse," he advised. "You don't want the worry of them here."

She tried to laugh. "I don't mind!"

"No," he said. "Avery House is being closed up. Let me leave you safely with the ladies at the warehouse, moving them to a new home with the money you have so cleverly earned for them, with your little treasures stored safe. I will go north and make everything ready for you there."

"I don't like you to go so far away!"

"I shall be back as soon as I can."

"We should announce our engagement now," she pressed him. "Before you go." She had a superstitious fear that if he left London without her, he would never return.

"When I come back," he promised. "But I have to see my aunt at Northside Manor and tell her that my circumstances have changed. I have to tell the minister I want the banns called, and then we can announce our betrothal and I will send for you."

"But this will all take so long!"

"There's so much to do."

"I shall miss you so!" She tried to press herself against him, to remind him of desire, but the front door stood open and Glib was coming and going and James did not dream of embracing her in public. "Oh, James, don't go! Write and tell them to do everything! Surely you can just write?"

"My love, I would if I could; but I must—I really must—tell my aunt of our betrothal. I cannot write such news to her, it would distress her. I must tell her in person, I have to see her and explain. She would never forgive me if I thrust you on her without giving her time to prepare. She will want to order new curtains, and new carpets, for Lady Avery's parlor, and new sheets for the bed. Give us time to get your new home ready for you."

"But I want to choose my own things!"

He smiled. "You shall make it over if there is anything you don't like," he promised. "Besides, you have Matteo to care for, and you have to go on with your instruction in the Church of England, and a new house to find for the ladies. You have too much to do already!"

"I can't get my money from the goldsmith's without you," she pointed out. "And I need money to put down on a new warehouse for them." She put her hand on his sleeve. "I can't do it without you," she said softly.

He hesitated, hearing the rumble of wheels on cobbles as the carriage came to the door.

"At least stay another day and take me to the goldsmith's," she pressed him. "I have to have my money to pay for my shipping from Venice."

He threw a harassed glance towards the front door which stood open, the carriage outside. "How much do you need?"

"Fifty pounds for the shipping," she lied quickly, guessing that he would not know. "And a pound for Alys's housekeeping."

Glib was carrying smaller boxes past them and James stopped him. "Put that one down."

Glib put the small chest down and stepped back. "You can load the others," James said to him, and when the footman turned away, he took a small key from his waistcoat pocket and opened the chest.

Livia's gaze raked the box which was filled with promissory notes and a few purses of coins. "Are you not afraid of thieves?" she asked.

"I have to have coin in Yorkshire." He lifted a small purse from the chest and counted out coins. "Fifty-one pounds," he said. She watched him put the purse back in its place.

"And you will send for me?"

"I will," he promised. "Of course." He locked the chest and gestured to Glib that he should load it in the carriage. "I can't keep the horses waiting," he said.

"James!" she whispered urgently.

But he was blind and deaf to her, thinking of his long journey to his beloved home. "Glib will take you back to the warehouse," he promised her.

A swift kiss on her hand, not on her mouth, then he bowed to her and walked out of the hall, down the three shallow steps to the street, and got in the carriage. The door was closed on him, the horses strained against the harness and, in a moment, he was gone.

Glib escorted Livia to the water stairs, called a boat with a shrill whistle, and accompanied her as the boatman rowed them down the river to the wharf. The tide was ebbing, he held the boat steady at the foot of Horsleydown Stairs. She climbed the greasy steps, rising up from the stinking low-water level as if she were coming up from a dank hell, Glib following her. In front of the warehouse she turned to him. "Come for me the moment that your master tells the household that he is returning," she said. A silver shilling went from her gloved hand to his.

He took the coin, the first she had ever given him. "Won't he send for you himself?" he asked.

"I am ordering you to come and tell me before he arrives," she repeated, her voice sharp. "Of course, he will send for me, but I want to be ready. I want to know the moment he plans to return to London. Do as you're told, and I will pay you again."

Glib bowed and palmed the coin.

"And bring me any other news," she added. "If he writes to say the house is to be opened. If he writes to say the house is to be closed. Tell me his plans."

"Won't he write you himself?" Glib asked impertinently, but then wilted under the dark look of spite that she shot at him.

"When I am Lady Avery, and you can be very sure that I will be Lady Avery, shall you want a place in my household? Because I will be Lady Avery and I will be the one that hires the household staff. Or dismisses them."

He dropped his head. "Yes, your ladyship. Of course I want to keep my place."

"Then I have told you how to earn it," she said, and turned to the warehouse door, clicked the latch, and went in.

Alys was in the counting house at the high clerk's desk. Livia came in taking off her cape and leaned against her sister-in-law's shoulder, seeking comfort. Alys put an arm around her but kept the page open, finishing her work. Livia ran her eye down the column of figures. "Is that all?"

"Yes, that's all."

"It's hardly worth doing?"

"It keeps us."

"It wouldn't have paid for my shoes in Venice!"

"I expect you had very lovely shoes," Alys said with a smile. "We earn enough to keep a household; but there's very little profit. We're too far from the legal quays to pick up waiting ships, and I can't afford to bribe the lightermen for them to bring us trade."

"We have to buy a new warehouse. You have to borrow the money, Alys. We have to move upriver. You know I'll help."

"I know." Alys turned and kissed her sister-in-law on the lips. "You are the greatest good in my life, in every way."

"My second batch of antiquities will come soon," Livia observed. "We should buy the warehouse now and show them there."

"Livia . . ." Alys took a breath, determined to tell Livia that Sarah would come home with the antiquities. "Livia, I have to tell you . . ."

Livia crossed the room laid her cheek against Alys's. *"Mia amica del cuore."*

"What does that mean?" Alys leaned from the clerk's stool into Livia's arms.

"My sweetheart," Livia whispered. "My heart."

DECEMBER 1670, VENICE

Sarah and Signor Russo dined in a little canalside restaurant and then he took her home by gondola, seating her in the stern and smiling at her delight. Behind her, standing tall, was the gondolier, who poled them down the canal with casual grace. When they entered the Grand Canal it was clear that all of Venice was boating on the clear frosty night. Some gondolas had little cabins and when the doors were closed and the lights flickered from the windows there were hidden lovers inside, enjoying an assignation. Other gondolas carried single ladies, robed in capes, masks held over their faces, weaving through the crowded river so that they could meet their friends and attract attention. Single noblemen reclined in the prow of their gondolas, scanning the boats for new beauty, novelty. Young men shared a bottle of wine and someone was singing, a clear tenor voice echoing over the water.

"They meet? People meet each other?" Sarah asked, trying to hide her shock at the open licentiousness.

Signor Russo smiled at her. "I told you everything was for sale," he said. "And everyone."

They turned down the canal that washed at the great doors of the Russo house, and with careless skill the gondolier spun his craft around and swirled them into the internal quay. Signor Russo helped Sarah from the rocking boat and guided her up the stairs to the hall. The house was scented with the light smell of clean cold water.

"And now, are you tired, would you like to go to your bed? Mamma will make you a hot chocolate to help you sleep? Or would you like to see the Nobildonna's collection?"

"I should like to see her collection," Sarah replied. "If it's not too late for you?"

He smiled. "Ah, I am a night owl. Like justice, I never sleep." He smiled at her. "That's what they say at the Doge's Palace, you know? That justice never sleeps. It's to remind us all that they can arrest anyone at any moment."

"It must be . . ." Sarah could not find the words. "Uneasy?"

"They do the torturing at night," he remarked. "So as not to disturb the clerks working in the nearby offices during the day."

"They torture?"

"At night. We never forget that we are being watched," he told her. "We never forget that they are listening. To be a Venetian is to be continually under suspicion. But there is a pleasure in knowing that your neighbor, your friend, even your husband is under constant suspicion too." He laughed at her shocked face. "So! We trust nobody."

He opened his jacket and took a key from around his neck. He went across the grand hall towards the back of the house, and opened a small locked door. "The Nobildonna's collection," he said. "And my humble store."

The long vaulted room was cold and eerie in the light of the candles. All around, on the floor, on tables, and mounted on their own ivy-winding columns, were bodies, and pieces of beautiful bodies, their sightless eyes gazing at Sarah as if they were a frozen ballroom of dancers. Sarah recoiled on the threshold and looked around her, towards the back where cleft and clipped torsos were stored on shelves, where odd arms faced right and left with exquisite fingers and perfect nails. At the foot of the shelves were beautifully shaped calves and the dainty feet of nymphs and the sandaled feet of heroes with arched insteps. On the top shelf were chipped heads with braided stone hair, ribbons fluttering forever in an ancient wind, and the occasional noble profile and the strong smile of a hero.

Stone dust made the floor snow white, ghosts filled the room like stone mist.

"They were real people?" the girl whispered.

"I don't know," he said casually, as if it did not matter. "They are beautiful. And old. That's all we care about now."

"But this woman—" Sarah gestured to the top half of a face, sliced by a plow, whose eyelids still crinkled in a smile. "We don't know who she was, nor where she came from? Not who she's looking at, to make her smile on him?"

Signor Russo was interested, for a moment. "She's looking down, so perhaps she was smiling at a baby in her lap. Venus with Cupid? But we don't know. It's not our task to—you know—part the veils of time. It's our task to find the lost, to show, to admire. Of course, to sell!"

"And how much of this is . . . the Nobildonna's dower?"

He threw a grand gesture. "She can claim all of it!" he declared. "Her husband was an outstanding collector of ancient sculpture. I store it for her. I have my own collection, of course, and on the floor below I have my workshop where I make, repair, and polish, but it is nothing to hers. You can choose from all of this."

"All of these things are hers?" Sarah pursued.

He shrugged. "We don't quarrel about who owns what. We have an agreement."

"An agreement?"

"A partnership. But you know what she wants to ship? Or was the list stolen with the letter of authorization?"

Sarah picked her words with care. "The list was stolen with her letter to you. But I know what she wants."

The chill of the storehouse, filled with icy marble so near to the dark, slowly moving canal, made her shiver. "The Caesar heads sold well, and the smaller pieces, like the fawn."

His warm smile never wavered, she could not tell if he believed her.

"So let me show you some things, and you shall choose."

He led her deeper into the warehouse where the shelves were filled with little scraps of things, the heads of babies, the wings of cherubs, a fat little foot of a child not yet walking, a clenched fist held against a giggling mouth. The farther they went into the gloom the more that Sarah felt that these were real children, horribly frozen babies.

"Nothing like this," she said faintly. "She can't sell anything like this."

"It distresses you?" he asked acutely. "The row on row of stone babies?"

She felt herself choking, as if on the dust of their bones. She nodded.

He laughed as if he found her charming. "Then let me show you this . . ." He turned her around the shelves to another rack where small animals seemed to play. "Mostly off friezes. We think the country people sawed them from the facades of old palaces and temples. Made them into little gods. People are such fools. But they are pretty? Are they not?"

It was like being in a wonderland of an English forest. Little rabbits stood up on their hind legs, their ears pricked, squirrels flirted fat tails. Nests of baby birds opened their beaks and harassed mother birds bent to feed them, a wriggling worm rendered in stone before the open maws. There was even a stone pond with stone ripples and a leaping salmon.

"Oh! It is exquisite!" Sarah exclaimed, and then turned to the birds: blackbirds and robins and a speckled thrush, tits with long tails and tipped heads, and the adorable nest of a house martin with the mother bird hanging on the lip and half a dozen nestlings craning out.

"You like this? She would want this? This is what they like in England?"

"I love it!" Sarah declared. "We should have many small pieces. But she wants big pieces too. Grand pieces."

"Grand?"

"The king is back on his throne and they all want portraits of Caesars and great men," Sarah tried to explain. "All the lords are building big houses, they want to feel like returning heroes. They want to believe they are part of the Greeks, of the Romans, that great power descends to the new men, even though none of them ever risked anything, and none of them fought a battle."

"You sound as if you despise them!"

"I do!" she said. She remembered she was supposed to be a servant and corrected herself: "Not that it's my business, I know. I'm just a milliner."

"And so who are the true heroes now in England? In the opinion of a pretty milliner?"

"People like Mrs. Reekie," she told him truthfully. "People who have a vision, and hold to a vision. Not because they think they are better than everyone else; but because they know what is right in their hearts. People like Mrs. Stoney, her daughter, whose word is her bond, who smiles only rarely, but who is full of love that she doesn't show. She never changes either. People like Mr. Ferryman, who left England and may never come back, because he will not live under a king again, after being free."

"You sound as if you love them, your employers?"

"I do!" Sarah said, and then corrected herself with a shrug. "They're good mistresses," she said. "And that's hard to find."

"We live in changeable times," he observed. "Most people prefer not to give their hearts and find it easier to change with the tides."

"Good people know what's right," she argued. "And she—Mrs. Reekie—is like a lodestone. She can't help but point the direction."

He was silent for a moment. "Was it she who told you to come here?"

Sarah recovered herself, and smiled into his handsome face. "She allowed me to come, but it was Lady Reekie, the Nobildonna's business, of course."

"They like her? These good women in this great London merchant house? They admire her? She is happy? Does she say when she plans to return here?"

"They adore her," Sarah said firmly. "Everyone adores her."

"She has many friends?"

"Only Sir James, who shows her statues in his house."

"Ah, she has an admirer? He's a young man?"

"No, he's quite old."

"And what do you think of her? What is the opinion of the milliner of the Nobildonna, her Italian mistress?"

"I think she is the most wonderful woman," she assured him, sounding completely sincere. "But I don't say that I understand her."

He laughed shortly. "Ah, she's a woman!" he said. "If you cannot understand her, a woman and her own maid, I am sure I would never try to do so. Now, see here . . ."

He led her into a second room, off the first, crammed full of treasures, carefully arranged and stacked, some of them packed for travel, some of them laid on the floor. There were pillars piled one on another like carved logs. In the middle of the room were the larger pieces, many of them seated women. Some of them had been designed to serve as fountains, tipping empty jars into the darkness. All around them were random pieces of stone, some of them half-carved, others were blocks cut or fallen from a bigger piece, like a giant puzzle. And there were heads of great men, their stern brows crowned with laurel, and shields with inscribed poetry proclaiming heroism.

"I had no idea she had so much!" Sarah said. "How will she ever . . ."

"Sell it all?" he asked. "It is the collection of a lifetime, for a lifelong fortune. She can only sell a dozen or so pieces at a time. The English collectors want their statues one by one, not in their hundreds. I would never show a customer all of this, all at once. This is for you, only. When we have established a name, she will not have to sell pieces one at a time. The agents will come to us from England and France and Germany, we will have a showroom with just a few, a very few big pieces and they will order what they need and we will send it. The buyers like to see only a few pieces at a time, it makes them look rare."

"They're not rare?"

He held up the lamp so that she could see that every part of the room was filled. "They were carved for centuries in great numbers," he said. "For tombs and public places, for houses and temples, for libraries and government offices, for roads and for overlooking the harbors. We are a country that has carved stone since the beginning of time. Of course, there are more statues than there are people in Venice! Now that they are admired, now that they are given a value, we find them, we dig for them all over and we trade them."

"And you mend them and polish them?"

"No! Never say it!" he said laughing. "All we do is clean them and we sometimes mount them on a plinth so they can be seen. But we don't alter them in any way. They have to be authentic."

"You don't copy them? Or carve your own?"

"The skills have been lost," he said firmly. "That's what gives these survivors their value: that they are so old and can never be made again. To pass off modern work as that of the ancients would be a fraud. These are worth a fortune because they are antiquities. A modern copy would be worth only the price of the stone and the wage of the mason. An ancient statue is worth ten times that. We take great care that all our things are truly old, truly beautiful."

"And you share everything?"

"Let us say we are partners. We were partners when she first saw them in the Palazzo Fiori, we were partners when we rescued her share, and we are partners now, as we sell them."

"Her palace must have been very beautiful," Sarah ventured.

"It was one of the finest."

"And then she married Mrs. Reekie's son. That was surely a comedown for her?"

"Ah, the doctor? Little Roberto? Did you know him?"

Sarah found that she was bristling at the casual dismissal of her uncle. "No, I never knew him. He'd gone to Venice before I went to work for Mrs. Reekie. I know of him, for they talk of him often. They loved him, they mourn him . . . But I wouldn't know him if I saw him."

"And of course, you'll never see him," he reminded her gently.

"No, of course. It was a great shock for the household when the Nobildonna wrote and told us that he was dead."

"It was a great shock for us also," he said. "A tragedy. So? You have seen our store. You can take your pick. How many things do you want?"

"About twenty things," Sarah said. "And Captain Shore is to ship them back to England, as before."

"Will you choose them now?" He handed her the candelabra and leaned against the wall as she walked around the crowded room, looking at one thing, stretching around something to inspect another, and bending down to admire the stored columns.

"I should take columns," she said. "I know she wants four or five. Some of the bigger animals—people like them for their gardens. Lions especially. Some vases, and I think—the Caesar heads, another set of them. And a few little things, for showing on tables."

"You like the Chimera?" he asked, showing her a lion with the head of a goat bursting from its spine, being bitten by the lion tail, which was itself a snake. Sarah recoiled. "It's horrible!"

He laughed. "Little Jolie—nothing is horrible. Nothing is beautiful. It is just what people like now and then. And this is amusing as it shows a brute that preys on itself. Like Man perhaps. It is not charming but it is in fashion. All we care for is fashion. All we want is money. You can start packing them tomorrow. Your taste is very good, it's just what I would have chosen myself."

He led the way out of the room and closed the door behind him. Their nighttime candles were burning on the marble side table in the shadowy hall. Sarah was suddenly acutely aware that the house was silent and that they were alone together, and that his dark gaze was on her face.

"Now," he said quietly. "Would you like to sleep in your bedroom? Or would you prefer to come to mine?"

Sarah shot one horrified glance at his smiling face. "No!" she said. "I'm not . . . I'm not . . ."

"Not that sort of milliner," he said understandingly, not the least embarrassed. "In that case I will give you your candle and bid you good night, Miss Jolie."

DECEMBER 1670, HADLEY, NEW ENGLAND

Ned went through the laborious process of loading his basket with goods, strapping on his snowshoes, shooing Red out of the door, and heading into town. Red bounded through the snow, sinking and leaping, his thick fur ice-tipped. Ned did not need to dig out his garden gate; the drifts were so high that they stepped over the top of it and onto the wide featureless snow plain that was the village common. On either side Ned could see the roofs and the shuttered top-floor windows of the houses. One or two settlers had dug out their front doors; but most had abandoned the front of their houses to the snow and only dug out their yard so they could feed their beasts and get to their stores. Every house carried a cap of snow, every house showed a streamer of smoke at the chimney, as if to say that the village was fighting to stay warm, burning huge stores of wood every day to try to get through the ordeal of winter.

Ned traded venison from Norwottuck as he went, picking up a small cheese from a dairywoman whose cow was still in milk, and admiring some knitted woolen gloves. Though his fingers were red and chapped from the cold, he did not think he could afford to trade food for gloves.

He made his way down the street to the minister's house where the slaves had arduously dug a path to the front and back door and to the meetinghouse. Ned, carrying his basket, went round to the back, and knocked on the kitchen door.

"You have to push it open, the wood's warped," came a shout from Mrs. Rose inside.

Ned put his shoulder against the door and fell into the kitchen. "Beg pardon," he said, flinching from her glare as snow from his hat cascaded on the clean floor. He stepped back out again, took off his snowshoes, shook himself like a bear, and then came inside, leaving his oiled cape, coat, hat, and mittens on the hooks at the side of the door. "I am sorry," he said.

"Never mind, you're in now," she said. "Is it cold out?"

"Very. I left my dog in one of your stables."

"Will he be warm enough there?"

"Yes, I won't be too long. I brought you some meat."

She glanced into his basket. "Thank you. They're all upstairs," she told him. "The cellar's too cold in this weather. And no strangers come in this season, anyway."

Ned hesitated, wondering if he should say something more intimate to her. "I'm glad to see you," he said. "You're looking well."

She threw him a little smile. "And I you," she said. "I think of you, beside the ice river, the last house of the town."

"It's not that far away," he protested, as he always did.

"Look at you!" she replied. "Wearing half a bear just to get to the minister's house."

He nodded. "John Sassamon came the other day and he was wearing half what I put on, and he was warm. I must get him to trade me his furs."

She turned her head at once. "He'd rather have a red or a blue coat," she said. "They all would. They all want proper clothes; but they won't work to earn it. You shouldn't buy his native clothes, and he should stay in his proper trousers and shirt. Why would he run around in buckskin when he's got a perfectly good proper house in Natick? A wife? A ministry? What's he even doing this far north?"

"That's what I've got to talk to the minister about," Ned said.

She nodded, compressing her lips on what she might have said. "He'll be spying," was all she said shortly. "Running about the woods and spying on us."

"He came openly to see me," Ned protested. "Boot's on t'other foot. He took me to spy on them."

"Well, you can go on up," she said, silencing him. "They're all three together upstairs."

Ned made an awkward little nod to her and went out of the kitchen and up the staircase. As he climbed, he called: "It's Ned Ferryman!" and the door at the head of the stairs opened and the minister looked out.

"Good to see you!" he said. "All well with you?"

"Aye, I came to see that all was well with you?"

"Praise God, yes. Come in."

John Russell opened the door and Ned edged into the room. The three men were sitting on hard high-backed chairs with the single bed pushed back against the wall to give them more room. A mean fire burned in the grate, there were frost flowers on the inside of the window. A Bible was on the table, open at the Psalms.

"Ned!" William said warmly. "Good man!"

"Good to see you, Ned Ferryman," said Edward.

Ned smiled at them. "I'm sure you need no guarding," he said.

"The weather will keep everyone indoors. But I thought I would visit, and I brought you some fresh meat for your dinner, venison from my neighbors over the river."

"You've never crossed the river?"

"John Sassamon led me across. I don't mind admitting I was fearful."

"Is he this far north again?" John Russell asked.

"Yes," Ned said. "Again. I've come to speak with you about him, and the Pokanoket. Indeed, he asked me to speak with you, and with these gentlemen."

"What's the matter?" The minister took his seat, and waved Ned into a stool by the fire. "What does he want?"

Ned squatted on the stool. "Thing is," he started. "He trusts you, sir, as a man of God, a minister far superior to him, and a man who has risked his own safety for his friends."

"Rightly," William said.

"And he trusts you two," Ned said, turning to his former commanders, "after taking you out and bringing you back to Hadley last summer. He knows you have the ear of some of the great men of the Council, he knows that you know the governor, and the great men: Josiah Winslow and that Mr. Daniel Gookin keeps your cattle, and that you have friends throughout the land."

"How does he know all this?" Mr. Russell asked, surprised.

William nodded, not taking his level gaze from Ned's face. "We are blessed with good friends," he said. "What of it?"

"John Sassamon says that the settlers aren't staying within their agreed bounds," Ned said earnestly. "They're buying land, though the Council forbade them to buy. The Indians are selling to them, though the Sachems forbade them to sell. The country is driven by buying land and no law seems to be able to stop it."

"Amen. It's true," William said seriously.

"Amen," Edward said. "The Indians are right to complain if we bring them not to God but to Mammon."

"The Massasoit has all but lost his kingdom," Ned said. "They say he can see a roof and a chimney from every side of Mount Hope where once there was nothing but forest. He can't even get to the sea without crossing settler farms. That's very bitter for them—his prayers in the morning are to be said facing the rising sun over the sea."

"He'll have sold it himself," Mr. Russell pointed out.

"Not freely," Ned went on. "They say that we get them into debt, and then we suddenly foreclose."

"That is illegal, the Council are firmly opposed to it. All deeds have to be good, and signed in good faith. They should make a formal complaint and we will prosecute the settlers," John Russell said firmly.

Ned looked away, embarrassed. "Yes, but it's the old governor's son," he said miserably. "He's suing an Indian for a ten-pound debt. Says he'll take twenty pounds' worth of land for it!"

"Says who?" William asked indignantly.

"They say," Ned admitted. "The debtor is the nephew of the Massasoit—King Philip. The father, who is Sachem of his tribe, is handing over a hundred acres of land to the trader to forgive the debt."

"Josiah Winslow is doing this?" Edward asked.

"It's worse than that—he's got a debt on King Philip himself." Ned looked from one grave face to another. "If they force the Massasoit to sell land, when he has sworn he will not—"

"It makes him look bad," John Russell said. "It makes him break his own word. It humiliates him."

"They say that when they were all-powerful and the English newly arrived and starving, they were good to us. They were generous. They say that now we have guns and cannon and a militia and we are stronger than them, they say we should be generous to them."

"Are we stronger than them?" Edward the old commander demanded. "If it came to war?"

Ned looked at him, unable to lie. "I don't know," he said. "I've not been to Mount Hope—Montaup, the sacred home of the Pokanoket—and I've never seen one of their gatherings. But I know they're having big gatherings and that other tribes are attending."

"To make alliances? To go to war?" John Russell asked.

"They say it is to dance. John Sassamon came just to warn me, he told me to warn you. He showed me a village that's arming and building defenses, a Norwottuck village, just over the river, as close as Hatfield, and they are arming and building a palisade that would withstand cannon. I swear they're stockpiling weapons, perhaps even muskets. He showed me, so that I should tell you what I've seen with my own eyes. He asked that you pass it on to the men you know on the Council. I've seen him many times this autumn and winter; and he's clearly traveling for the Massasoit. He's talking to kinsmen and tribes, it certainly looks like they're mustering. If the governors don't meet with him and make a treaty about leaving the Indian lands alone, I'm afraid it will be war."

The two older men, who had made war on their own people up and down England, and even in Ireland, looked bleak. "A war of the Pokanoket and their allies against us would be deadly," Edward judged.

"It would undo all our work," John Russell said. "We've told Boston, we've told Plymouth before. But we'll have to warn them again. We'll have to make them understand. They might survive a war with the Pokanoket in the cities; but we would not!"

"And which side would you take, Ned?" William challenged him. "You and your Indian friend? Aren't you and he both in the same boat? Warning both sides against the other? You can't spend your life crossing from one side of the river to the other. You're going to have to choose."

DECEMBER 1670, VENICE

Sarah woke after strange haunted dreams of her aunt Livia as a monster of stone, as a sculpted sea serpent, as a white marble widow, as a disinterred goddess, and came downstairs, pale and dark-eyed, to have breakfast in the salon served by Mamma Russo, who was not as charming as she had been the night before. The marble-floored salon was cold, the whole house was chilled stone built on icy water.

Sarah tried to throw off her unease, and spent the morning wrapping the smaller statues in scraps of sheep fleece, and then sewing them into a coarse sailcloth, and handing them to the Russos' servant, who crated them for her: building little cages of wood around the irregular shapes. She could not rid herself of the sense of working among a mortuary: every now and then she looked around, and the sightless eyes were watching her. Even the little stone animals seemed to silently yearn for a sun that had been lost.

At four, as the light from the warehouse window darkened and the canals gleamed with gondola lanterns reflected on their still waters, the whole family gathered together in the first-floor dining room for their evening meal: the mother of the family, Signora Russo; her handsome adult son; her little son; and the sulky daughter, Chiara. Sarah, as guest, took the foot of the table opposite Signor Russo, and when the children withdrew after dinner and his mother put a bottle of brandy before him, she set three glasses and sat with him and Sarah, as if Sarah were a gentleman guest, a man of quality, who should be served with honor.

"You enjoyed yourself today among the antiquities?" the young man asked her.

She did not tell him that she had looked for him all day, and had been wishing he would stroll into the storehouse and flirt with her.

"Yes," she said. "They are all things of such beauty, I kept looking around and surprising myself."

"One day I shall take you to the feather market, and we can visit a milliner's also. You might like to see how they work here. They make masks as well as hats, their speciality is masks and crowns and fantastic headgear, and beautiful creations which cover the face and the hair, for those ladies who wish to be unknown."

"You would take me?" Sarah asked, and felt her face warm in a blush as he smiled at her.

"It would be my pleasure," he said.

"When I first arrived, I saw some ladies in masks and standing very tall on pattens, so high that they had to be held up by maids."

"Those are our courtesans," he said. "The courtesans of Venice on their chopines. Pattens, as you say, but so tall they are almost like stilts. Very expensive, very famous, very beautiful."

Sarah felt herself flush hotter. "I didn't know. In London, of course, especially at court there are . . ."

He took a sip of his wine. "The whole world knows of the London court, and the ladies who whore for the king. But you are not of that world?"

"No," she said, falling back on her usual excuse. "I don't know anything about it. I'm just a milliner."

"I believe that Signora Nell Gwyn was just an orange seller. But it didn't prevent her making her fortune from favor. D'you never think of that life? You have such beauty that you would surely be a success?"

Sarah knew she was blushing furiously. "No," she said. "My mother is a woman of great . . ." she could not find the words. "Great . . ."

"A puritan, in fact," he helped her.

"Yes," she gasped. "Very respectable. I would never . . ."

"But you like pleasure? You like beautiful things?"

"Yes I do . . ."

"And you hope to marry? You are betrothed perhaps?"

"I have no thoughts of marriage." Sarah tried to compose herself. "I've just finished my apprenticeship. I have to make my own way in the world. I cannot afford any luxuries."

"You call a husband a luxury?" he laughed.

"In my world, a lover or a husband is a luxury," she managed to say. "And one I can't afford."

"I toast you!" he said, raising his glass to her. "A young beauty who thinks of men as expensive luxuries. Indeed, you come from a country which has turned everything upside down. The English throw down their kings and then bring them back, raise young women who cannot afford to marry! What a novelty! Bless you, Bathsheba Jolie!"

His mother smiled and raised her glass to the toast in English, which she could not understand. She asked her son a quick question in Italian.

"She asks me what I have said to make the English rose blush red?" he reported.

Sarah smiled and shook her head. But she knew that those had not been the words. The woman had spoken too quickly for her to follow, but she would have recognized the words "rose" and "English." She was almost certain that she had heard Livia's name in the stream of rapid Italian.

"If you had been raised as I have been, you would think the same," she told him staunchly.

"No father?" he asked. "Me neither."

"No father; but the hardest-working mother that ever blessed a home, and a grandmother who never complains, who understands more of this world and the next than any ordained minister. A home where we don't really live together, we cling together while the world turns upside down and back again."

"A little business?" he asked sympathetically.

"Clinging on," she said. "So my brother and I had to make our own livings. He—Johnnie—is doing well, he has a head for numbers. He's apprenticed to a merchant and they think well of him, and I have my millinery papers. When I go home, I'll look for work as a milliner and leave service."

"And is that what you want?" Signor Russo asked, his dark eyes on her animated face. "Now you have come so far and seen Venice? Is that all you want—to go home to a new millinery shop, with a box of feathers?"

She hesitated. "It's hard not to want more," she admitted. "Now I'm here, even though I've seen only the port and the streets on the way to here . . . it's hard not to imagine more."

He got up from his seat, came to the foot of the table, and leaned over her chair to pour her another glass of wine. "Imagine more," he counseled softly in her ear. "This is a city where imaginings can come to life. Marco Polo went from here, overland to the court of China: just because he dreamed it was possible. We live here without a king, without an emperor: because we thought it could be done. We won't run out of great leaders and fetch a king back like the English did. This is a republic that is built to last. Every wall here is painted by a Master: because we love beauty; look up when you walk around and every corner is beautiful. Even the courtesans make a fortune: because we know that beauty is fleeting and precious. Imagine more, Bathsheba, and see where your dreams take you."

She found she was smiling, filled with excitement. "I must be drunk." She resisted the spell his words were weaving around her. "I can't be imagining and dreaming. I have too much to do. I have to pack up my mistress's goods and go home."

He laughed. "Then I will light your candle for you to go to b[...] drunkard," he said. "Good night, Bathsheba."

"Good night, Signor Russo, good night, signora," she repli[...] rising from the table and going to the beautiful marble-topped sid[...] table where her candle stood ready in a beautifully wrought gold candlestick.

He lit her candle from one of the branch on the dining table and as she took it, he held her hand. "You may call me Felipe," he said quietly. "You can say: *Buonanotte*, Felipe."

She glanced at his mother and saw her smiling, dark-eyed nod, and then turned back to his intense gaze. "*Buonanotte*, Felipe," she repeated, and took her candle and walked from the dining room. She felt him watch her all the way to the foot of the stone stairs, and she walked, shoulders back, head set, proudly like a little queen, as beautiful as a statue, all the way up the stairs while the candle flame bobbed excitedly beside her.

DECEMBER 1670, LONDON

Johnnie came home the Sunday before Christmas and found his mother standing precariously high, on a clerk's stool, pinning greenery above the corner cupboard in the parlor.

"You know, when I was young, it was forbidden to take a holiday on Christmas Day?" she said, stretching to make the last adjustment. "This is such a pleasure."

"But why was it forbidden?" he asked.

"Oliver Cromwell," she said shortly. "And the minister said it was pagan. But now it's all turned around."

The court takes two weeks to celebrate," he said. "Drunk for a ⸱tnight. And then they start all over again for Twelfth Night."

Alys laughed. "You're a puritan like your uncle Ned," she told him, as he helped her down. "Our minister, the puritan one at St. Wilfrid's, used to say—where does it say in the Bible that you should get drunk to celebrate the coming of the Lord? And Old Ellie from East Beach would shout from the back: 'He didn't turn water into wine to make vinegar to put on His cabbage, you know!'"

"She did?"

"Aye, they would punish her every Twelfth Night for one thing or another. But they didn't even call it Twelfth Night when I was a young woman. We didn't have Twelfth Night nor Christmas."

"Did you have presents?"

She turned from him to put berries on the coat hook on the back of the door. "We had no money for presents. But Rob and I used to look for the little tokens that your grandma loves so much. We'd search for them all year, and give them to her for Christmas. And she'd give us fairings, anything sweet. Lord, we loved anything with sugar."

"You and your brother, Rob," he confirmed.

"Yes, God bless him."

"And Sarah is away, looking for him, this Christmas Day?"

She gave her son a long level look. "Oh—so you know too? You've known all along? And kept it from me? The three of you knew: your grandma and Sarah and you?"

He nodded. "I'm sorry, Ma."

"You should have told me, Johnnie. We've become a family of secrets."

He hesitated. "We've always been a family with secrets."

She shook her head. "Why wouldn't she tell me?"

He looked awkward. "She thought you'd tell Livia."

"I would have done!" Alys exclaimed. "I should have done! Who better than her to tell your grandma and my daughter that they were chasing after rainbows! What does she think? That Livia is not Rob's widow? That he's not dead?"

"They're very sure that something's wrong," Johnnie said gently. "Grandma was convinced."

"She's taken it into her head that Rob is alive, and that Sarah will somehow find him, and Sarah took it as an excuse to go off on an adventure. Of course there's nothing to it. God keep my daughter safe and bring her home."

"Amen," Johnnie said. "I miss her."

"I miss her," his mother confirmed. "And what are we going to tell Livia when Sarah steps off the ship from Venice? Tell me that!"

DECEMBER 1670, VENICE

The feather market was held in one of the great warehouses not far from the Rialto Bridge. Sarah and Felipe Russo walked through the narrow streets, across the market, where the money changers and moneylenders were setting up their stalls, under the arches of the court. Each man had a scale weight, and an abacus on his stall, a quill and paper to write a note of the debts, and a chest of coins safely underneath the table, guarded by a young man who stood behind the money changer and never took his eyes from the box.

"You'd do better to change your English money into gold," Felipe told her. "You're sure it's a good coin?"

She nodded. "Will they give me the true weight for it?"

"They would not dare to cheat a Christian," he said. "They're Jews. They lend money and change gold and ply their trade in usury and sin by permission of the Doge. If any one of them so much as dreams of cheating he'd be denounced and publicly executed by sunset. They're probably the most honest men in Venice. Certainly, they're the most frightened."

"You'd have to be a reckless man to break the law in this city," Sarah remarked.

"Only for a very great profit," he agreed.

"How do I choose which moneylender?" Sarah asked, hanging back from the downcast faces of the men in their long black gowns, each with a yellow star sewed on the front of his black coat. "They all look equally . . . tormented."

"I use this man," Felipe pointed out. "Mordecai." He guided her up to the stall. "English guinea for gold," he said shortly.

The man bowed, and took up his scales. "May I have the coin, your ladyship?" he asked Sarah in perfect English.

"How did you know I was English?" she asked, startled.

He kept his head bent but she could see his smile. "Your fairness of face, ladyship," he said quietly. "All the English have that fair skin." He glanced at Felipe and spoke in Italian: "So like the Milord doctor."

"Just give her the money," Felipe ordered quietly in Italian.

Sarah kept her face impassive as she watched the moneylender's lad open the chest under the stall and hand up gold coins and little pieces of gold chain. She did not betray for a moment that she had understood the brief exchange. She put her hand in the placket of her skirt, drew out Alinor's guinea, hesitated for a moment, and then handed it over.

Mordecai the moneylender put the coin on one side of the scale and added coins and links of a gold chain until they balanced exactly.

"And some for luck," Felipe said in English, a little edge to his voice.

"Signor . . . it was fair measure and an agreed price."

"You'll sell a good English guinea at a profit, you know you will, you old sinner. Give the lady a little, for luck."

"I don't—" Sarah began.

"As I say."

Without another word, Mordecai added three links of a gold chain and the scales tipped and wobbled to Sarah's advantage.

"Hold out your purse and he'll pour it in," Felipe instructed.

Sarah did as she was told. "There you are," he said as she pulled the strings of the purse shut and carefully tied it on her belt.

He guided her away from the stall, and they left the square and climbed up the steeply canted Rialto Bridge. On either side were little stalls selling beautiful pieces of glassware, exquisite metalwork: daggers enameled with glass, set with jewels. Spice sellers had colored and scented powders that Sarah had never seen before, there were perfumed soaps and sprinkling dust and oils on another stall, while another had yards of silks and velvets in the shadow of a huge oiled and painted parasol. Even the air smelled strange and exotic, scents of patchouli and lemon and rose billowed about them as they walked. Sarah stopped to smell the sharp wintry scent of myrrh.

"Does it make you dream?" Felipe asked her quietly as they arrived at the warehouse door.

"I think it is a city of dreams," she said. "I can't understand how Liv . . . how my mistress can bear to live anywhere else."

"Ah, she left wearing black, her dreams drowned," he said with ready sympathy. "Is she still in mourning black in London?"

"Yes."

"She's the sort of woman who will never leave it off. She loved her husband very dearly. She grieved for him like a woman driven mad with sorrow."

"And it suits her," Sarah pointed out, which made him laugh.

"Yes it does."

"They were very much in love?"

"At first they were inseparable. She would walk with him on the marshes and go with him on his visits. He insisted on going to the poor—he had an interest in quatrain fever—and she was quite un-afraid. They went together, in doctors' masks like a pair of black her-ons. You know?" He smiled.

"Herons?" she repeated.

"They wore the black gowns and the great masks of doctors, the long beaks stuffed with herbs to protect from infection, the eyes like holes. The gowns black. I used to laugh at them, going together like a pair of birds with big beaks like egrets on the marshes."

"Did she show him the antiquities?"

"He saw them when he first met her, in her first home. She was enthroned among them, a beauty among beauties, in her palazzo. She was a wealthy wife, rich in everything but happiness. When her first husband died and she condescended to marry the doctor, she brought all of the treasures to him as her dowry. Of course, he had no idea what we had in the store." Felipe guided Sarah up some steps to a great storehouse.

...d he never see her store? Did he visit your house?"

...lipe turned the handle of the pedestrian door in the great door-
y. At once a wall of sound billowed out. He smiled. "Listen! That
, the sound of people making money!"

Sarah laughed.

"Now, this is the weekly feather market," he told her. "The great
hunters and collectors go all around Europe, all around Asia and
Africa, they deliver feathers in their millions. The feather merchants
buy them here, in the raw, and also treat them, dye them, clean them,
sculpt them, and bring them back here to sell to milliners and costu-
miers. This is where the feather dealers sell sacks of feathers to traders
taking them on to London and Paris, to their own markets. So you
will see everything here from a dirty pelt to a completely finished
single feather. You can buy in any amount."

Sarah was starting through the door when he put a hand on her
arm. "But not with that face," he said.

She turned to him, surprised. "Am I dirty?" she asked, brushing
her gloved palm across her cheek.

He smiled. "You are eager," he said. "Never look eager in Venice.
You put up the price just by the way you walk into a market. This is
a market for haggling, in a city which admires indifference. You will
show me what you like—discreetly show me—and I will halve the
price. But I cannot do it if you look like a child on the morning of
Christmas Eve, opening presents."

She laughed and composed her expression. She did not know it;
but she was enacting Livia, at her most disdainful. "There? Do I look
above it all, and very indifferent to everything? Very bored?"

"Like a queen," he said, and stepped back to let her precede him
into the hall.

She was glad he had warned her of what to expect. One side of the hall
was like a butchers' shambles, piled high with bleeding pelts, some
of them stinking of the dead birds' dung, some of them inadequately

cleaned and rotting already, sharp with the stink of vinegar that had been poured over them during quarantine to prevent the spread of disease. Wings that had been savagely hacked off dying birds lay in mountainous piles, birds that had sported fine crests had been roughly beheaded so that the crests were perfect but the necks were blood-clotted stumps. Bodies with beautiful breast plumage, showing long colorful tails, were piled on the floor. Sarah turned her head: "Disgusting."

"*Allora,* every trade has its dirty side," Felipe said philosophically. "And all these have been in quarantine on the Isola del Lazzaretto Nuovo. Anything that might bring an infection into Venice has to go to the island and be cleaned—aired, or smoked, or soaked with vinegar. Only when it's clean may it come here."

"Oh, the Captain, Captain Shore on my ship, said something about this."

"Yes, of course. If you had sickness in London, the Captain, his crew, and even you would have to kick your heels for forty days on the island before you were allowed into Venice. Any goods you brought in would be cleaned while you waited, to see if any infection showed. The merchants hate the delay; but it keeps us free from illness."

"And after forty days they are released?"

"Of course," he said smoothly. "So everything here is clean. It might stink but it's not infectious."

"But it is . . ." She could not find the word. "Cruel?"

"A severed head? Of a bird? And this from the nation that beheaded a king? I thought you were bolder than that! You know, someone always gets hurt if there's a profit. But if you are so squeamish, come and see the finished feathers. There are no broken necks here!"

There were a hundred stalls made from boards on trestles lining the long hall and a double passageway down the middle, each heaped with a speciality. Sarah could see sheaves of peacock tails, the strangely sculpted feathers of birds of paradise. There were drifts of snowy white feathers from egrets, and the enchanting dapple—like speckled bronze on marble—of barn owl feathers. Cormorant pelts shone an iridescent green-black, a pile of parrot tails showed a violent almost luminous blue. There were sacks of tiny feathers sold by weight, sorted by color, the deep reddish-brown of feathers shaved from dead pochard heads, the black-cobalt of male mallards.

On the middle stalls the feathers had been cleaned and dyed. Jet-black feathers—the hardest color to achieve—made a pool of darkness in sack after sack, graded by size. There were feathers that had been expertly styled and finished, cut into scalloped edges, shaved to a single bobbing frond. Some had been dusted with gold so they glinted and glittered, some had been set with sequins, all of them were beautifully worked and stroked so the fronds sat together in lustrous perfection.

"Oh," Sarah said, taking in the riches all around her.

"Face," Felipe said.

Sarah bit down a giggle and composed herself. "But I have no more than half my guinea for spending," she whispered urgently.

"Do you want quantity or quality?" he asked.

He could see her yearning look at the perfect single plumes, then she resolutely returned to the sack of kingfisher feathers. "How much of these would I get for my half a guinea?" she asked.

He turned and spoke in rapid Italian to the stallholder.

"They charge by their weight in gold," he said. "Do you want a guinea's worth of this sort?"

Sarah gulped, but she knew that she could sell them for five times that price in London. "Half," she said. "I have to keep some back, in case of trouble."

He laughed. "I will keep you safe, little cautious one! There will be no trouble for you! But half a guinea, it shall be."

The woman behind the stall proffered a large set of scales with a tray for money on one side and a basket on the other. She showed that they weighed true with matching Venetian coins on either side, and then Sarah put a handful of her gold into the tray. The woman tipped an avalanche of turquoise feathers into the basket until the scales trembled and swung, and then balanced themselves evenly.

"And for luck?" Felipe reminded her, and she threw in another handful.

"You are content with your purchase?" he asked Sarah.

Dazzled by the color, the basket of sapphire, she nodded, and the woman poured them like a stream of light into a bundle of soft cloth, tied the top into a loop for easy carrying, and shoveled the gold into a pocket of her apron.

DECEMBER 1670, LONDON

Johnnie's master called him into the inner office on Christmas Eve, and he stood before the great desk, loaded with ledgers, while Mr. Watson finished checking a column of figures and then peered at him over the top of a set of small eyeglasses.

"Ah, Master Stoney," he said pompously. "Your time with us is up."

"Yes, sir," Johnnie replied.

"You have your contract of apprenticeship?"

Johnnie unrolled the scroll with the fat red seals at the bottom and Alys's plain signature beside his master's scrawl.

"Completed to the day," Mr. Watson said. "You sign there."

Johnnie made a clerkly signature at the foot of the page and Mr. Watson signed his own name with a swirl.

"You will stay on?" Mr. Watson inquired. "Senior clerk at five shillings a week?"

"I should be glad to," Johnnie said. "Till Easter, if I may?"

"You hope to move to another House?"

"I have been fortunate," Johnnie told him. "More fortunate than I could have hoped. I have a patron who has mentioned my name. I have visited the East India Company and they have offered me a post. They say I may start at Easter."

"Good God!" Johnnie's master dropped his chair back to four legs. "You're flying very high," he said with a hint of resentment. "I've not got a place at that table. Who got you in?"

"My aunt from Venice knows an investor," Johnnie said. "He was so good as to recommend me."

"You have an aunt from Venice?"

"Yes, sir."

"That's new, isn't it?"

"It is, sir, and unexpected. But my uncle has just recently died and his widow has come, and is living with us."

"And what do you have to do for her? For your patron? For this is a more than cousinly favor you have here?"

Johnnie laughed, a little embarrassed. "It seems I have to be her advisor, and her friend," he said. "She lives with my mother and grandmother at the warehouse, and—it seems that she wants my support in a plan that she has for the business."

Mr. Watson looked dourly at the young man. "Well, you can go home to your family, befriend your aunt over the holiday. If she wants to invest any money in cargoes I rely upon you to bring her here; bear in mind what I've done for you, lad. I expect to see her in the New Year."

"She has only her dower," Johnnie said. "She's not a wealthy woman."

"She has wealthy friends," the merchant said flatly. "I'd like to meet them too."

"I'll tell her," Johnnie said awkwardly. "I'll definitely mention your name."

"Aye. Well and good. Off you go now. Start again, day after Christmas, and God bless you all."

Johnnie hesitated, in case there was a Christmas box—and left without any gift.

DECEMBER 1670, VENICE

Early in the morning, before the household was stirring, Sarah woke and dressed in silence, in the half-light of the moon reflected from the canal to her dappled ceiling. As she moved to leave the room, Chiara, still asleep in bed, stirred, and muttered something. Sarah froze, and then crept to the door on the creaking floorboards. She made no sound at all on the stone stair, and with her slippers in her hand she slipped down to the street door like a ghost. It was unlocked, the kitchenmaid had already come in and climbed up the stairs to the kitchen, to light the fire and start baking, so Sarah swung it open and went out into the quiet streets.

Venice was awake—Venice never slept. There were street sweepers plying their brushes, pushing the dust into the canal where it floated like a pale scum, and there were street waterers, hauling water from the canal and sloshing it over the pavements. The sellers were walking to the markets, their wares in balanced baskets swinging from the yokes on their shoulders. There were plain wooden gondolas and sandoli going up and down the canal carrying goods. The collectors of trash and soil were heaving the neighborhood baskets into their boat. There were one or two glossy black gondolas laden with drunks wallowing low in the water, heading home from a late night. One gondola with a closed cabin showed a flickering candlelight where clandestine lovers were holding back the day.

Sarah retraced her steps from yesterday, to the Rialto square where the moneylenders had their tables. She was too early for all of them, but one young boy, dressed in black with a skull cap on his head, and a betraying yellow star of cloth sewed on his little shirt, was waiting for his father by the fountain. Sarah went up to him.

"I'm looking for Mordecai the money changer."

He bowed low, clasping his shaking hands before him, too afraid of the Christian woman to find his voice.

"Mordecai, the money changer," she repeated.

"He walks here," he replied reluctantly. "He will come at eight of the clock."

"Can I go to meet him?"

"Your ladyship must do as you please," he said in his little-boy treble.

"Will you guide me?"

His anxious look around the square showed her that he did not want to walk with her, but he knew he could not refuse a Christian lady anything that she might demand.

"Of course, your ladyship," he said.

He trotted away from the square; Sarah strode beside him. "Where are we going?"

"Towards the ghetto, your ladyship."

"What is that?"

"The old iron foundries . . . where the people of the Book have to live, all together. Locked in at night."

She was going to ask more, when the boy looked up, and said with evident relief: "There is Mordecai now," and she saw the man walking towards them, the deep canal on one side of him, the dark wall on the other, with his young apprentice following his footsteps, carrying the chest of money.

"Signor Mordecai?"

The boy shot an imploring look of apology to the older man. "I am sorry, signor," he said in Italian. "She insisted, and I could not refuse." He vanished into the shadows of the lane.

"Your ladyship," Mordecai said in English, showing no surprise.

"You knew me for English, yesterday?"

He bowed. "I did."

"You said I looked like the Milord doctor."

He bowed in acknowledgment. "You understood me when I spoke Italian?"

"I did; I was not mistaken."

"I meant no harm, signora."

"I know that you didn't. I have come to you—because I think you are an honest man."

"I should not be speaking with you."

"We can say I am changing money. Did you mean Roberto Reekie? The English doctor?"

"I knew him," he said reluctantly. "But I knew nothing of him. I told them."

"You told who?"

"The men who inquired."

"Who inquired?" Sarah asked.

He frowned a little. "The authorities," was all he said.

"Signor Mordecai, may I trust you with a secret?"

"No," he said firmly. "It is not safe for me to know secrets. And you should trust no one."

He turned to walk away, shaking his head; but Sarah ran after him and stepped in front of him to bar the way. "I have to trust you," she said. "I have no one else to ask but you. The Signor Roberto was my uncle. That's why I look like him. As you say. You knew at once. He was my uncle, my grandmother grieves for him, she wants him home. I have to ask after him!"

He turned. "You are under the protection of Signor Russo. Of all men in Venice, he knows all the secrets. You ask him."

"I don't know him," Sarah gabbled. "And I am not under his protection. I have told him a false name and a pretend reason for being here. I have no friends in Venice, and I don't know where to begin. My grandmother has sent me to find Robert Reekie. She is a woman of wisdom—she knows things—and she says that she knows, without doubt, that he is still alive."

His face was graven with lines of sorrow. "Then she is blessed," he said. "To know that your son is alive is a blessing for any mother. Many mothers do not have that confidence."

"If you care for them, then care for my grandmother too. Let me tell her that her son is alive?"

He sighed and paused to allow her to speak.

"When did you last see him?" Sarah pressed him.

He thought for a moment. "Three-quarters of a year ago. Nearly a year."

"Where did you see him?"

"We met at the house of a friend. He too is a physician. He and your uncle were friends, they worked together, they were interested in physic and how it worked. They were interested in preventing fevers—marsh fevers. They were working with patients, they thought they might find a cure."

"An herbalist?" she guessed, and when he looked yet more grave, she continued: "Worse? Worse than that? An alchemist? A Jewish alchemist?"

"I don't know what they did," he said flatly. "I sometimes sold them metals for their work. Always, I had a license. Never did I disobey the law. May I go, your ladyship? I should set out my stall."

"Wait." She put a hand on his arm and he recoiled from her touch as if she were a danger to him.

"I am forbidden to touch you," he said. "Do not harm me, signora, I pray you."

"But it was I that touched you! What's wrong with that?"

He shrugged as if he did not expect justice, but only that the law would be used against him. "I am forbidden."

"Please! Where is he?" she asked simply, stepping closer to him and looking up into his face. "Where is the English Milord? My uncle?"

He pitied her enough to bend his head to whisper. "Alas, he is as good as dead. His mother is right and wrong at the same time. He is not dead; but he is in the well."

She leaned closer, thinking she had misheard him. "In the well? Did you say he is in the well? What is that? What do you mean—the well?"

"The well is what they call the cells below the Doge's Palace," he replied. "Where they keep the prisoners. Those who are awaiting torture and questioning, those who have been accused while evidence is being gathered against them. Those who will be executed."

"They are killed?" Sarah was breathless with shock.

"They die of the cold and the damp, they are below the canal, lying on damp stone, without light. They die of the heat in summer, and in winter, like now, of the cold and thirst and madness."

"Thirst?"

"They lick the water from the walls, they are starved."

"The prison of the Doge?"

"A prison that is itself a death sentence. Most likely he is dead already."

She was as white as a ghost, but her hand tightened on his sleeve. "But he's not drowned? He was not drowned in an accident? He was not drowned in a stormy night in dark tides?"

"Denounced," he said, his face filled with pity. "Far worse than drowned. Denounced."

DECEMBER 1670, LONDON

Johnnie found the table laid in the parlor, the walls pinned with evergreens, the fire lit in the hearth, and his mother, his grandmother, and his aunt Livia waiting for him.

"This is nice," he said, looking around at the copper coal scuttle newly polished, and the candle flames dancing over wax candles. "This is so nice! You must have worked hard all week."

"Your mother did," Alinor told him. "She has been fetching and carrying every day and Livia pinned up the leaves."

"I did nothing." Livia put her hand on his knee and smiled at him. "I just told Tabs what to do. I am a most idle daughter-in-law."

"She knew how to make things lovely," Alys defended her.

"I thought you would at least have put up a couple of Caesar heads for us to dine with," Johnnie joked.

She slapped his leg and made him blush at her touch. "Naughty boy to tease me!" she said. "We'll have to wait till your mamma has a grand dining room, and then I will fill it with marble. Don't you think we should sell up here and buy a bigger place upriver?"

He opened his mouth to answer, and was spared by a shout from the yard at the back of the house. They heard Tabs answer and open the warehouse doors and shout: "Mrs. Stoney! It's a man from the Custom House," she said.

"An officer?" Alys started, suddenly pale, rising to her feet and opening the door.

Johnnie exchanged one appalled look with his mother. Alinor went white and grasped the arms of the chair.

"Nay!" Tabs said dismissively from the hall. "A porter from the Custom House. He's got a box for you."

"Oh, of course, of course." Alys put her hand to her pounding heart and laughed with relief.

They all crossed the narrow hall into the warehouse and found the porter pushing his barrow loaded with barrels and boxes through the half door of the warehouse. The wintry air blew in with him. "Delivery for Reekie," he repeated, resting the barrow on its legs. "And duty to pay on the goods." Alys felt in her pocket for a shilling and paid him for the delivery. "I'll come down and pay the duty after Christmas," she said.

"Aye, it's not a gift!" he joked.

Alys managed a strained smile as Johnnie took a crowbar down from the wall and began to lever the top off the first box. At once the storehouse was filled with the heady scent of strange herbs. Alinor leaned over the barrel and inhaled the perfume.

"Sassafras," she said. "No wonder it brings such health."

"No wonder it's so expensive," Alys exulted. "Uncle Ned has sent us a fortune, just as we need it. Will you make posset bags with it?"

Alinor was rifling in a box of bark and roots. "And here are some seeds for us to set, and some other herbs."

Johnnie loosened the ring and took the lid off a barrel. "Dried fruits," he said.

"God bless him," said Alys. "It couldn't have come at a better time."

"You read his letter." Alinor dusted it and handed it to Alys as Johnnie carefully replaced the lids and followed his mother and grandmother into the warm parlor. Livia slipped ahead and took a seat beside the fire.

Alys cut the seal, opened the single sheet of paper, and read the letter telling of his preparation for winter. Alinor looked out of the window towards the river, listening intently to the list of goods, his preparations for the season, and his blessing. When Alys had finished she said only: "Read it again." After the second reading she breathed out slowly, as if she had almost been holding her breath, and said: "I always used to garden with him, it's strange to think of him working alone."

"It sounds as if he is doing well," Alys said cheerfully.

"Aye—what does he call the marrows?"

"Squash. And the berries are called cranberries. But other things sound the same—thatch and hens—Ma. Think of him having bees? Just like you used to do! Some things sound just the same as England. And some things sound better? Being free, without a master and without a king."

Her mother nodded. "He'll like that," she said. "And what he says about how you can just pick up your bed roll and musket and go. He always wanted to be free to leave Foulmire; and now he is. I must be glad that he's free."

"And he thinks of us," Alys pointed out. "He thinks of you when you think of him, at the full moon."

Alinor smiled. "I suppose it's the same moon," she said. "The same moon shines on my brother as it does on me. It shines on us all, wherever we are." She took the letter and turned it over in her hands.

"I'd give so much to travel!" Johnnie said. "But I'd go East rather than West."

"Oh, would you?" Livia asked limpidly.

"He's always wanted to join the Honorable East India Company," Alys told her. "But you need to have a patron to get a place in the Company. That's what they call it—as if it needs no other title—the Company."

"A patron?" Livia asked, as if this were news to her, and Alinor glanced at her. "What sort of patron?"

Johnnie was excruciatingly embarrassed; but could do nothing but answer her. "You can only enter the Company with a patron, Aunt Livia."

"Someone like the noblemen who purchased my antiquities?"

"Yes, those sort of gentlemen," he agreed shortly, wondering why she was leading him on to lie to his mother. "Someone like them, I suppose."

"But I know people like this!" Livia exclaimed smiling. "They buy my goods—they would not buy anything from here, but they buy my goods on the Strand."

"I know," he said awkwardly. "But it's a far cry from buying your antiquities to sponsoring a young man from nowhere. There's no reason they should recommend me, just because they like a column twined with ivy."

Livia flickered a dark gaze at him like a lover's secret glance. "Not so far," she said. "And it was honeysuckle."

"We know no one whose help we want," Alys ruled, looking from Livia's half-hidden smile to her mother's gray gaze which was fixed, speculatively, on Livia's downturned face.

"We'd rather make our own way than depend on someone's favor," Alinor supported her daughter. "Wouldn't you, Livia?"

"Oh, I suppose so," Livia concurred, glancing up at Johnnie almost as if she would wink.

DECEMBER 1670, HADLEY, NEW ENGLAND

On his Christmas Eve in Hadley Ned was surprised to hear a whisper of displaced snow at his door and a quiet tap from a mittened hand.

"Who's there?" he shouted. He did not reach for the musket, but nor did he think for a moment that it was Mrs. Rose.

"I don't know!" came the laughing response in a deep voice. "Am I John Sassamon, or Wussausmon?"

"I think it depends what you're wearing?" Ned said, opening the door and welcoming the tall man dressed in Indian winter clothes into his room.

He brushed snow from his head, from his shoulders, from the iced fringes of his buckskin leggings and then stepped inside. "I will make a lake here, where I melt," he said.

"I see you, Lake," Ned said. "But come in anyway, and get warm. Will you stay the night?"

"If you will have me? I leave for my home at dawn. I said I'd be there for Christmas Day."

"Lord, is it Christmas Day tomorrow?" Ned asked.

"Heathen," Wussausmon said comfortably. "Did you not know?"

"It makes no difference to a godly man." Ned followed the old ruling of Oliver Cromwell. "It's not a celebration ordered in the Bible so it's an ordinary day of prayer to me and all true Christians. Certainly to all of us in Hadley. So who's the heathen now?"

Wussausmon laughed shortly, shook off his undercape, and came to the fire. "Ah, you've let your dog in," he said as Red came to sniff him. "I wondered if he would spend the winter outside."

"He sleeps out," Ned said defensively. "I'm not making him soft. He's a working dog."

The Indian raised his hands. "Why would I care?" he asked. "You Coatmen are so strange with your animals. Both tender and cruel. You put your dog out but you sleep with hens?"

Ned laughed. "I do," he said. "Don't tell anyone."

"It shall be our secret," Wussausmon promised. "Please God we never share any worse between us."

"Will you take a glass of cider?" Ned invited. "A small glass, and don't get drunk and sell me your fields at Natick?"

"A small glass, and then I must sleep. I will have to leave at dawn."

Ned poured a tiny measure for him and his guest and the two men stretched their feet to the fire and sipped.

"D'you know the name of the translators for the Coatmen who first came?" Wussausmon asked Ned.

"No," Ned replied. "No, wait, someone told me. When the English first arrived on the first ship, the *Mayflower*? You mean, translators like you?"

Wussausmon smiled. "Maybe they were like me. I hope to God that they were not. One was called Squanto and one Hobbamok; they were rivals, they each told the English that the other was a Judas, a betrayer. Nobody could decide who to believe. Perhaps they were both liars, perhaps they were both betrayers of their people and their birthright."

"I told John Russell of your fears." Ned guessed that Wussausmon was speaking of his sense of being in two worlds and belonging to neither. "I told him of Norwottuck arming, I warned him as you wanted me to do."

"Will he pass on the warning to the Council? Will the hidden generals speak for us to their friends?"

"I think they will. I think they'll persuade the Council to make an agreement with the Pokanoket in spring. I tried to tell them of everything—both the wrongs against the Indians, and their arming."

"They believed you? They believed me?"

"Yes, they know what's happening. They weren't glad to hear me name Josiah Winslow as one of the merchants who are foreclosing on Indians; but they didn't deny it."

"I pass like a spirit from one world into another, I tell of what I have seen. But then I go back and speak of where I have been," Wussausmon remarked. "And every day I fear that I am not translating one to another; but just making the misunderstanding worse. I am trying to bring these two worlds together but all they do is grind against each other. They don't trust each other, nobody wants to hear what I say, and they both believe I am a liar and a spy."

"Is that like Squanto? And Hobbamok?"

There was a silence, as if Wussausmon could not bear to say yes.

"You know you were afraid of the forest and I told you to take every step with knowledge? Knowing where you were and what was all around you?"

"Yes?"

"I feel like I have lost my knowledge," Wussausmon said very quietly. "Sometimes when I am walking alone I feel that someone is watching me. Sometimes at night I wake in the darkness and I think someone is looking down on me. I feel as if someone is behind me."

"Who?" Ned asked. "Maybe an Indian? Maybe an English spy?"

"A ghost," Wussausmon whispered. "Perhaps Death himself is walking beside me these days, following in my tracks like a friend."

Ned shivered. "The times are bad, but you'll pull through," he said heartily. He poured another small cup of cider. "These are midwinter fears. Too much cold and darkness!"

Wussausmon did not argue. He sipped his drink, his eyes on the red embers of the fire. "I'll tell you something strange about those two," he said.

"What two?"

"Squanto and Hobbamok. Something no Coatman knows—unless they know our language well. Squanto had been kidnapped when he was a boy, poor child. He was taken to Spain to be sold as a slave, and then to London; he lived among you Englishmen, he knew all about you. He found a ship that was sailing for here and he got himself on board, he knew what he was doing, he was determined to come back to his home. The Englishmen on board used him as a guide and he directed them to his own village, hoping to get back to his own people. But when he found his village it was empty, completely silent."

"Why?" Ned asked uneasily.

"It was the killing disease that the Coatmen first brought. All his people were dead, all his friends and family were gone, died of the Coatmen's illnesses, the Coatmen's curse. He guided the ship onwards to where they met with some people who were still alive. He told them he was a child of the dead and his name was Squanto."

"Yes?" Ned said cautiously.

"His name was not Squanto."

"It was not?"

"No. Never. That was the name he used when he came back to his own people, and found them dead, when he brought the Coatmen to his fields where they would release their own dirty animals. He took a new name that the Coatmen would not understand, and he went to his own people under that name. He spoke to his people under a name that they would understand. As a warning, so they knew what he was, and that he was false to them."

"Squanto?"

"Squanto is the name of a bad god: a devil, you would call him. One that brings mischief and despair."

Ned shivered though the fire was warm. "We were guided here by a man who called himself a devil?" he asked.

"And Hobbamok."

"What does that name mean?"

Wussausmon shrugged. "It's almost the same. Hobbamok is another of our gods: a trickster god, one who loves wickedness and cruel play."

"The guides who brought us here were devils? Roaming the world to set us against one another?"

Wussausmon nodded as the men sat in silence, as if they were listening for a ghost to answer them.

"It makes me think, Ferryman. What did they know, those men who crossed from one world to another, who tried to live between two worlds? What did they know that they both named themselves for the bringers of grief, of trouble, of death? Did they know more than you and me? Do you think they knew that if you go from one world to another you are bound to destroy them both? Do you think they were saying that a go-between is always a translator from one hell to another?"

"Have you told anyone this?" Ned asked. "Does Roger Williams have these names in his great dictionary of your language?"

"I've told no one but you," Wussausmon said quietly. "Who would listen but another man who goes from one world to another doing the devil's work?"

"I'm not doing the devil's work," Ned said staunchly.

"How do you know?"

DECEMBER 1670, VENICE

Sarah walked briskly to the quay where Captain Shore's ship, *Sweet Hope,* sat before the wide warehouse door loading goods for the return voyage, scheduled to leave within two days. As she had expected, Captain Shore was on the quayside, negotiating with much hand waving and miming to overcome the language difficulties, with a merchant who was sending Venetian glass to London. Sarah waited at a distance while the two men haggled. When they finally shook hands and the merchant turned away into the Custom House to declare his goods and get his permit, Sarah stepped forwards.

"Eh?" Captain Shore remarked. "You here, Bathsheba? All going well? Found your antiquities?" He lowered his voice. "Where's the husband?"

"No," she said awkwardly. "There is no husband. I'm sorry, but I lied to you, Captain Shore. And my name's not Bathsheba Jolly either."

He was horrified. "Never mind me, child! You lied to the port officers? The papers you signed?"

"I never mentioned a husband. They know nothing of him. But I lied about my name."

He turned on his heel and then came back to her. "It's not safe! It's not safe!" he exclaimed. "Venice is not a city for amateur deceivers! They burn people in public for forging coin, behead them for forging letters—this is a merchant city, your word has got to be good. Your name has to be known for straight dealing. If you lie—you must never be caught. And now my paperwork is wrong too. Fool that you are—I'll have to report you. I've got no choice, but I'll have to report you. What's your real name?"

"Sarah Stoney," she told him, and saw him slowly realize what she had said.

"Not Mrs. Stoney's girl, of Reekie Warehouse at Savoury Dock?" She nodded.

"Christ's teeth! Does your ma know you're here?"

"No. My grandma does. She sent me."

"Good God! Have you run away from home? And I helped you? God spare me! I'd do anything not to offend your ma!"

"No, no. My grandma asked me to come, and she'll have told my mother by now. She asked me to come and find my uncle Rob. He was reported drowned, you see, but my grandma is sure . . . she felt . . ." Sarah trailed off.

"Your grandma—the healer?"

Sarah nodded.

"And she wanted you to find her son?"

Sarah nodded again.

"The drowned one!" he exclaimed.

"Yes, she doesn't think he drowned."

"But why not send your brother? Or Mrs. Stoney herself? I'd have been proud to carry her. She could have had a cabin for free!"

She had no answer. "It was only my grandma who wanted me to come. She was certain, she felt she just knew."

"Does she have the sight?" he lowered his voice to ask. "The sailors who buy her teas against fever say she has a gift. Do you have it?"

"I don't know," Sarah said cautiously. "It depends who's asking."

He laughed unwillingly at that. "You're your mother's daughter," he said. "No fool. But—Lord—you've got us into trouble here. How will you set about finding him?"

"That's why I came to see you," she said. "Someone told me that my uncle was not drowned, but in the well. D'you know what that means?"

The Captain's anxious face was suddenly as grave as if she had told him of a death. "Of course, I know what it means. They make sure that everyone knows. It means he is lost to you, child. The well is the stone cellars of the Doge's Palace, the worst of prisons. Nobody comes out from there, but to the scaffold."

"There must be people who are released! People who prove their innocence?"

He looked at her. "Maid, I'm sorry for you. This isn't England. They're denounced, they're taken up, they're tried, and then they're gone. If they ever come out at all it's to be hanged in the square, but mostly they just disappear, no one ever speaks of them again. If they're in the *piombi*—the cells under the lead roof—they die of the heat in summer. In winter, they die of cold. If they're in the well, they get sick from the mists and the damp of the canal. And if they're accused of heresy or treason, they put them in a cage and dangle them over the canal and let them starve to death in public."

"He won't have been a heretic," Sarah said firmly. "None of us would die for our beliefs. We're a family that wants to live. But what could he have done that someone would denounce him? He was a doctor, a physician. He made people better and saved lives! I spoke to someone who knew him—he was trying to find a cure for quatrain fever. Who would denounce a man like that?"

Captain Shore shrugged. "That's what the Bocca are for. Anyone could have denounced him for anything. An unhappy patient? A rival physician? A woman? Someone who thought he was a spy because he was English? Probably, we'll never know. Did he make enemies?"

"I know nothing about him but that he married the Nobildonna, on the death of her first husband!" she exclaimed.

"Nobildonna da Ricci, or Peachey, or whatever she calls herself today?" he asked. "Her that has more furniture than any woman on God's earth?"

"You call her da Peachey?" Sarah confirmed.

He shrugged. "I call her what she tells me to call her. That's the name she had put on the cargo manifest."

She nodded. "I'm staying with her steward. He doesn't know I'm her niece. I gave him my false name."

"Signor Russo?" he asked, looking at her under his sandy eyebrows. "Handsome as a devil and charming as a snake?"

Sarah blinked at the critical description of her only friend in Venice. "That's him," she agreed uncertainly.

"Not a good place for you," he said flatly.

She drew closer. "Captain Shore, why not?"

"Not my place to say," he hesitated.

"You wouldn't want me to be in danger . . ."

"I don't want you to be here at all!" he said, goaded.

"My ma would want you to protect me if you could."

"I know! I know!" he said miserably.

"When we get home, I will tell her how kind you have been to me."

"If we ever get home at all!"

"Help me," Sarah urged him. "It's my mother's brother."

"Step over here." He led her to the prow of the ship and they faced out over the water, so that no one on the quay could see their faces or guess what they were saying from the movement of their lips. "That Russo—he's not just a collector of antiquities."

She waited. "He was my aunt's steward," she volunteered, and saw him quickly shake his head.

"He's an ambidexter, a cheat. He's got more statues than could ever have come from one house. I've shipped hundreds of big crates for him, stones, friezes, figures, statues, one so big that it had to lie on deck and we had to clamber round it."

Sarah looked down the deck of the galleon, trying to imagine a statue as big as he described.

"He sells a lot?"

"That's what I'm saying, he's a trader, the biggest trader. He handles them in their hundreds."

"But surely, that's not illegal?"

"Not illegal if he buys them, and doesn't steal them," he confirmed. "Not illegal if he has the paperwork to export them. Not illegal if he doesn't falsify the paperwork, saying he's sending one thing when really he's sending something else. Not illegal if he's not forging them: copying and then chipping them and darkening them to pass them off as old. Not illegal if he's not putting lots of different parts together and then saying it's a rarity—a whole figure."

"Are all these crimes?"

"The Venetians don't want all their statues and old goods flying away to the new houses of France and Germany and England," he said. "You're only allowed to ship so much. You have to have a permit, and you can only get a permit if you're an ambassador. Didn't your mother herself tell me it was the Lady's furniture—not antiquities but furniture?"

Sarah nodded fearfully. "I thought that was so the Nobildonna could avoid paying duty in England."

"She should have paid in both countries," he said dourly. "She's committing a crime in two countries. And so is anyone who ships and stores for her. She's got your mother smuggling for her."

"My mother! You didn't warn her?"

He scowled at her. "She wouldn't hear a word against the widow."

Sarah checked at the thought of the trust her mother had put in Livia. "They're sisters-in-law," she said.

"Not very sisterly to get your mother into a crime that could ruin her and her warehouse. The fines would bankrupt her."

Sarah was white. "But all this is nothing to do with my uncle. Why was he denounced?"

Captain Shore shrugged. "Look, maid: Lord knows what she and that steward of hers were doing. Your uncle was in a nest of thieves, if not a thief himself."

"Then why was he denounced but not the two of them?! Livia and Signor Russo! They're both free! She in London, living as Rob's widow, and he is here in Venice, with no blame at all! Why is it my uncle is under arrest in the well and they are free? How can I find him? And how can I get him out?"

He shook his head. "That you can't do," he said with finality. "I'm sorry for you, maid, coming all this way on a wild-goose chase. But you'll never get him out. There's no appeal against the Doge. Not in Venice. Once a man goes in, he never comes out."

Sarah waited in the red-and-white checkered hall of the Palazzo Russo as Felipe's mother came down the stairs and unlocked the inner door to the warehouse of statues without a word, without a smile, dour as her daughter. Guiltily Sarah wondered if they had discovered her identity, or seen her talking to Mordecai.

"*Grazie,*" Sarah said awkwardly from the statue-lined hall. The woman nodded and labored back up the stairs. From the first floor her daughter stared down at Sarah, and then followed her mother out of sight.

Alone in the warehouse, Sarah did not set to work at once but looked with fresh eyes at the shelves and shelves of statues, some of them wrapped, some of them polished and ready for sale, some of them chipped and dirty. Now that she looked carefully she could see that they were in very different styles, and some of them older and more worn than others. Now it was obvious to her that they were not all from the same collection, they must have come from many different sources. Irritated by her earlier naivety she walked down the line of the shelves on the back wall, seeing that there was no attempt at order—as there would have been if they had been properly collected and arranged for show; they were tumbled in, pell-mell, just as they had arrived. They looked as if they had been found, dug up, shipped at random, and heaped together, all waiting for sorting and cleaning and polishing. There were stains from different-colored earth, dark silt, red clay. A market of figures, like the market of feathers: a jumble brought together only to make money, severed, dirty, thrown into one place for the convenience of a buyer looking for profit, not for beauty. This was material newly found, with mud still drying on it.

Only on one side of the warehouse, where Sarah had been invited to make her choice, were the sculptures ready for examination. Here was a selection of statues of matching colors, cleaned and polished; here was a harmony of style that looked as if it could have come from the collection of a famous connoisseur.

The shelves of the warehouse ran the length of the house, beneath the high windows that overlooked the canal. The other side was shelved from floor to ceiling, piled with fragments of statues and some big single pieces. Sarah went all the way along, looking at the beautiful old stones, some of them chipped and dirty, some of them hacked from their bases, but all of them newly delivered to the warehouse, the dusty stone floor marked with tracks where they had been dragged in on cloths, or wheeled in on barrows. At the end of the row Sarah realized that some tracks led, not from the inner door to the house, but to a curtain of sacking at the far end of the warehouse. Sarah followed the trail to the curtain, and when she lifted it, she saw behind it another double door set into a circular stone tower, like a stair.

"Signora?"

Sarah dropped the curtain with a gasp and turned around to find old Signora Russo looking in from the door to the hall.

"*Si, si!*" she said, coming swiftly forwards, into view. She had been hidden, she thought, by the projecting statues, the old woman would not have known she was at the doorway at the far end of the warehouse. But she would certainly have seen that Sarah was at the opposite end from her workbench, in an area of the storehouse where she had no business to be.

The woman mimed eating, pointing at her mouth and at the ceiling above her head.

"It is time for dinner upstairs? I'll come at once!" Sarah nodded, came quickly to the door to the hall and followed the signora up the stairs.

"I should wash," she said, showing her dusty hands. She ducked into her bedroom, poured water from the jug into the ewer, and washed her hands, drying them on a piece of fine old linen. When she entered the dining room Felipe was not there. There was a place set for one and a glass of wine beside the bowl of soup.

"Just me?" She pointed at herself and the older woman nodded.

Awkwardly, Sarah sat at the table and spooned her soup in silence. Behind her the old woman left the room and came back with a bowl of pasta and a plate of freshly washed fruit. She put both down and left Sarah to eat alone. Clearly, Signor Russo was not coming home tonight, and in his absence the women ate in the kitchen and did not bother to entertain the visitor. Sarah wondered if she were in disgrace for going out so early in the morning, or if they suspected her of spying on them. But there was nothing in the silent service of the mother or the sulky behavior of the girl to tell her either way. The warm friendliness of the first two nights had disappeared; Sarah felt uneasily as if they were watching her.

As darkness fell, the old woman came with an ancient gold candelabra staked with wax candles, but Sarah did not want to sit in the echoing dining room with the statues like frozen companions around the walls.

"Signor Russo?" Sarah mimed beckoning, asking if he was coming home.

The old woman shook her head. "*Domani,*" she said.

She made a gesture to indicate prayer.

"Oh," Sarah said. "At church. Christmas, I suppose. Oh well. *Demain!*" she said, as if she only spoke French. "Tomorrow! Ah well! So, good night, signora!" She took her single candle, lit it from the glorious candelabra, and went carefully up the stairs to her bedroom. Chiara, having dined well with her mother in the kitchen, was already asleep in the bed. Sarah undressed, slipped in beside her, and waited for the house to be quiet.

DECEMBER 1670, LONDON

A messenger came down the quay to the Reekie warehouse, disdainfully picking his way as if he might stain his shoes. "This must be for you," Alys said to Livia as the three women in the parlor saw the cockaded hat go past the window.

Alinor looked up from the cheesecloth bags. "You can get it," she said quietly, as Livia hesitated and then quickly went to open the front door before the man had even knocked.

"Nobildonna Reekie?" the man asked.

"Da Ricci," she corrected him. "Yes."

"A letter," he said, and handed it over. It was franked by Sir James, with his name signed in the corner, so there was nothing to pay.

"I'll read it in the kitchen!" Livia called through the doorway, not wanting to face them in the parlor, and went down the hall to the kitchen where Tabs was scouring pans. "Out," she said shortly.

"Out where?" Tabs replied mutinously. "For I'm not going out into the yard; it's freezing."

"Oh, stay there then!" Livia said irritably. She glanced at Carlotta, nursing Matteo before the fire. "Isn't it time he went to bed?"

"No, your ladyship."

"Take him up," she said irritably. She found she was shaking with apprehension. This should be an invitation to come to the distant house in Yorkshire. There should be a guinea under the seal to pay for her travel. Better yet, if it announced the carriage would come for her the next day. Best of all, if he was coming himself.

She seated herself in Tabs's chair by the fire, took a knife from the table, and slit open the paper.

My dear Livia,

For so I shall call you.

First news! I am snowed in and not able to come to London, nor send for you until the ways are clear. I don't even know how long this letter will take to reach you. We have had extraordinary weather, and my aunt and I have been housebound for days. We doubt if we shall get out till the New Year. Quite an adventure. It's not uncommon for us to have snow, but this is early and uncommonly deep.

I hope you are well, and that you are not troubled with such harsh weather. I have often observed that the south of the countries are warmer than the northern regions, and I hope that is the case for you in London.

Livia paused in her reading and gritted her teeth on her temper at her fiancé's untimely interest in climate.

As soon as the snow clears, I will come to you, and— good news—my aunt is determined to make the long journey to see you also. As soon as we have arrived at Avery House I will send for you. I am sorry for this delay, but I am sure you are having a happy time with your family, and I can only trust you will be glad to greet—

Your obdt servant
James Avery

"Cattive notizie?" Carlotta asked her, disobediently hovering in the doorway, holding the baby. "Bad news?"

"No!" Livia lied. "Not at all. Sir James writes to me that he is coming to London, as soon as the roads clear."

"Un matrimonio?" Carlotta asked her, gleaming.

Livia glanced at Tabs, who was openly listening. "Don't be ridiculous," she said coldly. "To sell the antiquities of course. They will be here soon."

DECEMBER 1670, VENICE

Sarah slept and then woke with a start, but it was still night; the shutters threw bars of the shadow and moonlight on the floor, the canal outside the window was quiet, except for the lapping sound of a passing boat or the call of a disturbed gull. Sarah slid from under the covers, drew a shawl around her shoulders, and tiptoed to the door and down the stairs into the hall. The warehouse door was locked, but she knew the key was kept under one of the statues on a shelf in the hall. She went down the row, sliding her fingers under the base of each one to feel underneath, until she touched the cold shank. Quietly she drew it out, went to the warehouse door, fitted it into the keyhole, and turned.

The warehouse was ghostly in the moonlight that filtered through the greenish glass windows. Sarah went silently down the rows of shelves, past the looming pale statues, till she reached the curtained door, set in the curve of the wall around the secret stair.

It was locked, but it was a double door, slumped on its hinges, and she could just pull it apart, leaning on one heavy door and pushing against the other until there was enough of a gap between the two of them for the old lock to release and she could slip through. These service stairs spiraled upwards to the kitchen and downwards into darkness. The cold dank smell of the canal rose up to greet her. Sarah blinked into the gloom, trying to see, but all she could make out was the pallor of the stone stairs, winding down into blackness, the only sound was the eerie lap of invisible waters against the bottom steps.

Sliding a bare foot along each step to make sure that she could feel her way, her hand against the rough stone of the curved wall of the staircase, Sarah went down, one step after another, the sound of lapping water becoming louder, almost as if it were coming to meet her, as if a flood were rising. Finally, she was at the bottom, and there was a door before her; she put out a trembling hand. It was unlocked.

Gently, she pushed the door and found herself in a downstairs warehouse, a match for the one above, in almost complete darkness. The noise of lapping water from the water gate and the greenish light from the far end of the room guided her down a narrow path between benches loaded with more goods. The door at the end to the water gate was bolted from the inside, but the bolts were well oiled and slid silently back. There was no more than a little click from them and then she opened the door to the dancing illumination of moonlight on the canal. She found herself standing on a little quay, in the Russo water gate. To her left the marble steps ran up to the main house; opposite her, beside the bigger quay, the Russo gondola rocked, its head bobbing up and down like an eerie black horse.

Sarah was on the narrow storehouse quay, on the opposite side from the great steps, a place for unloading household goods; she turned and went back into the store, leaving the door open for the light.

At first glance it was a mirror image of the storerooms upstairs. Under the windows set high, away from the water, was a disorganized heap of statues, some big rounded amphorae and a jumble of little animals curled noses to paws, who looked as if they had been frozen and turned to stone as they slept together on the broad shelves.

There was a big workbench in the middle of the room, and towering over it, supported by a hawser on a pulley set in the roof beam, was a huge block of stone, the base carved roughly to look like a cliff, and on it, farther up, arms spread as if preparing to leap off the precipice into flight, an angel, a boy, naked but for a pair of exquisitely carved wings, plumage like an eagle. Sarah looked up into the sculpted face of Icarus and saw a creature as beautiful as Michelangelo's *David*, feathered like an archangel.

To her right was a small plaster cast of what the finished statue would look like, dotted with guide points so that the stone mason could measure from point to point to reproduce in stone what he had cast in plaster from his clay model.

For a moment Sarah was stunned by the beauty of the statue and by its size. It was at least twice life-size, carved to be seen from the ground on a tall pedestal or mounted on a building, high near the roof. The beautiful face looked down on her as if the boy were measuring his distance to earth, and something about those wide eyes and the formed lips made Sarah want to shout a warning to him, stone though he was, that he should not jump, not trust the fantastic feathered pinions that sprang from his muscled shoulders. As she checked her impulse, she realized why she wanted to speak to the stone face; it was compellingly real. Sarah realized she was looking at a work of art of exceptional beauty and importance. But it was a new work, in the process of carving from the plaster model. This was the workshop where Signor Russo's stone mason carved exquisite fakes.

Behind her, on the back wall, were slabs of marble, each as thick as a tabletop, stacked one on another. Each shelf had a pile of them, some of them nearly as long as the entire wall, others were shorter, some of them showing new cuts, where the whiteness of the inner stone contrasted with the aged patina of the surface. These were genuine, these were old, probably ancient. Raised on her toes Sarah could see the top of one pile of slabs and understood why they were so long and thin— each one was a single side of a stone box, plain on the inside, magnificently carved on the outer side. As she went along the shelf, she saw more and more pieces that matched in length, two long pieces, beside two short. Sarah imagined it assembled into a magnificent frieze, rider following rider or grand horses with tossing manes and tails in a long ribbon of marble. She could tell it was old, the marble was stained brown as if it had been buried in clay, and some of the horses were chipped and scarred and missing their tack. From the odd stud of a nail and a little of a rein, she guessed that the saddlery had been richly wrought, the horses bitted with gold and harnessed with bronze. But even disassembled, even shelved in a jumble, this was a band of stone fit for a palace wall.

She was so dazzled by the beauty of it that she went one step after another, deeper into the warehouse, hardly aware of where she was going; until the last stone panel gave way to a collection of what she took to be more statues, wrapped in packing material. They were stiff still figures, without spreading arms or angel wings, feet bound together, not proudly astride, but rolled in cloth or loosely wrapped, some white with dust and some discolored. Sarah looked closer, took one of the heads in her hand to gaze into the wrapped face, took the end of a sheet of packing cloth to lift and see the carving beneath and then froze. It was the smell that alerted her that there was something wrong, terribly wrong. It was not the scent of stone, clean stone, but of earth, of decay.

Sarah froze and gently replaced the head that she had thought was stone back in its place, at the top of a line of white vertebrae, dropped the winding cloth that she held in her hand. Convulsively she wiped her palm down her nightgown again and again. Staring, her eyes widened in horror, she could now make out the jumbled goods piled on the open shelves. They were bodies, human bodies, some long dead, some more recent, pulled from their stone coffins and thrown into the shelves, like so much waste. Some were stiff from death, locked rigid into the coffin shape, bandaged arms strapped over their chests, hair growing grotesquely through the bandages which bound their heads; others had been broken by being dragged from the ground, heaved from their last resting place, with arms hanging limp and the shrouds torn to show gray decaying toes and lolling blackened heads. Some were even older and the flesh had rotted away and gray bones of toes protruded from worm-eaten feet.

Sarah's sharp gasp of horror frightened her, as if it were them panting at her, and she clamped her hand over her mouth. But she still heard her little whimper of fear. She could not take her eyes from the horror before her, and she could not press past corpses to get to the safety of the inner stair.

She could hear her breath rasping against her throat as she fought not to retch in disgust at the smell, at the sight of the rotting limbs. She knew she must move but it was as if she were frozen, as still as they, whose bodies were piled one on top of another like the dead in a plague pit. At the thought of plague she heard herself give another little moan, her feverish mind thinking that the smell of decay was the stink of infection and that she too would become a tumbled corpse, piled up here with the others.

She could not take her eyes off the bodies, she was too horrified to turn her head, fearful that if she once turned away from them, turned her back to them, that they would rise up behind her and follow her down the long workshop, that she would look back to see them stiffly approaching, their bandaged eyes staring, their desiccated hands reaching out bony fingers, extending towards her. Instead of turning and running—and she knew her legs could not run, it would be like a nightmarish dream of slowness—Sarah stepped backwards towards the far end of the room, the water gate, one hand holding her steady on the shelves that held the sarcophagi of the tumbled dead, her eyes never leaving the awkward reaching hands, the pathetic bony feet.

The soft touch of the sacking curtain behind her made her jump and shudder, but then she realized she was at last at the door. She parted the curtain, and stepped out over the floodguard onto the narrow quay, reached inside, and slammed the storehouse door on the secret charnel house inside. As soon as the door was closed she heard her own whimper turn into frightened sobs, tears of terror cold on her face. She turned to the brightening water gate, the light of dawn reflecting on the lapping water, and there, on the opposite side, on the grand marble staircase, was Felipe Russo in a red velvet cape, with a candle in a gold candlestick, watching her.

Sarah did not hesitate for a moment. Crying hysterically, she ran around the narrow quayside at the back of the water gate, and Felipe dumped his candlestick on the steps, and received her into his arms.

"You know! You must know!" she gabbled, her teeth chattering so that she could hardly speak. "You know what's in there."

"Hush," he said. "You've had a fright. Yes, I know. Come."

"You know!" she cried.

"Yes, yes." Skillfully he drew her up the stairs, one step after another as her knees buckled beneath her, until they reached the beautiful hall, where she shook with horror and could not release her convulsive grip on his velvet sleeve. She turned her face into his shoulder and breathed in the smell of warm fabric, the scent of vanilla and bay, the smell of his skin, so warm and alive, so safe.

"My God," she whispered. "You know? But you must know!"

"Come," he said again, and led her up the inner marble stairs to the dining room, holding her firmly under the elbow so her knees did not give way beneath her. "Come in," he repeated gently, and led her into his private study beside the dining room.

"I did . . . I did . . . I went . . ."

"Hush," he ordered her, and turned to the sideboard and poured her a large glass of deep red wine. "Drink this, before you say anything." He pressed her into a chair and took a stool to sit beside her. In the room, watched by the sightless statues on the walls, she sipped until he saw the color come back into her white face.

"Now, you can tell me," he said quietly.

"I have nothing to tell you! It is for you to explain! You must know what I have seen!" She was trembling, the wineglass shaking in her hand. "You must know what is down there!"

He bowed. "I am sorry that you had such a shock."

"What are they? They are dead, aren't they? They have been pulled from their graves?"

He spread his hands as if in apology. "Alas, if you want antiquities you have to seek them with the ancients."

She put down her glass and gripped her hands under the table to stop herself from crying out. She felt so far from home, and so incapable of understanding what was happening. "What d'you mean? What d'you mean?"

He went to the sideboard and poured a glass of wine for himself, and poured more in her glass. "Drink. You have had a fright."

Obediently, she took another sip and still felt the terrible tremor inside her belly as if she were going to vomit.

"Did you see the beautiful panels?" he asked her. "The stone panels?"

She nodded.

"They were carved by artists, craftsmen—you agree?"

Silently, she assented.

"They should be seen, don't you think? Works of such beauty should not be hidden?"

"I don't kn—"

"They are stone coffins, coffins of pagans, not Christians. There is no reason that they should not be taken up, and shown to people who will love them, collectors. Connoisseurs. Cognoscenti!"

"But the bodies!" was all she could whisper.

"Of course there are bodies! These are coffins, they were each one carrying a body. But they are all so very old. It is not as if they were family! They were not Christians, they are not from a churchyard. And I make sure that we rebury them, reverently, respectfully."

She did not have the voice to argue but she could still see, behind her closed eyelids, the tumbled heap of corpses, the rotting flesh.

"Just thrown in . . ." was all she could whisper.

"It takes time to arrange a proper burial," he said. "Sometimes we have to keep the bodies for a little while. I am sorry that you had such a fright."

She shook her head, her eyes fixed on her face. "What?"

"My dear," he said gently. "Every profit comes at someone's cost. We make a great deal of money by tomb raiding. Yes—for that is what it is. And the people who paid for their beautiful burials are robbed. But they know nothing of it. What harm is it?"

Again she shook her head.

"But—of course—you were spying. I had not invited you into that part of the warehouse. You were not invited there, no one but my stone masons go there. It is not the behavior of a good guest to—how do you say it? Intrude."

"I'm sorry," she said stiffly. "I wanted . . ." She realized she had no excuse. "I wanted to look at the Nobildonna's dower, her beautiful pieces, for packing tomorrow, and I went farther down the warehouse and then through the door."

"Through the locked door? The one that is hidden behind a curtain?" he pointed out.

She felt simply in the wrong. "I was just working . . ."

"No you weren't," he said coldly, and she swallowed a little gasp on her new fear of him.

"Suppose you tell me the truth?" he suggested. "It is nearly morning, and my mother has told me you had your dinner and you went early to bed. I know you are lying with this talk of working for the Nobildonna; but I don't know why, nor what you are really doing here?"

She trembled again, her mind frozen in this new shock. "I'm not lying."

"Obviously you are." There was ice beneath his pleasant tone. "You are lying to my face and spying on me. First of all: what is your real name?"

She shivered; she did not know what she should say.

"Better that you say." His voice was silky.

"My name is Sarah," she said in a very small voice. "Sarah Stoney."

"And how do you know the Nobildonna?"

She looked towards the door, to the windows overlooking the canal. There was no escape from this interrogation. "I want to go to bed," she said childishly.

"Not till you have answered my questions. Remember, you are in my house under a false name. I could denounce you for spying right now and I would be paid a fee for arresting you."

"I'm just a milliner!" she protested.

"Now, that, I believe," he agreed. "You truly loved the feathers."

"I did. I really did."

"So, are you the Nobildonna's milliner?"

"Yes," she said, grasping at the lie.

"And why did she send you here?"

"To find her husband," Sarah invented rapidly. "She's so grieved— her heart is breaking—and she thought he might be alive. She thought he might be in prison: not dead. So she asked me to come . . ." Her lie tailed off as he rose and went to the window and looked out at the canal. His face was hidden from her but she could see his shoulders were shaking. She thought he was weeping, perhaps for sorrow at the loss of Rob—so she rose too, uncertain what she should do. Carefully she approached him and put her hand gently on the velvet sleeve. "Are you distressed, Felipe? Did you know him?" she asked.

Felipe Russo turned, and showed her the tears in his dark eyes, but they were from laughing, he could hardly stop laughing to gasp: "Child, I swear that you will be the death of me! For God's sake stop lying to me. That is the funniest thing I ever heard. You will never know how ridiculous! It's a terrible lie, a stupid lie, a clumsy lie. She would never send a girl like you to save her husband from prison!"

"But why not?" Sarah demanded. "She loved him. She would want to know he is safe. She would surely want him found? Why should she not have sent me to get him out?"

"Never! Never!"

"But why never?"

"Because it was she who denounced him! Little fool! She put him in there, herself!"

DECEMBER 1670, LONDON

"And where is Sarah?" Livia asked the one question Alys had been dreading. The two women were in bed, wrapped up in shawls against the cold, ice flowers frosting the inside of the windows in the winter London dawn.

"Still at her friend's house."

"She does not come home? Not for Christmas? Is she coming for Twelfth Night? When will she come?"

Alys moved out of Livia's embrace and leaned up on one elbow, so she could see the beautiful face on the pillow, the dark plait over the bronze shoulder.

"She will come soon," she said.

"You do not send for her, and order her home?"

"No. She will come . . . perhaps next month."

"So, tell me the truth."

Alys felt dread in her belly. "The truth?" she repeated. She knew she could not bear to tell Livia that she was so deeply mistrusted, that her own mother-in-law would not love her, would not receive her money, would not accept her child as a grandson.

"Have you sent her away because you did not want her to see us?" Livia whispered.

"See us?" Alys repeated; she had no idea what Livia was saying. "See us together?"

"Why should she not see us together?" the older woman repeated.

Livia stretched deliciously, like a lazy cat, her arms above her head, the dark hair in her armpits releasing an erotic scent of musk and oil of roses. "Since she would see—as your mother, for all her wisdom, does not see—that we are friends, that we are lovers who will never be parted, we will be together forever."

Alys felt her world turning around her; she put a hand on the head-board, as if to anchor herself against seasickness. "We are sisters," was all she could say. "We love each other as sisters."

"Oh my dear, call it what you will! Do you not love me and want me to stay here forever? Do you not wait, through the long cold day, for when we shall be alone together at night? Have we not found, together, true happiness? We are loving sisters who have never found love like this before in our lives. No husband has understood me or been tender to me as you, and you have never had a husband at all. Am I not dearer to you than anyone you have ever known?"

"Except my children," Alys temporized. "Except my mother."

Livia waved them away. "Of course, of course, except our children. Is not this the first true love you have known?"

Alys thought of the young man who abandoned her on her wedding day and left her and her mother to face disaster alone. "All he gave me was a cart," she said with old bitterness. "And I had adored him, I risked everything for him."

Livia laughed. "But I will give you a fortune," she promised. "We will move to a bigger, better wharf with a beautiful storehouse where you will show art and antique collections and we will be true in love and true in business. The world will see us as loving sisters, and we will keep our desire hidden. I will never tell of it and you will be mine, heart and soul. Send for Sarah, she can come home. We will be discreet. I will let everyone think that I am pursuing Sir James—" She put up her hand before Alys could protest. "I know you don't like him but let everyone think that I am chasing him for his money. That's what your mother thinks already, isn't it?"

"Yes," Alys admitted.

"So let her think that. I will visit him and work with him, but it is all, only, to make a fortune so we can have a business, a home, and a life together. Everything I do is for us to have our house together and we shall have a love that is true."

Alys, thinking that Livia had accounted for Sarah's absence all on her own, leaned towards her and kissed her yielding mouth. "True," she repeated.

DECEMBER 1670, VENICE

The room was deathly quiet when Felipe had stopped laughing at Sarah's stunned face.

"Livia denounced him?" Sarah asked. "She denounced her own husband? Robert Reekie?"

"Wait," he said. "I will answer your questions, when you answer mine. We shall speak truly to each other now, shall we? First tell me: who are you? For never in all her life would the Nobildonna send her milliner to rescue her husband. Not this husband. And Lord! Not this milliner! The moment I saw you on my doorstep I knew you had not come from her."

Sarah took a breath. "I'm Sarah Stoney. My mother is Alys Stoney, and my grandmother is Alinor Reekie."

"Reekie?" he demanded. "Reekie? You mean Roberto Reekie's mother?"

"Yes. She's my grandmother. It's her that sent me to find him."

"Did she not believe that he was dead?"

Sarah shook her head. "Not for one moment."

"But why not? Livia was in full mourning black? She threw herself on your pity? She cannot have been less than convincing."

Sarah shrugged. "My grandmother is a very wise woman. She never trusted Livia. She didn't like her saying that Matteo could take Robert's place."

"Lord! Did she think he was not Rob's child?" he demanded.

"No, no," Sarah corrected herself. "Just that he could not take Rob's place. She was completely sure that Rob was still alive."

"She had a vision?" he asked scathingly. "She has magical powers, your grandmother?"

Defiantly, Sarah nodded.

"*Dio!*" he said blankly. "I sent Livia into a madhouse."

"Why did Livia denounce her husband?" Sarah pursued.

"To be rid of him," he said simply, as if it were obvious.

"She put a letter in the Bocca?"

"Yes, I arrested him myself."

Outside, the constant lapping of the canal grew a little more urgent, like a speeding heart, as a boat went by and the splash of the wake lapped against the walls of the house. Sarah looked at Felipe, her eyes dark, her face blank: "Did Rob see the warehouse? Was she your partner in the lower workhouse as well as the upper one? Did Rob see the bodies?"

"Yes," he said, and poured a glass of wine for himself. "Alas, he did. He wanted to purchase a body, you understand? For his studies.

He and the Jewish doctor needed to examine a dead body, to understand how the muscles worked, how the breath comes. He was especially interested in the lungs—especially interested in people who drowned."

Sarah wrapped her arms around herself so she did not shudder. "You told me that you buried them with respect?"

"I do, when I can. But I also sell them to the hospitals, and the doctors, and the artists."

"This is legal in Venice?"

"No," he conceded. "So, we keep each other's secrets. The Jewish doctor brought Rob to meet the man who could supply a corpse, and there—*ecco!*—was I in my storeroom!" He broke off. "Roberto had known me as Milord's steward, and Livia's trusted servant. He was very surprised to find me in such a grand palazzo, selling corpses. He was determined to know, he pushed into my workroom . . . he saw . . ."

"He saw what I saw?" Sarah whispered. "The terrible dead? The unburied? And their tombs. He was here?"

Felipe bowed. "He was here. He was just like you—shocked like you were. He dashed away, he went straight home and accused his wife of terrible crimes: defrauding her dead husband, trading in grave goods, lying to him, deceiving him with me."

"As her criminal partner?" Sarah confirmed.

Felipe bowed. "As her lover," he said very quietly. "He guessed that too."

"Is that why she denounced him?" she asked. "So he could not accuse her, and you, of what you have done here?"

"Really, she had no choice. And besides, her husband's family were saying he was murdered. It was quite obvious that she should blame it on the doctor."

Sarah was aghast. "She accused Rob of murder? And you sent him to his death?"

"Really, he left us with no choice."

Sarah rose from the chair and pressed her trembling hands down on the highly polished table to hide their shaking. "Then what about me?" she asked him. "For now I know too. What are you obliged to do to me?"

DECEMBER 1670, LONDON

Twice a week Livia made the long cold journey from the south bank of the river to the north, to the fashionable church where Sir James had suggested that she should meet with the minister. Twice a week she sat in the minister's book-lined study, with his housekeeper as chaperone, darning in a corner by the door, while he taught the principles of the Protestant Church, the catechism, and the prayers in English. He praised Livia for her command of the language, her punctuality, and her diligence, but he found he could not warm to the beautiful young woman who occasionally tapped a long fingernail on the desk and muttered, *"Allora!"* at some particularly obscure theology. He feared she was preparing for baptism and confirmation for worldly gain—so that she might marry Sir James—and not because she knew in her heart that the religion of her family and childhood had fallen into heresy. When he tried to gently question her as to her heart and her conscience Livia widened her dark eyes at him and smiled her enchanting smile. "Father," she said, though he wished she would not. "Father, my soul is pure."

"The world is full of temptations . . ." he started, hoping she would admit that she was tempted by Sir James's wealth and position.

"Not to me," she said quietly. "All I want is grace."

Livia never told anyone where she was going, nor what she was learning. She said that she was walking for her health and that she could not remain cooped up in the little warehouse every day of the week, especially in this miserable weather when the fog lay low on the icy tide. Alys made no complaint, and never questioned Livia

351

about her outings. Occasionally, Livia brought home some little fairings: a ribbon for Alys, or a toy for Matteo, or some special herbs for Alinor. She said then that she had been shopping, or visiting the Royal Exchange, she said she had been walking towards the City and stopped to look at a market in the street. She said that she could not be expected to see nothing day after day but the cold rise and fall of a dirty winter river.

Some days she walked past Avery House on the Strand, taking care to cross the road to walk in the shadow of the imposing wall so that she could not be seen by any servants cleaning or tidying the empty house. She would pause at the corner and glance back at the shuttered windows, imagining the rooms where the furniture was covered, and even the chandeliers were bagged and dark. There were no signs that Sir James was expected, and there was no way for her to cross the road and knock on the front door to ask. She would not have demeaned herself by inquiring for him, when he had told her that he was snowed in at his country house. And anyway, the valuable brass door knocker had been taken off the door.

DECEMBER 1670, VENICE

Felipe rose to his feet and poured the rest of the bottle into Sarah's glass. "Of course, you raise a very difficult question," he complained. "Perhaps I had better just strangle you and drop your body in the water gate."

"Captain Shore knows where I am," she said defiantly, but her voice trembled.

He shrugged: "Does he care? Would he look for you?"

"I can offer you an agreement," she said unsteadily. "If you will help me rescue my uncle, I will never speak about the . . . all this. I will forget all about the workshop and what you do. We will never mention it again."

He cocked an eyebrow.

"And I can pay you!" she said desperately.

He openly laughed at her. "Half a guinea? Or will you throw in the half guinea's worth of feathers?"

"I can send you money from England. If you will only help me."

"Obviously, I'm going to get money from England, and far more than you can raise."

"But what if you don't?" Sarah challenged. "What if you don't get any money? What if you are working to your plan, and risking everything, but she isn't?"

He turned his head and looked at her over the top of his glass. "What do you mean?"

"Because she's not sent you any money, has she?" Sarah gambled. "And she's certainly not paid us anything. I think she's keeping it all to herself. The antiquities were for sale—I saw them for sale myself! But she has a new partner now."

"Who? She was to sell them in your warehouse? With you bearing the costs."

"She's got another plan now!" Sarah grew more confident. "She's got another partner. We carried the costs, but she showed them in his house. He's an English lord, she chased him since she first arrived in England. She's ditched you, she's ditched us! She's got another patron altogether. She's a whore like one of those women on their chopines, and she's moved on from you and left you behind."

He shook his head, confidently smiling. "She would never double-cross me."

"How can you be so sure?"

"Because we are promised to marry."

"Not her!" Sarah swore. "She's going to marry Sir James Avery, and give him the son he wants. Matteo will be an English boy. You'll never see either of them again. She'll marry him—an Englishman, far richer and grander than you will ever be—and she'll never ever come back here."

DECEMBER 1670, LONDON

Livia shivered in the stern of the little skiff as it crossed the river, a cold wind blowing in from the sea, the water stairs at Avery House glittering with frost, the garden a monochrome of tree trunks, white on one side and black with damp on the other, the twigs and the boughs outlined, as if a limner had been through the orchard to make every branch a thing of startling beauty.

"Here," Livia said, putting a penny begrudgingly into the man's hand.

"You're welcome, my pretty," he taunted her, and let the boat rock as she stepped from it to climb up the stairs, her boots making dark tracks in the white frost of the steps.

"I shan't be long, you can wait," she said.

"You hiring me to wait?" he asked hopefully.

"No! Of course not! Why should I pay for you to do nothing? But if you wait, I shall come in a moment and pay you to take me back to Savoury Dock when I'm ready."

"I'll wait unless I'm called away," he said, resentfully. "I'll wait for free and then I'm sure it'll be my honor to escort you home. To Savoury Dock—known for its aroma. To the Reekie Wharf—known for its elegance."

"*Chiudi la bocca,*" she muttered under her breath, and turned to walk through the garden. Ahead of her a robin gripped a swinging bough, sang to her, a sound of piercing sweetness. Livia did not hear it, did not see the tip-tilted bright head. The statue of the sleeping fawn was curled at the foot of a gnarled apple tree, drifted snow was white on the white marble of its back. Livia strode past it, eyes on the blank windows of the house.

Glib, the footman, had reported that the staff had been instructed to light fires, air the linen, and open the shutters and that the master would return within the week, but Livia had heard nothing from Sir James himself, neither letter, nor invitation. She did not know why he had not invited her to his house, not written to her again from Northallerton and sent no present. She had been hoping for a diamond ring as a Christmas gift and a betrothal. She had received nothing. Livia gritted her teeth and walked up the beautiful terrace, sparkling with frost in the hard bright sunshine of winter.

She felt no gladness when she saw that the curtains of his study were drawn open. She felt no joy when she saw the back of his head and shoulders as he sat at his desk. She raised one dark gloved hand and rapped on the window. He jumped at the sudden knock, turned and saw an ominous figure in a dark dress; she saw the shock on his face, and then he recognized her.

He rose to his feet and opened the tall glass door. "Livia," he said weakly. "What a surprise."

She marched in.

DECEMBER 1670, VENICE

Sarah woke late, to a silent house, and went apprehensively downstairs. The beautiful hall was the same as always. Sarah had the strange feeling that she must have dreamed the night before, but when she turned to glance at the front door she saw it was bolted tight. She was imprisoned in the quiet house.

Felipe's mother Signora Russo had a milky hot drink ready for her, and bread and jam to eat in the dining room, but when Sarah took her seat at the table, the woman stood and watched her, as if she were on guard. Felipe Russo came up the stairs from the water gate, directly from Mass at the local church, holy water still wet on his forehead, said one quiet word, and his mother left the room.

He took a seat opposite her. "You told me last night that the Nobildonna would not come back here," he started abruptly. "You told me she was to marry an Englishman."

"You told me last night you might as well drown me in the water gate," she said defiantly.

He gave her a quick warm smile. "You know I would not. But what you said about Livia: was it a desperate lie to save your skin?" he asked.

She hesitated before answering him. "No. It's more than that. I've never met anyone like Livia in my life before, so I can't say what she might do. I don't know what promises she has made to you. But truly, when I left she looked very much as if she were planning to marry an English baronet—he's called Sir James Avery. At first, she said that she had come to live with us, that she wanted an English family, she wanted nothing but to share our life. Then she started to complain that we aren't rich enough for her, the warehouse is too small, in a poor part of town, a long way from the City. She said that my uncle Rob had led her on to think we're grander than we are." She flushed. "We're working people," she said. "My grandma sells herbs and possets to apothecaries, Ma runs a little wharf."

"But you do have a warehouse?" he pressed. "I sent the first load? Reekie Wharf?"

"It's just a little storehouse beside the wharf, we load corn and apples and coasters' loads for shillings at a time. We don't earn much, we could hardly afford the shipping for her first load." He heard the resentment in her voice. "She talked my ma into paying for her."

"We agreed she should arrive penniless." He laughed shortly. "We thought it would be more persuasive. We thought you were wealthy and you would be bound to help her if she came in, in tears, with the baby in her arms."

Sarah scowled as she remembered Livia's tragic appearance. "Oh, she did that, she did all of that. And we did help her. She's got my mother wrapped around her little finger, risking our whole business in not declaring the goods. When you bring goods into England you have to pay the Excise—but the Nobildonna didn't declare it."

He gave a little laugh. "Of course not!"

"The first rich man she met was Sir James, and straightaway she got him to let her sell the antiquities at his big house on the Strand. I saw them together, as close as lovers. She sat at his desk to open her letters, she looks like she owns the place."

Sarah betrayed all of the Nobildonna's secrets without hesitation. "If she catches him, she'll surely have no interest in trading antiquities, she'll never want to see you again. She'll want to leave you far behind, and us—she won't come back to our wharf when she's Lady Avery; she'll be an English lady then, thinking of nothing but her children and her dogs."

"But he's an old man? You said he was old?"

"He is, he must be about forty."

"Forty is no age at all!"

"It seems very old to me," she replied. "Old enough to be my father."

He looked at her from under his dark eyebrows "I am thirty-four. Do I seem very old to you?"

She could not help but laugh. "No! You're . . ."

She blushed and could not describe him and he understood her stammering halt, and beamed back at her. "Thank God for that," he remarked. "Did she really send for a second order of antiquities? That was true?"

"Yes," Sarah said, recovering from her betraying embarrassment. "She said she made a fortune on the first load. Did she send any money back to you? Captain Shore could have carried a letter? Have you heard nothing from her at all?"

He rose from the table and went to the window, looking down at the canal as if he would find an answer in the green lapping waters and the crisscrossing boats.

Sarah rose from the table to stand beside him and follow his gaze. "So . . . now you know this of her, will you help me to get Rob released?

There's no reason for you to leave him in prison now. Not now that she's betraying you. You've done all this: you've lied for her and denounced an innocent man, and smuggled for her, and now she's gone away with your money and will marry someone else."

"You talk like a child," he said angrily. He turned from the window and threw himself in his ornate chair at the head of the table.

Sarah stood before him. "I speak simply," she conceded. "And I'll tell you why. Just because she is complicated, doesn't make me stupid. I'm no fool. She's played me for a fool, and she plays my mother for a fool, and plays Sir James for a fool, and even—I think—she's made a fool of you. But not my grandmother, who knew the truth the moment she saw her and her baby. We don't all have to dance to Livia's tune. You can help me save Rob, and that will be one thing where she has not had her own way. My uncle is a good man, I believe, and his mother loves him. There's no reason that we should help Livia to have him imprisoned, and maybe die in prison, and break my grandmother's heart."

He was silent, considering this. "One should never do business for spite," he remarked.

"But why should you do so much, and risk so much, to get her into Sir James's beautiful London house? With the next shipment of antiquities you will lie for her, supply her with forged goods, help her marry another man, and you're not even going to be paid!"

He nodded slowly. "I am not disposed to do that."

"Then help me."

"Perhaps I could save Roberto," he conceded. "Unless he is already dead. But it will not be easy, and why should I?"

"Because I believe you are a good man," she said earnestly, putting her hand on his. "A good man who has done bad things. But this can be put right. You can put it right; indeed, you should put it right."

He looked at her with a smile in his dark eyes. "For the sake of goodness and justice?" he asked her. "So that I can be a better person? You talk like a Protestant!"

"Yes." She did not flinch at his cynicism. "But there is another reason."

"I'm listening."

She smiled at him, suddenly confident. "If you get Rob released, and he comes home with me to England, then she can't marry any-one, can she? She's still married to him. Her plan to break her prom-ise to you, and steal your goods, and marry another man and take Matteo with her—it all fails. She can't marry Sir James: she's al-ready married."

There was silence in the cold room. Outside on the canal, a boat-man went by singing a love song. Gently, Felipe took up her hand from the table and kissed it. She could feel the warmth of his lips on her fingers. "What a clever girl you are," he said caressingly. "Under that straight gaze, under that fair skin, what a clever mind works so quickly! Almost, you could be Italian. Almost you could be the No-bildonna herself. She made a grave mistake when she did not enchant you along with all the rest of your family!"

Sarah felt her cheeks warm at the kiss on her hand, and at his words of praise. "I don't think she even saw me," she told him. "She was far too busy being charming to my mother, and my brother, and then Sir James."

"Foolish," the Signor said. "Foolish to miss such a one as you. I imagine you are as clever as all of them together."

DECEMBER 1670, LONDON

James Avery rushed to pull out a chair for Livia. "Please, sit!" he begged her.

She sank down into the chair opposite him and found her sweetest smile. "I'm so glad you are home!" she said. "I could not wait to see you! I could not wait another moment for you to send for me!"

He flushed, shuffled papers, stacked them into a pile, and then put them in a drawer. "I should have sent the coach tomorrow," he said. "I have only just arrived. The house is not ready for visitors."

"I'm no visitor!" She made her eyes warm on his face, her gaze on his mouth to make him think of kisses. "I am the mistress of the house. I am ready, Beloved."

"There were difficulties at home," he said awkwardly.

"This is your home."

"No, no, this is my London house. The London house of my family. I always think of my home as Northallerton. Northside Manor, Northallerton. And there were difficulties. My aunt . . ."

She laughed as she stripped off her black leather gloves and dropped them, like a gauntlet in a challenge, on the desk. She unwound a shawl of black lace from her neck, as if she were undressing before him, as if next she would open her bodice. "Your aunt?" she repeated, as if to invite him to share a joke. "The English aunt?"

"She requests, indeed, she insists, that she meet you before the banns are called. So she is . . ."

She widened her eyes. "The aunt wishes to inspect me? As if I am a horse?"

"No! No! It's just that she has been as a mother to me, and she longs to greet you as a daughter."

"And I her."

"And she wants to prepare you for your life as the lady of Northside Manor."

"Does she know that I am a Nobildonna, and that I had a palace in Venice?"

"Yes, I told her," he said miserably. "I did tell her."

She raised her beautifully arched eyebrows and she smiled at him. He felt his anxieties melt away under the warmth of her beauty and confidence. "I think I can run a little house like yours," she assured him.

"She insists," he said haplessly.

"Then we will welcome her," she assured him. "Together. When does she arrive?"

"She's here now. We came together in my coach."

She raised a white finger to reprove him; she did not show her temper. "Now that was very wrong, my love, to invite her here without agreeing with me. But—*ecco!*—I forgive you. I should have liked to have been here to welcome her—but no matter. The English have no manners, and I daresay she is not offended. I shall order the cook to prepare dinner for us and she shall dine with us. Where is she now?"

"Out," he said shortly.

"Out where, *cara mia*?"

"She has gone to visit my brother-in-law."

"The brother of your former wife?" she specified, as if she did not know in a moment who he meant.

"Yes."

"The gentleman who accused me of fraud, and malpractice?"

"You remember, he withdrew his words, and apologized?"

She shot him one sharp look and then she looked down, her long dark eyelashes brushing her cheeks. "I remember everything," she whispered. "I remember what you did. I remember what you did to me—that afternoon in your bedroom. I remember what you promised me."

"I did," he said grimly. "I was wrong, but I do not forget it."

"I will never forget it," she told him. "It was the happiest of ordeals for me as it proved to me that you loved me—beyond restraint." She let that sink in. "So I shall tell the cook to prepare the dinner for later—when the aunt returns. I suppose she dines in the afternoon? Will she bring the brother-in-law with her?"

"She may invite him. She has every right to invite him to this house. She is my honored guest and she has lived with me for many years. This house is as her home."

Livia rose in a rustle of black silk. "Of course. What a pleasant dinner we shall have."

DECEMBER 1670, VENICE

Felipe Russo walked down to the ship with Sarah to meet Captain Shore. "I will take this young lady to an officer of immigration, he can be trusted to change her papers," he said, almost as soon as they had climbed the steep gangplank. Captain Shore greeted them at the top, as if he did not wish them to come on board.

"I'd rather we kept this between ourselves," he said, shooting a horrified look at Sarah. "She didn't tell me she had another name when we sailed from London. We sail tomorrow. No reason to trouble the authorities. She's done nothing wrong beyond giving another name. A girl's trick. Not important. If we can get in and out again without bringing it to the attention of the authorities I'd much prefer it."

"On the contrary," Felipe overruled him. "She's going to right a great wrong. She's going to attend the Doge's Palace and give a deposition. She's going to free an innocent man."

"Nothing to do with me," Captain Shore said sternly. "Look, signor, we've worked together in the past. I've shipped some valuables for you and never questioned you on the source of them, or the license to export. I've shipped what you've loaded, accepted the description on the docket, and never opened a case to check it. Neither of us have been overly fussy about the paperwork."

"We have always worked well together," Felipe conceded.

"I'd rather not draw attention to myself."

"No more would I," Felipe agreed. "But it's not as if we were smuggling—"

"Ssh! Sssh!" Captain Shore cast an anguished glance at the

quayside where idle men could be loitering and listening. "Not I! Never out of this port! The closest I've ever got has been your business! Your own business! When you dispatch huge boxes, and tell me it's the private property of an ambassador. When you wrap a ton of statues and tell me it's the lady's private furniture. Again! She has a lot of furniture, I must say. And all of it in crates as heavy as stone! And this is the second time I've shipped her poor widow's mite to London. And do you know what she does with it there?"

Felipe shrugged. "Sits on it? Dines off it? Since it is her furniture?"

"You know very well what she does with it."

"You have nothing to fear. I assure you. I am an agent of the state myself. I will change the registration of this lady—"

"Just a milliner, really," Sarah added.

"I will go with her into the Doge's Palace and she will make a deposition."

"So why are you so right and tight and aboveboard all of a sudden?" Captain Shore growled.

"This lady has convinced me," Felipe said, smiling down at Sarah. "I am persuaded."

"Is this what you want?" Captain Shore asked Sarah with desperate honesty. "Because if it's a Banbury game, say so now." He was gambling that the elegant Italian would not understand the London slang words for "a lie."

Felipe looked from one to the other. "Speak alone," he said, waving them for'ard. "You need not speak in your barbaric language to elude me. Speak freely."

Captain Shore took two paces with Sarah. "What's going on?"

"He is who he says he is," she said breathlessly. "A state spy. He put my uncle in prison, and he can get him out again."

"Lord!" the older man said miserably. "But why would he?"

"He's on my side now," she claimed. "I'm going to change my name on the ship's papers and go as myself, into the Doge's Palace and set my uncle free."

"Child," the Captain said to her. "You don't know what you're doing. You go in there, you'll never get out again, and your grandmother will mourn for the two of you dead, and your mother will never forgive me. You'll breathe your last in the icy air under the *piombi* as so many good men and women have done before you."

Captain Shore thought she was like her mother: brave and determined, her jaw set square, looking as her mother did when she received a bill she could not manage. "No, I won't. For I'm going to free my uncle and get him home."

"Why would he help you? A cutthroat like him?"

Her whole face lit up, as she leaned forward to whisper to him. "He's sweet on me."

"Lord!" he moaned. "There's no safety in that!"

"I have to take the chance on it," she said, her eyes still bright. "He's the only chance I've got."

"Look," he said. "If you go in there, with or without him, sweet or not, I won't be able to get you out. I'll have to sail without you. Don't think I'll be any help because I won't be, I can't be. Your uncle is almost certainly dead already, God rest his soul. And I can't take that news back to your mother and tell her you're gone too."

She gritted her teeth. "I'm doing it," she said. "I'm going in there."

The fight went out of him in a muttered curse and he turned back to the Italian who was waiting at the head of the gangplank, watching the quay below where a load of carpets was being noisily valued and crated for export.

"I hear you're a reformed character," the Captain said bluntly to him. "Transformed by love. Sweet on her?"

"Is that what you think?" Felipe asked Sarah, a laugh in his voice. She met his gaze. "Yes, I do. Is it not true?"

"Sweet?" he confirmed the English word. "You mean to tell him that I am in love with you?"

She shot him a flirtatious glance. "Not yet," she said carefully. "It's as if you're disposed to fall in love with me."

He nodded. "That's quite right. I am disposed to it, Miss Jolie. And you? Are you sweet on me?"

"If you could do this some other time," the Captain interrupted. "I could get on with loading my ship."

Sarah dragged her gaze from Felipe and giggled. "I'm sorry.

Of course. I'll just take my papers and we'll change my passport."

"I'll follow behind you," Captain Shore promised her. "I'll see you in. I'll wait outside. If you're not out within the hour, I'll go to the English ambassador."

"What can he do?" Signor Russo asked with interest.

"Nothing," Captain Shore said miserably. "As you very well know. But he's the only man in the whole of this city who ought to take an interest in this woman—young enough to be my daughter—walking into that circle of hell. And you taking her. What's to say you're not arresting her and getting the bounty for her innocent neck?"

"This innocent neck was certainly born to be hanged," Felipe told him. "And besides, we are all agreed I am sweet on her. Have you got her false papers?"

Captain Shore opened the ship's log and handed Sarah's papers over.

"First we'll correct them at the Custom House and then we'll go up to the palace."

"Aye," the Captain said. "And pray God you come strolling back again. I'll come to the gate, and watch for her to come out, God spare her. And to watch you." Sarah and Felipe went down the gangplank, and as the Captain followed he muttered under his breath. "And I'm not the only one that hopes they arrest you and fling you down somewhere very deep."

Correcting the papers was easy with Felipe Russo's fluent explanation about Sarah concealing her name until she could claim his help. "A friend of the family," he murmured as the papers were stamped and sealed with wax.

The three of them took a traghetto across the canal, and then walked, with Captain Shore trailing behind, to the entrance to the Doge's Palace. Sarah gave a little shudder as the shadow of the great gateway fell on her, and Felipe took her elbow and guided her in.

"Here to see His Excellency Giordano," he said pleasantly. "Signor Russo and a guest."

The clerk at the gatehouse entered their names in a register and stamped a pass. "You know where to go?" he asked.

"Of course, we are old friends," Felipe said, and guided Sarah across the courtyard, through the double doors, and up a marble staircase.

"Are all these rooms prisons?" she whispered.

He laughed, his voice echoing on the quiet stair. "Oh! No! These are all offices. A thousand clerks work here like maggots in cheese, reporting on everything: trade, plague, religion, inventions, people, gold, Ottomans (we keep a watch on the Ottomans for the rest of the world), silks, sea currents, heresies. Whatever there is in the Republic we watch it and note it and report on it. The Council of Ten know everything there is to be known, and their advice to the Doge guides his decision, which is never wrong."

"It was wrong when they arrested my uncle," Sarah said stoutly, though she was unsteady on her feet with fear.

"The advice was wrong then," Signor Russo agreed. "My advice, actually. But the Doge cannot be wrong. Remember that. It's illegal to say he is."

Sarah paused and looked at him incredulously.

"Remember it," was all he said.

"What will they do to you?" Sarah asked nervously as they climbed up and up the stairs. "For bad advice?"

"Oh, they'll make me rewrite my report," he said casually. "And set me to capture the real murderer."

"I hadn't thought of that!" She suddenly paused. "The Nobildonna's husband was truly murdered? So there is a real murderer out there?"

"Almost certainly," he said nonchalantly. "Come on now. They know how long it takes to get from the gate to the office, we can't be late."

"They're watching us now?"

His face was completely serious as he nodded to the darkened internal windows all along the corridor. "Oh yes. They are watching us now."

DECEMBER 1670, HADLEY, NEW ENGLAND

Ned set off early up the road of snow to the minister's house, with only some dried fruit in a little box in his basket. He did not want to stop on the way for trade or conversation, he was haunted by what Wussausmon had told him, that the English had been guided to their New World by men who named themselves devils. He was desperate to talk to the minister, to confirm that it was God's will that the English came to the New World, that it was their destiny, Ned's own destiny, to conquer the land and to show the rest of the world what a divinely inspired nation could be.

He timed his visit for the morning prayer meeting in the minister's home. He wanted to hear the simple clarity of the prayers, he wanted to hear the long sermon. Since it was winter and everyone had work to do, John Russell kept to the point: these were the hardest days in a hard year, the darkest of nights in uncertain times, God was guiding them, they must never doubt but that God was with them.

"Amen," John concluded the prayers, and said good-bye to his congregation as they went out into the cold.

Ned paused in the hall. "Minister, I have doubts," he said very quietly.

"God be with you, Ned. Doubts come from the devil," John Russell replied simply. "Do you doubt that you are elect, one of God's chosen?"

"No," Ned said uncertainly. "I am doubting our mission here, my work in the world."

The minister nodded. "Come on upstairs," he said. "All of us doubt our mission, and those of us who have been defeated and have to endure the calumny of the world have a hard road to tread." He led the way up the stairs. The spare-room door was open, for William and Edward to follow the service, listening in silence. Ned greeted them.

"Did you get my warning to the Councils?" he asked. "Will it have to wait for spring?"

"I wrote, and sent a letter downstream," John said. "The river is open lower down and a native in a mishoon was going, even in this cold weather; he said he'd take it to the coast. The ships for the coastal trade should be sailing, between storms, so it should get to Plymouth and then Boston, it'll take days, or even weeks. But yesterday I had a message overland from the Council brought by the militia they were so anxious to get news to the outlying towns. It's bad news. Very bad. They confirm what you say, Ned."

Ned looked at the grave faces of the three other men.

"They've had reports from all around the country that King Philip has been holding feasts and dances at his winter quarters," John Russell said grimly. "Not even this weather can stop him."

Ned nodded in silence.

"They didn't know he was sending scouts out. How do they even get messages through?"

"They have ways," Ned said, thinking of the snowsnake track, and the smoke signals. "They're not afraid of the forest, they walk on the frozen river. They aren't trapped in their houses like we are by the cold."

"The Council says that someone has seen that King Philip is stockpiling weapons and his *pnieses*—his men at arms—are in black warpaint."

"What does that mean?" Edward asked.

"It means they're preparing for war," Ned said unhappily. "If the Council would just talk to him . . ."

"As soon as it thaws they will summon him to Plymouth and he will have to answer for his acts. They swear that this time they will teach him a lesson he'll not forget. He's not allowed to prepare for war— that's rebellion against our rule. We will accuse him of rebellion and he will face the greatest punishment."

William nodded. "Hanging," he said shortly.

Ned, shocked, looked from one royal rebel to the other. "We can't hang him for rebellion. He's not subject to our laws, he's not under our rule. He's a leader on his own lands. The treaty—"

"The treaty said that he should stay on his lands and we on ours," John Russell interrupted. "That we should live in peace. That his enemies would be ours, and ours would be his."

"And they're stockpiling weapons," William pointed out.

"We sell them weapons!" Ned said despairingly. "We sell them the very weapons we're complaining about!"

"We sell them for hunting," Edward ruled. "Not for them to be turned on us."

Ned turned to John Russell. "All this could be peaceably resolved," he said. "But if they summon King Philip and treat him like a traitor, they will shame him before his people; that will anger him, things will get worse. If they would meet him halfway somewhere, and give him gifts and treat him like the friend that his father was. If they would speak to him like an equal and promise to stop buying land and cheating his people out of land! If they would take away the cause of war, then it won't come to war. Surely! Isn't that in our interest? Isn't that the best outcome for us all?"

William shook his head. "It's too late, Ned. Remember the old king, Bloody Charles? There comes a point where you can't keep asking someone to give their word and change their ways. There comes a point where you have to capture them, arrest them, and kill them."

"It'll be the same with this king," Edward agreed. "He's growing overmighty. We have to stop him now."

"He doesn't even call himself a king!" Ned protested.

Grimly, the three men shook their heads. "It's God's will," John Russell said simply. "Who are we to question?" He dropped a heavy hand on Ned's shoulder. "Are these the doubts?" he asked gently. "Are these your doubts, Ned? Are you doubting God's intention for us?"

Ned knew he could not argue with God. "Mercy . . ." he said quietly. "Mercy for the Massasoit . . ."

"As soon as the thaw comes we're ordered to muster and train the town militia," John Russell told him. "You'll be summoned, Ned, and we'll need you more than anyone. You're one of the few who has seen action. You'll be made a captain."

Edward leaned forwards and clapped Ned on the shoulder. "You'll be a commander, Ned! And we'll advise. We'll stay out of sight but we'll order the drilling and training, and we'll plan defenses."

Ned remembered Wussausmon saying that the fences would not stop a deer and that the People could command fire to go where they wanted. "We've only got stock fences," he said. "Nothing that could defend us against an attack."

"They won't directly attack us," John Russell said. "They wouldn't dare. I expect them to creep up on a few deserted farmhouses. They'd no more attack us than fall on Springfield. They know we're too strong for them."

"But you should come into town, Ned," William said. "You're too remote, out there by the river, and they could scalp you in the night and get away by canoe and we'd not even know it. You'd better come into town and then you can supervise the defenses."

Ned thought for a moment he must have taken a fever he felt such a rush of sickness and weariness. "I can't leave the ferry," he said miserably. "If the people from Hatfield want to come over in spring, especially if they feel in danger, I have to be there to bring them over. And I can't leave my beasts in the winter and I can't drive them in through the snow."

"The Hatfield people must fall back inside our palisade as soon as they can travel," Edward ordered. "And the ferry ropes cut, and the raft sunk, so the enemy cannot use it."

Ned shook his head, at the thought of destroying his ferry, at the thought of Quiet Squirrel and her people being named as enemies, at his sense of the world falling out of control, falling from godliness and certainty into fear and war.

"You'll have to come into town," his old commander told him, and Ned heard the order. "Your place is here, with your own people. Now that it's war."

DECEMBER 1670, LONDON

Dinner with his aunt and Livia was even worse than James had feared. From the first introduction it was a joust of beautiful manners.

"May I present the Nobildonna da Ricci—" he started.

"Peachey," Livia corrected him.

"You don't know her name?" his aunt turned to him.

"My *fidanzato* mistakes," Livia said smiling, curtseying low. "It is my accent! I am learning to speak English, you know. My name is pronounced Peachey."

James's aunt, who had known Sir William Peachey of Sussex in the days before the war, gave her nephew a long considering look, and curtseyed very slightly to the widow. "Any relation to the Sussex Peacheys?"

"Very distant," Livia answered truthfully.

"This is my aunt, Dowager Lady Eliot," James said.

Livia returned the curtsey. "Ah! You are a widow like me?" Livia tipped her head on one side to convey sympathy and smiled tenderly.

"Indeed," her ladyship said, immune both to sympathy and the smile. "And you have children?"

"Four: Sir Charles my son, my daughter Lady Bellamy, and my daughter Lady de Vere, and another daughter."

"Not married?" Livia was as fast as a hound on the scent of the sole disappointment in this list of social triumph.

"Married but not to a nobleman; she is Mrs. Winters."

"I am surprised you do not live with them?"

"A glass of wine?" James interposed. "Before dinner?"

"I live at Northside Manor. To keep James company after his loss."

"And now I will be able to comfort him," Livia assured her. "And you can be released to their ladyships and the little Mrs."

"I expect I will stay at Northside," her ladyship said firmly. "I lived very happily with dear Agatha."

"White or red?"

"Agatha?" Livia's laugh tinkled out. "Ah, forgive me, this I cannot say at all. Who is dear Athaga? Agatta?"

"Lady Agatha Avery, James's late wife, as dear as a daughter to me."

Livia's head tilted to the side again. "And at last you can return to your own daughters," she said. "How they must have missed you, while you were staying on and on in my dear Sir James's house!"

"When you are settled in, and you know how things go on, in one of the great homes of Yorkshire, I shall perhaps move; but only to the Dower House nearby," her ladyship said firmly. "I have agreed it with Sir James."

"My *fidanzato* cannot be wrong," Livia declared with a little smile at him. "His judgment is perfect. If that is what he prefers I am sure it should take place at once. Perhaps you had better go to the Dower House now?"

"Surely, they will serve dinner soon!" James remarked.

"It is delayed?" Livia was all concern. She smiled at Lady Eliot. "Is this how you keep order in the great house of Yorkshire? I shall have to learn your patience! In my home, in the Palazzo Fiori, I was very strict."

DECEMBER 1670, VENICE

The Doge's Palace was like a warren of stone. Felipe and Sarah took a small stone staircase at the side of the building that climbed up and up with unending little passages running off to one side and another. Felipe followed the official, Sarah behind him, and a guard brought up the rear. The official turned into a set of rooms and they followed a twisting corridor paneled with wood, which went past one tiny office and another. All of them had open fanlights so every office could eavesdrop on the talk in the corridor; all of them had windows set at an angle so they could observe who went past, without the visitors seeing inside the offices. All of them had double doors so that no one loitering outside could listen to a quiet conversation in the room.

They came to a double doorway; Felipe tapped and confidently led Sarah through the first door into the tiny lobby and then through the second. It was a small room, with space only for a fireplace and a desk. A clerk sat behind a table, pen poised; he rose as Felipe entered and greeted him as a friend. Briefly, Felipe explained that his accusation had been incorrect, that Roberto Reekie was innocent and here was his niece come to beg for his release. Sarah apologized for giving a false name on arrival in Venice and said that she was seeking her uncle who had been wrongly arrested. The clerk made her sign the document in triplicate and then Felipe Russo opened the door and she waited outside in the twilight, a narrow slit of a window far above her head. She could hear nothing through the thick double doors but inside the room Felipe explained to the clerk that Roberto Ricci was innocent and should be released. He was in there for more than an hour and when he came out his face was grave.

"My uncle?" she demanded, her hand against the carved paneling, to keep her steady. "He's not . . . he's not . . ."

"He's not dead yet," he said flatly. "But I'm sorry, we're not in time to save him."

"What?"

"I'm sorry . . ."

"Please tell me," she whispered. "Please tell me what's happened."

He took her arm and started down the winding corridor, his voice very low. "They knew he was a doctor, they knew that he worked with patients with quatrain fever, studied old documents with the Jewish doctors and translators of the Arab physicians."

"Is that wrong?"

"No, that's allowed—you have to have a license—but he had one. But since he was an expert, accused of a crime and formally denounced by witnesses, they sent him to the Isola del Lazzaretto Nuovo—the quarantine island for people suspected of the plague or sick with other fevers. You'll have come past it when you sailed in—did you see the ships flying a yellow flag to show infection?"

Sarah was still stunned. "Yes, yes."

"The ships' masters fear the island worse than the plague itself. If your ship is suspected of disease you have to moor up, and go ashore and live there until the doctor clears you."

"The doctor?"

"Now the doctor is your uncle Roberto."

"But how long do you have to stay in quarantine?"

"For forty days—more than a month."

"Then Rob will be able to leave?"

"No, it is the foreign crew that can leave; but Roberto is appointed as doctor, permanent doctor. He will have to stay there, checking the food, checking for disease."

"For how long?" she asked. "How long does he have to stay?"

He looked at her with sympathy and he paused in his reply as if he could not think how to tell her. "This is a death sentence," he said gently. "Though they don't strangle him as a murderer, he will stay there for the rest of his life, till he takes the plague and dies. You must think of him as a dead man now. He may be dead already."

He watched her curiously. First, she took in the shock of the news, that the terrible risk they had taken—entering the Doge's Palace and confessing a deceit—had been for nothing, that her uncle would die on a tiny island, within sight of the shore. He saw her color come and go, and then he saw her eyes slide out of focus and she looked dreamy, as if she were listening to music from far away or thinking intently of something else. When her dark gaze returned to his face, it was as if she had returned from the other world to this one.

"No," she said with sudden clarity. "No, he's not dead."

He took her arm and led her down the stairs, thinking she was too shocked by the news to speak sense. "You're upset," he said. "But this is the truth. I've withdrawn my evidence but they won't change the sentence. There's nothing we can do for Rob, now he's been sent there. No one escapes. And if he gets the plague"—he corrected himself—"when he gets it, or cholera, or yellow fever, or whatever the sailors happen to have, they will send him to the Lazzaretto Vecchio—the old death island—and he will die there."

"I can't believe it," she repeated.

He guided her out of the gate and nodded to Captain Shore, who followed them back down the quay to his ship, walking a few paces behind them as if he was indifferent to the Italian's scowl and the girl's tranced blankness. The three halted on the quayside under the prow of the ship, sheltering from the icy wind that was ripping down the Grand Canal.

"Not good news, I take it?" Captain Shore asked, his eyes on the ashen-faced girl.

"He's been appointed doctor at the Lazzaretto Nuovo," Felipe said quietly.

"Ah, God bless him and take him to His own," Captain Shore said. "Well, he's lost to you, maid. I'm sorry for it. You can't go there, and he can't get away."

Sarah nodded.

"You've taken it hard," the Captain said quietly to Sarah. "Bound to. Will you come on board?"

"I'll take her back to my house," Felipe said. "She'll come back tomorrow and we'll load her goods in plenty of time."

"The Nobildonna's furniture?" Captain Shore inquired. "That's still to go ahead?"

"Of course. It's business," Felipe said. "Nothing to do with this . . . this . . ."

"This what?" Captain Shore asked him. "This little play you have put on for her? For reasons of your own? For what reason of your own, exactly?"

"This tragedy," Felipe corrected him. "A niece has lost an uncle. A mother has lost her son. It's very sad."

"But business is still business," the Captain said, looking at the handsome Italian from under his sandy eyebrows.

Felipe bowed, and tucked Sarah's hand in his arm. "Business is still business," he repeated. "Will you take another passenger? I wish to travel with the Nobildonna's antiquities to London?"

"You?" the Captain was surprised. "Small beer for you, I should have thought?"

"Small beer?" the Italian repeated.

"Nothing compared to the shipments . . . the other shipments you've made."

"Ah, I see. No, it is beer of an appropriate size. I wish to accompany the young lady, and the Nobildonna's goods are my concern. I wish to visit the Nobildonna and see how she is in London." He paused. "Bearing up under her grief," he said with a smile.

DECEMBER 1670, LONDON

Sir James and Lady Eliot struggled to make conversation over dinner. Livia's laughter tinkled out, but nothing seemed to amuse her companions. More than once, Lady Eliot looked puzzled at her vivacity, and James made a little embarrassed grimace. The ladies withdrew after dinner to the parlor and sat there for only a few minutes before Sir James joined them. It was as if he did not dare to leave them alone.

"Have the ladies from the warehouse moved into their new home?" Sir James asked his fiancée.

She shrugged. "Not yet, I am looking for them."

"They're still in that cramped cold warehouse! Through this weather?"

"I am still there," she pointed out. "Nobody feels the cold worse than me."

"You won't like Yorkshire then." Lady Eliot smiled.

"And Sarah is still away?" James pursued.

Livia spread her hands in a pretty gesture of bafflement. "Apparently

English girls may go away from home with whoever they like and return when they wish. No Italian girl would dare. It's hardly respectable. I have spoken to her mother, but she says nothing more than that Sarah can be trusted."

"Where is she?" Sir James asked.

"Staying with a friend in the country. She said she would be a few days but she has stayed on, and on. I think there must be a young man in the question. Don't you? But her mamma does not order her home. I cannot understand it."

"Young girls have far more freedom than when I was a girl." The Dowager finally found something on which they could agree. "Quite shocking."

"But they are quite poor," Livia explained, "so it does not matter so much. The girl is a milliner and the ladies—I call them that—but they are nothing but very small merchants with a little warehouse. They are workingwomen."

James was irritated by this exchange. "I left you with money to get them a better house!"

"And I have it still," Livia said limpidly. "But Mrs. Reekie will not move until Sarah comes back from the country, and they insist on a warehouse upriver, where they could sell things as well as import them . . . At least I achieved one thing: the boy Johnnie will join the East India Company at Easter. Your letter was introduction enough."

"Yes, yes?" James said, distracted.

Livia turned to the Dowager with a little laugh. "I wish to help them, though I am afraid they have grown greedy since I shared my dower with them."

The Dowager nodded. "It's an unfortunate address for you," she said. "That side of the river, and so far out of town. I couldn't call on you there."

Livia flushed. "Exactly, and I cannot be married from there, I was telling Sir James. We need to call the banns in the north, in Yorkshire, do we not?"

"You can't live in Northside before your wedding," the Dowager ruled. "It looks so odd. As if you have no address of your own."

"I thought so myself," Livia said smoothly. "So would it be better if we were married in London? In this parish?"

James glanced from his aunt, to the exquisite face of his mistress. "Yes, I suppose so. You can only have met with Mr. Rogers—what? A dozen times?"

"Oh yes!" she said. "I have studied with him twice a week, and I have attended his church twice a week as well. Crossing the river in all weathers! I am completely prepared; he agrees that I am completely ready."

"You must have at least four months' instruction."

"Yes, yes, I can do that, of course. I can complete my instruction while they are calling the banns."

"But the baby must be baptized after you," James said. "You have to bring him to the church."

Livia threw up her hands, laughing prettily. "*Allora!* I agree! I agree! Don't make me press for my own wedding day before your aunt, she will think me shameless."

Lady Eliot raised an eyebrow but said nothing, as if this was exactly what she thought.

"Matteo and I can be baptized into your church together, when I have completed my instruction," Livia offered. "We can be married. It will be . . ." She counted on her long fingers in the black lace mittens. "The end of February. How will that suit you?"

Sir James tried to laugh at her pretty challenge. "Very well," he said.

"Alas no," Lady Eliot said in quiet triumph. She leaned forward. "Lent. You can't get married in Lent."

The look that Livia flashed at her was far from daughterly. "Why not? It's not as if you are of the tru . . . the Roman Catholic Church?"

"Yes, but even so. You cannot marry in Lent. Can she, James?"

"No," he was forced to agree. "It will have to be after Easter, my dear."

Livia tried to smile. "No, no, I can take extra instruction next week, and we can marry before Lent. In early February."

James hesitated.

"There is no reason for delay," Livia told him.

"Certainly," he agreed. He took her hand and kissed it and glanced nervously at his aunt. "February, in St. Clement Danes."

"And do you have no family in England at all?" Lady Eliot pursued. "No one to stand as your godparent when you are baptized? No one to give you away when you are married? You are as solitary as . . . as an orphan?"

"I have no one." Livia blinked on a tear, daring Lady Eliot to challenge her any further. "I know nobody in England but my late husband's family, women wharfingers with a little warehouse. I make no pretense! I married beneath myself when I engaged with him and his family. But with my dear Sir James I will return to people of my own sort—nobility."

"Oh, will you?" Lady Eliot said, with one eye on Sir James's face. He was looking into the fire, downcast. He did not look like a joyful bridegroom only six weeks away from his wedding.

DECEMBER 1670, VENICE

Felipe Russo and Sarah took a gondola from the Custom House; Sarah sat wrapped in her cape, in the middle seat, while Felipe took the seat in the prow.

"A song?" the gondolier asked agreeably. "A song for young lovers?"

"No," Sarah said irritably, and hardly saw the beautiful houses, the white marble church, the pretty canals as they passed by.

"Are we not lovers now?" Felipe asked her teasingly.

Absently, she shook her head. "Do you have a chart of the lagoon?"

"To see Roberto's island?" he asked with ready sympathy. "Yes, I will get one out for you. But you know . . ."

"I know I cannot send a ship for him," she said.

The gondolier spun the gondola to arrow them into the water gate of the Russo house, mooring beside the Russo gondola so they had to disembark on the warehouse side. Sarah shrank from the lower store-house door, knowing what was behind it, and they walked around the quay and climbed the wide marble steps.

Sarah hesitated in the hall at the top warehouse door. "Will you show me what was hers, from her palace, just the things she truly owns?"

"That's easy," Felipe said. "Come on up to the dining room."

He led the way to the room where the cold watery light was playing on the painted ceiling. Sarah looked at the walls lined with the beautiful silent statues.

"Not them," he said, closing the door behind him.

She glanced at the ornate chandelier.

"Not that. Nothing. Nothing is left. As soon as she married the old Conte and entered the Palazzo Fiori she started smuggling pieces out for my workmen to copy. She was selling pieces that we had forged back to her husband. If he had a column and we could find something to put on top of it, we would blend them and polish them and sell them to him as a new thing. Once he took to his bed we were free to make copies of his collection, borrowing an original, making a mold from it, putting the copy back, and selling the original."

"Forgery," Sarah said flatly. "And theft."

Gently he cupped his hand on the cold white calf of a statue of a nymph pouring water. Her sightless eyes looked out over the canal, the carved water fell, eternally, from the mouth of the vase. She smiled a little, as she had smiled for centuries—or perhaps for only a week. "To me there is a truth to beauty. I don't really care who made it, or how, or when. If people are so foolish as to pay more for something that is old and was despised until I found it—then they may."

"But not if they are paying Livia for your work," Sarah said astutely.

He bowed with a smile. "Not then," he agreed pleasantly. "Which is why I am going to come to England with the antiquities. I shall see for myself where she shows them and how much she is earning for them. I shall see this Sir James for myself."

"Very well," Sarah agreed.

"And in return for my help today and in the future, you will not denounce me: not for grave robbing, nor exporting without a license, nor covering up a murder, nor wrongful arrest, nor theft and fraud—" He broke off. "That's all, isn't it?" he asked.

"That's all I know of," Sarah said cautiously. "But that's not to say that's all you've done."

He gave a crack of a laugh. "Ah, Miss Jolie—you are well to be cautious, but truly that is all that concerns you and me. So we shall be partners? Now that you know the truth of me? You are the only woman that has ever known the truth of me, which is—I admit—very bad indeed, but I did not kill the Milord my master, I did not hate Roberto, I did not denounce him myself, and I will not drown you in the water gate."

"You want to be partners with me?" she asked cautiously.

He took her hand to his lips. "Partners, and perhaps we will be lovers, since you tell the good Captain that I am 'sweet on you.'"

He watched the color rise into her cheeks, and turned her hand over to put a kiss into the palm. "It is nothing but the truth," he said. "I am very sweet on you, Miss Pretty. You know, you will always be Bathsheba Jolie to me."

Next morning, when Sarah came downstairs, she found the dining table covered by a huge map of the islands of Venice, and only a corner left free, for a pastry and a cup of chocolate for her breakfast. Felipe was standing at the window drinking a tiny cup of coffee, he turned and smiled as she came into the room, and he pulled a chair from the table for her to sit. "Did you sleep well, *cara*?"

Sarah nodded. "Is this the map of the Venice lagoon?"

"Yes." He pointed on the map to where one tiny island was marked in green to show that it was above the level of high tide. "That's where Roberto is imprisoned, that's the Isola del Lazzaretto Nuovo."

Around it was a speckle of sandbanks, of reedbanks, of mudflats and wetlands and underwater shoals. It was a world that was never still, it was a coastline that could never be mapped. Every high tide the land became water. If there was a storm surge, even the islands with quays and stone seawalls would be inundated. But every day new houses and islands were created from stakes driven into the lagoon bed and built up with boulders. Old islands were eroded by the sea and were reborn as marsh. Venetians and the sea were in continual dialogue over what was land and what was water.

"But this is just like his home." Sarah pored over the map, seeing how the little island, crowned with a building like a castle, was surrounded by marsh, sandbars, reed beds, and deep channels. "The people who lived on land called Rob's home 'wandering haven' because they never knew where the harbor channel was running, it changed every storm. Only my grandma and her two children, Rob and my ma, who lived right on the edge of the mire, knew the paths, knew the dry places, the sinking sands and the hushing well."

"He always liked the lagoon," Felipe said doubtfully. "We could not understand it. He was always out with a gun in a shallow boat, or in a skiff with a fishing line. When he was not studying, or with his patients, he would go out walking the margins: the shoreline between water and land. He liked that it was so uncertain underfoot. He liked that it was lonely. We thought it odd—we like a marble quay not a *barena*."

"*Barena?*"

"As you say, land that is land for half the day and water for the other half."

"And he's not free to walk or boat anymore. He's kept on this tiny island?"

"He'll never leave it," Felipe said quietly. "As the doctor, he will live in a small house inside the walled area, not in a cell like ordinary crew; but he will be guarded like a prisoner. He will have a small garden inside the walls perhaps, for his herbs. But a wall runs all around the warehouse, and there is only one entrance—a great bolted gate that faces the lagoon, towards Venice, with a quay where the ships are unloaded. The gate is locked at night, and even during the day unless there is a ship at the quay for unloading. There are guards with swords and pikes who watch, night and day, that no one escapes. In the west and southeast corner of the compound is a stone-built store for black gunpowder, which the Arsenale keep here for safety. It is a fort, as well as a prison."

"How big is the island?" Sarah said, nibbling on the pastry and drinking her hot chocolate, looking at the stipple of land and sand-banks in the blue of the map.

"Hardly bigger than the outside walls," he said. "You can walk around the perimeter in half an hour, though it's all mud and drain-age ditches."

"They never let him out?"

Felipe shook his head. "Besides, where would he go? This is an is-land. And no ship would pick up anyone from a lazaretto—it would be like signing your own death warrant, you would not know what illness they carried. Everyone on the island is only there because they are suspected of breeding a fatal illness. Who would pick them up until their cargo has been sweetened and they have survived forty days?" He hesitated. "Darl . . . Miss Jolie, we don't know that he is not sick already. He has been there for weeks, for months, nursing people with blood vomit, or cholera, or scarlatina, or plague. He might already be sick. You have to prepare yourself: he is probably dead."

She shook her head with silent conviction.

"Ah, you think you are like the old grandma—that you would know by magic?"

"We never speak of magic," she said quickly. "But my grandma would have said prayers for her son's soul if she had felt his death in her heart."

His dark eyes were filled with sympathy. "*Cara,* perhaps you should tell her to pray."

"Could we write to him? And see if he's still alive?"

"Yes, we could write to him. But anything you write would be read by the governor of the lazaretto. They would probably not allow him to reply—and any reply would be passed through smoke or dipped in vinegar to clean it before it could come to you. It would take days, weeks. If he's alive at all."

"But we could get him a message?"

He shrugged. "If you wish it. But what is there to say to a man condemned to death, and waking each day knowing death is coming?

What is there to tell him? He'll know by now that his wife denounced him and left Venice."

"He doesn't know she went to London and is stealing from my mother!" Sarah said sharply.

He looked at her with compassion. "Why torture him?" he asked. "He can do nothing to help his sister or punish his wife."

She turned to the window and looked down at the busy canal below. He saw her shoulders slump in defeat. "You're right," she said. "You're right. It would be to torture him. I won't tell him that. I will write only to say that we have not forgotten him, and that his mother loves him, that we all miss him. That's all she asked me to do—to see that he was not dead. I can go home and tell her that at least."

"Nobody could ask for more," he assured her. "Nobody could do more. And you are right not to fight against a certainty. Just write to say good-bye."

She nodded, her face grave. "If I write a farewell, can you promise me that you will get it to him?"

"I can try," he said. "Don't write anything that would incriminate me. And remember that it has to be left open—anyone can read it, everyone will read it."

He turned to the sideboard, pushed the map aside, and gave her a quill and a bottle of ink.

DECEMBER 1670, LONDON

Sir James sent Livia home to the warehouse escorted by Glib. Silently, the two of them took a skiff to the Horsleydown Stairs, and sulkily he walked her to the warehouse door.

"When does she leave?" she demanded.

"Who?" he asked, pretending to ignorance.

"The old crone. The aunt."

He shook his head. "She stays in the house till we all go north."

"He listens to her? She advises him?"

He hesitated.

"Servants know everything," Livia said to him sharply. "Don't dream of lying to me now."

"He listens to her," he agreed. "And Lord! She's a tyrant! We all jump to her bidding."

"Tell them that they will have an easier mistress with me," Livia said rapidly, pressing a silver sixpence into his palm. "Tell them that it would be better for us all if she went to her Dower House now—and left him alone in London. Promise them that I will be a new mistress, generous with leftovers for those in the kitchen, and with my old clothes to the maids. Everyone will be bettered when I come to Northside Manor and Avery House. You, especially."

"I'll try," he said, unconvinced. "But she's well liked in Yorkshire."

"Pffft!" Livia waved away the objection. "She is nobody. I am the new mistress of Northside Manor. Tell them they had better think about me and pleasing me!"

"And when's the wedding?" Glib asked as they parted at the warehouse door.

She looked sharply at him as if she suspected him of insolence, as if she feared that the servants knew all about this too. "Before Lent," she swore. "And you remember that!"

DECEMBER 1670, VENICE

Dear Uncle Robert,

I am your niece, Sarah Stoney, come to Venice on the ship Sweet Hope with a message from your mother. She sends her blessing — she says you always found your own way widdershins on the ebb at the full.

This is a letter to say farewell, but your ma, my grandma, knows best and she is certain we will meet on a celestial shore.

Sarah

She handed the letter to Felipe.

"These English words!" he said. "How can you even write them?"

"My grandma is a countrywoman," Sarah said carelessly. "I thought Rob would like to hear her, as she speaks. Can you get it to him?"

"They have food and drink delivered every day," he said. "I'll take this to the Fondamente Nuove, and get one of the boats to take it."

"And send this," Sarah said. From her placket she drew out an old worn purse, which had once been red, but was now rusty brown.

"The porters will steal any money," he warned. He hefted it in his hand. "Light," he said at once, though he heard the coins chink.

"It's not money. It's valueless to anyone but my grandma," Sarah said. "She used to collect little tokens and clippings of old coins. As soon as he sees them, he'll know I am who I say. It'll give him comfort."

Felipe tossed the purse in the air and caught it. "You are the strangest of families," he told her. "Are all English people quite mad?"

She laughed. "That's nothing," she said. "You should see my grandma with a sick baby, you would think she was breathing life into it."

He crossed himself. "I'll send this now," he said. "And we have to pack the last of the Nobildonna's treasures."

"You're going to send her all that she asked for?" Sarah asked curiously. "You're still doing her bidding?"

"Of course. Business is business, she can sell them, and give me my share," he said. "And besides, they are on the cargo manifest. You forget how we Venetians are about reports. Captain Shore would rather sink to the bottom of the lagoon than go into the Custom House and change his cargo declaration."

Sarah laughed and folded up the map. "May I keep this?"

"If you wish."

"I'd just like to know the island as we go past it," she said. "To say good-bye."

DECEMBER 1670, HADLEY, NEW ENGLAND

Ned went out through the kitchen door to give the dried fruit to Mrs. Rose. She was stewing a pot of succotash in the fireplace, native food in an English kettle.

"I brought you these." Ned put the woven basket of fruit on the table.

"I'm grateful," she said, and tipped them into the storage jar and gave him back the basket. He could see her hands were shaking with fear.

"You'll have heard the news?" he asked.

She looked strained. "I was in the room when the minister read the letter from Plymouth to the guests," she said. "It's just as I feared. Only worse. It's war, isn't it? Between us and the Indians?"

"They've ordered me into town," he said. "I'll have to leave my home and my land and my ferry as soon as it thaws."

"We'll have no chance against them out here," she said. She tried to put a cork into the top of the storage jar and she fumbled with shaking hands.

Ned took it from her and corked the jar. "It may come to nothing," he told her. "We've had scares before, and it's come to nothing. We've marched out before and . . ."

"We've done more than march, we've wiped them out," she said fiercely. "Over and over again. Last time, against the Pequot, we burned their village and them inside it. Those children that weren't roasted alive, we sent into slavery. We told them to forget their families, to never say their tribal name. We wiped them out, ended their line. But they just melt into the forest and then they come back. They keep coming, from the west, from the south, and the more we kill, the more spring up. And they never learn, they go on refusing us, blocking our way."

"No, no, they are just like us," Ned protested. "They just want to keep their own lands and us on ours, they want to live at peace."

She shook her head. "I can't bear it," she told him flatly. "When my time is up I'm going to ask the minister to find me a servant's place in Boston rather than a plot here. I want to be among my own. I want to be in a town with a stone wall around it. I want to be somewhere that the savages are ordered to come to answer, where they are hanged on the green, where they are enslaved, not somewhere that they can stroll up the street whenever they like, or pitch one of their houses on our common, as if it was shared land."

"Leave here?"

"You could come too!" she said boldly. "You could get a post as a servant, a footman, or a groom or something. Or perhaps you could be an agent to a slave trader? Shipping men into slavery in the Sugar Islands and sugar and rum on the return voyage? That's a good business! You could get a job with a factor, we could go together? We could find work together?" Her color rose as she tried to persuade him, her face strained with anxiety. "It'd be hard work but better work than stuck out here waiting to be scalped. If you don't want to fight for settlers, you don't have to! You don't have to command the militia if you have no stomach for it. We could be safe in Boston."

"I'm not afraid to fight!" Ned was stung into objection. "It's not that I won't serve! It's that they're not my enemies. I won't kill men who are not my enemies."

"They're not now," she pointed out. "But they will be in the spring. You won't open your door to your friend then. You'll open your door and get an arrow through your gut and feel a tomahawk cleave your forehead."

DECEMBER 1670, LONDON

Alys was lighting Alinor's fire, on her knees before the fireplace, carefully placing the pieces of coal on the kindling, then sitting back with satisfaction when the little blaze licked its way along the sticks and then caught.

"At least the evenings are getting lighter," she said. "The year has turned."

"And who knows what this new year might bring," Alinor said.

"Ma, you're not thinking that Sarah will bring Rob home, are you? Because you know that's really . . ."

"Really?"

"It's not possible, Ma. Whatever we might wish. Whatever you might feel. I just pray to God that she comes back safe."

"Captain Shore will guard her."

"I know he will. But for you to send her all that way!"

"She's got a good head on her shoulders, I trust her."

"You could say all the same for Rob; and he never came home."

"I believe he's coming home now. I dreamed of him. I'm sure."

"I know it," Alys cut across her mother. "I know you're sure. But I'm waiting and waiting for her and I don't have your certainty, and I don't have your dreams. I am too earthly to have your visions. I just want my little girl home again."

Alinor heard the tremor in her daughter's voice. "Be brave," she said quietly. "Be patient. And trust her."

There was silence in the little room.

"Where's Livia today?" Alinor changed the subject. "Does she still go to the house, though she has nothing to sell?"

"Not every day," Alys replied. "There's nothing for her to do here, until her antiquities arrive."

"And then she will sell them again? As she did before?"

"Aye, and repay us for the voyage and storage again."

"And then again, and again?"

"Yes, that's the plan. And move to a warehouse where she can show her goods to customers and sell them there. You know this, Ma. Why ask me?"

"She puzzles me now, as she's always done. She leaves her child with us: you have him most mornings, and his nursemaid brings him to me in the afternoon. What's she doing all day? How come she's Rob's widow, and yet lives off us, making you pay for her shipping even when she's got money at the goldsmith's? She complains that we're poor, that Tabs isn't a proper maid, that the food is badly cooked; but we've seen nothing of her sale money? She says she wants us to get another warehouse to ship her goods; but not how much she'll put into it? She asks you to borrow for it. She's young and might look for another husband, and so I wonder if that's what she's doing when she's out every day?"

Alys flushed. "She is a perfectly good mother. She loves Matteo."

"When she's with him."

"She brings in more money to this family than she costs! She's repaid for the first shipping and storage and she'll repay for the second when it arrives. And she's going to buy the new warehouse with us?"

"A gift? Her gift to us?"

Alys bit her lip.

"And she will remain here with us, and not remarry?"

Alys turned to her mother. "Ma, she's such good company for me. It's such a pleasure for me to have her here, and little Matteo. It's like we have a beautiful bird in the house. I want her to walk out freely and come back to us, without being questioned. I want her to make her home here with us. I love her as a sister, I don't want her to think about remarrying and leaving. I don't want her to think she has to pay rent, or provide for us. I want her to live off us, and live with us. I want her to stay forever. I am happy to provide for her."

"My dear, d'you really think she won't remarry?"

"You never did! I didn't!"

Alinor nodded, her eyes on the flames. "I don't think Livia is a woman like us," was all she said.

DECEMBER 1670, VENICE

The *Sweet Hope* was to sail on the ebb tide of the evening, lit by a huge cold moon, which sat, bright as a gleaming globe, on the horizon, making the canal into glassy black and turning the brightly colored houses into shades of gray. The canal was busy with workers going home for the night, and with merrymakers starting to go out; all the gondolas carried bobbing lanterns on their prows and lights gleamed on the waters from the open water gates of the great houses.

Captain Shore, on the quayside before the Custom House, blazing with flambeaux, had a brusque nod for Felipe and a smile for Sarah as they waited to have their papers checked at the gangplank, but he did not speak to either of them until the officials had released them and they were ready to board.

"All well?" he asked shortly. "For we sail as soon as the *pedotti* says so, we're taking on fresh stores at Sant' Erasmo, and we can't be delayed."

"All well," Felipe said. Sarah nodded.

"Stow your things," the Captain commanded. To Sarah he said: "You can have your old cabin, my dear." He turned to Felipe: "You'll have to share with the first mate, unless you want to pay extra for a private cabin?"

Felipe bowed his head. "I'll pay, Captain," he said smoothly.

The Custom House official came with a sheaf of papers and seals. Captain Shore checked them meticulously, signed, and exchanged documents, paid his mooring fees and the duty on the goods he was shipping, and then stepped up the gangplank. Behind him followed the *pedotti*, who unsheathed his knife. He cut off the official seals from the wheel of the ship and nodded to the Captain that they were ready to leave. Captain Shore shouted the order to cast off for'ard, the gang-plank was shipped aboard, the fore line was thrown, caught, and taken in. The current swung the ship so that it nosed out into the channel, as Sarah came out of her cabin to see the little barges fix their lines on the ship and draw her forward. The *pedotti* shouted for the stern line to be released and the barges guided the ship out into the main channel where the ebbing tide drew them smoothly down the Grand Canal, past palaces, the glimpse of St. Mark's Square, past the Doge's Palace: every window lighted bright, as justice never sleeps, and then out into the lagoon. They passed the island of Vignole on the port side, and saw ahead the flicker of the torches burning on the end of the pier of Sant' Erasmo. As the *pedotti* shouted commands, the barges drew the galleon to the pier, and the farmers started carrying their baskets of produce towards the ship.

Felipe joined Sarah on deck as she stared out into the gathering darkness. "You are looking for your uncle's prison?"

She nodded. "Is that it?" She pointed north over the flat farmland, dark against the dark water, to the rooftop of the great building, which gleamed in the moonlight like a huge granary, one story with a huge barn door, bigger even than the Venice Custom House, pale in the moonlight. "The place that looks like a castle?"

"That's it," he said. "But those are chimneys, not castellations. Every cell has its own fire and chimney so those who are quarantined don't mess together. Your uncle Rob will have lived in the doctor's house, under guard. The big doors open to a double warehouse for the goods."

"Lived?" She picked him up on the word. "You believe he is dead?"

He spread his hands. "*Cara mia,* neither of us knows, and the people who know don't care. If he is not dead now, he will be soon. *Ahimè,* alas, if not now then later. Say a prayer for him, say good-bye to him."

The order came to run the gangplank on board, cast off, and raise the sails as the barges released the ship and she moved into the deep-water channel south of Sant' Erasmo. One by one, the barges took in their lines, and peeled off back to Venice. Sarah waited till the barges had left, and then went to the companionway and called up for permission to come on the quarterdeck.

"Aye, you can come up," Captain Shore said; he was standing behind the *pedotti,* who still had command of the ship. The Captain was looking skywards, at his unfurling sails stretching to take the light wind. The moonlight was so bright it was like a silvery dawn, with mist rolling along the dark water.

"Captain Shore," Sarah said quietly.

"Aye?" he said with a little impatience. He shouted an order to one of the crew who was reefing the sail.

"I know you have a great regard for my mother."

She had caught his attention. "Deepest respect," he said, embarrassed. "Not that she knows it. Not that I have given her any hint."

"I know you would be very glad to tell my mother that you brought me safely home, from the Doge's Palace, safe home to her."

"Aye," he said more cautiously.

"So if you were to lose me, in some mishap, I ask you to wait for me."

"Eh?"

Unexpectedly, she reached up and pecked him on his cheek. "Don't fail me," she said.

393

"What?" he demanded, but she slipped away from him into the waist of the ship and reappeared at Felipe's elbow.

"I want you to raise the alarm, two men overboard," she said to him urgently.

"Sarah?"

"I can't explain. Just give me a moment and then shout, 'Man overboard—two men!'"

He turned to her and saw that she was undoing the ties of her cape. He stared disbelieving, as she stripped it off and thrust it into his hands. She was wearing nothing underneath but her linen shift, which left her neck and shoulders bare; underneath she had a pair of boy's breeches.

"Sarah?" he whispered. "What are . . . ?"

Before he could say another word, his hands filled with her heavy traveling cape so he could not reach for her. She put two hands on the rail and vaulted, lithe as a boy, over the side of the ship, and he heard the splash down below, as she plunged into the icy water. "Sarah!" he shouted, and leaned out. He could see her head, dark as a seal in the moonlight, and then she disappeared.

"Sarah!" he shouted again. He raced to the companionway and seized a lantern, leaned out over the water. He could see nothing but a waste of water and the mudbanks and reed banks and sandbanks, a canal, a brackish pool, and then more water.

"Dio onnipotente," he groaned. "Sarah!"

He turned and dashed to the stern of the ship. "Captain Shore?" he called up the companionway.

"Not now," the Captain said grimly, and when Felipe put one foot on the stairs, he glared at him from under his impressive eyebrows and said: "Nobody comes on my quarterdeck without invitation."

"I beg of you! It's Sarah! She's gone!" Felipe burst out. "Into the water."

"You let her?"

"How was I to know?"

"You saw her?"

"That way!" Felipe gestured towards the lazaretto where the windows showed a few gleams of light from the different cells.

"Can she swim?"

"How should I know? Yes! She was swimming away from the ship."

The Captain scowled. "Madness! Madness! And she said to me . . . what the hell is she doing?"

"I suppose she has gone to Roberto?"

"Christ's wounds!"

"You must stop the ship and send out a boat!"

"I can't! I can't take her back on board!"

"You can't leave her to drown!"

"God Almighty!"

"Exactly."

The two men stared at each other. "Ah! She told me to wait for her," Captain Shore finally said. "That's what she was saying. Wait, for her mother's sake."

Felipe saw the *pedotti* turn his head from his careful scrutiny of the channel, and glance at them.

"Man overboard!" Felipe yelled. He sprang up onto the quarterdeck. "Man overboard! Two men! Stop the ship! *Uomo in mare! Due uomini!*"

"Avast! Heave to!" Captain Shore shouted.

At once, the sailors dropped the sails.

"Let go anchor!"

The Captain turned to the *pedotti* for a quick bilingual argument. Felipe stood alongside Captain Shore and explained to the irritated pilot that two crew members had fallen overboard, simultaneously, and the Captain would launch a dinghy to find them.

"I'm damned if I'll have it row to the quarantine island," the Captain swore in an undertone to Felipe.

"You don't have to," Felipe said. "But you do have to launch it, now you're heaved to. Please God she comes back to us quickly."

"What is she doing? Little lass like her into the water on an ebb tide?"

Felipe was ragged with fear for her. "How would I know? How the hell would I know what she is doing? Get the dinghy out, I'll row out for her."

"I'll wait for no more than a minute," the Captain ruled. "And if she doesn't come, we'll sail without her."

"We can't leave her!"

"She left us," the Captain snarled.

"Captain, I beg you to lower a boat for her. I'll go alone, we can't just let her go!"

"We don't know where she is," the Captain pointed out furiously. "What are you going to do? Row round the reed banks? She could be drowned already."

"She can't be drowned!" Felipe exclaimed in horror. "It's not possible that she could have drowned!"

"Just what she said about her uncle!" the Captain crowed. "When your mistress had told everyone he had been caught by the dark tides. Not so funny when it's someone you love, is it? Not such a clever story when you're at sea yourself."

Sarah, swimming north against a strong ebbing current, knew that she was in trouble. The bulk of the ship was behind her, she even heard the loud rattle of the anchor chain, but she was being pushed back to it and away from the island by the tide. Though she swam as strongly as she could, the lights of the Lazzaretto Nuovo were steadily receding. The stone and brick walls, clear in the moonlight, came no closer. Sarah glanced behind her and saw there were sandbanks all around her, some topped with saltwort and sea lavender, so she let the current sweep her towards them, and felt silt and shells under her feet and clambered out of the water. She was on the shoals and sandbars that made up the island of Sant' Erasmo, she could even see the lights of the Lazzaretto Nuovo, but between her sandbank and the island was a broad stretch of water, more than half a mile wide, with the moonlight dancing on the ripples of the fast-moving tide. She thought that perhaps she might be able to swim across, when the tide turned and it was slack water—but the tide would not turn for hours—and the *pedotti* on Captain Shore's ship would never let him wait that long. She started to walk along the shore, trying to get as close to the quarantine island as possible, stepping carefully from one patch of vegetation to another, shying back when her foot sank. Sarah had a terror of quicksands, from childhood stories about the shifting paths of Foulmire. She gritted her teeth, which were chattering for fear and for cold, and went one step at a time, hoping that this sandbank would connect with another and that she might paddle her way towards the Lazzaretto Nuovo and find a shallow crossing of the deadly fast water.

In her note to Rob she had told him to go "widdershins," trusting that he would guess that she meant him to come out of the front door of the Lazaretto and turn left, "widdershins" in the old country word, counterclockwise, the witch way. She had told him to go on the ebb tide, by the light of the full moon, the Yule moon which shone above her now. She had told him the name of her ship, the ship that had brought him to Italy ten years ago. She had to hope that the purse of tokens had convinced him to read the hidden meaning to the letter, and that he had been able to get out of the fort. But it was, she knew, a desperate chance, a forlorn hope.

Carefully she slid her foot forward and saw ahead of her something that looked like a path on the next sandbank. She paddled into the icy water that flowed between the two, and found it came no higher than her knees, and as the silt shifted warningly under her feet she dropped to hands and knees and crawled across. The neighboring sandbank had a well-trodden path. It was narrow—so narrow that she went one foot before another, but it went on firm ground and it led to another reed bank. Sarah, shivering with cold, went a little more quickly on the narrow track, wrapping her arms around herself to try to keep warm, her cold feet bruised and cut by sharp shells and thorns, and then she froze as she heard a whistle, just like that of a reed warbler—but warblers roost at night.

She squinted into the darkness towards the Lazzaretto Nuovo and saw, in the shadow of the wall, at the southeast corner—just where Rob should have been waiting for her—a single pinprick of a light, come and gone in a moment, like a spark from a tinder box.

"Rob!" she whispered, her voice echoing across the water.

In the darkness she could just make out a small craft, a punt for hunting wildfowl, slide into the deep channel and come towards her, a figure pushing it along the shallow channel. The prow grounded on her patch of dry land.

"Rob Reekie?" she asked.

"Are you Sarah?"

"Yes. I feel I should ask . . . Like a password."

"Ask anything."

"What's our name for Wandering Haven?"

"Foulmire," he said at once. "Foul for it stinks like a foul thing, and mire for you are trapped in it forever. And God knows why we miss it so much." He reached out a warm hand and she took it and he pulled her on board. "You must be freezing," he said. "Take my cape." He swung it off his shoulders and around her. Sarah clutched it to herself.

"I'd have known you," Rob said. "Though you're grown. I would have known you for little Sarah."

She looked at him, trying to trace her memory of him on his thin prison-pale face, her mother's features on his gauntness.

"Where to?" Rob asked. "I thought you had a ship?"

"I hope I've got one waiting," she said. "Off Sant' Erasmo."

"The Captain'll never take me on, if he knows I've come from here."

"He will," she said. "It's Captain Shore. He's sweet on my ma."

"On Alys?"

She nodded, still shivering as he pushed them off from the sandbank with the pole, and then started to move the punt, kneeling in the stern so they were low in the water and less visible in the moonlight.

"How did you get the boat?"

"Governor's boat," he said. "He lends it to me for fishing, and hunting. We don't get the best food on the island, so he lets me fish in secret."

"Could you be infected?" she asked.

"I think not," he said. "We've only had a few fevers since I was sent there, and no plague at all. Please God, I'm clean. I've got no signs."

Sarah said nothing more, watching this uncle that she had never known, looking into his square face and his brown hair, tracing the resemblance to her mother as he knelt up and poled the boat along.

"What will we do, if he doesn't let us on board?" she asked, sharing her fear.

"You'll go on board," he said. "Back to England. And I'll ask him to tow me, as far as he will, out of the lagoon, towards the mainland. You've given me hope. If I can get out of the lagoon, and out of rule of the Republic of Venice, I'll get home somehow."

They were silent as he poled them into the main channel and Sarah felt the flow of the water take them quickly away from the lazaretto.

"There it is!" she said as she saw the dark bulk of the ship in the darkness. "He's waiting for me."

Rob let the little craft nudge alongside the waiting ship and looked up. A rope ladder tumbled down to them and Captain Shore peered over the side. They could see the muzzle of a pistol before him.

"Who's there?" he said, his voice a low rumble of anger.

"It's me," Sarah said, speaking through chattering teeth. "Captain Shore! It's me! And I've got my uncle Rob. An Englishman, you know, and the brother of my ma—Alys Stoney."

"Is he sick?"

"I'm not," Rob said, standing in the rocking boat and lifting his face upwards. "See? No marks, no symptoms, and I've not been with anyone with plague. That I swear. There's no disease on the island but a few fevers, and there's been none since I was sent there. Let me on and I'll go straight into a cabin and not come out for forty days."

"She can come aboard. Not you," the Captain replied. They heard the clink as he armed his pistol and they saw the black muzzle aimed down into the little craft.

"I won't come without him," Sarah said flatly. "He comes up first. Then me. And if you don't take us on board I go straight back to the Bocca di Leone and denounce you."

"What for?" came the muted roar. "What the hell for, you little bitch?"

"Smuggling," Sarah said flatly. "Smuggling antiquities. And you've got a forger on board with you. Taking a criminal out of the country, with his forged goods."

"Bathsheba!" Felipe reproached her, peering down at the boat.

"They're your own damned antiquities!" Captain Shore roared.

Sarah shook her head. "All his," she said. "His and his accomplice, the Nobildonna. Forgers, perjurers, and grave robbers. And everyone knows you've worked with them before, carried forged papers, and sold to foreign courts without an export license, and you're aiding his escape from justice now!"

"You, madam, are a little whore," the Captain swore. "And keep your voice down."

Sarah, knowing she had won, beamed up at Captain Shore and held the ladder for her uncle. "Just a milliner," she said.

JANUARY 1671, HADLEY, NEW ENGLAND

Ned, snowed in at the ferry cabin, not knowing what he thought, not knowing what he felt, not knowing the right thing to do, went from one bitter conclusion to another. He was trapped indoors by a relentless blizzard that made it dangerous even to dig out a path to feed the beasts, who were warm behind a wall of snow. Getting into town to see his old commanders or his minister was impossible. He was in a rage of indecision which seemed to be echoed outside his cabin by the wild storm of the weather.

He was bitter and isolated but not lonely. He did not miss the company of the townspeople, he felt that he did not care if he never heard another of the hateful words they said. He did not want to see Mrs. Rose with the hot spots of anger on her cheeks and the strain in her face. He did not want to see Quiet Squirrel or hear her steady counsel either. He could not think of her without wondering if the snowsnake path had brought her a message to fall on the people of Hadley the moment that the Massasoit received his summons to go to Plymouth and answer for his actions. The people at Hadley might think that they could order the Massasoit to attend in secret, and that none of the scattered tribes would even know, but Ned knew that he would never obey men he did not regard as his equals, let alone his superiors, and he had friends and allies all around them.

The hope that other tribes would not know was folly. Ned knew that all the neighboring tribes would know at once. They had been communicating all winter, they had probably agreed a signal. The moment the Massasoit got an insulting summons, the English would find themselves isolated and outnumbered even in the biggest towns. A little place like Hadley could be obliterated in one night.

There was only one person that Ned wanted to see, there was only one person whose opinion he wanted to hear, there was only one person who was, like him, between the two worlds: John Sassamon, the Christian Indian, minister to the congregation at Natick, and Wussausmon, the same man but in different clothes, the advisor and translator to the Massasoit, the translator and advisor to the English: the go-between in the heart of this crisis.

Ned was so anxious in the days when dawn did not come till halfway through the morning, and then it was often a sky dark with snow clouds, that he thought he might summon Wussausmon by wishing for him, as if he were the devil, like his brother-translators. Or he might call on John Sassamon through prayer—like a disciple in the Bible stories. But one day, as Ned was pouring a jug of boiling water into the earthenware bowl of ice in the cowpen, he heard a shout from where the wicket gate was buried under the snow and saw Wussausmon himself waiting courteously outside the garden where the fence should have been.

"Come in! Come in!" Ned shouted. "Am I glad to see you!"

"I can't stay," Wussausmon said, gliding towards him on his snowshoes. "But I was going downstream and thought I would come to say good-bye."

Ned splashed water on the straw as his hand shook. "Good-bye? Won't you step inside and get warm?"

"No, I'm warm as it is. But I would not go past your house, *Nippe Sannup*, without a greeting."

"Don't go," Ned said quickly. "You can eat with me? I have some succotash on the fire."

Wussausmon dived into a pocket under his cape and brought out a strip of dried meat. "Try this," he suggested.

He held it out to Ned and Ned nibbled the end. The rich warm taste of dried moose tongue filled his mouth. "That's good," he said ruefully. "Better than my succotash!"

Generously, Wussausmon tore off a strip. "Put it in the succotash," he said. "It will flavor the whole pot. And don't forget to give thanks."

"But where are you going in such a hurry?" Ned asked. "Oh—Wussausmon, are you going to Montaup?"

"There are many gathering there," Wussausmon said. "You told them? You warned your people?"

"I did. But it didn't do any good," Ned said, looking away from the direct dark gaze and staring instead at the bare black trunks of the trees and the white stripes of snow on their bark, at the delicate lines of ice on every twig. "I am sorry, I said everything that I could—but they are determined that King Philip—Massasoit—shall answer to them. They know of the gatherings, they know he is stockpiling weapons. I told them it all but they're not going to make peace; they're going to summon him to answer."

"I will have to warn them," Wussausmon said. "I will go to Plymouth myself. As the Massasoit's translator I must be believed. I will tell them that he must have his rights under their own law. I know the law, I can read it. I will have to make them listen to me."

"They're frightened, they won't listen," Ned said, and at once cursed himself for telling an Indian that the white men were frightened. "Lord, I shouldn't have said that to you. Wussausmon, we have been friends, we cannot be on the brink of being enemies. Mrs. Rose—the minister's housekeeper—she's talking about leaving here altogether, going back to Boston."

"Will you go with her?"

Ned looked from the frosted trees to the great river flowing under the thick ice, the forest on the other side, and the snowcap on his little house where the chimney sent a single stream of smoke into the translucent sky. "How can I? How can I leave here? This is my home!"

A dark smile crossed Wussausmon's face. "Ah, do you feel it now? That you belong to the land and it belongs to you? That you cannot leave?"

"Almost," Ned said tentatively.

"I shall look for you here when I come by again, if I ever come by again," Wussausmon told him. "But Mrs. Rose is right: none of you are safe here."

"I wear Quiet Squirrel's moccasins every day," Ned objected. "My roof is thatched with the reeds she traded me. Are you saying that I am in danger from her now?"

"All of us who have been living between the worlds will have to choose," Wussausmon said. "You're on the very edge here, *Nippe Sannup*, between water and land, between tribal lands and English village, between one world and another. You will have to choose."

"And you?" Ned asked his friend. "Between the praying town with your wife and children and the warpath at Montaup. Will you have to choose too?"

Wussausmon turned to his friend, his face impassive but his eyes bright with tears. "I will have to betray someone," he said quietly. "I am Squanto."

JANUARY 1671, LONDON

In the new year Livia tried to create a habit with her fiancé that she would dine with him every Sunday, after church, and then every other day throughout the week. But he was often dining out, and sometimes at business, and even when she did arrive at dinnertime to find him at home, Lady Eliot was always there too. Sometimes, Livia would swear the older woman had been about to leave the house, but as soon as Livia arrived, she shed her cape, and said she would stay for dinner. Sometimes, even worse, Livia was certain she had seen a glance between Sir James and his aunt that had prompted the older lady to stay.

"We have to have a chaperone, for your good name," he told her one day towards the end of January.

"We don't need one. We will be married in two weeks." She came a little closer to him so that he could smell the perfume of roses in her dark hair. "I am baptized and confirmed, the banns are being called, why should we not be together?"

He stepped back and felt the edge of his desk against the back of his thighs blocking his retreat, as his betrothed came forward until she slipped into his arms and pressed herself against his body.

"We don't need a chaperone," she whispered. "For we are friends and lovers, and betrothed to marry, our wedding within weeks, and we have been everything to each other. Tell her to go out, and let us be together!"

"That can't happen again," he said; but she could feel his arousal. "Not until our wedding day."

"Send her away for tonight, and let me dine with the man I love alone," she whispered.

"I can't," James said. "In all honor, I should not be alone with you, Livia. It is for your good name, as much as my own."

She looked up at him, her eyes inviting. "Do you want me so much? Should I be afraid of your passion?"

The way she spoke to him, the tremble of her voice on the word "afraid," made him cool abruptly. There was something calculating about her, the lilt of her accent sounded suddenly affected. "No indeed," he said, stepping away from her and putting the desk between them. "I would be ashamed to make a lady afraid. The incident, when I forgot myself, was, as you know, an accident that I will not repeat."

She turned to the window for a moment to hide her frustration, then she turned back to him with the sweetest smile. "Ah, I know. And you must forgive me. I just long for the time when we can honorably and truly love one another. When I can give myself to you," she whispered. "When we can give your great name an heir."

A tap on the door saved him from answering her and Lady Eliot threw the door open. "Look who's coming to dinner!" Lady Eliot said, taking in the room in one swift glance. "Dear George. George Pakenham."

Livia stepped forward, her hand held out for him to kiss. "Ah!

How glad I am to see you again!" she said, as if she were genuinely delighted. "And not one word about my beautiful things, this time, for they are all the property of Sir James. And he won't hear a word against them!"

She turned a laughing face back to James, who was silent behind his desk.

"How come?" Sir George said, kissing Livia's hand.

There was a moment's pause. "Oh, did you not know? We are to be married!" Livia announced. "Aren't we, *caro marito*?"

"Yes," James said, coming round the desk to greet his brother-in-law. "Yes. Her ladyship has condescended to make me so happy."

"Really?" George demanded.

"Next month," Livia triumphed. "In two weeks! You must come to my wedding."

JANUARY 1671, AT SEA

Felipe was in the prow of the ship, at noon, wrapped in a thick cape against the cold wind, watching the hypnotic smooth parting of the waves under the wooden bow. Sarah came up on deck as if drawn to him, and stood beside him. Without a word, he opened the side of his cape and put it around her shoulders, like an embrace. They stood, side by side, enwrapped in the cape, but not embracing. Their shoulders brushed against each other on each roll of the ship.

"You could have drowned." Felipe was coldly furious.

"I can swim," she said calmly.

"You could have been arrested. We nearly left you. The *pedotti* should not have let us launch the dinghy that close to the quarantine island. He would not have allowed us to wait for more than a moment longer."

"But you persuaded him?"

"I had to tell a mouthful of lies."

She smiled up at him. "That must have been torture for an honest man such as you."

"This is not amusing to me," he said furiously. "I thought you would die in the water. I felt—" He broke off.

"What did you feel?" she asked.

"Terrified," he said, as if the truth were forced out of him. "I thought you were—"

She waited.

"I thought you were lost. I thought I had lost you."

Still wrapped in his cloak she turned towards him and put her hands on either side of his face. "Forgive me," she said earnestly. "I had to lie to you, I knew you would never have let me go; but I will promise to never lie to you again."

He put his hands on her slim waist; but he did not draw her close. "You will be true to me?"

"I will," she said solemnly.

"You know that I cannot make a promise to be true to you? I am what you called me—a counterfeiter, a forger, a fraud, a grave robber, a thief, and a liar."

She nodded very gravely. "I know. But you could change?"

He shook his head. "*Cara*—I cannot promise to reform, I have lived a life—my whole life is dishonest. My business is forgery."

The look she gave him would have converted any sinner. "But you could change? You could repent?"

He bowed his head. "I am not worthy of you. Even if I were free."

"I see I would have to save you," she said, with a hopeful little smile.

He swallowed down his reply, and he released her and she turned away so that they stood shoulder to shoulder again, watching the sea.

"Our worlds are oceans apart," he remarked. "And soon there will be a sea between us again. Will you go back to being a milliner?"

"Already Venice feels like a dream," she said. "I feel as if I will

406

wake up to London and the shop and the hats, and the girls will ask me where I have been and what I have done, and I'll never be able to tell them."

"What would you tell them about me?"

She shook her head. "I'll never speak of you."

For a moment they were silent, looking at the waves.

"Will you sell your feathers at a great profit?" he asked.

"I'll sell some, but I'll keep some back. I'll make my own hats and headdresses and sell them on my own account."

"I shall think of you in your milliner's shop, when I am home again," he said. "I shall think of you every day."

She looked up at him and for a moment he thought he could not resist pulling her towards him and kissing the sadness from her mouth.

"Don't do that. Because I shan't think of you at all," Sarah said determinedly. "Not at all."

FEBRUARY 1671, HADLEY, NEW ENGLAND

Ned was smoking meat in the chimney of his house, long strips of venison that Quiet Squirrel had given him earlier in the day when she had crossed the river for trade. She said that she wanted some pins for sewing, an excuse so transparent that Ned did not even count the pins he poured into her sack, and neither did she.

"Want news?" he asked her, thinking that his grasp of the language was so poor that he could never convey to her his anxiety about what was to come, especially his fears for her, and the little village with the new palisade around it.

She nodded, her eyes on his face. "If you know anything, Ned."

"Massasoit must go to Plymouth, understand? He must make answer, he must say: sorry."

She sighed and he thought it was impatience at the childishness of his speech in their tongue. "I wish I could tell you that I know all this," she said to him in her own language, knowing he would grasp one word in ten. "I know all this! We've all seen it coming. What I want you to tell me is when the men at Hadley, even the old soldiers that we helped to hide, are going to come against my people? I know they will. I don't ask if, I ask when." She took his hands and looked into his face as if to summon his attention. "Hadley men?" she asked him. "Are they going to march against us? Against my children?"

He understood at once what she meant. "No," he said, then he checked himself. It was not for him to reassure her so that she trusted her neighbors when they were arming themselves, when they were talking of teaching a lesson to this wise old woman and the village. "Maybe," he said, his face grim. "Maybe."

"They are arming?" she asked him. "They are drilling?"

Before he could answer her head jerked up to listen to a noise outside, and at the same moment Red raised his head from his paws and growled.

"Someone at the door?" Ned asked, and turned back to her, but she was already gone. She had melted to the back of the room and slid herself under Ned's big winter cape on its peg and stood perfectly still.

The hammer of a fist on the door echoed in the snow-silent cabin and Ned shouted: "Who's there?"

"Selectman!" came the reply.

Ned opened the door and wrapped his jacket around himself against the cold as the man jumped down from the drift of packed snow into the house. Ned slammed the door behind him.

"Long way to come in the snow," he said.

"I didn't think I'd get through." The man gestured at himself. He was dusted with snow from head to feet. He had been struggling through waist-high drifts up and down the common lane. "I'm going into all the houses this end of the village. You're mustered: town militia. You're to attend first Saturday on the meadow if fine.

Next Saturday if snowing. One after that if still bad. You're to bring your own weapons. D'you have a musket?" He looked above the door where Ned's gun hung. "You're to bring it."

"What're we doing?" Ned asked him.

"Drilling," he said. "Practicing marksmanship, practicing marching."

"To defend?" Ned asked, his last hope.

"To attack," the man said. "To march with other militia under commanders appointed by the Council. A force of all New England, advancing together. You're to be captain."

"Marching against who?" Ned asked.

"Against the savages," the man said generally.

"Who?" Ned demanded. "What tribe?"

The man made a lordly wave. "All of 'em," he said. "They're all as bad as each other. D'you accept your summons?"

"Yes," Ned said. "Of course."

The man turned, opened the door, and grunted as he heaved himself up the big bank of snow. He set off at once, without saying good-bye, struggling through the thick snow, falling, picking himself up again. Ned shut the door against the cold and Quiet Squirrel came out from his cape.

"What will you do?" she asked him, her face as tender as a mother to her son. "*Nippe Sannup*—what will you do?"

FEBRUARY 1671, AT SEA

True to his word, Rob had gone straight into the cabin that Felipe hastily vacated and did not come out for forty days, a self-imposed quarantine that he would not break. His food and beer were left at the door, and he returned the plates scraped clean, throwing the scraps and his slop bucket from the porthole. A bowl of vinegar stood outside his door and his plates and cups were soaked in it before they were collected. An old sailor, who had survived the triangular trade to the killing coasts of West Africa with one of Mrs. Reekie's plague purses sewn around his neck, swore he would catch nothing, and served Rob, steeping his clothes in seawater and vinegar and then boiling them in hot water, pressing them with a scorching iron to kill the lice.

"He's cleaner than I am," he said with satisfaction on the fortieth day of the voyage when it was thought safe that Rob should come out.

"Really, that's not the highest accolade in the world," Felipe said.

Sarah giggled, but tapped on Rob's cabin door. "Will you come out?" she said.

"Does the Captain give permission?" he asked from inside.

"He does."

They heard the noise of the bolt being shot and then Rob opened the door and stood before them, newly washed, newly shaved, in pressed plain clothes. He was a strikingly handsome young man of thirty-four years old, brown-haired, brown-eyed, with a square open trusting face and an easy smile that warmed his face and lit his eyes when he saw Sarah. "My little angel," he said. "You were just a child when I left London and look at you now!" But then he saw Felipe, and the smile was wiped from his face and he fell back.

"You! What are you doing here? You damned serpent! God! What trick is this that you have played on me?" Furiously he turned on Sarah. "What have you done? Tricked me? Where are we going? How could you?"

"I didn't, I didn't," Sarah said hastily.

He would have flung himself back in his cabin and slammed the door on them but they both went forward with him and Felipe caught the door with his shoulder.

"She hasn't betrayed you, fool," he said sharply. "You blame the wrong woman. You misunderstand—as usual. *Dio!* I had forgotten how persistently stupid you are!"

"Traitor!" Rob accused Sarah. "You sent me my mother's coins and I trusted—"

"I freed you," Sarah said quickly. "That's the truth. The ship's sailing to London and the Captain is honest. I am who I say I am, your niece and your friend. It's all as you thought. It's Felipe that is different. He's with us now."

"My enemy!"

"Not now. He's on our side."

"He's only ever on his own side!" Rob accused.

Felipe gave a little ironic bow. "Alas, that was once too true. But listen and stop raving. I helped Sarah set you free, I didn't realize she was going to be quite so"—he paused to search for the word— "dramatic. I didn't realize she was going to fling herself off the boat, nearly drown herself, nearly freeze to death, and bring back a plague carrier. But I did tell her where you were, I did help her find you."

"It wasn't very hard to find me!" Rob spat. "Since I was committed to the prison where you sent me."

"True," Felipe conceded. "But nonetheless we did find you."

"You left me to die in there."

"I did, but she rescued you. You've nothing to fear from her. She's always been true to you, came here to find you, and wouldn't stop till she did."

"You are?" Rob turned to Sarah, desperate to believe in her. "You are true to me? You are my niece? You did come for me?"

Sarah nodded, and put her hand to her heart. "I did come to find you, I did rescue you. I promised your ma that I would find you, or I would put flowers on your grave."

Rob nodded. "But him? Do you know what this man is? This cold-hearted brute?"

"Yes," she said boldly, "I know the worst of him; but he helped me. I could not have found you if he hadn't helped me. And he's coming to London to accuse Livia. He's turned against her. It was her who stole the goods from her husband's collection and now she's using our family to sell the goods."

"You have nothing to fear from me. I am your friend," Felipe told him cheerfully.

"You will never be my friend," Rob assured him.

Felipe hesitated in the face of such determined hostility. "Very well, as you wish; but we share an enemy." He glanced down at Sarah. "And we share a most gallant friend."

Rob turned from him and took Sarah's hands. "You are truly my niece, Sarah?"

"Yes, I am."

"And you came here to Venice to find me?"

"Yes. It was your mother who asked me to come."

"You have been misled and betrayed by this man," Rob warned her. "He can be no friend to you."

"No, he's told me everything, I think."

"Sarah, it was he that arrested me and threw me into the well. Nobody gets out of the well. They only freed me to go to my death on the Lazzaretto Nuovo."

"Could have sent you to the Lazzaretto Vecchio," Felipe pointed out, provocatively. "Far worse. Far more certain a death. And life is always a chance, here or in the well."

Rob ignored him. "He plotted my death so that he could steal and trade antiquities with my wife," he told Sarah. He expected her to be shocked but the face she turned to him was completely calm.

"I know this," she said. "He told me himself. And now, in turn, Livia has betrayed him. She's in England, selling the antiquities for her own profit and planning to marry an English lord."

"Livia? She's in England?"

"She came to us," Sarah told him. "She went to your ma and told her you were dead—drowned."

Rob was horrified. "She never told Ma that I was drowned! Not drowned!"

"It wasn't as wicked as it seems," Sarah said fairly. "She didn't know your ma wouldn't be able to bear such a thought. She didn't know what she was saying to people like us, people from Foulmire."

He shook his head as if to clear his thoughts. "How did Ma bear the news?" He looked quickly at Sarah: "It didn't make her ill?"

She beamed. "That's what's amazing. She was unhurt. She didn't believe Livia for a moment!"

"She didn't? But why not?"

"There's something about Livia that Grandma doesn't like," Sarah said honestly. "She's never said what. But she never believed her, not from the first. Livia is beautiful, and so tragic—you know—she told a story that would break your heart. But Grandma just looked at her and said, 'Oh yes.'"

"Oh yes?" Rob repeated.

Sarah felt a little bubble of laughter at the thought of her idiosyncratic grandmother. "It was when Livia put Matteo into her arms and said he would comfort her and be in the place of you."

Rob was smiling now too, imagining his mother. "She didn't like that?"

"It should have been really moving; but apparently your ma just held him, looked into his face, and said: 'I don't think it quite works like that.'"

"Lord, I can hear her! I can see her!"

"But why?" Felipe asked. "This woman is like a stone!"

"She's not a fool to be played by a mountebank," Rob snapped. "She'd see right through you."

"Later, when she asked me to look for you, she told me she would know if her son was dead and I believed her," Sarah told him. "I knew what she meant. I'd know if Johnnie was sick or dead. I'd just know it. Grandma never believed that you were dead, and she was certain you weren't drowned. The only time she had a doubt was just when I was leaving, and then she was afraid. She asked me to bring back something of yours that could go into her coffin at her death. And to put flowers on the water where they lost you."

"What flowers?"

"Why does that matter?" Felipe asked, who had been following the rapid speech.

"Forget-me-nots."

Rob grimaced. "Ah God, I'd never have wanted her grieved! And all this time, in the well and on the island, I've been thinking that Livia was breaking her heart and going to everyone for my release." He glanced at Felipe. "I thought you'd acted on your own, and that she would be fighting you, trying to get me freed. I imagined her entrapped by you, fighting to be free."

Felipe shook his head. "Not the Nobildonna! You never knew her

413

at all. She left at once for England, the moment they issued a warrant for your arrest. She was afraid they would call her as a witness to the death of her first husband. The day you were arrested was the day she sailed for London. She went like a princess, with a beautiful trousseau of black gowns—from when she was mourning the Conte—and she hired a maid to care for Matteo."

"And we took her in," Sarah told him. "And Ma believed her. She showed her antiquities in London, she sold them, and she said she would use the money to buy a bigger warehouse, in a better part of town, with better rooms for us."

"Her antiquities?" Rob turned to Felipe.

"Indeed." He gave a little bow. "Those that she stole from her husband and those that I make. And now she has ordered more from my store. We've got them on board now. We're taking them to her."

"She doesn't know that Ma sent you to Venice?" Rob asked Sarah.

Sarah nodded. "She doesn't know. At least—she didn't know when I left. I don't know what she'll have got out of my ma while I've been away."

"She won't know that you're coming to London with her antiquities?" He turned to Felipe.

The Italian smiled. "She can't know that. I did not know it myself."

"Why did you bring him?" Rob turned to Sarah.

"Perhaps she is going to save me?" Felipe said provocatively.

"In fact, it's an ambush," Rob named it.

"She deserves it," Sarah said grimly.

"She's still my wife."

There was a pause. "You can't still love her?" Sarah asked cautiously. "Are you going to forgive her? She nearly killed you."

"I have thought of her night and day for nearly ten months. I can't suddenly see her as an enemy. I can't believe that she has done what you say. I can't change how I feel, like that!" He snapped his fingers. "In a moment."

Felipe raised his eyebrows at Sarah. "As I say," he reminded her: "persistently stupid."

"I can't understand how she can have done the things you say, when I think of how she was with me," Rob explained to Sarah, ignoring

Felipe. "It's as if you're talking about a stranger. The thought of her trying to rescue me was all that kept me alive. I knew she would never stop trying to save me—and now you tell me it was she who put me there?"

"But this is her!" Felipe exclaimed. "This is what I love about her—the very thing that you never saw! That she can change her very self in a moment! She understands that the only way to make money is to be constantly deceitful—she stops at nothing."

Rob shook his head, as if he could not follow his own thoughts. "When I first met her, she was a young wife, lonely and ill-treated by her husband's family, a beautiful widow, lost in a grand palazzo with a family that hated her. I loved her. I fell deeply in love with her. I rescued her from them. I can't imagine any other Livia."

"There are a dozen others," Felipe told him. "And you're not the first man to love the face that she showed him."

"And not the last!" Sarah added. "She's doing it right now! She turned to Rob. "I'm sorry that you still love her, Uncle Rob. But I think she's planning to marry this English lord. The one who helped her to sell the antiquities to other gentlemen."

"Who is he?" he asked.

"Sir James Avery," she told him.

He thought for a moment and shook his head. "Never heard of him."

"He came to the warehouse," Sarah told him. "Someone from the old days at Foulmire? Ma hates him, but Grandma said she would see him, just once. Wasn't he your tutor? When you were a boy? On Foulmire?"

"That was James Summer," he exclaimed. "James Summer was my tutor. Not Avery. But I suppose—could it be the same man?" He looked astounded. "He came back to Ma? But how does Livia know him?"

"Livia got her claws in him on his first visit. He let her use his house to show the antiquities. By the time I left, she'd persuaded him to do a second show. That's what this shipment is for. She was very sure of him, in and out of his house, acting like she owned it. It looked to me as if she planned to marry him."

Felipe waited, his eyes on Rob's stunned expression. "Slow," he remarked quietly to Sarah. "Persistently . . ."

"She can't marry him; she's married to me!" Rob said simply.

"*Ecco!*" Felipe said triumphantly. "*Finalmente!* Exactly."

FEBRUARY 1671, LONDON

The line of ships waiting for the legal quays trailed down the river. Captain Shore, staring upriver, his blue eyes squinting against the light drizzle of a cold morning, called for a skiff to take him to the Custom House to ask permission to go straight to the Reekie Wharf and meet a custom officer there.

"You don't have to unload at the Custom House?" Felipe asked with interest, looking up to the quarterdeck and the Captain.

"Only if you're carrying special cargo, cargo that pays a royal duty, like coffee or spices, or from the East Indies, or cargo of high value. Our manifest says private goods, furniture and the like." Captain Shore scowled down at the handsome younger man. "And some barrels of oil, and wine. We can unload them all at Reekie Wharf and pay the duty there. If they *were* private goods, furniture and the like, then I would have no worries. You tell me they are?"

"I do. And you have an export license that confirms my word."

"Then of course I am reassured."

"Do you have to declare the passengers?"

"Of course. And I will," the Captain warned. "Proper papers. Mrs. Reekie's reputation is good, and I won't be a blackguard at her wharf. Proper papers, full declaration. The officer will see you at Reekie Wharf and you can pay your dues and get your passport there. Give me your papers to show at the Custom House."

Felipe handed over a much-signed document with many ribbons that attested he was Felipe Russo, a trader in antiquities, a member of the guild of stone masons of Venice, a freeman of the city, and entitled to travel where he should wish.

"What about Roberto?" Felipe asked.

"As he's an Englishman, he needs nothing," the Captain said. "He's just coming home. Like Miss Reekie. But they'll ask if any of us have been in contact with disease."

"We have not," Felipe said. "We are all come from Venice, which is—*grazie Dio*—free of illness."

"Aye, you have an answer for everything," Captain Shore said. "Wait on board, till I return."

"Aye, aye, Captain," Felipe said in a parody of obedience, and watched the older man climb down the ladder at the side of the ship and step into the waiting skiff.

"What do we do now?" Sarah asked, appearing at his elbow. "I can almost see my home from here."

"We have to wait," he said. "Did you think you would dive in and swim over?"

"No," she conceded. "I don't want to do that again."

"Then I should think you'll be home this afternoon, as soon as the Captain has permission to dock at your wharf. And then what will we do?"

"I'll take Rob to my grandma," she said, smiling in anticipation, "and then we'll see Livia—at home if she's there, and if she's not—we'll go to Avery House and find her. If you're still sure?"

"I'm sure," he told her. "I'm very sure."

"You'll unmask her?" she demanded.

"I'll see what she requires," he answered ambiguously.

She turned to go back down to her cabin, but he caught the edge of her shawl. "Stay," he invited her. "Tell me about your home. Show me the landmarks. I've never been to London before, tell me about the City?"

Her gaze on his face was very direct. "You'll find out soon enough," she said bluntly. "All you need to know for now is that here is the south bank, the poor side of the City where the Nobildonna lives with my family, and uses our space and treats us as if we were there to serve her, and over the river on the north side is where she is headed, where beautiful houses await a cultured and beautiful mistress, where people buy your fraudulent goods, thinking them real, where they enjoy her company, thinking her a woman of quality. It's an easy city to read. We live here, on this side, the poor side, the dirty side. We're honest on this side. But Livia is determined to spend her time on the other side. As anybody would. You as well, I expect. That's where you will 'see what she requires.' That side is for the nobility and the liars, those for who appearance matters more than truth. People like her; people like you."

He took her hand and kissed it, glancing up at her. "No," was all he said.

"No what?" Sarah said, pulling her hand away.

"I am ready to become an honest man, I no longer want to be one with the nobility and the liars. You can stretch out your hand and save me, Miss Jolie. Miss Pretty. Let me be on your side."

She looked at him as if she did not wholly trust him. "You are reformed?"

He smiled at her, shamelessly attractive. "If you will save me?"

FEBRUARY 1671, ST. CLEMENT DANES CHURCH, LONDON

Livia, wearing a new gown of navy blue silk, with a matching jacket trimmed with navy blue lace, an exquisite bonnet with a navy blue veil of lace caught back with a golden pin, walked down the aisle of the church, quite alone, her new shoes making a satisfying tap-tap on the floor. Behind her came Carlotta, carrying Matteo in her arms, as if the little boy must witness the marriage of his mother, and establish his rights to his stepfather. Matteo was sleepy and looked around him blinking his wide dark eyes and then tucked his little head under Carlotta's chin. Livia did not look back at him, but walked steadily forward, her eyes modestly downcast. She had no other companion.

Waiting for her, in his family pew on the right side of the church, was Sir James, Lady Eliot beside him, Sir George Pakenham beside her. In the pew behind them were the upper servants from Avery House, allowed to come to church in the afternoon to witness the wedding of their master. As Livia walked up the aisle they craned and stared and whispered.

Livia, pretending to hear nothing, carried a small posy of primroses, tied with a dark blue ribbon, and a Book of Common Prayer. As they heard her heels tapping on the newly laid stone floor, Sir James rose from his knees, where he had been praying in his family pew, and took his place before the altar, so that when she came up he was ready, like a man standing in a dock.

She thought he was very pale and drawn; she raised her eyes to him, in a parody of modesty, wishing he would look more like a man on his wedding day, and less like a man facing a slowly closing trap. She whispered a word of greeting and he gave a grim nod to acknowledge her and turned to face the minister. Sir George came out of the pew to stand at his side, as Lady Eliot begrudgingly rose to her feet, to witness the wedding.

Livia peeled off her dark blue lace mitten from her left hand. George placed the ring on the open book that the minister held towards him. It was the wedding ring of Sir James's first wife, George's sister's wedding ring, a slim gold band inset with diamonds. Livia had insisted upon having it. She would not have a new ring; she wanted the old one. She wanted everything that the first Lady Avery had owned, as if her ring and her embroidery frame in her parlor, her cut-glass perfume bottles in her traveling case, would make the title real. The minister took a breath, looked from the drawn face of his parishioner Sir James to the exquisite beauty of his young bride, and started the service:

"Dearly beloved friends, we are gathered together here in the sight of God, and in the face of this Congregation, to join together this man and this woman in holy Matrimony . . ."

The minister had rehearsed the service several times with Livia so that she should understand the significance of each word in a church that was not her family's church, in a language that was not her own. He always had the sense that she was learning her lines like an actress, rather than repeating them as a prayer. Even now, as he intoned the introduction to the marriage service, he thought there was something rather theatrical about the beautiful widow. She lifted the posy of primroses to her face and breathed in their scent, and then she lifted her dark eyes to his, looking at him soulfully over the butter-cream petals.

"... *Which is an honorable estate, instituted of God in Paradise in the time of man's innocency, signifying unto us the mystical union that is betwixt Christ and his Church.*"

He could not be mistaken: her smile gleamed at him as if she had enlisted him to help her in some trick, as a cardsharper in the street might use a bystander to lure a fool and take advantage of him. The minister continued with the words, but he could not bear Livia's smiling gaze.

"... *Which holy estate Christ adorned and beautified with his presence, and first miracle that he wrought, in Cana of Galilee; and is commended of Saint Paul to be honorable among all men: and therefore is not by any to be enterprised, nor taken in hand, unadvisedly, lightly, or wantonly, to satisfy men's carnal lusts and appetites, like brute beasts that have no understanding; but reverently, discreetly, advisedly, soberly, and in the fear of God ...*"

The minister glanced at his other parishioner, Lady Eliot, rigid with disapproval in the family pew, visibly unhappy at this second marriage and bitterly resenting this foreigner. At the bridegroom's side, George Pakenham stared blankly at the stained-glass window behind the minister's head as if he wished he was elsewhere. The minister hesitated, any man on God's earth would have hesitated, looking from the white-faced Englishman to the smiling Italian widow. And as he paused, Livia lifted her pretty face and snapped: "Go on."

Sir James flinched at her order. Then he confirmed it: "Yes, Mr. Rogers, please continue."

The minister recited the sacred reasons that the two should be joined in matrimony, unconvincing even to himself. He demanded if there was any reason that they should not be married? And that anyone should speak now, or forever hold his peace. He made the traditional pause for any reply, and Livia's upward glance at Sir James was sweetly trusting.

Lady Eliot held her breath, looked at Sir George, opened her mouth as if to speak, and then subsided. There was nothing she could say to prevent the wedding going ahead. There was nothing anyone could say.

The minister held the Prayer Book towards Sir James, the wedding ring resting on the open page, and James put his dead wife's ring on Livia's finger, reciting the wedding oath: *"With this ring, I thee wed, with my body I thee worship, and with all my worldly goods I thee endow. In the name of the Father and of the Son and of the Holy Ghost, Amen."*

It was a little too large; Livia clenched her hand in a fist to hold it tight.

"Let us pray," the minister said, and he led them through the prayers for the marriage and then went to the altar to prepare Holy Communion. Livia, now baptized and confirmed into the church, went with her new husband to the chancel steps and received the bread and the wine. She was followed by her new aunt Lady Eliot, Sir George, and her household. When the service was completed, they prayed again and the minister said to James: "You may kiss the bride."

Livia, still holding the primroses to her cheek, turned up her face for his kiss so that he kissed warm lips and felt the flowers against his cheek, and smelled the delicate sweetness of their scent.

"So that's done," Lady Eliot remarked sourly to Sir George. She picked up her Prayer Book from the shelf in the front of the pew, and turned to leave, as the big door at the far end of the church banged open and a swirl of cold air blew in. A crowd of strangers strode down the aisle, one, two, three men in traveling capes, and among them Sarah and Alys Stoney—the last people Livia would have expected to see here on the Strand, the last people she would have wanted at her wedding.

"Stop the service," Rob Reekie said very calmly. "Minister, I bid you, stop the service. This woman cannot be married to this man."

James Avery, scowling at the rudeness of this interruption, fearing scandal before he even knew what was happening, saw Rob, his former pupil, but did not recognize him in this fully grown confident brown-haired man who looked at him so grimly, with two strangers behind him, and bringing up the rear: Alys Stoney and her daughter, Sarah.

"Stop the service," Rob repeated. "This woman cannot be married to this man. She is my wife."

In the stunned silence, it was Lady Eliot who took control of the situation. She stepped forward and put up her hand to Rob. "Not another word more," she said, and when he would have protested, she said: "I mean it. Not another word more."

For a moment Livia thought she had found an unlikely defender. But Lady Eliot was only thinking that the servants must see and hear as little as possible. "You can go." She turned to the Avery House steward, to the Avery House cook, and to their underlings. "Apparently, there is a difficulty, a mistake here, which we will resolve privately. Go back to Avery House now, and we will come later, and you can serve the wedding dinner then. And mind that it's perfect. However delayed."

The servants dawdled out, as slowly as they dared, but the nobility and the strangers were silent, as if frozen in their places like statues, until the door had closed behind the servants, and they were alone.

"Shall we . . . ?" helplessly Mr. Rogers gestured towards the vestry. "You will want to be alone?"

"No," Livia said flatly, daring anyone to contradict her. "I'm not going anywhere. Anything anyone wants to say can be said here. There is no obstacle to me marrying this man. And in any case we are married now, and anyone who says different is a liar." She did not even look at Rob, as if he were not there, as if he were still imprisoned on a plague island, as if he had never been.

A slight gesture from Felipe caught her eye and for the first time she saw him, realized that he had come with Rob, and that there was a new and dangerous alliance against her. Even now she showed no fear, she did not hesitate for a moment. "This is a true marriage," she repeated defiantly, directly to Felipe. "It is in everyone's best interest that it is not challenged. I speak to you complete strangers, as I do to my loved ones, as I do to my new husband and family. All of you, *all* of you will do better if you leave this marriage unchallenged. I did not undertake it lightly. It is in the best interests of us all."

Felipe hid his smile. He took off his hat to her and bowed.

James Avery swallowed on a dry mouth. "Who are you?" he asked Rob, and then he said, more uncertainly, "You're Rob, aren't you? Rob Reekie? Good God, Rob! I thought you were dead. They all thought you were . . ." He took half a step towards the younger man as if he would embrace him; but Rob did not respond at all, did not open his arms, made no move beyond a stiff little bow, and James's joy died away in uncertainty. "I wouldn't have believed it!" he said more quietly. "What a miracle! And your mother!" He turned to Alys. "Have you told her, Mrs. Stoney? Has she seen him? Does she know?"

"Aye," Alys said shortly.

"This is your first thought?" Livia asked him with an edge to her voice. "Your first question is—if his mother knows?"

He did not even hear her. "And . . . Sarah? Miss Stoney? You're here too?"

"We came straight from the ship," Sarah said. "We've just landed at Reekie Wharf. I went to Venice to find him."

"I thought you were staying with friends?"

"I thought so too," Livia agreed with her husband. "That's what they said. That's what they all said." She looked over the top of her flowers at Alys. "That's what you said, Alys. Did you lie to me?"

"Aye," Alys repeated, her mouth closed in a hard line.

"My grandma sent me to Venice. She never believed her—" Sarah's contemptuous tip of her head indicated Livia, standing with her nose in her posy of primroses.

"But the marriage?" the minister interrupted. "We have performed a marriage here. A solemn . . . Are you saying this lady is precontracted?" He turned to Livia. "Nobildonna, you should have told me . . . is this true? You made a solemn declaration on oath, you gave your word before God that you were free to marry. You have taken instruction for weeks and you never—"

"She's my wife," Rob interrupted. He glanced back at Matteo who was sleeping in Carlotta's arms. "And that's my son. He carries my name. This gentleman"—he gestured at Felipe—"was her steward. He knows her as my wife. He witnessed our wedding in Venice, he witnessed my arrest and her running away from Venice. She's been living with my family as my widow. She lied to them. She told my mother that I was dead."

"This is very serious," the minister began.

"I thank God that you are alive," Livia said with quiet dignity to Rob. She did not rush to embrace him, but nor did she step towards Sir James. She stood alone, poised, looking from one man to another, as if she were deciding what to do. But she never so much as glanced towards Felipe, as if she counted on him to stay silent, while a new fraud was forged.

"You truly thought he was dead?" the minister asked Livia.

She tossed her head as if he were interrupting her thoughts. "Well, of course I did. I was told he was dead," she exclaimed. "I was told that he was drowned. Why should I question it when he went out every night on the dark tides? I went into mourning for him, I left my country in the deepest grief, I came to England and I broke the terrible news to his family and tried to comfort them." She shot a dark gaze at Alys. "My sister-in-law will confirm that I tried to comfort her, that we shared our sorrow. We wept in each other's arms."

Alys, with a face like stone, said nothing.

"Then you are guilty only of a genuine mistake," Mr. Rogers assured her. "If it was a genuine mistake?"

"What else could it be? I was told without doubt that he had drowned. Praise God that he is alive." Her eyes flicked once to Felipe. "I was told that he was drowned. Everyone in Venice said it. No one would contradict me."

Felipe did not contradict her, though Sarah glanced at him, expecting him to speak. His gaze was fixed on Livia's beautiful face and the primroses that trembled beside her cheek.

"She denounced me to the authorities," Rob said flatly. "I was arrested, not drowned. This is her lover and confederate." He gestured to Felipe. "It was he who arrested me. I was accused of murder and I was imprisoned for life."

There was an aghast silence. Sir George let out a low whistle. Livia bent her head over her flowers to inhale their perfume.

Rob nodded. "This is her partner—in business and in crime: Felipe Russo."

"The ancient steward and friend of the family," Sarah supplemented spitefully, one eye on Livia.

Livia flicked her eyes towards Sarah and took in her new confidence. "A mistake," she said to the primroses as if to prompt Felipe to speak. "Rob, you are mistaken, perhaps your imprisonment has driven you mad, your word cannot be trusted. Perhaps you have a fever now. Clearly, this is not my steward, not my old steward, this is the son of my old steward, I don't know him well; but I am sure he will confirm what I have said." She turned to him, her eyes narrowed, and she held his gaze, a small smile playing on her lips. "He will support me, he will confirm my story. Won't you, Felipe? Won't you?"

They all waited for his answer, Sarah watching his face. Felipe Russo bowed to Lady Eliot and to the gentlemen. "Alas, the Nobildonna defrauded me," he said simply. "She was betrothed to me and we were partners. Together, we stole antiquities from her first husband, and we copied them and sold the forgeries. She married Roberto to hide our crime and when he caught us, she denounced him."

Sir George cleared his throat and leaned a little towards James, as if he wished to shoulder him out of the church and away from these people. "Perhaps we could go now?" he suggested quietly. "Report all this later?"

But James stood still and silent, his gaze on Livia's beautiful impassive face and the trembling primroses that she held to her cheek.

The minister shook his head, as if he could not begin to understand. "These are very grave claims, very serious accusations," he said. "They should be made before a magistrate."

"I'm a magistrate," Sir George volunteered promptly.

"Someone unconnected with any of the parties," the minister ruled.

"I can get one," Sir George offered. But the minister had already turned to Livia. "Your ladyship, these are most serious accusations that are being made against you. You should have someone to defend you . . ."

"It is all untrue," she said coolly. "But by all means let us go to a magistrate so that I may clear my name."

"You should have an advisor, someone to speak for you! You cannot face this alone."

"I have someone," she said calmly. "My husband will speak for me." Livia put her hand in James's arm and rested her head, crowned with the enchanting blue hat, against his shoulder. "Sir James is all my family now. My good name is his. I am Lady Avery of Northside Manor—who is going to speak against me?"

"But . . . but . . ." The minister was lost for words as Lady Eliot and Sir George exchanged looks of mutual horror.

Sarah watched Felipe smile at Livia, as if he were watching an exceptionally skillful player at a game of chess.

"I?" James said flatly. "I am to speak for you?"

"Obviously not." Lady Eliot came out of the Avery pew. "You gentlemen must find a magistrate at once, and he must question this woman. If needs be, we will find her a lawyer to speak for her. Though I think she is very able to defend herself. But not in Avery House."

"In my home if I wish it," Livia defied her. "In Northside Manor if I wish it! Lady Eliot, you will have to learn that these are my homes now, and I shall go to them whenever I like."

"Better come to the warehouse," Sarah said.

Lady Eliot gasped. "South of the river?"

Sarah glanced at her mother for permission. Dully, Alys nodded.

"Not there. We cannot distress Mrs. Reekie," James said urgently. "She should not be disturbed."

Livia flicked a contemptuous glance upwards to his pale face. "She will not be distressed," she promised him. "Why should she care if your marriage is challenged? It's not as if she could ever be a wife for you?"

He flinched from the contempt in her tone. "I don't want to trespass on her time," he said weakly.

"The justice of the peace in our parish is Mr. Peter Lucas, a member of the City Corporation," Sarah suggested.

"Send for him," Lady Eliot told Alys Stoney.

Alys raised an eyebrow at being ordered by a stranger. "Aye," was all she said.

The only room in the warehouse large enough to accommodate the magistrate, Alinor's family, the wedding party, Captain Shore, and

Felipe was the counting house, with the doors thrown open to the storeroom. Everyone could see, at the back of the store, the newly unloaded crated antiquities, each clearly labeled "Nobildonna da Ricci" in Sarah's writing, as if to declare, before anyone had even spoken, that Livia was Rob's wife doing business under his name. Carlotta, holding a sleeping Matteo, stood near them, uncertain what was taking place.

Johnnie, summoned from his work, hugged his sister tightly and whispered: "Glad you're back!" He took in the assembly, the many strangers in the warehouse where visitors were a rarity, and gentry had never come. "What's going on? I just got a message from Ma that you were home, that you'd brought Rob with you, and that I was to come at once. I thought we would be celebrating!"

She squeezed his arm. "You'll see. It's all right."

She meant that there was nothing here that would hurt their mother or grandmother and he was reassured. "And you? Are you well?" he asked quickly, and was surprised at the radiance of her sudden smile. "Wait a minute! What's happened?"

"Tell you later," she whispered, and pushed him towards the clerk's stool beside the magistrate, Mr. Lucas, who was already poised behind the tall counting desk. The portly City merchant pushed pen and paper to Johnnie. "You'll write down what's said when I give you the word," he ordered. "Write neat, so we don't have to make a fair copy after."

Alinor had come downstairs to be with her son, and she stood, her arm in Rob's, leaning slightly against him, as if she wanted to be sure that he was truly there, in reality, and not a dream. "I always knew you were alive," she said to him quietly. "And here you are. Nothing matters more than this. Whatever they say here, nothing matters more than that you are alive and have come home to us."

"Nothing matters more," he agreed. "But Ma—she has to answer to this: that she should have imposed on you . . . that she should have said I was drowned . . . and . . ." He lowered his voice. "What's happened to Alys? She looks so ill? Is it Livia? Did she rob her?"

Alinor looked across the warehouse at her daughter's closed expression, and the hard line of her mouth. "I think Livia betrayed her," she said.

"The antiquities? Did she make Alys pay for the shipping? Is she in debt?"

"Yes," Alinor said, knowing that there was so much more.

James came quietly before them. "May I speak with you?" he asked Alinor, ignoring Alys, who stepped forwards, as if she would protect her mother.

"You can," Alinor said. She did not move from Rob's supporting arm and James had to speak before the three of them.

"I wanted to say that I am very sorry," he said quietly. "I have been a fool, I have been played for a fool and now I am shown as a fool in front of you, the one woman in the world whose opinion I care for. I hoped that she would help you, I gave her money to help you, I only went along with all of this—the shipping of the antiques, their sale at my house—to help you. I wanted to make your life better, I wanted you to be able to afford medicines. I wanted you to live in a better house, a healthier situation, I wanted you to have a garden again . . ." He trailed off. "I thought I was helping you, through her. And then . . . like a fool . . . I was compromised . . ."

"It doesn't matter," Alinor spoke with genuine indifference to his shame. "All that matters to me is that my son is alive and has come back to us."

"I'm glad for that," Sir James said with a swift glance at Rob. "But Alinor . . ."

Rob tightened his grip on his mother's arm. "I don't think you should speak, sir," he said quietly. "I don't think you should speak to my mother."

"I wanted to make . . ." He was lost for words. "I wanted to make reparation."

"I want nothing from you," Alinor said firmly. "We never did."

Sir James bowed his head as a man who accepts a life sentence and stepped back in silence. Livia, at the side of the warehouse beside her looming wrapped antiquities, regarded them all with tepid interest, as if they were a theater performance that might start at any moment. The only person she did not watch was Felipe; as if she were confident that he would say no more.

"Right," said the magistrate. "Gentlemen, if you're ready, let's get started."

They drew closer to circle the desk, the gentry putting themselves forward as always, as the most important people in any room. Lady Eliot was beside Sir George with Sir James on his right. Livia came forward to stand beside her new husband, her hand tucked confidently into his sleeve, her other hand holding her posy of primroses to her face. Alys, Alinor, Rob, and Sarah faced them on the other side of the circle. Captain Shore stood a little behind Alys, Felipe beside him, immediately behind Sarah. The minister from the church, silently wishing he was elsewhere, stood beside the magistrate and Johnnie at the desk.

"This is a preliminary inquiry by me, justice of the peace of this parish of St. Olave's, into an allegation of bigamy against Nobildonna Livia Reekie or, in her married name, Lady Avery." He nudged Johnnie. "Write that down."

"Da Ricci," Livia remarked. "Or Peachey, as it is sometimes pronounced."

The magistrate nodded. "Now, evidence . . ."

Rob stepped a little forward and explained that he had come to Venice as a newly qualified doctor and been appointed to the elderly Signor Fiori and so met his beautiful wife, the Nobildonna. Livia, sniffing the primroses, apparently uninterested in the retelling of her story, released Sir James from her grasp, and strolled again to the back of the warehouse where the antiquities were crated up, as if the silent shrouded stones were of more interest to her than the two men who had married her, the three men who had loved her, and the silent Alys. Rob concluded his statement saying that since he was alive, Livia was his wife, and this marriage to Sir James was bigamous.

"Is this true?" the magistrate asked her. "Madam? Would you reply to this charge?" He looked up from overseeing Johnnie's notes and saw that Livia had strolled away. He repeated more irritably: "Madam! We are waiting for you! These are most serious charges."

Confidently, she turned and walked towards the desk, her heels tapping on the floor as they had tapped down the church aisle just two hours before, her dark blue gown brushing the dusty floor. She smiled at the magistrate, conscious of her own beauty.

"It's mostly true," she said judiciously. She turned to Rob. "One thing I should say, and you should know. I did not denounce you, my dear. That was Felipe. I loved you then, as a wife can love a husband who has brought her more happiness than she ever knew. I would never have hurt you or betrayed you. I would have died first."

She bent her head to the posy of primroses as if to see if Felipe would argue, and when he remained silent she looked up, like a beautiful actress timing her lines. She smiled tenderly at Rob as if they were alone together in the room. "All our sorrows came from Felipe," she said softly. "He ruined our lives. He controlled me completely for years, he trapped me into working for him when I was married to the Conte—yes—he ruined my happiness there too. I was bound to him by a hundred secrets, and I should have known he would never let me go. When you found out about his business, he wanted to be rid of you. It was not I." Meltingly she looked at him. "Never would it have been me. You know that I loved you. I would never, never have denounced you. But when he arrested you, I did see my chance to escape him. I did leave Venice, I did run away. I was afraid . . ." She lowered her voice. "You know how much I was afraid of him. This was a man who murdered my first husband and had my second imprisoned! I was terrified of him, and I was all alone without protection. Of course I ran away."

"Murdered your first husband!" the magistrate exclaimed, looking from her serene face to Felipe.

Livia did not trouble herself to answer, she turned to Alys. "And of course I came to you. You know how unhappy I was when I first came here," she said softly. "You know how deep was my grief at the loss of Roberto, your brother. You know how much I loved him. You will remember me crying in the night, crying till our pillow was wet with my tears. You know how you comforted me."

Alys's face was flinty. "Aye," was all she said.

"You know how you comforted me," Livia repeated. "You held me, you dried my tears, you took me in your arms."

Alys nodded, still saying nothing.

"No one will ever know how good you were to me," Livia said. "That tenderness will always be just between us, our secret."

Alys's mouth was shut in a hard line.

"And now I am pledged in all honor to Sir James and married to him." Livia turned back to Rob. "My dear, I thought you were dead. Felipe assured me you were dead and there was no possibility of my ever seeing you again. Of course I told your family that you were drowned! I could not have borne to tell them that you were arrested and executed for the murder of my husband! I would never have shamed your name like that. I was trying to make a new life, and to love those that you loved. I was comforting them and supporting them." She glanced back at Alys. "My dearest Alys will witness for me that I have been a good daughter to this house and a most loving sister to her. No one has ever loved you more—have they, my dear?"

Alys said nothing.

"But this was not a valid marriage," the minister interrupted quietly. "Whatever your reasons for leaving Venice, you cannot be married to Sir James as you have a previous husband still alive. Since you have a living husband, the service of marriage which I have just undertaken was invalid and will be annulled."

"Annulled?" Sir James inquired.

"As if it never happened," the minister confirmed.

Livia made a little gesture with her hand, as if she were waving away something unimportant, as if she alone had the power to decide. She looked around the circle of rapt faces and saw no one who could oppose her.

"No," she said simply. "It is not going to be annulled."

Johnnie's pen paused and he looked up to watch her. She exchanged one long pointed glance with him as if to remind him that he too was indebted to her, that he too had secrets with her. She held the attention of the room, as she ignored the minister and spoke directly to the magistrate. "Not so."

She stepped a little closer to the desk so that she was standing halfway between the two parties, center stage, the complete focus of their attention. Johnnie could smell her perfume of roses. She gave him a warm confiding smile.

"It was my marriage in Venice that was not valid," she explained slowly to the magistrate, speaking in her clear low voice. "I understood this, when this good man Mr. Rogers"—she gestured to the minister, who blinked and swallowed convulsively—"undertook my spiritual instruction, and admitted me into the Protestant Church. Then, only then, did I realize all that had to be done to make a valid marriage.

"My marriage in Venice to Rob was recited in English, which I did not then understand, a language that was foreign to me. So it was not valid on those grounds alone. It was in the Protestant Church in Venice where I was not a communicant. I had never been there before. I had no pew, I had no fellow parishioners. I was then a Roman Catholic, a communicant and confirmed member of the Roman Catholic Church. So it was not valid for that reason too.

"Of course, my church does not recognize your services, it does not recognize your ministers. In the eyes of my church it was never a marriage. And since I did not speak the language, and was not a communicant, it was not a valid marriage service in your church either. My marriage to Roberto Reekie"—she paused to smile tenderly at him—"my beloved Roberto—was invalid from start to finish."

Johnnie had ceased to write anything, his pen suspended over the page, a blot of ink forming slowly on the nib. The minister looked blank, the magistrate was silent.

Livia turned to Rob. "I am so sorry, Roberto. But we did not know. We were young and so much in love! How should we know? The minister of your church should have told us, and baptized me, so that we might truly marry. He should have prepared me and confirmed me into his congregation in your church, as this good man has so carefully done. I would have done that for you! You know that I would have done anything for you. But he failed us, and since I was not a member of your church, since I did not understand my vows, the service was invalid. We were never married."

The magistrate turned to Rob. "Is this true, Dr. Reekie?"

"Yes," Rob replied hesitantly. "It's true that we married in my church . . . I didn't know . . ."

"If the couple are of different faiths the marriage is invalid," the minister confirmed. "If she was not prepared for communion in our church and did not understand the vows then it is true: you were not married. All this time you were living in sin, God forgive you both. And the child . . ."

"Good Lord," Lady Eliot said, truly shocked. "What has she said? Will she make her own child a bastard?"

Everyone turned to look at Matteo, who had woken and was struggling to get down from Carlotta's arms to crawl on the floor.

"Oh, the child is mine," Felipe spoke up.

Rob turned on him.

Sarah watched him give a little shrug as if he did not care what the admission might cost him. "The boy is mine."

"Heavens save us!" Lady Eliot said, and gave a little stagger.

Livia shot one fierce glance at Felipe. "The child has been baptized and is the son and heir of Sir James Avery," she stated. "Nobody else can claim him." She stepped towards James and slid her hand into his arm. "He is our son," she said. "Matthew Avery."

"I doubt that Sir James wants him now," Felipe remarked. "An Italian bastard as the heir of an English lord?"

Sir James made no answer and did not respond at all to Livia's clutch on his arm, neither taking her hand nor shaking her off. He stood, completely still as if frozen, his eyes on the magistrate like a man awaiting sentence.

"Who witnessed your Venice wedding to Dr. Reekie, madam?" the magistrate asked her.

"I did," Felipe volunteered conversationally. "I and a colleague of mine, a member of the stone mason's guild."

"Although the woman was your mistress?"

Lady Eliot closed her eyes as if she were about to faint, and then opened them again to see Felipe's face as he answered.

"Yes," Felipe agreed. "Would that make it invalid in your church?"

"It makes it scandalous," the magistrate told him with distaste. "It makes it a disgrace. But not invalid. It was invalid because she was not of our religion, and she now declares that she did not understand her vows. So she was never married to Dr. Reekie, whatever you witnessed, it was not the sacrament of marriage in the Church of England. She was indeed a widow when she came to London, as she declared herself, but she was the widow of her first husband: the Signor Fiori."

"Wearing the mourning clothes she bought for his funeral," Felipe confirmed cheerfully. "That was a valid marriage. I witnessed that too."

"So she was, in fact, able to marry me?" Sir James asked coldly. "Our marriage is valid in law and in the eyes of the church?"

"She was able," the magistrate ruled, and the minister nodded.

"And she did marry me?" Sir James confirmed, his eyes like ice.

"She did," the magistrate agreed.

"So the case of bigamy is dismissed?"

"No case to answer," the magistrate declared.

Sir George let out a quiet oath, and Lady Eliot exhaled a trembling sigh, but no one else responded at all. Mr. Lucas tapped Johnnie's arm to remind him to record the judgment. "This lady's second marriage in Venice to Dr. Robert Reekie was invalid, her marriage here was properly undertaken." He glanced down at Johnnie's notes. "You're a married man, Sir James, like it or not."

White-faced, his arm gripped possessively by Livia, James Avery bowed slightly. "Thank you," he said without any hint of gratitude.

"This is an outrage!" Lady Eliot stepped towards the desk, bristling with fury. "After what has been said about her? She is little more than a Venice whore! A criminal. A counterfeiter and fraudster! She cannot be married into the Avery family!"

The magistrate was gathering up Johnnie's notes.

"Better say nothing more," he advised her quietly. "Since she is married into the Avery family. She is Lady Avery."

"But the alleged crimes?" Sir George asked. "The . . . er . . . fraud? The false denunciation? The stolen and forged antiquities? This whole caper?"

The magistrate shook his head. "Out of my jurisdiction." His dry tone indicated that he did not regret it. "You'd have to take it up with the Venetian authorities, if you want to do that." He turned to Alinor and Alys, who stood, very still and quiet, with Sarah and Rob on either side of them as a family might watch a tide rise to their doorstep and lap at their livelihood.

"Good day," he said. "I shall send this in as my report. If there is any duty unpaid on the lady's cargo, you should pay it at once. Any false reporting of the goods will be noticed." He turned to James. "Any claim against her for goods that are forged or fraudulent will fall on you as her husband. You might wish to speak to her customers. You might wish to compensate them, to protect her name, which is now yours."

Lady Eliot visibly shuddered.

Captain Shore glanced at Alys. "The tax will be paid tomorrow before the noon gun." He turned to the magistrate. "I'm obliged to you, sir. I'm just remarking that the good name of the warehouse is unchanged. This was none of their doing. They had a good business before this . . . fell on them. They'll have a good business after. There will be no gossip about the Reekie warehouse. They are innocent of any misdoing."

"I'm aware of it," the magistrate said, glancing towards Livia, who stood, slightly smiling, her arm entwined with James. "You would almost call it an act of God."

"Not God!" the minister exclaimed indignantly.

"Nothing godly about the widow," Captain Shore agreed. "But she is no fault of the warehouse."

"I'll bid you good day," the magistrate said shortly, glancing around the silent storeroom. Johnnie led the way and showed him and the minister out of the front door and came back to the warehouse, leaving the door to the quay open, as if to hint that the others might leave also.

"We'd better go," Lady Eliot said to Sir James, her frozen lips barely moving. "I hardly know where we should go. I suppose she will have to come too? Perhaps she will accept an allowance, and a house somewhere in the country? Unless we can send her back to wherever she came from?"

Livia laughed shortly; but James seemed deaf. He stood unmoving, looking across the room at Alinor, with Livia's hand still tucked firmly in his arm as if she would nail them together.

"James!" Lady Eliot prompted him.

Finally he turned to her. "I have ruined myself," he said quietly. "I have shamed my good name and ruined myself." Gently he detached himself from Livia, unfastening her hand and pushing her gently away from him. He crossed the room to Alinor, who still stood, pale and unmoving, her family around her. He stood before her as if she had far more authority than any magistrate, as if she were judge and jury to him.

"When I was a young man, a foolish young man, I broke my word to you," he confessed, his voice very low. "I did not speak up for you. I loved you and I let them half drown you though I knew you were carrying my child. All I thought of then was my good name and that I could not bear to be shamed. So all the shame fell on you."

Her dark gray eyes were steady on his pale face; but she did not speak and he went on: "And now—in a sort of justice—my word is given, when it should not have been given, and this woman will hold me to it. I have ruined myself to a far worse degree than I risked with you. I did not claim you, and marry you when I should have done, so that I might claim and keep my position in the world; and now I have pushed myself into the gutter and my name is as mud."

She was silent for so long that he thought she would refuse to speak to him; but then she took a breath: "I am sorry for you." Her voice was filled with pity. "I wish you nothing but well, James."

"May I . . . ?"

Livia came up to him and slid her hand in his arm. "No," she said simply, speaking without doubt that she would be obeyed. "You will not visit here, nor write. She has told you more than once, and she is a better judge than you will ever be. And I am your wife, and I forbid it. We will go now to Avery House." She managed a laugh, a pretty light laugh. "I doubt the dinner will be edible, but your aunt ordered it to be ready for our return. It is I who will have to speak to the cook!" She turned to the hall and gestured with the posy of primroses that Carlotta should follow them.

"So you're going through with your marriage to this man?" Felipe asked her, casually, as if he were only slightly interested. "And you intend to take Matteo—my son?"

"He is my son," she said. "Perhaps Rob fathered him, or perhaps it was you, but I have decided that he shall be Matthew Avery, and that is final. In time he will be Sir Matthew Avery of Northside Manor, which is more than you or Rob could do for him."

"Never," Sir James said quietly without heat.

Livia glanced up at him. "I don't think you can refuse me."

"He can stay here," Alys spoke for the first time. "He can stay here, with us."

Livia checked. "Why would you want him?" she asked coldly, as if it was another ruse to overcome; and then she suddenly realized that Alys was speaking from love. "You want him?" she asked in a quite different tone. "You want to raise my son? You want to care for him?"

"Not because he's yours," Alys told her. "But he's happy here. He doesn't know that we're lowly and poor. He doesn't despise us. He likes it here, and he's settled with us. I love him for himself, whoever his father is; and so does Ma. You've got no time for him, you never have any time for him, and Sir James once again loses a child through his own pride." Her eyes flicked over him with contempt. "You neither of you know how to love him, nor how to love anyone. Give him a chance and leave him in our keeping."

Livia did not even glance at James to know his opinion. "You will love him for me," she whispered to Alys.

"I love him for himself," she replied steadily. "And this is the only place where he will be loved."

"Leave him here," Rob advised her.

"I agree," Felipe said.

"Very well," Livia decided, her voice carefree. "What a good idea! He shall stay here for now. I shall send for him when I want him, and he will go to school where I decide. But he shall stay here for now."

Sir James and Alinor exchanged one long look. "Another son and I don't see him?" he asked bitterly.

"He's best left here," she told him. "Neither of you will be loving parents in that great house. You're not going to be happy."

He bowed his head, as if under a penance. "I know it."

"And I?" Felipe asked Livia. "Your fiancé? And the father of the child?"

For a moment she hesitated, quickly thinking what she might pull from this disaster of her business. "Of course, you are still my business partner . . ." she began. "Nobody here is going to speak of this outside these walls. If you are prepared to overlook all that has been, we still have a fortune stored in your warehouse, and since you are here, and you have brought the antiquities, you can sell them and we can share the profit . . ."

"Good God! No!" Sir James started, but it was Sarah who stepped between Felipe and challenged her aunt.

"No, Livia. He's not in business with you anymore. And this load is in our storehouse, shipped by us, owed to us."

"He is not?" Livia asked, smiling at her niece. "He is no longer my partner, when we have been hand in glove for years? You know this? When we have committed every sin we chose and every crime that made a profit? For years? And you have had two weeks in Venice and you are now an authority?"

"Yes, I am," Sarah said, ignoring the sarcasm. "I'm going to sell the antiquities. Not him, and not you. He is not your partner, he was not your fiancé; he never was."

For the first time, Livia lost her smiling calm. Shocked, she looked from Felipe to Sarah. "What is this folly? Does the child have a fever that she thinks she can speak to me like this? Does she think she can claim my antiquities? Does she think she can claim you?"

Felipe did not even hear Livia's outrage. The handsome Italian turned to the English girl. "I am not her fiancé? You have decided this, Miss Jolie? On your own account?"

"Yes," she said bluntly to him. "She's married another man, she's given up her child. She runs everything as if she is a woman of the world and knows how it turns; but in truth she knows nothing. She knows about money but not about value. She knows everything about profit and nothing about love. I saved Rob from her. My ma has saved Matteo from her. And now I'm saving you."

Felipe laughed out loud and caught both her hands. "Ah! Bathsheba!" he exclaimed. "Jolie! I knew you would not fail me! You have decided? You have finally decided in my favor though I am so very, very unsuitable and neither the uncle nor the grandmother will ever approve of me? And the mother will know I am not good enough for you—and she is right?"

"Yes," she said. "I'm saving you."

FEBRUARY 1671, HADLEY, NEW ENGLAND

Ned was preparing his toboggan for travel, tying new buckskin leads to the wickerwork frame, fitting the harness over his oilskin winter cape, his essential foods packed at the back of the sledge, his warm clothes in the middle where the waxed leather cloth would keep them dry, and his tools and gun at the front where he could easily reach them. His cow and sheep he had pushed and driven and urged to his nearest neighbor, breaking them a path through the snow, telling the neighbors that the roof of his stable had collapsed under the weight of snow and asking them to house the animals. He had produced hens from under his arms and asked them to keep them warm. He could not bring himself to tell them the truth, he was not even sure of the truth himself.

He wanted to leave before the thaw, before the white world turned dirty brown, before the muster, so that his name was never called and there was no answer. He felt dishonored—an old comrade who was no longer guarding the north gate. He felt faithless—a traitor to his people; he felt loveless—a man who could not court a woman and take her where she wanted to be. But he knew he could not bring himself to serve in another army, especially one that would march with guns against people with bows and arrows.

He wanted to leave without saying good-bye to his friends, the men he had hidden and guarded and served for so long. He wanted to leave before the Council summoned the Indian king to stand before them at Plymouth and the Indians all around the Dawnland rose up in their righteous anger and their pride to defend him. He wanted to leave without saying good-bye to the men he had guarded for years. He could not bear to face them and tell them that, though he would have laid down his life to protect them when they were persecuted by a tyrant, he could not support them when they turned tyrant themselves.

He wanted to leave before the thaw so he could go by sledge on snow and across lakes, and on frozen ground. He was going north, away from the settlers into the forest, which had always frightened him, hoping to find empty lands, unclaimed unused lands, where he could live without choosing sides, where he could be himself: neither master nor man. Ned thought that it was as painful to leave the little village where he had made a home and the men he had promised to guard, as it had been to leave England. But in some ways, it was the same questions—the unanswered questions that had haunted him, for all of his life: what side was he on, what man must he obey, what did he want to protect?

The sledge was ready, he shut the door of his house with pointless care, he whistled to Red, who came to his side at once, bounding through the deep snow. Ned leaned forward, took the weight of the toboggan and stepped forward on his snowshoes, finding the sledge slid easily behind him, and Quiet Squirrel's snowshoes made shallow tracks. He turned east, going alongside the river past the gate at the end of the common lane of Hadley, unrecognizable in drifted snow, and then into the trees of the pine plain of Hadley forest, and then beyond the settlers' stone marker post, bearing the initials of the friend he would never see again, into the forest of the new lands.

He walked for an hour, following the river as it curved to the north, his eyes dazzled by the sunshine on the snow. There was a frozen lake to his right and Ned, glancing up from the way before him, checked as he saw a figure through the haze of snow which was making the whole world into a blinding mist.

It was the silhouette of a man, crouched on the ice, a cape thrown up over his head so that he could look down into the icy water below. His left arm moved slightly, as he jiggled the little decoy fish, dancing it in the water so that the big fish that dozed on the bottom of the icy water would come up, the other hand holding the spear, ready to stab the hidden fish in the dark waters below. The figure was so clear that Ned bit back a shout of greeting, and started to undo the harness to the toboggan so that he could approach Wussausmon quietly. As his cold fingers fumbled with the bindings he knew that he was deeply glad to say good-bye, glad that they would have one moment together before their ways went forever apart. He loosed himself from his burden and stepped towards the lake, as he thought that only to Wussausmon could he explain why he was going. The only man in this new world who would understand the division of loyalty that was pulling him north, into unknown country, and away from both his own people, and the strange people that he had come to love.

He got himself free of the harness and stepped onto the frozen lake and then hesitated. Now he looked again, there was no one there. There was nothing in the blank whiteness, no figure bulky in furs bending over the hole, no fishing bag laid on the ice, no spear, no freshly dug ice hole filling with black water—nothing, there was no one there but the unbroken ice of the lake and the whirling drifting whiteness of the snow.

"Wussausmon?" Ned whispered. "John?"

There was no answer. There was no figure bending over a hole in the ice. The long level whiteness of the pond stretched forever, there was no one there. There had never been anyone there.

A cold wind, whispering up the river valley, reminded Ned that he had to make ground away from Hadley before he set a camp for the night, and that there was no time to linger here, looking for ghosts. He thought that his mother and his sister would tell him that this was the sight, and that he had said good-bye to Wussausmon for the last time, as the man waited for his fish, poised with his spear in his hand, most truly himself in his furs, on the ice, hunting as his people had done for hundreds of years, listening as he always did for the sounds beneath the wind, watching as he always did for the movement in the dark water below him.

Ned retied his harness, looking down at his dog. "You didn't see him, did you, Red?" he confirmed. The dog wagged his tail, stood to leave.

"Good-bye then," Ned said uncertainly into the wind, and took the weight of the toboggan for the first pull, as it shifted from the snow and then glided behind him. He walked slowly and steadily, turning north, tracing the course of the frozen river, the setting sun coldly bright on his left cheek, following a native path that was somewhere under the snow, the story holes hidden but still there, leading him one step before another, with a bleak determination, as if the only way to be a free man is to walk, one step before another without stealing, without lying, without leaving anything more than footprints which were quickly blown away in the snow.

AUTHOR'S NOTE

John Sassamon/Wussausmon's frozen body was found in Assawomp-set Pond beside an ice-fishing hole, the day after warning the Plymouth authorities that his leader, Massasoit Po Metacom, was preparing to make war against the settlers. Without any conclusive evidence of murder, the Plymouth Council tried, found guilty, and executed three Pokanoket men for his murder. It was claimed that they were assassins: punishing Wussausmon for treachery—though this would not have been Pokanoket law or tradition. In response to the execution of his men without his consent, and enacting his earlier war plan, Massasoit Po Metacom launched a defense of his lands that would cost the lives of thousands of settlers and American Indians, and take the New England colonies to the brink of destruction. His defeat and death were part of a campaign to eliminate his nation forever, even banning the Pokanoket name. The persecution of all American Indian people, the obliteration of their history and culture, and the theft of their goods and lands continue to this day.

The sections of the novel set in New England are based on historical research, and while Ned is a fictional character, as is Mrs. Rose, the other people in the tragic story of one race colliding with another were real. The regicides, Edward Whalley and William Goffe, escaped the revenge of the restored King Charles II to hide out in New England until their deaths. Most of the time they were at Hadley, at the home of the minister John Russell. There is a traditional story that William Goffe appeared when the town was attacked by American Indians and mustered the troops for defense: the so-called Angel of Hadley.

I am deeply grateful to the historians at Historic Deerfield, who were so generous with their time: Anne Lanning, Barbara Mathews,

Claire Carlson, Phil Zea, James Golden, and Ned Lazaro. Their conversation and their notes have been invaluable. I owe Professor Peter Thomas particular gratitude for his interest and guidance and the privilege of a long correspondence about the detail of early life in Hadley.

During my time in New England, I also had the pleasure of visiting the wonderful Mashantucket Pequot Museum and was very grateful to Joe Baker for his welcome, and Kimberly Hatcher-White, Nakai Northup, and Matt Pina for their time and expertise at the best American Indian museum I have ever visited.

I was honored with an invitation to Montaup (Mount Hope) to meet the current Sagamore of the Pokanoket Nation: Po Wauipi Neimpaug, William Winds of Thunder Guy; the Sachem of the Tribe: Po Pummukaonk Anogqs Tracey Dancing Star Brown; First Council Person: Quogqueii Qunnegk Deborah Running Deer Afdasta; and two of the Tribe's Pinese: Po Kehteihtukqut Woweaushin William Winding River Brown and Po Popon Quanunon Ryan Winter Hawk Brown. I was deeply moved by their knowledge of and passion for their history and their willingness to share it with me.

I am very thankful for the help given to me during research for the Venice sections of the novel by Roberta Curiel and Sara Cossiga, who patiently took me all around a flooded Venice, and even to the extraordinary Lazzaretto Nuovo, where the curator was kind enough to admit me. I am also very grateful to Silvia Cardini for her knowledge of and enthusiasm for Florence, and especially to Clara Marinelli, for welcoming me into her family's foundry and marble workshops. To see marble carved in the old way and in the new was an unforgettable experience. Franco Pagliaga was kind enough to meet me and talk about his work on forged paintings.

My friends and fellow historians Malcolm Gaskill and Stella Tillyard were kind enough to read the manuscript and advise. I owe a debt of gratitude to them and to Zahra Glibbery and Victoria Atkins for their support through research, travel, writing, and the pursuit of accuracy.

Writing this book has been a moving experience at a time when our modern life has sometimes seemed as anxious and uncertain as the lives I am describing. The present seems to echo the past to tell us that we will only survive if we live tolerantly and generously with one another, treating nature with respect and welcoming strangers as did the Pokanoket, imagining a better world like Ned and the *Mayflower* generation.

Philippa Gregory,
2020

BIBLIOGRAPHY

NEW ENGLAND

Brooks, Lisa. *Our Beloved Kin: A New History of King Philip's War.* New Haven, CT: Yale University Press, 2019.

Captivating History. *American Indian Wars: A Captivating Guide to a Series of Conflicts That Occurred in North America and How They Impacted Native American Tribes, Including Events Such as the Sand Creek Massacre.* Sundsvall, Sweden: Moliva AB, 2019.

DeLucia, Christine M. *Memory Lands: King Philip's War and the Place of Violence in the Northeast.* New Haven, CT: Yale University Press, 2018.

Dunbar-Ortiz, Roxanne, and Dina Gilio-Whitaker. *"All the Real Indians Died Off" and 20 Other Myths about Native Americans.* Boston: Beacon Press, 2016.

Ellsworth, Patricia Laurice. *Hadley West Street Common and Great Meadows: A Cultural Landscape Study.* 2007. Landscape Architecture & Regional Planning Masters Projects. 44. Accessed January 21, 2020. https://scholarworks.umass.edu/larp_ms_projects/44.

Fraser, Rebecca. *The Mayflower Generation: The Winslow Family and the Fight for the New World.* New York: Vintage, 2018.

Gaskill, Malcolm. *Between Two Worlds: How the English Became Americans.* Oxford: Oxford University Press, 2014.

447

Gookin, Daniel. *History of the Christian Indians: A True and Impartial Narrative of the Doings and Sufferings of the Christian or Praying Indians, in New England, in the Time of the War Between the English and Barbarous Heathen, Which Began the 20th of June, 1675.* Worcester, MA: Transactions and Collections of the American Antiquarian Society, first published 1836.

Hämäläinen, Pekka. *The Comanche Empire.* New Haven, CT: Yale University Press, 2008.

Jenkinson, Matthew. *Charles I's Killers in America: The Lives and Afterlives of Edward Whalley and William Goffe.* Oxford: Oxford University Press, 2019.

Judd, Sylvester, and Lucius Manlius Boltwood. *History of Hadley, Including the Early History of Hatfield, South Hadley, Amherst and Granby, Massachusetts.* Springfield, MA: H. R. Huntting & Company, 1905.

Kupperman, Karen Ordahl. *Indians and English: Facing Off in Early America.* Ithaca, NY: Cornell University Press, 2000.

Leach, Douglas Edward. *Flintlock & Tomahawk: New England in King Philip's War.* Woodstock, VT: The Countryman Press, 1958.

Lepore, Jill. *The Name of War: King Philip's War and the Origins of American Identity.* New York: Vintage, 1999.

McGaa, Ed. *Mother Earth Spirituality: Native American Paths to Healing Ourselves and Our World.* London: HarperCollins Publishers Ltd., 1990.

Miller, Marla R., ed. *Cultivating a Past: Essays on the History of Hadley, Massachusetts.* Amherst, MA: University of Massachusetts Press, 2009.

Moore, Jay, and Charles Rivers Editors. *King Philip's War: The History and Legacy of the 17th Century Conflict Between Puritan New England and the Native Americans.* Ann Arbor, MI: Charles Rivers Editors, 2016.

Oberg, Michael Leroy. *Uncas: First of the Mohegans.* Ithaca, NY: Cornell University Press, 2003.

Orr, Charles. *History of the Pequot War: The Accounts of Mason, Underhill, Vincent and Gardener on the Colonist Wars with Native American Tribes in the 1600s.* Pantianos Classics, first published 1897.

Pagliuco, Christopher. *The Great Escape of Edward Whalley and William Goffe: Smuggled Through Connecticut.* Charleston, SC: The History Press, 2012.

Parker, Bernard. *Indian Wars in Colonial America 1637–1763: The Parker Family in the Connecticut Militia.* Self-published, 2018.

Philbrick, Nathaniel. *Mayflower: A Voyage to War.* London: HarperCollins Publishers Ltd., 2011.

Savinelli, Alfred. *Plants of Power: Native American Ceremony and the Use of Sacred Plants.* Summertown, TN: Book Publishing Company, 2002.

Schultz, Eric B., and Michael J. Tougias. *King Philip's War: The History and Legacy of America's Forgotten Conflict.* Woodstock, VT: The Countryman Press, 2017.

Silverman, David J. *Red Brethren: The Brothertown and Stockbridge Indians and the Problem of Race in Early America.* Ithaca, NY: Cornell University Press, 2010.

Silverman, David J. *This Land Is Their Land: The Wampanoag Indians, Plymouth Colony, and the Troubled History of Thanksgiving.* London: Bloomsbury Publishing, 2020.

Utley, Robert M. *Indian, Soldier, and Settler: Experiences in the Struggle for the American West.* St. Louis: Jefferson National Expansion Historical Association, Inc., 1979.

Wackerbarth, Doris H. *The Guardians of the New World: Pioneering in the Connecticut Valley.* Winchester, CT: The Country Squire, 1980.

Weatherford, Jack. *Indian Givers: How the Indians of the Americas Transformed the World.* New York: Random House, 1988.

Weatherford, Jack. *Native Roots: How the Indians Enriched America.* New York: Fawcett Books, 1992.

Wilbur, C. Keith. *The New England Indians: An Illustrated Sourcebook of Authentic Details of Everyday Indian Life.* Guildford, CT: The Globe Pequot Press, 1978.

Zelner, Kyle F. *A Rabble in Arms: Massachusetts Towns and Militiamen during King Philip's War.* New York: New York University, 2009.

LONDON

Brotton, Jerry. *The Sale of the Late King's Goods: Charles I and His Art Collection.* London: Pan, 2017.

Engels, Friedrich. *The Condition of the Working Class in England.* Oxford: Oxford University Press, first published 1845.

Jordan, Don. *The King's City: London under Charles II: A City That Transformed a Nation—and Created Modern Britain.* London: Little, Brown Book Group, 2017.

Keay, John. *The Honourable Company*. London: HarperCollins Publishers Ltd., 1991.

Mortimer, Ian. *The Time Traveller's Guide to Restoration Britain: Life in the Age of Samuel Pepys, Isaac Newton and The Great Fire of London.* London: The Bodley Head, 2017.

Pepys, Samuel. *Diary of Samuel Pepys—Complete*. Scotts Valley, CA: CreateSpace Independent Publishing Platform, first published 1669.

Picard, Liza. *Restoration London: Everyday Life in the 1660s.* London: W&N, 2004.

Porter, Linda. *Mistresses: Sex and Scandal at the Court of Charles II.* London: Picador, 2020.

Prior, Mary, ed. *Women in English Society, 1500–1800.* Oxford, UK: Routledge, 1985.

Searle, Mark, and Kenneth W. Stevenson. *Documents of the Marriage Liturgy.* Collegeville, MN: Liturgical Press, 1992.

Stone, Peter. *The History of the Port of London: A Vast Emporium of All Nations.* London: Pen & Sword History, 2017.

Trevor-Roper, Hugh. *The Crisis of the Seventeenth Century: Religion, the Reformation, and Social Change.* Indianapolis: Liberty Fund, Inc., 1967.

Uglow, Jenny. *A Gambling Man: Charles II and the Restoration.* London: Faber and Faber, 2009.

VENICE AND ART THEFTS AND FORGERIES

Amore, Anthony M. *The Art of the Con: The Most Notorious Fakes, Frauds, and Forgeries in the Art World.* New York: St. Martin's Press, 2015.

Brown, Patricia Fortini. *Private Lives in Renaissance Venice*. New Haven, CT: Yale University Press, 2004.

Davis, John. *Venice: A History*. New Word City, Inc., 2017.

Greenhalgh, Shaun. *A Forger's Tale: Confessions of the Bolton Forger*. Sydney: Allen & Unwin, 2018.

Sicca, Cinzia, and Alison Yarrington. *The Lustrous Trade: Material Culture and the History of Sculpture in England and Italy c. 1700– c. 1860*. London: Leicester University Press, 2000.

Stevens Crawshaw, Jane L. *Plague Hospitals: Public Health for the City in Early Modern Venice*. Oxford: Taylor & Francis Ltd., 2012.

Watson, Peter, and Cecilia Todeschini. *The Medici Conspiracy: The Illicit Journey of Looted Antiquities—From Italy's Tomb Raiders to the World's Greatest Museums*. New York: PublicAffairs, 2007.

ABOUT THE AUTHOR

PHILIPPA GREGORY is the author of many *New York Times* best-selling novels and is a recognized authority on women's history. Many of her works have been adapted for the screen, including *The Other Boleyn Girl*. She graduated from the University of Sussex and received a Ph.D. from the University of Edinburgh, where she is a Regent. She holds honorary degrees from Teesside University and the University of Sussex, is a fellow of the Universities of Sussex and Cardiff, and was awarded the 2016 Harrogate Festival Award for Contribution to Historical Fiction. She is an honorary research fellow at Birkbeck, University of London. She welcomes visitors to her website, PhilippaGregory.com.

DARK TIDES

PHILIPPA GREGORY

This reader's guide for Dark Tides *includes an introduction, discussion questions, ideas for enhancing your book club, and a Q&A with author Philippa Gregory. The suggested questions are intended to help your reading group find new and interesting angles and topics for your discussion. We hope that these ideas will enrich your conversation and increase your enjoyment of the book.*

INTRODUCTION

In *Dark Tides*, two unexpected visitors arrive at a shabby warehouse on the south side of the River Thames on Midsummer Eve, 1670. The first is a wealthy nobleman seeking the lover he deserted twenty-one years earlier. Now James Avery has everything to offer: a fortune, a title, and the favor of the newly restored King Charles II. He believes that the warehouse's poor owner, Alinor, has the one thing he cannot buy—his son and heir.

The second visitor is a beautiful young widow from Venice in deepest mourning. She claims Alinor as her mother-in-law and has come to tell Alinor that her son, Rob, has drowned in the dark tides of the Venice lagoon.

Alinor's brother, Ned, in faraway New England is making a life for himself in the narrowing space between the worlds of the English newcomers and the American Indians as they move towards inevitable war. Alinor writes that she knows—without doubt—that her son is alive and the widow is an imposter. But how can she prove it?

TOPICS & QUESTIONS FOR DISCUSSION

1. The novel begins with a letter from Alinor, the protagonist of *Tidelands*, to her brother, Ned, bringing news that her son, Rob, has reportedly drowned in Venice. She does not believe this can be true. How does this letter set up what is to come? What role do letters and communications play throughout the novel?

2. Ned tells a selectman that he didn't come to the New World " 'to be a king looking down on subjects, forcing my ways on them in blood. I came here to live at peace, with my neighbors. All my neighbors: English and Indian.' " How does Ned abide by this intention, especially as tensions mount between the settlers and American Indians in New England? How does his previous support for Cromwell and the republicans affect his life during this period?

3. When Alinor is presented with Matteo as a replacement for Rob, she tells Livia, " 'I don't think that one child can take the place of another. Nor would I wish it.' " Consider this in terms of all the characters and children in the novel. Can any of these characters or children stand in for one another? How does this affect Matteo's fate at the end of the novel?

4. Alinor, Alys, and Livia form an unusual trio of women, all living without the protection of a man, all operating in a man's world. How does each woman respond to the challenges of the patriarchal society in which she lives?

5. Alys explains to Livia that the Reekie family was " 'always on the edge, between poverty and surviving, between friends and enemies, in the tidelands between water and fields. We were on

the edge of everything. At least here we are in a world with a firm footing. At least Uncle Ned is making a new life in a new land as he wants.'" How do the characters exist in the space between land and sea? By the end of the novel, how do you think the family's position has changed?

6. When James asks if Livia is willing to give up her ideals in order to get ahead, she replies, "'If it was exiled: let it return. If it burns down: rebuild it. If it was robbed: restore it. If it is free—let us take it.'" How does this reflect Livia's point of view? Has she lived by this edict?

7. Alinor believes that Sarah shares her gift of sight. She explains that "'for some people, this world is not quite . . . watertight. The other world comes in . . . sometimes we can reach out to it. It's like Foulmire—sometimes it's land and sometimes it's water. Sometimes I know this world, sometimes I glimpse the other. Don't you?'" How does Alinor's sight affect her perception of the world around her? Do you believe that Sarah has her gift?

8. Livia says to Alys, "'I am a beautiful liar, if you like. I am all twists and turns and misdirection. You cannot trust me. I recommend that you do not trust me. I am not actually evil; but I am not straightforward. I am not simple.'" Livia tells Alys exactly who she is. Why does Alys refuse to believe her? How do the other characters react to Livia's treatment of Alys?

9. Mrs. Rose feels trapped by her circumstances, having come to the New World for the "'same reason as everyone. . . . I came in the first place as I had hopes of a better life. God called me and my master ordered me. I didn't know it would be like this. I hoped for better, I still hope. And I don't have the money for my passage back home anyway.'" Do others in this novel feel hemmed in by their lack of opportunity as they search for better lives?

10. Alys rebukes her mother, stating, "'You were a fool once for love! Are you going to be a fool for spite?'" How do characters act as fools for love in this novel? Does anyone become a fool for spite?

11. When Sarah arrives in Venice, Signor Russo tells her that "'Everyone here is either a spy or a villain. Or both.'" Does Sarah find this to be true in Venice? Do you believe that Signor Russo is a villain? Do you believe that the Reekies are heroes, as Sarah later suggests? Or does the complexity of these characters exist outside of the concept of heroes and villains?

12. Wussausmon, Ned's friend and advisor to the Massasoit Po Metacom, says, "'I pass like a spirit from one world into another, I tell of what I have seen. But then I go back and speak of where I have been. . . . And every day I fear that I am not translating one to another; but just making the misunderstanding worse. I am trying to bring these two worlds together but all they do is grind against each other. They don't trust each other, nobody wants to hear what I say, and they both believe I am a liar and a spy.'" How do all of these characters live between worlds? Between the lives they have and the lives they aspire to? Between who they are and who they could be?

13. Signor Russo instructs Sarah that "'Every profit comes at someone's cost.'" What are the costs in this novel? Who do you think pays the greatest cost? Why?

14. The ending of *Dark Tides* mirrors that of *Tidelands*. Then, Alinor and Alys had been driven from their home and were setting out on a journey to a new life; now, Ned leaves his home in search of "unclaimed unused lands, where he could live without choosing sides, where he could be himself: neither master nor man." Why do you think the author chooses to end the story in this way?

ENHANCE YOUR BOOK CLUB

1. Get out a map and identify the places where this story takes place. Does anything strike you about the physical distance between these locations, especially given the time period during which the story takes place?

2. Visit a museum with Greek and Roman art galleries or the Metropolitan Museum of Art website at https://www.metmuseum.org /about-the-met/curatorial-departments/greek-and-roman-art to view the kinds of antiquities Livia and Felipe might have exported. Which are you most drawn to?

3. Has anyone in your book group read other novels by Philippa Gregory, either *Tidelands* or her previous books? How does this book compare?

4. Visit the author's website at PhilippaGregory.com to learn more about her work and the Fairmile series.

A CONVERSATION WITH
PHILIPPA GREGORY

Dark Tides is the second book in a planned series about the fictional Reekie family, spanning generations and continents. What drew you to writing an ambitious family saga at this point in your career?

It's been a long career and deeply enjoyable! And I have learned the confidence to embark on a long project like this, certain that there will be extraordinary, little-known stories that will turn up in research that I can incorporate into the story of the family's rise to prosperity and the greater story of the changes in England and in the world. I know a little of my family history, and many other individual and small histories, and I want to go from the personal to the global with an international long-term story. I've always disliked the snobbery of much of traditional historical fiction when it focuses on the well-known and grand people, so this is a challenge to that style. And in addition to all of that, I was rereading *The Forsyte Saga* and was inspired by the journey Soames—a wealthy Victorian Londoner—makes to what he regards are his roots: some muddy fields. Go back far enough, and all our families come from muddy fields; I wanted to celebrate that.

Although you're best known for your work in royal historical fiction, you've spoken about working on a history of what we consider "ordinary" women, who have been overlooked and invisible throughout much of history. How does this nonfiction work influence and inform your fiction and vice versa?

My interest has always been in women in history; it was the obscure women and not the famous men that have always interested me. So it was a logical development that I should want to write a history of women who rarely make any mark in the records. I have been working for some years now on a history of women of England and this is my major work, but it is inspiring and supporting my fictional writing. As always, what really happened is so much more dramatic, extreme, and unlikely than anything I would dare to invent.

The first book in this series, *Tidelands*, was set in the marshlands of Sussex, where you lived for a time. This novel takes place between London, Venice, and the land that became Connecticut. What drew you to these settings?

Pagham Harbour, the setting of *Tidelands*, was the destination of many childhood visits, and I lived beside it for five years, sharing a house with the warden and sometimes helping him with his conservation work, so it was a powerful place for me to invoke in my first novel of this series. London is the center of the development of global Western trade at this time, a natural destination for disgraced women who might hope to make a living obscured by the crowds, and a wonderful starting point for a story about a trading family. Venice was a famous trading city, especially in luxury goods and the objects that drove the Renaissance: classical artifacts. I've visited the city many times and I love the urban architecture and history, but for this novel I also went to the Isola del Lazzaretto Nuovo. I was honored to have a tour by the curator and was able to walk around the waterside path outside the boundary walls of the old quarantine castle. It was so striking to see the wildness of the Venice lagoon, the mud banks, the reed banks, and the bird life. At once I realized that Rob would see the similarity to his home, and would be as sure-footed here as on the Saxon shore. It was the landscape which inspired the escape, a part of the story I particularly like, as it came to me so vividly. I visited New England also, meeting historians and people of the Pokanoket and Pequot nations. Here too the landscape was hugely inspiring, and I could trace the settlement of Hadley on the bend in the river, and try to imagine the people who lived there for so many centuries before the coming of the settlers.

You write beautifully about the natural world. The space particularly between land and sea holds such significance for your

characters. How does your experience of nature and landscape influence your writing?

I think the truth is more that nature and landscape influence me very deeply as a person, and it comes out in everything I do. I even have very vivid and detailed dream landscapes! I have lived for most of my adult life in the country, and one of my greatest pleasures is being out in the countryside. I have a sense of peace and belonging in a rural landscape, and I feel at home in woods and fields in a way that I never do in towns. I like to be connected to the animal world—I care for two ancient ponies that were my children's ponies, and I have a dog and sometimes raise abandoned ducklings. I feed and house a rescued barn owl who flies freely out of my barn, and has lived as my neighbor (by his own free choice) for twelve years, bringing a female back every year and raising chicks. Earlier generations who lived off the land were far closer to the natural world than we are now, and I try to reflect this in my characters' love of their home landscape, and their knowledge about the natural world. I am in awe of the historic American Indians' integration with their world: they felt a kinship with the animal and natural world which was incorporated into every aspect of their lives.

A tremendous amount of research went into this novel—there's such authority and ease to your voice when explaining both the process of art forgery and the relationship between settlers and American Indian nations in the New World. How did you go about researching this novel? Did anything surprise you during the research process?

As always, my research was a great deal of reading and some visits. My biggest early surprise was the extent of art and historic artifacts forgery, even today. *The Lustrous Trade* and the other books about art forgery listed in the bibliography were real eye-openers! I had no idea of the extent of grave looting and forgery which continues even today. Other fascinating snippets were the early international trading companies of London—Johnnie did not long to be a member of the Company any more than I longed for him to join them! I learned about the value of herbs and semiprecious stones in *Restoration London*, and the use of sassafras. The strangest and most inspiring material was the research into

American Indians, where everything is different from English history—from religion to diet, women's rights to transport. Studying, visiting, and talking was like entering another world.

Were there any scenes—either due to their content or the research involved—that were particularly difficult to write? How did you work through them?

I was especially aware that in the American Indian history, I was writing about people who are not my ancestors, and whose descendants have already suffered from land and cultural theft. Indeed, they have suffered at the hands of people who *are* my ancestors. That gives me every reason to approach with sensitivity, caution, and awareness. That was one of the reasons that I made Ned a man between the worlds, so that he too was cautiously approaching a world he did not know. It also meant I was not attempting to tell the story of the American Indians directly—of course, they have their own storytellers. Instead, I was telling the story of a man who wanted to live in a New World without the cruelties of the old, and there were some like Ned but not, tragically, enough to change the course of that cruel history. I read extensively from histories that were sensitive to these issues, and I am indebted to the readers from the Pokanoket nation for their advice and support.

You started your writing career writing about a fictional family, then transitioned to detailing the lives of Tudor and Plantagenet women. What do you feel is the greatest difference in writing wholly fictional rather than historical women?

In my first novel, *Wideacre*, there were no historical characters; the family lived in a historically accurate landscape of agricultural and political change, but they did not meet any recognizable historical characters. *The Wise Woman* also was wholly fictional against a historical landscape. But since then, I think all my historical fictions have had characters who were real people, and have been subjected to my increasing desire for history. I find the research much more interesting when it takes in whatever might have come up at the time—it is really rich and thought-provoking. And it leads me to characters that otherwise I would never have heard of! I'd never have researched Jacquetta, Duchess of Bedford—a woman almost forgotten by history—if I had not written a novel about her daughter Elizabeth Woodville.

I really thought this series would be more fictional, but quite unconsciously I started the novel at a time when Charles I was in captivity, and I located the opening scene a mere twenty miles across the sea from him. As you may know, Charles I is featured in the novel and his failed rescue attempts are key to the action of the story. I don't seem to be able to get away from historical events—nor do I want to. We are all determined by the times we live in, and to write of characters as if they were independent of their culture is not only unrealistic, but it is to miss one of the most interesting aspects of a life: how it is shaped by the times.

The technical difference is that writing about characters who have been recorded by history is about ten times more demanding than writing about wholly fictional ones! There are constant problems of location and action. Very few characters are fully recorded and many accounts are contradictory, which poses lots of problems as to which accounts should be trusted. There are the problems of historically recorded characters who just vanish from the records for years at a time. A historian can cheerfully leave a gap—but in a fiction all characters have to be plausibly accounted for. There are problems of controversial characters when I have to decide, as the author, whether I go with the traditionally accepted view of a historical character, or think for myself how they might appear to my fictional observer. But all these problems are worth the benefit of writing a fiction which is perfectly aligned with the known history and with the biographies—while keeping the liveliness and the authorial voice of fiction.

Your work now spans more than twenty-five novels, both historical and contemporary. What is your process for beginning a new novel?

It's such an enjoyable process now, for I can trust it. I do a lot of general reading around the wider period and stay alert for anything that I think will be interesting—however unlikely it seems. For this series I am now reading Japanese, Chinese, and Indian history, as I think my story will take me to the East. I start to think about the characters—some will be carried forward from previous novels, but some will be new, and I think about what they will bring. I have an idea of what will be the events of the novel and I think about certain scenes in a quite detailed way. Then I start my specific research into historical characters who will occur and events that will happen, I create a strict historically accurate timeline—this goes on a massive chart, sometimes with overlays!—and I start the detailed plotting of the individual stories and scenes into the historical event. At the back of my mind is the broader question of what is happening in the history: Is there a notable historical trend during this time? And the question of my intent: What do I want to say in this novel? What do I want to learn in the course of writing? And now that I am in the midst of a series: How shall this novel end and what can I take forward to the next? One of the greatest guides is when I can't bring myself to either read or write anything else but the new novel—that's when I know I am ready to start. And then I simply do start, at the beginning. It's important to get a lot of work done in the first few weeks so as not to lose momentum or confidence, but once I am about thirty thousand words in, I generally feel that I know where I am going. Then I read and write in tandem till I can write *The End*—which I always ritualistically do (though it's not published like that), and then I can start thinking about how far I have achieved what I set out to do—and then rewrite.

Can you give us any hint of what comes next in the Fairmile series?

Oh! I'm very excited about it. It's partly the story of Matteo, who is going to be his mother's son, ambitious like her, and attach himself to the court of James II. Ned is going to come back to England with his son and try for one last push at a rebellion. Sarah and Felipe have established a legitimate business in Venice and London, and Johnnie is going to be an entrepreneur with the East India Company and make a fortune. The family is going to continue expanding the business with the ethics of Ned and Alinor in contrast to the increasingly ambitious and greedy world of the eighteenth century. That's the plan now—it will be quite different in the writing, I know!

Don't miss the beginning of the story!

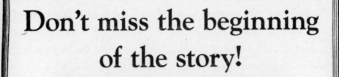

NEW YORK TIMES BESTSELLER

Philippa Gregory

A NOVEL

TIDELANDS

"Superb ... A searing portrait of a woman that resonates across the ages." —*PEOPLE*

Available wherever books are sold or at SimonandSchuster.com

80332